3-6-18

To Peggy,

You are such a giving and kind soul. Just know that I appreciate you and your caring friendship. Thank you!!

Crystal Bickers

ALSO BY CRYSTAL HICKERSON

Street Corners

The Magician: The Awakening

Wanted

Other Media Works available at

www.trinitymovies.net

Official Website

www.crystalhickerson.com

The Volunteer

A Novel

**Crystal
Hickerson**

Lillie Mae Publishing
Detroit, Michigan USA

LILLIE MAE
PUBLISHING

PUBLISHED BY LILLIE MAE PUBLISHING (USA)

Distributed by Lulu Publishing (www.lulu.com)

First printing, April 2012

No part of this book may be used or reproduced in any manner whatsoever without written permission, except in the case of brief quotations embodied in critical articles and reviews.

This is a work of fiction. Names, characters, places, and incidents are products of the author's imagination or are used fictitiously and should not be construed as real. Any resemblance to actual events, locales, organizations, or persons, living or dead, is entirely coincidental.

The cataloging-in-publication data is on file with the Library of Congress.

ISBN 978-1-105-67447-1

Copyright © Crystal Hickerson, 2012

All Rights Reserved.

Printed in the United States of America

Visit Crystal Hickerson on the World Wide Web at:
www.crystalhickerson.com

~ for Laurie ~

*Dedicated to all the
hospice volunteers around the world.*

ACKNOWLEDGEMENTS

This novel was really a journey of love. When I first thought of writing this book, one of my volunteers, Marie Appleberry, was standing in my office giving me report on her visit with a very special patient of hers. I listened intently, and as she was speaking I was thinking, "This would make a great story!" and here began the feverish typing until a year later, you are reading this now. Words cannot accurately express how much I appreciate Marie for not only being my muse on this project, but for taking on the enormous task of editing!

When I finally finished the writing, I was discussing with Marie the next step which was editing the manuscript. She immediately said "I would love to edit your book." I explained that this is a huge job, but she was fine with it. Well, she got into the work, and she admitted it was daunting, but she persevered! I am so happy she did, but not only did she correct my horrible grammatical mistakes, she offered amazing insights and notes! I was so ecstatically happy that she stuck with it, you have no idea. So THANK YOU SO MUCH, Marie!! Also, did I mention she is a STAR hospice volunteer? She could write her own textbook on the subject!

I would also like to thank Lynn Leithauser and author, Royce B. Smith for also providing their invaluable editing skills. When Lynn came into my office, fuming at how incredibly insensitive one of the characters were, I knew I had done my job in character building!

And lastly, but definitely not least, I would like to thank all of the people who sign up to volunteer with hospice. These are selfless individuals who give of their time and compassion to those who are in the final stages of their life. Whether they are reading, talking, or just being present with the patient, they give so much. Thank all of you so much for doing what you do. **This book is dedicated to YOU, the HOSPICE VOLUNTEER!**

The Volunteer

A novel

By Crystal Hickerson

ONE

The awning was dark blue with brilliant white letters. The ruffles on the bottom of the rounded canopy fluttered lightly in the early spring breeze. The letters were in the recognizable Verdana typeface. It read simply: Community Hospice, two simple words that brought tears to her eyes, tears that slowly made their way toward her chin. The words invoked the image of her mother as she lay dying in her hospital bed while the cancer raged through her body like a runaway train. Nothing could be done; say your goodbyes, the doctor had advised. It was much too late for words. Although her mother's chest was still rising up and down, the time for words was over. Jenna Steele knew this. She did not need a doctor, nurse, or any so-called relative to tell her what she needed to do. Though her mother had not been a woman who lived life to the fullest, Jenna knew her mother would not want to live hooked up to a machine. She demanded the plugs be pulled, and pulled they were. As Jenna sat in the room alone with her mother, holding her mother's hand she felt the warmth escaping as her mother took her last breath.

Jenna sat behind the wheel of her car and lit a cigarette, a habit she had recently picked up again. Her mother would have disapproved, she knew, but, after everything, she felt a bad habit or two were warranted. It had been a year, almost to the day, that she had buried the only family she had in the world, at least the only one Jenna had considered family. There were people who showed up at the funeral, people who commandeered her mother's kitchen and house, and people who acted as if they belonged there. Jenna supposed they were family members, but she did not consider them as such. After her grandmother had died years before, she rarely even saw these people. When her mother was ill and all of her money went to paying off medical bills, and when Jenna left college to care for her mother, she rarely saw family at all. Sure, there was an occasional phone call, an occasional remark of "if there is anything we can do," but their presence was not felt. It was she alone who sat with her mother, cleaned her mother when she could no longer do so herself, and read to her when it was too painful for her mother to even open her eyes. Jenna just simply sat with her mother when that was all a daughter could do. Where were they then, *these people*?

There were people who did help her, however, strangers whom she had known all of her life, it seemed, strangers who taught her how to care for her mother correctly, and who instructed her on medications with names Jenna never learned to pronounce. These strangers took the place of the family who wasn't there for her, strangers who were just like the people inside the building with the blue awning.

Jenna reached inside her purse, pulling out an oversized envelope. It was a form that folded down into a mailer. She unfolded the sides and retrieved the personal check she had written out for her donation. *Was it enough? Maybe I should have just mailed it,* she thought, but she only lived a few miles away from the office, and it was a nice day, why not just deliver it? *Is it presumptuous to bring it in person? No, what difference does it make?*

"This is stupid!" she said aloud. Jenna extinguished her cigarette and exited the car before she changed her mind and drove to a post office box. The double glass doors of the building were emblazoned with the name and a large tree of life logo. Inside was a spacious foyer with a cherub wall fountain. The flowing water added to the serene atmosphere. On either side of the fountain was a planter filled with pleasant greenery. On the other wall to the right was an elegant seating area equipped with a flat screen television. Directly in front, a few feet away, sat the receptionist window. It was your typical office set up, but, the room was decorated with particular attention to comfort with accents and color that gave you the feeling of an opulent home rather than an office.

"Hello, may I help you?" the secretary asked as Jenna approached the window. Her nametag read Marie. It was pinned to a light peach sweater twinset. Marie Marano wore a pearl choker and had her strawberry blonde hair pulled back in a loose bun. Her pleasant face revealed her age to be in the mid-fifties; yet, with each tilt of her head, she seemed so much younger. Her eyes were those of an eighty year old, however, full of depth and wisdom.

"I .... I would like to volunteer," Jenna stumbled over her words, words she barely realized she had uttered.

Marie smiled at her warmly, "Are you sure, hun? You don't sound so sure."

"I am," Jenna answered more confidently. "I would like to get more information on how I can volunteer with hospice." She had not meant to say those words at all. She had actually come to ask about making a donation, and was this the right place to drop off her envelope, but she had blurted out this odd comment about volunteering. True, she had thought about volunteering, but not in any concrete way. The words had escaped her mouth before she realized this was what she really wanted to do.

Marie gave a look of "knowing" and offered her a nod. "Have you gone online to fill out the application?"

"No ma'am."

"Your name please?"

"Jenna Steele."

Marie reached over, produced two pieces of paper from a nearby file folder and placed them on a clipboard. She handed Jenna the board and a pen. "Jenna, please fill out this application, and I will see if Mr. Ames has a moment to speak with you." Marie only called the Director of Volunteer Services, Matthew Ames, mister, in front of the public, but, in private, she called him Matt. Marie had been working for Community Hospice for about fifteen years, and the entire staff had a kinship where formalities were relaxed.

Jenna sat down in one of the chairs and began filling out the application, a standard application form with demographics and the like. A few questions tripped her up, however, the first one was: *What is the reason for wanting to volunteer with hospice? And* the second was: *What are your views on life and death?* Repeating each question in her head conjured up many memories.

There was a memory of her mother lying in her bed holding up a weak hand for Jenna to stop at the doorway while a nurse positioned her to administer a pain shot, and all the while her mother was trying to maintain a smile. Her mother was ever the guardian trying to protect her then 28 year-old daughter as if she was half that age. There was also the memory of a house full of people she barely knew, but they each had a title such as aunt, cousin, neighbor, or friend of the family. Jenna remembered escaping the house and sitting alone in the backyard staring at her mother's garden. Without her mother's care, the garden was overrun with weeds. On this particular day, she noticed a male figure sitting in the weeds on the ground. Jenna recognized him to be her first cousin, Adrian. Like her, he sat alone staring down into the wild grass. He must have felt her looking at him and returned a clear yet sad smile. He got up and walked over to her and placed a gentle hand on the top of her head. He whispered, "She's gone." Then he disappeared into the house. Her mother's funeral was over and the reception was going full blast with laughter and talk. Jenna had nothing to share with any of them so there she sat.

Jenna had actually wished Adrian would return, but he did not. Instead, she remembered an older woman of sixty coming out and sitting beside her. The woman never spoke a word, she only held her hand. Her name was Patty, and she was her mother's hospice volunteer who, for months, came in to do caregiver relief, thus allowing Jenna to run errands. Jenna didn't know how Patty knew, but by not saying a word, by just holding her hand, Jenna was able to feel her mother's presence there in the garden. It was what she desperately needed. Jenna never saw Patty again after that day. She hardly saw anyone else from the funeral after that day either.

Shifting her weight in the chair she continued to remember a night when she sat alone in her mother's empty room filled with a hospital bed, bedside commode and other abandoned medical equipment. It was all to be picked up the next day. She recalled having a very strong desire to destroy each piece of equipment with her bare hands. They were just remnants of a futile war: a battle fought, a battle mercifully lost. While she sat in the dark room, an image of a monument she had seen on a high school trip to Gettysburg came to mind. It was of two soldiers, one confederate and one union. The confederate soldier was dying in the arms of the union soldier. Something about that image resurfaced inside her and never left since that night.

The monument reminded Jenna of sitting at the bedside with her mother in the early morning hours before dawn, as her mother drew her last breath. Jenna's mother had whispered two words before the cancer finally engulfed her; she had mumbled simply "Live strong." It was the kind of saying you would leave with a fellow soldier on the battlefield like "fight to the death" or simply, "WIN!" Her mother had never really been a fighter, vibrant and strong. Cancer had struck her with one hard punch and down she went, never to stand again. It took only one year for the final count.

Jenna's mother died in that bed and Jenna had crawled in next to her, curling up into a fetal position like a small child. She had laid there in her mother's dying arms, crying silently, for more minutes than she could remember. If she could have done so, Jenna would have stayed there for the rest of her life.

"Miss Steele?" The voice of Matthew Ames penetrated Jenna's thoughts drawing her back from the memory of when her mother died.

"Yes." she said, returning to present time.

"I'm Matthew Ames, Director of Volunteer Services. Are you about finished with that?", he asked gesturing at the form in her hand.

"Almost, some of these questions require thought." She replied.

Matt smiled at her. "That's the whole idea."

Jenna looked directly at him for the first time and immediately noticed his hazel eyes. His features were interesting, a squared jaw, extremely masculine yet also quite boyish. Jenna had a hard time placing his nationality, not that that it mattered but it intrigued her, causing her to stare. His hair was brown tipped in blonde. It was cut neatly and close to his head, and he wore a meticulously groomed, very faint, shadow beard. She pondered whether he was Italian or Russian, with perhaps a hint of African American heritage, or all of the above. She couldn't figure it out. Because of that, she knew they had something in common. With her dark hair and easy to tan skin people often asked her "what are you?" Jenna promised herself she would never ask that question of him. She would just think of him as having a fascinatingly dark Paul Walker/Jesse William-*ish* look, if that made any sense at all.

"You can finish the form in my office; come with me." he told her, then led her through the door leading her further inside the building. Another seating area was located in front of two large double doors labeled "Conference Room". A smartly dressed young woman sat behind a mahogany L-shaped desk typing feverishly at her computer. She looked up at Jenna and flashed a smile, full of teeth. Her name was Shannon Silverman, the executive secretary who assisted all of the managers. Marie was her direct supervisor. Marie had her own office inside the main staff area.

Jenna followed Matt down a long, wide hallway, which lead to several offices with large windows. The first office was Matt's, and there were three more offices on down that side of the hall. Jenna would later learn those were the marketing, grief support and spiritual care offices. The hallway ended at the public restrooms. On the other side there was a door labeled "meeting room" and another door that simply said "Staff Only." Behind the "Staff Only" door was the main section of the building where the field staff had cubicles, along with the medical administrative offices and employee lunchroom. The staff entrance was on the other side of the building where employees could come and go easily.

Matt's office was very nicely decorated with masculine touches such as sports memorabilia and hockey trophies. On the wall behind his desk were photos of him smiling into the camera with many different people. Jenna only recognized two of the people pictured with him. One was the governor of Michigan, Jennifer Granholm, and the other was President Barak Obama.

"Is that you?" She pointed to the 5x9 photo of him with the leader of the free world.

Matt didn't have to follow her gaze to know which photo she was referring to. "Yes I did a bit of campaign work for the Michigan Democratic Party so this picture was actually of Mr. Obama before he became president. It was taken at one of the rallies we had in town." He pointed at the picture of him and the governor. "Governor Granholm came to our annual volunteer appreciation dinner and spoke. It was such an honor to have her. The rest of the photos were taken at various events the volunteers attended throughout the year. Some are personal photos from volunteers sent to me. I try to update them when I can. I get so many photos, in fact, because we take a lot of pictures at events, and these are placed the Volunteer Family Album." Matt pointed at the large book sitting on the table between the chairs in his office.

Jenna took a seat in one of the chairs positioned in front of his desk and leafed through the photo album. Inside were endless photos of the volunteers smiling faces. There were photos of volunteers smiling above patients, smiling next to him, and smiling alone, as the volunteer was happily caught in a moment of giving. She instantly wanted her smile captured in this album. The faces Jenna saw in her family albums she mostly did not recognize, and the faces in her memory were rarely smiling, or was it her own face that wasn't smiling? She couldn't quite remember.

"These pictures are very nice. Are they all volunteers?" Jenna asked looking up at Matt as he sat down in his black leather executive swivel chair that seemed to belong more to a CEO than a manager.

"Yes. I'm famous for taking pictures at each event. There are also photos that the volunteers themselves have taken of their patients. I add them to newsletters as well as use some for advertising and recruitment purposes."

"Very nice," she repeated the sentiment, a little perplexed that a man would get into such a job. *Is he gay? A minister perhaps,* she thought to herself a bit bemused. She immediately dispelled the first because he struck her as quite masculine. And once again the phrase "what difference does it make?" entered her mind, making her privately ashamed, yet the thoughts of him lingered strongly in her mind.

"So, Ms. Steele," he read off her application. "You are interested in becoming a volunteer. Can you tell me a little about yourself?" He readied his pen to jot down information as she spoke.

"Well, about a year ago my mother died from ovarian cancer, and we had hospice come in. Everyone was so wonderful; the nurses and aides helped us so much. She was only on hospice for a few months. She was diagnosed in April and died in August."

"I'm sorry to hear that."

"I know it hasn't quite been a year yet, as it says on the application that your loss should be at least a year old but I am fine, really."

"That is really a guideline for people." Matt explained. "I have known people to volunteer under a year and they've worked out fine. And I have known people where several years have gone by since their loss, and they are still not ready to volunteer."

"What are you looking at, their reactions to the patients?" she asked.

"After you experience a loss some people have different ways of reacting to it. In hospice, you are dealing with death every day. You are volunteering with patients who are dying, and your own grief issues can resurface quite strongly. Therefore, we ask that a year pass so the volunteer can work through those issues first."

"Should I wait until August?"

Matt thought about that for a moment. He hated to turn down a person who wants to volunteer for a couple of reasons. The first reason was when a person gets the idea that they want to volunteer it could be a passing thought if they have to wait and easily forgotten. Sometimes that is good because it could mean that maybe they are not truly interested in volunteering. However, another reason he hated to turn people away was because there was always something a person could bring to the program, a talent or a personality, and he wanted to give them the benefit of the doubt. Something motivates each person to walk through the door to volunteer, and he never wanted to deny a person his or her journey.

"How do you feel about it?" Matt asked her. "Do you feel you are able to handle seeing patients in similar situations as your mother?"

A frown swept across her face briefly. Jenna remembered a day she had walked into her mother's room. Her mother had been sitting by the window staring out at the rain. She had a blanket wrapped around her legs, and, for the first time her mother seemed very old to her. Possibly, it was the way her hair hung down limply over her shoulders instead of being pulled up tightly in a ponytail or maybe it was the way her eyes seemed to be more sunken as the gray light from the sky fell onto her unwashed face.

"Come closer," her mother had said to her. She had not turned around, but, she knew her daughter was standing in the doorway watching her. Jenna obeyed her mother and knelt by her chair. "You're going to need some help," her mother said. Her voice was raspy and weak.

"I can handle it." Jenna had sternly reminded her. Her mother's head slowly turned to her. Her eyes were distant and poignant. A frail hand rose up and cupped Jenna's chin. Their eyes locked for a moment, filled with silent words. Then her mother spoke in a voice so soft that it was only the movement of her lips that aided Jenna in understanding.

"No more," her mother shook her head for emphasis. "No more." She repeated, and then turned her attention back to the rain.

Jenna stood up, looking down at her dying mother. The first emotion that came to her was anger. How dare she quit like this. Tears invaded her eyes as she gently ran her hand down her mother's hair. She bent down and kissed her. "Ok."

"Ms. Steele?" Matt's voice penetrated her thoughts.

"Yes?"

"How do you feel about working with patients?"

"Fine. I can handle it." She sat up straighter in her chair. "I took care of my mother alone. There was no one else until hospice came in. I was so glad when they did come, because they helped her so much. I just want to give back." Jenna watched him nod and write.

"OH!" Jenna shouted suddenly, causing Matt to look up.

Jenna reached into her purse and pulled out the envelope containing the donation. She now handed it to him. "I almost forgot that I wanted to give this donation."

Matt took the envelope and pulled out her check. When he saw the amount, he looked up at her. He looked back down and counted the zeros just to be sure. He reread the words: Twenty thousand dollars.

"Oh my goodness, this is $20,000." He said it out loud just so she could hear it so as to be sure. She was a young woman, in her late twenties, not your average major gift donor. "Is this correct?" he asked.

"Yes, as I said, I just want to give back."

"Thank you, Ms. Steele. This is a very nice amount. We are non-profit so this will help a lot of people."

Jenna felt she needed to explain. "My mother inherited quite a bit from her father. She didn't vacation much and she lived modestly. She had been a librarian the last several years of her life. She kept to herself. Then when she died, I also learned that she took out a few large policies for me. Very large. I don't have any brothers and sisters. It was just me and her, really, so I think she felt it was a way for her to compensate for leaving me. You know?"

Matt observed as her face dissolved into an expression of profound sorrow that he physically felt. "Are you ok?"

"You know I am not doing a very good job at convincing you I can be a volunteer am I?"

"I can only imagine how hard it is to lose a mother. It also sounds like you two were very close."

"We were...we are." The tears escaped her and fell down her cheeks. Matt immediately snapped up two tissues from a nearby dispenser and handed them to her. "Thanks." She said wiping them away. "I do want to volunteer and I promise you I won't be a blubbering idiot when I'm with a patient. I promise!"

Jenna seemed very delicate to him at that moment. He felt it would be the perfect time to go into his hospice speech. "Let me tell you a little bit about hospice. Even though you have experienced it, I want to give you a bit more insight. You will learn a lot more in training."

Just hearing him say *training* meant that she was accepted, and that instantly relaxed her. "Hospice is for patients who are in their last stages of a terminal illness. It's is a program that is ordered by a physician, however, a family can ask for hospice before a doctor suggests it but a physician still has to sign off on it. When a patient signs onto hospice, they are saying that they do not wish to have any more aggressive treatments, meaning curative treatments. Hospice takes care of pain management and is a palliative care program. A physician is mandated to speak about hospice at the beginning of a patient's diagnosis of a disease that could possibly end up being terminal, such as cancer, dementia, etc. However, many doctors do not talk about hospice until the final stages of a disease."

"Why is that?" Jenna interjected.

"It could be for many reasons, but mainly the doctor may not want to scare the patient and family and bring down any hope that the patient will get better. Psychologically the patient may start to give up, and this can affect their physical recovery. However, once a patient is ready for hospice care it does not mean that they are giving up; it really means that they are accepting of their condition. In my opinion, it is a travesty for a patient to have to endure chemo or other treatments if it will not cure them. In hospice we focus on pain management; this way the patient can spend their last days, pain free and more able to interact with their family. During this time, they can heal wounds, see people they haven't seen in years and even say goodbye. In our American culture, we are focused on surviving and fighting until the end. In hospice we believe that a person should live their life until the end. Hospice care is not about death; it's about living the best quality of life possible until the end. You can't do that if you are plugged into machines and in a hospital. Most people want to die at home or in a home-like environment surrounded by their family and loved ones."

"When my mother told me she wanted hospice I was angry. I thought she was giving up. I wanted her to fight." Jenna put emphasis on the last word.

"Understandable."

"But when hospice came in she was herself again. She was off chemo; her color came back; she was able to speak, and for about a month or so before she started getting weak again, she was her old self. We had so many talks. You are right. She would not have been able to do that on a respirator." They both paused for a moment allowing this to sink in.

Then Matt continued. "Hospice has an interdisciplinary team of professionals. We have the nurse, physician, home health aide or hospice aide, a social work and spiritual care advisor. We also have a grief support counselor who helps the family after the patient dies. Sometimes they visit the family before the patient dies." Matt paused. He practically memorized his hospice speech. After nearly eight years of delivering it, he had it down to a science. Before he moved over to volunteer services, he was a marketer with the agency and he pretty much said the same thing.

"Now onto the volunteer," Matt continued. "The volunteer in hospice is a very important person. He or she is a member of the clinical team and can assist with so many areas of hospice. Medicare has stated that if a hospice agency does not have a volunteer program, and if those volunteers are not contributing at least 5% of the care of hospice then they can no longer call themselves a hospice. Volunteers founded hospice. Volunteer nurses and teams helped people in their time of need. It was a doctor, Cicely Saunders, who said that hospice should be a structured program." Matt went on to tell her about the different jobs and roles of the volunteer, giving her general information about what she would be doing as a volunteer as well as the mandatory requirements of getting a tuberculosis test and fingerprinting.

"Wow, that's a lot of information! I hope I can remember it all!" Jenna gasped.

"Don't worry about that, Jenna. In training you will get even more detailed information and you can make a decision whether this program is right for you."

"I am sure it is right for me. So when is training?" Jenna asked. Matt told her it would be in a couple of weeks. "I'll be there." She exclaimed. "So am I accepted?"

Matt laughed to himself. "Yes, you are."

"So that's it? That wasn't so bad."

"Well, the interview process continues through training. Once you get more of the details, you can decide if this is something you really want to do."

"And you can decide if you really want me as a volunteer." She cut in.

Matt chuckled, "We have to make sure it is a good match. Patients really depend on their volunteer. There are so many other places that a person can volunteer their time. We want to make sure it is the right decision for everyone." He reached across his desk and handed her his business card from the desk holder.

"Now, I am the Director of Volunteer Services so anything you need you just contact me, ok? If you are unable to attend this training or if you have any questions please feel free to call or email me. Once you become a volunteer, I will be your direct supervisor and point of contact. My job is to make sure you are getting the best out of your volunteer experience." He paused. "And Ms. Steele," Matt leaned in towards her. He seemed to want her to pay close attention to his next words.

"Jenna, please." She offered.

"Jenna, thank you again for your generous donation. You will receive a thank you letter in the mail and, at this amount; I believe you will be added to the major donor's list."

"Oh that's not necessary. I just wanted to help somehow." Jenna felt awkward repeating that sentiment over and over, but money sometimes makes situations uncomfortable. She thought that maybe she should have just mailed it in.

"It's standard. You will be placed on the mailing list for a newsletter and, I am sure, called upon again."

"Hospice helped us so much; I can't even begin to tell you. There was a nurse, Joyce Adams who was so kind and patient with me. I didn't know half as much as I thought I did. We didn't come here; my aunt chose the hospice program connected to the hospital."

"Programs are pretty much the same."

"I suppose, but I knew I wanted to make a donation to a hospice that was stand alone. I see your hospice sign all the time, because I live not far from here. Something just led me to your place."
Jenna stood up and Matt followed suit. She wanted to stop talking about her donation. "So I'll see you in a few weeks?"
"Yes, right at this office in the conference room there."
"Great. I look forward to it." Jenna remarked, and without realizing Jenna had batted her eyes. She didn't mean to act like a school girl, but it was Matt's hazel eyes that caused the innate reaction. Thankfully, he did not seem to notice, or at least decided to ignore it. He only escorted her out.

Matt watched his prospective volunteer leave, and then spun comically around to look at Shannon. He swiveled his hips and did a little jig. "I got 20, 000 dollars! I got 20,000 dollars!" He mimicked the tune Mike Meyers used in a '90s movie.
Shannon laughed at him. "You are so silly." She lowered her voice, cocking her head to the side, indicating the staff door behind her. "Heads up, brass is in the building."
Matt rolled his eyes coming over to her desk. "Ah, who cares? Bam!" He slammed the check he had been holding onto her desk. "Take a look at that."
Shannon picked up the cashier's check and looked at it. She had never seen so many zeros. "Whoa, where did you get this? Is this a donation?"
"Yes it is. The young lady who I just interviewed, my new volunteer, donated it."
"Your new VIP volunteer." Shannon corrected.
"All volunteers are VIPs and the same in my book."
"Yeah, but this one's rich!" Shannon paused and looked at him. "And she's pretty." She smiled, waiting for his response.
Matt grabbed the check away from her. "Your point is?"
"I often have no point," she said sarcastically. "just making an observation. She is young, has time to volunteer, has money, sounds like a good candidate to tame Mr. Ames."
"All those things are true, but you are forgetting one thing,"
"And that would be?"
"She is going to be a volunteer, which means I will be her boss, which means she is off limits. I always keep things professional."
"Do you?" Shannon stared up at him with a glint of menace in her eyes. Matt returned her gaze, instantly feeling as he had many times before in

the last year, remorseful. A stupid one-night stand after an unofficial office party with a few coworkers ended in catastrophe. Drinks mixed with loneliness are a lethal combination. Shannon had been with the company only a couple of months and was yet to be working directly with him as she was now. When Shannon asked him for a ride home he found himself staring more at her low cut blouse than the road. If only he had of been pulled over for intoxication, that at least would have sobered him up.

Shannon was aggressive, willing, and too damned gorgeous to resist. His large brain was swimming in vodka, while his little brain was alert and oriented. After the night ended, he hoped that she would see it was a one time only thing and for a while, it seemed she had gotten the message. The price he paid was these little innuendos or reminders of their night.

Today he did what he always did when confronted with it, he deflected. "So why is the brass here?" he asked, back to using his manager's voice.

"I take it you haven't checked your emails today?" Shannon asked well aware why he changed the subject.

"I've been a little busy."

"You never check your emails enough." She scolded.

"That's why I have you." He joked, and then wished he hadn't.

Shannon cut him a cold glance, then went on. "The CEO, Frank Jacobs, is speaking via video conference in an emergency meeting today at 2pm. The executive staff is at each site during the broadcast to run each meeting."

"So Dave is here?" Dave Chatman was the Senior Vice President of Service Operations and the Chief Operating Officer. Matt and Dave went to college together. Matt took the business degree route while Dave went into nursing, not to be a nurse but to be on the administration end of healthcare. When a marketing position opened up, Dave called Matt immediately. It was a great paying job with lots of potential for advancement. Matt took the job but within only three years switched over to volunteer management because it was a less hectic position travel wise. Matt and his wife were having major marital issues, and he thought being able to spend more time at home with her and their son, Jake, would save the marriage. It did not. During the time Matt was traveling his wife had an affair and they divorced anyway. However, Matt had grown to love working with the volunteers so he did not regret his decision. Dave took it personally, feeling that Matt made a terrible career mistake. He felt Matt was wasting his MBA. Things between them had never really been the same since.

"Yeah, he's in with Karen right now." Karen McBride, the Clinical Program Director, had an office on the staff side of the building. Shannon glanced up at the clock. "I have thirty minutes to get everything ready." She got up from her chair. "Let's just hope my damned cheese and crackers get here in time."

As if on cue, the doorbell rang. A man in a blue and gray uniform stood outside the glass entrance with two large boxes in his hands. "Excellent!" Shannon said, hurrying to the door.

"Need any help?" Matt asked her.

"Nope, thanks." She held the door open for the delivery guy. As an afterthought, and with a hint of icy grace, she said "Matt, you have a message from Connie." She pointed at her desk, and then presented a big smile for the delivery man as she guided him into the large conference room.

Matt went over to the wall mounted message bin and retrieved the pink paper from his box. He headed off to his office when the staff door opened. He almost ran smack dab into Dave Chatman. He was a full inch shorter than Matt was, yet Dave's suits seemed to always tower over his.

"Matt, how the hell are you?" Dave greeted, flashing cosmetically corrected teeth.

"Doing super, Dave, and yourself?"

"If I was living any better it would be a sin!" He let out one hardy *Ha!* Matt was really tired of that phrase. Dave was beginning to resemble a Hollywood producer more and more, Matt thought. "So what's this emergency meeting all about? Come to fire us all?"

Dave put on his corporate mask. "Well we have some uncomfortable issues to discuss today; lots of changes is all I can say. The rest you will hear in there from the big guy himself."

"Ok, well, I'll be right in." Matt turned, but Dave touched his arm stopping him.

"Let's get some drinks afterwards. It's Friday night, what you up to?"

"I have to pick up Jake, my weekend."

"He just had a birthday right?"

"Coming up in June."

"What is he, nine now?"

"He's turning eleven."

Dave made an exaggerated face. "Wow! Where in the world does the time go?"

"Out the door, Dave." Matt stated flatly.

Dave laughed. "I hear ya, man. How about that drink? I really need to talk to you."

"Can it wait?"

"Not really." Dave said with finality.

Matt took in a heavy breath, and even though Dave was a personal friend he was still his boss. "Ok, I'll work something out with Connie; I was supposed to pick Jake up from school but,"

Dave patted Matt's shoulder firmly, cutting him off. "Work it out. It won't take too long, but it is important. I gotta head in. See you afterwards." And with that he disappeared through the conference room's double doors.

Matt stood there for a moment before heading back to his office. He had been summoned by corporate for one of those behind the scenes meetings. Important decisions were made mostly in one of those clandestine conclaves. Matt felt he should be happy that he was occasionally privy to the inside track, but this time he wasn't. He smelled layoffs in the air, and this casual boy's get together only meant one of two things: Dave was letting him go, or he was giving him the goods on how horrible it was going to get for everyone else.

Matt was not looking forward to his meeting with Dave, but, he was looking forward to his conversation with his ex wife, Connie, even less. Dialing her cell phone was always brutal. He often wanted to start his conversations with her with an ice laced, *What is it now?* Or a *"I sent you your check."*

Connie answered on the first ring with the usual nonexistent greeting. "Matt, I need to verify that you will be picking up Jake today, on time."

Matt unconsciously breathed hard into the phone. "Look, Connie I..."

"Damn it, Matt, don't start this shit with me! Are you going to pick him up or not?"

"Yes I am but not after school. I will pick him up at your place."

"Unacceptable. I have plans tonight which I made because I assumed that you would do what you said you were going to do." Her tone was a controlled rage.

"I have a meeting, Connie! It was last minute, and it is important. I will still be there by 5pm as usual."

Connie paused after a long agonizing silence. "Pick him up at my mother's." The phone clicked and went dead. She had hung up on him.

Matt sat at his desk staring at his IPhone. "Forever the bitch." He cursed under his breath.

TWO

Jenna's ride home was much better than the ride over to the hospice office. There was a sense of unbridled accomplishment flowing through her. She had done what she set out to do. She had given the donation. The check was written; it was in the hands of hospice and she had given back. In addition, she had also gone a step further with a selfless contribution by signing up to be a volunteer. Would that squelch the guilt? She was not sure but it did make her feel better, and, at this moment, it was what she had desperately needed. She needed to feel better; she needed to be enlightened, to be touched by an angel, to walk with God, or whatever, she needed positivity to course through her heat-starved veins.

Turning onto Kirkway Road off of Long Lake Boulevard, she smiled for the first time in what seemed to be years. Even the sun glistening off Forest Lake made the water appear more radiant, more luminescent. Just glimpsing the water made her feel more at ease. She truly began to feel that her journey as a volunteer was going to be a good one. Yes, she made the right decision.

As she drove, taking in the beautiful scenery, Jenna thought about how much her mother would have benefited from living out here. After the funeral, Jenna needed to get away. She had the insurance money and the inherited money so she made up her mind to move out of her condominium and purchase a house of her own. Her mother had not done that. She had rented all of her life. The funny thing was she never needed to. Her mother had inherited a large amount of money from Jenna's grandfather. Instead of using it to buy a home, she had squirreled it away in a bank account that she never touched. It was this account that Jenna inherited.

Jenna's mother, Faye Steele, would sit for hours watching episodes of Star Trek over and over again, in the small house she rented from a friend for close to fifteen years. It wasn't in the best part of town; yet it wasn't in the worst part of town either. When Jenna learned, after her mother's death, of the money her mother had in a savings account, Jenna wondered why her mother didn't move to a better part of the city. Why would she live so modestly when she didn't have to? It was strange, but Jenna decided to buy a home, a nice one, out by the lake in a very wealthy part of town. Spiritually, she bought it for both of them. Her mother may not have allowed herself to live comfortably but Jenna was not going to deny herself that. Besides, this area was gorgeous, the lake, the green manicured lawns, the peaceful environment, all of it. If you had the means, why wouldn't you live here? Her mother used to complain about the noise in the neighborhood they lived in, the kids, the loud music in the cars riding by. She used to say, *"They're all a bunch of barbaric leeches."*

If she really felt that way, why in the world did her mother stay? Jenna knew exactly why; she was stuck. Her mother was stuck in space and time. She had given up and given in to her own sadness. When Jenna was about nine years old she saw a movie which spoke about this horrible force that was destroying a perfect world, it was called "the nothing". That is what she felt happened to her mother at some point in her life; she was eaten by "the nothing."

Jenna turned her car into her circular driveway. As the front of her new home came into view, a wave of sorrow swept over her without warning. It caused her to lift her foot off the gas pedal, quite unconsciously. The car rolled almost to a complete halt, her eyes watering, and then she looked to the left and saw a crème SUV parked directly in front of the entrance. It was her best friend Zabbie's car. Jenna detoured her heading from the garage, made a sharp left turn, and parked behind her.

Elizabeth Myers, or Zabbie to practically everyone who knew her, was sitting on one of the flat low steps leading up to the front entrance of Jenna's home. Her knees were bent high, and her head was hunched down while she stared intently into her cellular phone. She was, of course, texting. The sound of Jenna's car stopping, shutting off, or even Jenna shutting her door after exiting did not disturb Zabbie's fingers from racing over the touch screen.

"Wooooow, you seriously need counseling."Jenna said, stopping only a few feet away from the absorbed girl. Zabbie's response was a simple pinky finger going up briefly. Jenna stepped back, leaned on her friend's car and watched the whizzing fingers in awe. Zabbie's light blonde hair was parted and pulled back into a tight ponytail. When the sun hit it, Zabbie's hair glistened. Zabbie prided herself on her flat ironing skills.

Her peach painted toes and fingers matched her sheer blouse perfectly, not an accident. Underneath the blouse was a white tank to match the white Capri pants that hugged her slender legs elegantly. Jenna always marveled at how well put together Zabbie carried herself. It was easy to clean up when you had the money to do so, and Zabbie had never known a day where lack of money was an issue.

"Ok, all done!" Zabbie announced, jumping up and switching off her phone at the same time. She bounced over and kissed Jenna lightly on the cheek. "Sorry love, Zach is in Hawaii. He says hello, by the way."

"Hello back to Zach." Jenna responded. Zach was Zabbie's boyfriend. They had been dating for close to three years now. Every year he goes on vacation to Hawaii with his parents where he and his father spend most of their time fishing, and his mother, spends most of her time on the beach sipping rum concoctions.

"He was just finishing breakfast." Zabbie told her.

"Why don't you ever join them on these excursions?"

"His mother hates me." Zabbie grunted sporting a wry smile. "She calls me a WASP, a bug to be choked to death by spray poison, but I think she's Euro Trash so we're even."

"Wow." Jenna mouthed.

"She wants everyone to think that she is a descendent of the House of Savoy or some shit, when I know for a fact that her great-great grandfather was a grape stumper just outside of Naples." Zabbie stopped herself and glanced up at Jenna. "Sorry, they have money, old money, much more than my family. My family has *new* money. Bottom line, I'm not good enough for her little bambino."

"I think most mothers feel that way about their son's girlfriends. She will get over it, and if not, oh well."

"Oh well." Zabbie agreed darkly.

"All that matters is that Zachary loves you. She couldn't deny that if she wanted to." Jenna placed a finger under Zabbie's chin. "I've never seen two people more in love."

Zabbie beamed. "He does love me." She said almost as a question. Jenna nodded in complete agreement. "Well then she can go to hell!" Zabbie shouted.

"To hell with her!" Jenna joined in Zabbie's revelry.

Zabbie burst into laughter and Jenna quickly joined her. "What are you doing sitting on my stoop?" Jenna asked in mid stream of their hilarity.

"You forgot lunch with me again! I called and texted you a dozen times from noon to one; then I said screw it and I came over. That was about an hour ago."

"You have been sitting out here for an hour?"

"Not the whole time. Some of the time, I sat in the car. I was about to leave you know."

"I'm sorry, I went to drop off the donation." Jenna reminded her.

"It took you that long to do it?" Zabbie asked.

Jenna hesitated then spoke. "I also signed up to volunteer." She admitted.

Zabbie's head spun around. "What?" she asked incredulously. "I thought we talked about this?"

" Yes…" Jenna stumbled.

"Get in the car. I need crab cakes." Zabbie announced, with a point of her finger.

They drove in relative silence to "Big Fish", a seafood restaurant nearby, a place qualified to serve Zabbie crab cakes. They had talked about her donation a few nights prior. Jenna had struggled with the amount, was it too much or too little? Jenna had also wondered if she should volunteer and Zabbie thought it was too morbid. She didn't understand why Jenna would want to relive her mother's illness by watching others go through the same experience. It was a sentiment she decided to repeat now that they were seated at their table.

"Why relive it, Jenna?" Zabbie asked, pushing her menu to the side. She already knew exactly what she wanted to order.

Jenna buried her face in her own menu. She was hungry, but she was now very unsure if she wanted anything at all to eat. "It's not about reliving it. I don't even know what I will be doing. I don't have to work with patients."

"It's hospice," Zabbie exclaimed, "everybody's dying! Death, death, death! Why be a part of it? You should be embracing life right now!"

"I need to do this, Zabbie. I need to give back."

"You gave back, twenty thousand dollars worth! Isn't that enough?"

"It's just money." Jenna was grateful when the waiter came up and took their order. It would serve as a nice break in the conversation. Jenna ordered the caesar salad with a shrimp cocktail, and Zabbie ordered the Maryland crab cakes.

Zabbie snorted, picking up their talk where they had left off. "Only money my ass! When my mother donates to her chosen *charities of the year*, they kiss her ass ridiculously. Now she donates because my Dad wants a write off, and she wants to gloat and out do her friends. I mean they actually see it as a competition. It's really hilarious. But because of her donations they invite her to all of these lavish events etc." Then Zabbie reflected, "But the money does come in handy for the organizations and it means a lot to them. So it's not just money!"

"Maybe not, but I wanted to do more. There's nothing wrong with volunteering."

"I got it!" Zabbie burst with excitement. "Let's plan a trip! Let's go to Mexico- no, no Jamaica! Let's get our hedonism on!" her eyes were wide with excitement.

Jenna coughed on her water. "What? I don't think so! What about Zach?"

"We need to get you out of here and do something wild and different." Zabbie squinted her eyes in thought, and then a light bulb went off. "I got it, and this is even better- white water rafting in the Poconos!"

Jenna laughed. "Are you serious? I'm not getting in that water to be killed."

"Zach and I went last spring, it was great! No time to think. You go rafting, hiking, biking – it's amazing!"

"You know I can't swim that good."

"All the guides are so well trained. There is no way to get hurt. You sleep under the stars; you get back in touch with nature..."

"I was never in touch with nature." Jenna told her.

"Exactly. You need this. Let's do it. I can call my travel agent right now." Zabbie held up her cell phone and started clicking.

"Elizabeth, I am not going white water rafting in the friggin' mountains."

"We'll stay at a spa resort, that way we can raft, hike, or whatever all day long and come back to a comfy hotel room. We can stay at the casino hotel there! Oooooh come on it'll be fun!" Zabbie pressed.

"No!" Jenna protested. "Look it's not going to change my mind. I'm going to volunteer and that's the end of it."

Zabbie leaned back in her seat defeated. "I don't get it." She admitted after a long moment, just staring at her friend as if Jenna had just announced she was about to jump off a bridge.

"You don't have to." Jenna informed her.

"I just want you to be happy. You can't wallow in this."

"Wallow in what?" Jenna asked.

"In depression, grief, all this darkness!" Zabbie stressed her point with the wave of her hands.

"What are you talking about?"

"Your mother would want you to live life, to soak up all that is out there."

"I know." Jenna replied.

"How can you do that if you are watching other people die like she did? It's all so dark and morose. Don't you see that? You have to move on. It's been a year. Get...." Zabbie stopped her sentence abruptly.

Jenna looked directly at her. "Get over it?"

"I didn't want to say that."

"You've never lost anyone."

"I know I don't know how you feel." Zabbie conceded.

"No you don't. I feel like I took care of her all of her life, even before her illness. She was always so alone. No friends, no relationships to speak of. I used to sit there with her talking about the shows she watched, anything so she wouldn't be alone. Sometimes I don't know if she even realized I was in the room. When she died, I was sad of course but a part of me was happy for her. She was finally free of her pain." Jenna paused as their drinks and her salad was delivered.

When the waiter left, she continued, "Getting cancer was the best thing that ever happened to my mother."

"You don't mean that."

"Zabbie, she would have sat in that chair watching television for the next forty years. My mother? *She* was depressed. I am not depressed. I am doing something. I'm going to help people. I'm doing it whether you support me in it or not."

Zabbie agreed to be there for her friend even though she was very much against it. Jenna was obviously set on this course; therefore there was nothing left to be said.

The two friends sat in the restaurant and ate their meals, switching the subject to mundane topics like celebrity gossip, fashion and of course the relationship between Zabbie and Zach. Jenna had heard everything her friend was trying to say to her. Maybe Zabbie would prove to be right, that working with patients would be too much, but she had to give it a shot first; she had to try.

THREE

Dave Chatman offered to drive to the nearby mall bar and grill. Matt had squeezed his six-foot frame into the Mercedes two seater. The dark silver roadster was obviously brand new, and Matt was shocked when he saw the car Dave was leading him to. Is it mid life crisis time, Matt had thought, when they spun out of the parking lot.

"I won't tell you how much it costs but I will say it was worth every penny." Dave conveyed to him, as they sped down the road.

"It feels like a race car." Matt commented. He eyed the rich leather interior. The rounded panels and wooden accents reeked of mogul opulence. Matt didn't have to know the price tag; the car spoke for itself.

"V8 engine, and I could have gone for the AMG, but this is sleeker and sexier in a more business sense. This is where it's at, baby!" Dave flashed all of his teeth at Matt.

"Sweet ride." A gross understatement but the only one Matt could muster up to say. He thought about his Ford Explorer and wanted to puke. What's funny though, when Matt bought the Explorer, only a few months prior, he was excited about it. He even waited to get the color he wanted, dark copper metallic. Sitting in Dave's car made him snicker at his past exhilaration.

"I had to have it. It was a bit on the expensive side, but sometimes you have to take a risk. When I arrive in car like this, I've already won." Dave explained. He pulled up to the area of the mall near the restaurant, availing himself of the valet parking. He headed into the neon lit building with Matt in tow.

Inside, Dave ordered a Bellini Martini. "You gotta try these; sweet is not even the word." Dave recommended.

"I would rather not drink. I still have to pick up my son when we're done here."

"Come on, one drink." Dave directed the bartender to bring two glasses. He turned to Matt. "It's really a smooth drink."

"What's in it?" Matt asked becoming annoyed. He would allow the big boss to order the drink but he didn't have to drink all of it.

"It's a martini with peach schnapps and champagne."

"Champagne? That sounds like, if you'll forgive me, a woman's drink." Matt fished inside his jacket pocket and pulled out a pack of Marlboros. Dave held up his fingers and shook them.

"Uh, uh, uhhh, no more smoking anywhere, my man." Dave chuckled.

Matt looked at him and cursed under his breath. "Jeez, I forgot." He replaced the cigarettes.

"I quit myself, had to." Dave said. "Most people don't smoke anymore. And it's seen as a weakness. Plus I got sick of having to go outside to smoke, even in my own house. My wife hates the smell, and then I began to even hate it in my car. Besides it brings the value of the vehicle down. I have too many executives and board members in my car from time to time. Don't want them to smell tobacco when they get in, you know? "

"Really? How did you quit?"

"Cold turkey, the only way to do it. I just made up my mind and, poof, it was over."

"It wasn't hard?"

"Willpower, my man." Dave placed a hand on Matt's shoulder for emphasis and whispered. "Willpower."

Matt rolled his eyes and looked around. It was Happy Hour Friday night, and the place was beginning to fill up with white-collar workers ready to kick the weekend into high gear. The women, he observed, were a little young to be executives, probably the secretaries, coordinators and assistants to the executives. Matt also couldn't help but notice that they all were extremely attractive, and he was not alone in his scrutiny.

Dave poked him in the side playfully. "Yeah man, ripe for the picking." He laughed. "This is not my first time here, you know what I mean?"

The drinks came, and Matt took a sip of the fruity drink. "Not bad, I have to admit."

"Nothing wrong with a little sweetness every now and again." Dave was looking across the room eyeing a very buxom brunette.

Matt followed his eyes and sighed. "Dave, please tell me you didn't cause me to miss picking up my son, and yet again pissing Connie off, so you can pick up chicks."

"No, of course not, but pissing off Connie is just a bonus." Dave laughed heartedly. Matt was not amused. "Ok, man, lighten up. I'll get to the point."

"Thank you."

Dave gulped down the rest of his drink and then motioned for another. "Alright, here we go. Things are changing at the company; rearranging is probably a better word. There will be some layoffs."

"Yeah, I remember hearing that in the meeting today." Matt said, "I take it you know who?"

"Yes, a lot of contingents and a lot of redundant and unnecessary positions. It's gonna be brutal." Dave had the emotion of a sledgehammer.

"Due tell, should I start polishing up my resume?" Matt asked.

"Yes, but not because you're getting laid off. I have another position for you right here in the company."

"What would that be?"

"Remember Mark Tobolowski?"

"The marketing VP?"

"He go bye bye. Unfortunately, he doesn't know it yet."

"Wow, what did he do?" Matt asked more interested in finding out what a person has to do to get fired so he wouldn't do it.

"He's not producing, and when you don't produce, you get replaced. Now this will not take place until after the first round of layoffs."

Matt looked confused. "There was no mention of rounds of layoffs."

"No, to the employees it will just be layoffs. To the executive team it is categorized in rounds. We will start with the lower ranks and work our way up, so to speak. This will be a six-month process." Dave took another sip of his drink and another peek at the brunette.

"How many jobs are we looking at?" Matt asked his stomach sinking a bit.

"Like I said, it'll be a little brutal, but don't you worry about that. I'm here, unofficially, to let you know that an executive spot will be open in less than six months and I want you to have it." Dave paused as he waited for a reaction from Matt.

Matt repeated mainly to himself, "Vice President of Marketing?"

"Vice President of Business Development, Chief Marketing Officer, to be exact." Dave corrected. "What are you pulling down, fifty-grand a year?"

Actually, it was more like forty five, Matt thought, but who's counting? "About that." Matt lied.

"I'm talking eighty-thousand a year take home, to start," Dave continued, "and I haven't even mentioned benefits and perks!" Dave locked eyes with the brunette and winked. She returned a coy smile. "VP looks better on your resume than volunteer *coordinator*." He made sure to mock the last title.

"That's Director of Volunteer Services." now Matt's turn to correct, Dave. He made sure to stress the word director.

"Whatever. It's middle management at best, and I do mean at best. I'm talking about executive status. That title opens many doors, doors you didn't even know were there."

Matt was at a loss for words. Things had changed in his life, and he no longer needed the extra hours at home. He wasn't going home to anything now but an empty apartment and take out. He did enjoy home cooked meals and often cooked when he was married, but it began to feel ridiculous cooking a meal for one. He wanted to cook for Jake when he came on the weekends, but they often ended up eating pizza and burgers because that was what Jake wanted. Being with dad was fun time; at least that was what Matt wanted Jake to think of their time together. He knew that Connie made Jake eat sit-down meals at home, so when Jake came to visit Matt it was a boys' time together. He knew that Jake appreciated that.

Suddenly, Matt looked at Dave. Dave was an angler. He did nothing, or so it seemed lately, for anyone but himself. Matt had to ask, "What do you get out of this?"

"Woooow!" Dave said with exaggerated offense, "What's in it for me, huh? I couldn't just want my old friend to have a better career." He continued, "Listen, I know you are loyal to the company, you are a hard worker, not to mention you're not getting any younger, and Connie is not making it easy on you in the child support department, am I right?"

"You're not wrong."

"Look, man..." Dave said as he leaned in closer. "You think you're going to move up in the world by searching on Monster.Com? This is how it happens. You gotta have an in, and I am your in."

"I was hoping to someday get a shot at the VP of Volunteer Services." Matt responded.

Dave made the sound of a needle scratching a record on a turntable. "Oops, that's one of the jobs being eliminated."

"What?" Matt sat up, clearly shocked. "My God, does Sarah know that?" Sarah Evans was the current VP of Volunteer Services.

Dave shook his head. "Nope. So, as you can see, no real career path. If you wanna stay in Volunteer Services, fine, but this is as far as you go. Sorry, just being honest." Dave hunched his shoulders for emphasis.

Matt laughed sarcastically. "Do you people even realize how important volunteers are to hospice care? Do you know how much work goes into recruiting people to do this work for free? You have no idea. Without volunteers," Matt continued, "we wouldn't even be a hospice, and you wouldn't have the money to buy brand new sports cars."

"Hey, don't kill the messenger." Dave snapped back, "This is the game my friend, either you play the game or sit on the sidelines, your choice."

"What is it? You don't respect volunteers do you?"Matt asked, "You guys think volunteers are nothing, losers, bleeding heart idiots."

Dave frowned. "Look Matt, don't try and sell me the softer side of the industry. I know all about that. I'm a businessman, and this business is about making money, it's about being on the cutting edge. Don't be fooled by the Community Hospice title in our name. We are about money and progression, and don't ever forget that. You think our board or accountants give a shit about the community? They care about the bottom line. That's all that matters and all that will ever matter. As my fifteen year old niece says, – *don't get it twisted*."

Matt glared at Dave for a long moment, trying to decide whether to get on his soapbox or not, and talk about the trials and tribulations of volunteer services, but he thought against it. What was the point after all? Here is a guy who owns a two million dollar house and drives a hundred thousand dollar car. Clearly he does not care to listen to his grassroots speech. Matt moved on instead, asking: "Who will become our boss?"

"Corporate Director of Human Resources; it's all in the restructuring." Dave saw the shock on Matt's face. "That's why I'm telling you this now, buddy. You gotta strike while the iron's hot. You've got some time to think about it. Meanwhile, I'll talk you up, invite you to the fundraising ball to rub some elbows, and you do the rest."

"What's the rest?"

Dave looked him up and down. "Buy a few new suits, look the part, at least when you come to the corporate offices. I know you guys in your department are business casual but if you want to run with the big dogs, you gotta look like you have some bite, you know what I mean?"

"The big dogs, huh?"

"That's right." Dave looked at his watch. "Better get you back. Remember, mums the word. We never spoke about this, and no starting office gossip, *comprende*? Excuse me a second." Dave got up and made his way over to the brunette, who had been waiting for him to do just that. He expertly slipped his card into her hand while whispering something, no doubt x-rated, into her ear. Dave's whole player scene amused Matt. Dave's wife, Barbara, never seemed to mind the many affairs she caught him in as long as her charge card never got rejected at Nordstrom's.

It was all a lot for Matt to take in: layoffs, job eliminations, restructuring and a shot at a VP position, a lot to take in, for sure. Matt thought long and hard about their conversation for the rest of the evening. It never left his mind.

FOUR

Jenna was not sure if she was the first to arrive, but when she pulled into the Community Hospice parking lot for the first day of volunteer training, there were only about six or seven cars in the lot. The first time she came, which ended up being her impromptu interview, the lot was filled with cars. There were a few spaces empty for those marked "Visitors" but every other space was taken. The north end parking lot on the side was for employees; about five spots were held for "field staff", and the rest were for the office staff. Interestingly enough, Jenna pulled into the very same spot she had a few weeks prior, was it to become *her* spot, she mused. With millions of years of evolution, humans seemed to cling to their territorial roots.

Two cars were closest to the building, a late model silver four-door and next to it was a dark copper SUV with a University of Michigan license plate cover. Something told her the SUV was Mr. Ames' car. She couldn't see him driving any of the other cars; they appeared too plain, and he had struck her as kind of a man's man. A man's man would not be caught in a simple four door, not if he could help it. Something told her that Matt could help it. There was strength in his eyes, she remembered, when she looked at him, a stillness that was comforting to be around and safe. It was more than just a few times, she found, that his image would appear in her mind. Once she saw an actor that resembled him while she watched television; she had even popped in the DVD *"Joy Ride"* starring Paul Walker. She sat on her couch, popcorn at her side, and thought of Matt Ames, her soon to be volunteer boss. But not in a lingering way or even romantic. The actor only reminded Jenna of Matt; he wasn't really a dead ringer. Matt's skin was a bit tanner, and Matt's eyes were hazel whereas, Paul's were blue. This movie she had not watched in many years suddenly was a must-see on a lonely Saturday night.

Once Zach returned from Hawaii, Zabbie became quite busy and Jenna only saw her best friend once since their lunch together. The rest of their communication had been virtual, a Facebook comment here, a text there, so she could not be blamed for having a night of longings. Not that her thoughts were given to fantasy about Matt although he was attractive, she had to admit. He rather had this hot professor quality about him. Maybe Jenna had been watching too many Lifetime movies, she thought. This was more the truth she told herself, as she turned off the ignition to her car and settled in to await the arrival of the other trainees.

Jenna thought about the previous Saturday night when she had watched Matt's movie actor lookalike being terrorized by a psycho trucker. The evening did not remain lonely, though, for she did have a visitor. When the film had ended, she had shifted from movie watcher to music listener. There were times when her sadness overcame her and instead of squelching it with positive thoughts, Jenna often delved deeper into it, no doubt a behavior subconsciously learned from her mother. She had broken open a bottle of brandy, and she filled the air with sounds from Sia, an often times melancholy, always delightfully odd, Australian songster. The singer's voice was throaty and haunting, just what she had needed to immerse herself in self-pity. Calm, beautiful nights like those opened the door to her sorrow.

They say misery loves company, and around eleven that evening, when Jenna was contemplating retiring upstairs to her bedroom, the doorbell rang. Wearing only a tank and jersey shorts she paddled barefoot through the living room into the large foyer. Sometimes she wished she was back in her old condo because the walk from anywhere in the house seemed like miles in comparison. The expansive windows, which flanked the ornate wooden entry door, were tinted in such a way that allowed those on the inside to see out, but no one could see in. It was an interesting trick of the light done purposely for security. Jenna tilted her head to get a glimpse of her uninvited guest and instantly smiled when saw them.

"Adrian!" she yelled with glee, before even opening the door. Her exhilaration matched his, for as soon as the door opened two arms lifted her into a powerful hug.

Adrian whirled her around in the foyer, causing her loosely constructed ponytail to whip comically about her. "Jenna! Ahhh, a sight for poor sore eyes!" Adrian placed Jenna down and immediately kissed her forehead lovingly. "Have you put on some weight, Sis?" he joked.

"Fuck you!" Jenna laughed, punching his shoulder. She placed both of her hands through his wildly cascading curls. They had exchanged a long gaze that was filled with homesickness. They had missed each other's company, for sure. Jenna closed the door and led the son of her mother's sister further into the house. She had not seen Adrian since the funeral. The year had past so quickly, it seemed, but she had thought of him daily, wondering where he was and what he was doing. Adrian Franklin, her first cousin, was more like the brother she never had. They were more like siblings because within the family, they were the black sheep, as was her mother before her.

"Would you look at this fucking place?" Adrian said gazing dramatically around. "And you live here by yourself?"

Jenna gestured him into the slightly sunken living room that she never used. The designer she had hired to fill the house with furniture called this room high end traditional with rich paisley patterns and mahogany trims. It was the room where she displayed most of the family pictures. She aligned them on the fireplace mantle as well as on the grand piano, that she also never used. "That's right, you never saw this place. I had a house warming that you never came to."

Adrian sauntered around the room, stopping at the fireplace to gaze into the frozen expressions of their family. There he saw the faces of his mother, sister, and his aunts, just about everyone. He paused at the picture of Khaldun Moussa, who was featured prominently in the middle of them all. The man in the aging portrait had a stern look of ascendancy. He donned a white head wrap and a peppered beard. "So this is what grandfather's money wrought?"

"Mama never spent a dime of it so I did it for her." Jenna said, sitting down on one of the large sofas.

"That you did." Adrian commented absently, as he stared into the photo.

"You don't approve?" Jenna asked a bit insulted.

Adrian turned to her, when he heard the offense in her voice. "Look Jenna, it was your money. Money should never just sit and be wasted." He came over to her. "Hell, did my mother waste her inheritance? No, she did not, she spent it lavishly. She met my father, and her spending continued. Aunt Faye? She saved hers for you. She wanted you to live the way she never allowed herself to live."

"But why? You of all people knew how unhappy she was."

Adrian cupped Jenna's chin. "Money cannot bring happiness to the soul, Imzadi." The nickname "Imzadi" is what he used to call her when they were younger. It came from their love of watching Star Trek, it was a term of endearment. Adrian was five years Jenna's senior, and they were kindred spirits, part of the triad of outcasts, Jenna always felt. Adrian, Jenna's mother, and Jenna were off to the left of the rest of the family, the family for which, Aunt Gina, Adrian's mother, was the definite matriarch. Jenna was an outcast by association with her mother. Adrian made himself an outcast by pure personality and action. He had been accepted to Harvard, a virtual genius, but he only spent a semester at the prestigious school before dropping out and deciding to tramp across Europe and beyond. His ventures did not sit well with his mother who thought of his quitting as the final act of rebellion which she could not forgive, but Adrian didn't care.

Jenna watched as Adrian's eyes welled up with tears for the death of his aunt, Faye Steele. He missed her, she knew. Adrian was the only one her mother had truly opened up to. Jenna used to envy that, but she began to understand that there was something in common between the two of them; something that never existed between her and her mother: It was pure understanding.

Adrian broke away from her suddenly and quickly sat at the piano and began to play a song she did not recognize until he started to sing the words: "Someday when I'm awfully low, when the world is cold, I will feel the glow just thinking of you, and the way you look…tonight." Jenna's mood went from unchained sadness to one of reminiscent rapture. Steve Tyrell's version of the old song; 'The Way You Look Tonight', was her mother's favorite. She joined Adrian on the piano seat and began to sing along with him: "Oh but you're lovely, with your smile so warm, and your cheeks, so soft there is nothing for me but to love you, just the way you look tonight." That was Adrian's gift, to find the joy in the midst of pain. She was so glad he came. They spent the rest of the evening singing, enjoying brandy and sharing memories of her mother, memories she couldn't have shared with anyone else.

Now, as Jenna sat in her car outside of the hospice office she smiled despite herself, thinking of the sleeping soul she had left that morning. She almost hated leaving him, but she was glad she knew where he was, which was a rarity.

The cars slowly started to fill the lot. The trainees pulled in one by one. The sight of them drew her from her thoughts of her weekend with Adrian and into the present. This was the true beginning of her venture into hospice volunteering. This was also her last chance to start the car, pull out of the parking lot and drive home. Was she really sure about doing this? Wasn't the monetary donation enough? Twenty thousand dollars was a lot of money. She was sure that Community Hospice would put it to good use, but was it enough for her? She did want to do more, not just for hospice but for herself. Jenna wanted more for her life. All she had done was become a secretary, answer phones and greeted people. She never completed college. Her mother had gotten sick so she dropped out, but that was not the real reason she didn't continue. The college was only fifteen minutes from her house, and she could have continued. But she did not. The reason had less to do with her mother and more to do with herself. She really had no passion for secretarial work or for the business degree she was pursuing.

Jenna's initial plan was to get her business degree with an emphasis on finance. She would continue working while pursuing her MBA. Then she would work her way up the corporate ladder, a sensible plan, everyone agreed, including her mother. It, however, was not *her* plan. She really had no plan for herself. It was just the most logical thing to do go to school, get a college degree and make money, the end.

Now that she was entirely on her own, she could make decisions based on what she wanted and at her own pace. So yes, she concluded, she was sure about doing this. Jenna exited the car and headed into the building.

FIVE

The conference room was set up in classroom format. Matt had secured the help of two volunteers who assisted with all of his trainings. An elderly woman named Laura, who he affectionately called Miss Laura, prepared the coffee and always brought homemade cookies of varying flavors. The other volunteer was a man in his late 50's named Joe. He arranged the tables effortlessly along with handing out necessary papers to the participants. Joe was also the designated "gopher". He makes copies of trainee drivers' licenses, car insurance certificates and, any other documentation required, not to mention popping in and out to grab something from Matt's office if needed. When not helping with training Joe was one of the few handy men whose assignments ranged from building ramps for patients, mowing grass or shoveling snow. He was also known to help caregivers move furniture their loved one had died.

Miss Laura was the best baker Matt had ever known. She was a retired homemaker, as she called herself, and was known for her confectionery delights. She was always eager to bake for fundraising events and Matt's trainings and meetings, but her largest baking feat of the year was the hospice memorial service. Matt felt that her delicious pies and cupcakes were the only thing that lured the vast number of staff to the memorial service. The grief support manager was very appreciative of that!

"Hey, Miss Laura!" came a voice from behind him. Susan Cobbs had come in. Matt was so lost in his own thoughts he didn't even hear the door open. Susan was Matt's colleague from the South Branch office. Susan, the Director of Volunteer Services there, was here to help him with training. Their other colleague Brandon Thames, Director of Volunteer Services for the West Branch, would be there to assist Matt the following weekend.

Miss Laura looked up and smiled at Susan. Susan returned the smile; then she focused in on Matt. "Did you get my email?" she asked him.

Matt shook his head. "No. Did you need something?" He furrowed his brow and walked towards his office with Susan in tow.

"Yeah, I wanted to know if you had the HIPAA DVD?" Susan ask, following Matt into his office and sitting down in one of the chairs in front of his desk.

"Yes." Matt said, looking at her directly for the first time. "Brandon sent it back to me last week."

Susan put a hand to her chest. "Whew, good! I couldn't remember if I reminded him or not." In the last training which was held at her branch, she had left it, and Brandon had picked it up. She meant to email him to send it back to her, but she had completely forgotten. Susan basically had two full time jobs; for one she received a paycheck, and the other job was taking care of her husband and two boys. The boys' soccer and football games had turned her into a taxi service, and her mind was rarely clear. She was happy that the end of school was coming soon and they would be off to camp. This meant she would be able to focus better. And, speaking of focusing, "What's wrong, Matt? You look a million miles away."

"Do I?" he asked absently as he sat down in his chair. "Must be the training. I always feel as if I'm forgetting something."

"Bullshit." She disagreed. "I am the one who always forgets. Besides, you do training in rote mode. You know the material backwards and foreword. So tell me another one." Susan comically crossed her arms and awaited his response, which did not come quickly.

"Just got a lot on my mind." Matt finally offered after considering another lie.

"Like whether to take the executive position?" Susan asked while cocking her head to one side and lifting one eyebrow.

Matt looked at her in pure shock, "How did you-?" he started, then it came to him, "Barbara."

Susan hunched her shoulders. "It was the topic of conversation at lunch last week." Barbara Steiner, Dave Chatman's secretary was Susan's best friend.

"Barbara is such a busy body." Matt said, very matter of a factly, but Susan could see he was upset that his business was out there.

"Look, I'm sure everyone doesn't know. She just told me because it affects me."

"How does it affect you?" Matt asked.

"Well if my colleague leaves his position for another job then that makes more work for me."

"How so?"

"Between me and Brandon," Susan replied, "I am the senior director, which means I train, which means I take on both branches until they hire someone else. That is if they hire someone else. Heck, with the layoffs they are planning, I doubt they would replace you."

"I didn't think of that." Matt admitted.

"What are you thinking of? Are you going to take the job?"

"I don't know." Matt answered honestly.

"You will." Susan stated assuredly.

Matt looked at her for a moment. He almost felt guilty that he had been seriously thinking about it. "I don't know yet." He lied.

"Why don't I believe that?" Susan's response was met with staring eyes and silence. "You have to think about what's best for you. I know you haven't been happy with the job."

"I love my job." Matt retorted.

"I didn't say you didn't love it; I said you haven't been happy."

Matt glared at her. "And you have been? Come on, how many times do we have to fight to get respect around here? Hell, our job level is barely above a secretary! They think of us as fucking clerks!" Susan nodded her head in agreement. "I mean I am sick of it, aren't you?" Matt asked, desperately hoping for a kindred spirit in his emotions. He didn't quite get what he hoped from her.

"It will always be that way, Matt, I told you that. We've had this conversation before. We have to accept it." Susan told him gravely.

"I can't accept it! How can you?" Matt got up from his chair. "I was sitting with Dave, and man, all I could think about was his thousand dollar suit, his one hundred thousand dollar car, and what do I have?"

"Is this what's this is all about, Matt, money?"

"No. No...not just the money. I mean yeah I want more money; it would help Jake and, of course, keep Connie off of my back, but there's more to it than that."

"What more is there, Matt?" Susan asked in an unintentional motherly tone.

Suddenly Matt felt a bit foolish. What was it about? He didn't clearly know himself. Was it all just about the money? Possibly forty percent was, sure, yet is it wrong to want more money from a job you come to work at daily, sometimes doing uncompensated overtime? Was that wrong? Is it a sin to want to be prosperous? To be ambitious? Maybe Susan didn't completely understand. She was a woman after all, with a husband who was a successful engineer and earned enough to provide for his family. This job, for her, was a way to feel as if she was contributing, a way for her to feel worthy and gain independence. The respect, for Susan, had already been achieved, but Matt, he needed much more. Yes, he loved his job, but no, it wasn't enough.

"I'm sorry, I don't mean to lay this on you." Matt said. "Dave did tell me about the opening coming up, and yes I have been considering it." Susan nodded, as Matt spoke. "But that's all it is right now, a consideration, I haven't decided anything yet."

Susan stood and turned to leave. She needed get ready for her portion of the training. She turned and flashed a smile of understanding, at Matt, yet she knew Matt had already made up his mind. She was right. All that Matt was doing now was waiting for a reason *not* to leave.

SIX

As the new trainees made their way into the building, Matt busied himself with the setup of the computer for the PowerPoint presentations. He was expecting about twenty people. Periodically, he would glance up and smile at those who entered, checking them off mentally in his mind. He did not recognize a few of the trainees because they were coming from other areas. There were two other Community Hospice branches in the region, and volunteers were allowed to train at any of the three sites. It was Matt's turn to host the training. Susan was co-facilitating with him. She was great with the ice breakers. She usually had one or more of her three kids with her, but today, when he saw her walk in, she was alone. Matt breathed a sigh of relief because sometimes Susan's youngest boy, Tommy, would not sit still. Her teenagers were never a bother though, and often helped out when they were at a training.

When Susan came into the room a few beats before Matt, she had also made a quick visual sweep of the room as Matt had done counting her own trainees. She nodded at a few before walking up to Matt. "My husband decided to be thoughtful," She told him, "He scooped up the kids today, yet he left without waking me! *Idiot.* The only thing that woke me up was a damned chirping bird outside my window. I am shocked I woke up at all. I love Paul, but he sometimes misses the boat! The hilarity that is my life!" Susan chuckled.

"You mean I'm not going to see my little buddy today?" Matt quipped.

"Yeah right, like you wanted to see Tommy running around wreaking havoc?"

"I love Tommy!"

Susan looked at him and laughed. "The only people who love Tommy are me and soon his future parole officers." She nudged Matt with her elbow. "Am I right? Now where do you need me?"

"I think Miss Laura has the food set up and I have Joe making copies of a new handout for the HIPPA piece. Just get ready for your ice breaker." Matt responded.

"Oooooh, I wonder if she made those oatmeal cookies I love?" Susan said licking her lips dramatically.

"No, I think she made molasses this time."

"Oh my God. That woman is going to keep me fat! Oh and I have a new icebreaker, one with a ball. I think its going to be fun." She sped off to open the rolling brief case she brought in.

Matt frowned and smiled, at the same time perplexed at Susan's comment about Miss Laura keeping her fat. Susan couldn't have weighed much over 120 pounds. It amused him how much women were so focused on their weight. His ex wife was a curvy woman at about 150 pounds, but to hear her tell it she weighed well over 500 pounds. Matt thought it was all so ludicrous.

Everything seemed to be coming together nicely. He announced to those who were sitting in their seats that coffee and bagels were on the table and to help themselves. He checked his watch, noting that he had about ten minutes before the training was to begin. He thought he would sneak a moment back in his office to check a few emails. When he walked out of the room, he almost ran into Jenna who was just coming in.

"Morning Ms. Steele." He greeted her, as he grabbed hold of her arm to steady her before they collided.

"Oops, I'm sorry. Still sleep I guess." Jenna said.

"Then grab some of my liquid stimulant inside, as well as a seat. We should be getting started in just a few moments." Matt and Jenna exchanged a brief gaze and a smile. As she went past, Matt caught a whiff of her perfume. He couldn't place the brand, but the smell of it sent a curious surge through him. He promptly ignored it, but his colleague, Susan, caught it and smirked to herself.

When it seemed the participants had gotten their coffee and settled into their seats, Susan stepped up to the front of the room. "Hello and welcome to hospice volunteer training. I am Susan Cobbs, the Director of Volunteer Services for Community Hospice South Branch and in the back of the room standing watch is Matthew Ames, Director of Volunteer Services for East Branch where we are now. We are so pleased that you have decided to become a hospice volunteer. This could prove to be the hardest but also the most rewarding thing that you have ever. Each of you has your own experiences and reasons for sitting in that seat today, and as we go around the room, I want to hear what that is. Please be as brief or as open as you wish to be. Some of you may not know why you are here and some of you have very specific goals for your volunteer journey. First, lets' get the people who are being paid to be here out of the way. I am Susan Cobbs and I have been with Community Hospice for over ten years. My first 4 years were spent in the human resources department. I am in a sense, still in the HR department, but now I have a much nicer workforce to oversee." Susan laughed, and the crowd joined her.

"No, but seriously," Susan continued, "all of the staff I have encountered working in hospice are wonderful people. You will hear terms like angels on earth, or guardians, or special people. You will soon be called the same things, but I already know that you are which is why you're here. I have been married for over twenty years, which means I got married at age of seven." The trainees chuckled. "I married my high school sweetheart, and yes we do still exist for you youngsters in the room. I have three wonderful children and my husband is very supportive. My family are my source of strength. We will speak later about having a support system as we discuss self care. Having a support system is so very important when doing hospice work." Susan stressed. Then she gestured towards Matt. "Matt, could you introduce yourself?"

Bodies shifted in his direction. "Good morning all I'm Matthew Ames, I have been working for Community Hospice for about five years, and I absolutely love my job. I think of myself as the liaison between you and your hospice volunteer work. It has given me much joy and pride to do what I do, and I hope to continue doing this work for many years to come. To the left of me, sitting over to the side, are two of our most dedicated and gracious volunteers who have always helped me with trainings, Joe Carter and Laura Bingham or Miss Laura as I call her." Joe and Laura each waved respectively.

"Imitation of Life!" a trainee yelled out, and Matt smiled.

"You are absolutely right, that's where I got that from." He said pointing at the trainee who seemed quite pleased that she was right. "If you look at the packet in front of you should see the outline for the material we will be covering today, as well as next Saturday. Susan and I, as well as the other trainers will be doing a bunch of talking up here but we don't want to be doing all of the talking. Please speak up," Matt continues, "stop us, and ask questions. We want this to be an interactive training," he stressed. "and speaking of interactive I'll turn it back over to Susan who will start us off with your introductions and an ice breaker. Once again, welcome." Matt concluded.

Susan nodded at Matt and continued on with the introductions. Matt returned to his hands in pocket stance and awaited his next cue. He and

Susan had gotten volunteer training down to a virtual science. Even his introduction was rehearsed and memorized with minimal variations. Matt never mentioned whether he was married or not because he felt that was a bit personal. Besides, what would he say? Unlike Susan's glorious stable marriage, his sucked and he was now a divorced father of one, nope better to omit that altogether.

As he listened to each person give their name and reasons for being there he thought about his introduction. *Love my job.... Many years to come...?.* Was that the truth? It was partly true; yet, he had to admit, ever since sitting with Dave at the bar and being offered a higher level position that paid a lot more money, emphasis on a lot, he wasn't sure it would be for many years to come as he had stated. This may very well be his last year in volunteer services. On the other hand, Matt did not lie about loving his job. He really did. Now, if he could only figure out how to ignore the average pay, the lack of respect for the middle management role in the company, and his ex wife screaming about more child support, this could very well be a position he would gladly retire from. Was loving the work enough? He has a son to take care of and support, a son who will likely seek to play team sports, a son who will go to college one day, and all of these things cost money. And what about Matt? He did want to marry again and possibly have more children, and that would require a higher income. Matt wondered if he could really stay in this job forever? It didn't seem likely at all.

"Ok, everyone, stand up!" Susan yelled, jarring Matt out of his thoughts. She sliced her arm into the air. "Everyone to the right of my arm stand and look to your left. Everyone to left of my arm stand and look to your right." She picked up the soccer ball that had been at her feet. She began tossing it into the air. "Ok, now make a straight line so some of you are going to have to move."

Matt decided to join Susan at the front of the room not quite knowing what to expect. Susan continued. "Ok, this is what's called a Thumb Ball and on it are 32 phrases such as Best Thing I've Ever Eaten, My Favorite Vacation Spot, etc... I'm going to toss the ball to you, and you will read the phrase under your right thumb and then tell us your favorite place or whatever. Ok? Once you have answered," Susan continued, "You must then toss the ball to the person across from you. Alright, now I'll start it off by tossing the ball into the air."

Susan tossed the small silver and black ball into the air, caught it and read what the phrase said. "What makes me laugh? Hmmmm so many things makes me laugh," she said, "but what makes me laugh the most is my little dog Feathers. We named her that because her fur is soft like feathers. She can get into such a tizzy, and she'll run around the house chasing nothing. She'll bark, then she starts chasing her tail, round and round and round! It is the cutest thing," Susan declared, "but it is so hilarious! Feathers is in her own little world, and it is just the funniest thing to watch! My husband thinks she's psychotic, but it is so funny!" Susan giggled thinking about it, then tossed the ball to Matt. "Your turn!"

Matt caught the ball and looked under his thumb, "Most embarrassing moment? Wow, I've had so many," he said. Matt thought for a second; then it came to him. "Ok, one of my most embarrassing moments happened a few years ago. I was invited to a corporate dinner with a lot of the big wigs from our board of trustees. As I was at the table talking to our CEO and a couple of board members, I let out this extremely loud burp!" The trainees burst into laughter.

"I remember that!" Susan cackled.

"Yeah, well, I apologized," Matt said, "but here I was at this classy affair with my bosses, new bosses mind you, the first time meeting the CEO and trying my best to impress everyone and I let out a huge one. Embarrassed? I think I hid up at the bar the rest of the night!"

"We still call him Burp Man!" Susan said jokingly.

Once again red with humiliation Matt tossed the ball across to the first volunteer, and around and around it went. The class really got into it, and even though it took a little longer than some of the other icebreakers, it proved to be more successful.

The first eight hours of training are all about orientating the new volunteer to exactly what hospice is and what it is not, and dispelling the myths. Susan and Matt alternated subjects. Susan began with the toss across icebreaker, and next up was Matt with the Introduction to Hospice. Jenna noticed how calm and precise Matt was when he spoke. He chose his words carefully, allowing enough time for questions, although not many questions were asked. People were relatively quiet, but quite often you could see several trainees jotting down notes on the writing pad provided.

As Matt expounded on the vision of Dr. Cicely Saunders, the founder of modern day hospice, Jenna's eyes traveled lazily over the crisp blue collar of Matt's shirt. His suit was a simple charcoal grey, quite professional. The absence of a tie made his look more casual. The speech fell from his mouth with the ease of an experienced orator, each movement, each point to the screen, each poignant gesture, intended.

Jenna played a game with herself to pass the time as the lecture ensued. She would see how long she could trap his gaze each time his eyes reached hers as they traveled indiscriminately over the class. Sometimes it was just a quick glance; other times he held it longer. One second, two, three, and oh my, four full seconds! Jenna wanted to let out a hearty *yes!* though she was sure her co-trainees would not understand her gaiety. Instead she looked away after Matt did and smiled to herself.

Matt Ames spoke with his hands. He pointed his fingers up when he talked about the Medicare regulations. He rolled them slowly in front of him when he spoke about how hospice evolved in the United States from the first hospice in Connecticut all the way up to Community Hospice in Michigan. When Matt called on people to respond to why they felt hospice was under utilized in America, his head bobbed slightly in that person's direction.

As distracted as Jenna had become with Matt's appealing distinctiveness, she did hear things she was not aware of, such as how not all patients die on hospice. Some people do get better once their pain is controlled. Jenna did have to admit that she believed all hospices fell under the same umbrella, like a government agency. To learn that it is a philosophy and not just another regimented program was more comforting, and it made her decision to come for training more meaningful.

SEVEN

"So, am I boring you?" Matt asked a snack seeking Jenna on their first break.

She had eyed the sharp cheddar cheese cubes from across the room. As Jenna filled her plate with them, along with some pepperoni slices, she answered him. "No, quite the contrary, it's all very interesting." Jenna suddenly remembered the earlier game she was playing with herself. "Did I look bored?" she asked wondering if her expression was telling the tale.

"Sometimes, when I look at the crowd, I have to wonder if I'm losing people, that's all." Matt responded as he reached over and snagged an individual-sized bottle of orange juice.

Just then a petite, elderly woman appeared out of nowhere. "You weren't losing me, Mr. Ames. You have a way with words." She maneuvered herself a bit in between Matt and Jenna. "You know, when my husband died in hospice a few years ago, you all were so caring, I don't know what I would have done without you! A nurse named Thelma came in, do you know her?" The woman didn't give Matt a chance to answer, "She was wonderful. I don't know how many times she had to tell me about my husband's medications over and over. See Randolph, that was my husband, had rheumatoid arthritis something awful but that...."

Matt was trapped, Jenna observed, so, she continued down the table and got her own bottle of juice, then went back to her seat. Stocked well with cheese, she noticed she had a couple more minutes of break-time and thought it an opportune time to check on her houseguest.

Somewhere in the distance, the annoying digital sound of the phone filtered into Adrian's groggy ears. He was lying on his back with a pillow covering his face on the loveseat inside one of the three guest bedrooms. Adrian truly considered ignoring the phone, but a strange sort of curiosity struck him. The phone rang only once since he had arrived last night. Apparently, his lovely cousin was not dating anyone, or perhaps people just called her cell phone. Adrian did remember Jenna speaking about an ex-boyfriend a few months back. Maybe the call was from him, making an "are you still mad?" phone call check after a night of pining over her. It would serve him right if a sleepy, annoyed male voice answered Jenna's phone on a Saturday morning.

"*Hahlow?*" Adrian said, in the deepest voice he could muster.

"Are you still sleeping?" Jenna asked Adrian.

Adrian sat up a bit exasperated he wouldn't be pissing off Jenna's ex. "Nope, I'm up!" he lied. "What time is it?" he said as his eyes searched the room and finally found an ornate clock on the wall. Jenna told him it was going on eleven, confirming what the clock read. "Where are you?" Adrian asked Jenna. He felt the room spin slightly when he stood up and headed towards the bathroom. Vertigo was a morning-after sensation Adrian knew all too well.

"I'm at volunteer training; remember I told you about that." Jenna replied.

"Vaguely."

"I was calling to let you know that there is food in the fridge, help yourself. I'm also wondering what your plans are?"

Adrian finished relieving himself and flushed the toilet. "What, kicking me out already?" he quipped.

"No, of course not, just thought maybe we'd have dinner tonight, and go to a club?"

"Cool! Let's party and get our freak on!" Adrian said as he danced, watching his reflection in the bathroom mirror.

Jenna laughed. "No, I was thinking more of a lounge-type situation. Some jazz, you know where *grown folks* go?"

"Grown Folks? I'm sorry, but I'm not familiar with this term." Adrian responded.

"Yeah, ok." Jenna said. "Looks like they're starting back up here. I should be home by four, so be ready by seven? And the seafood's on me."

"Great Sis, the drinks are on me!"

Jenna clicked off the phone and watched as Susan Cobbs took her place at the podium. "The Role of the Volunteer" she announced and began to get into Section Three of their manual. Susan, though prolific, was a more rigid sort of speaker, leaving no games for Jenna to make up for her amusement. Instead, Jenna followed along in the book as the trainer spoke.

The rest of the day was spent learning about the Health Insurance Portability and Accountability Act or HIPAA, very stimulating material, but Susan made it make sense easily. She explained that you never know who you are talking to. We are only a few degrees away from everyone in the world, which is the reason why confidentiality is so important to the patients and families.

While Jenna learned about the rules of hospice volunteering, Adrian sat on her couch flipping through endless cable channels, even a few pay per view channels, to pass the time during his waking period. Waking up was something he tried to do less and less in the past six months. He had grieved his aunt's death in silence and in the shadows. Faye's death meant a life of being truly alone to him. She was the only one who understood his darkness. She was the only one who accepted it no matter his age. Unlike his mother, Faye saw him for exactly what he was, a man. She did not see a little boy for whom she bore ten hours of labor, or for whom she changed diapers; no, Faye saw a human being who existed, though separate from herself, along side of herself. There was no judging there. There were no ludicrous expectations of a life filled with imagined successes. No, Faye Steele saw him for just who he was, Adrian Franklin, nothing more, and definitely nothing less. In his Aunt Faye's eyes, he was incredible, unique, and rare; he was a person, and he was alive and real.

When Adrian stood alone over Faye's grave, in the dark long after the funeral was over, he knew that a physical part of him was buried with her. He was lost. He was unaided. That night, avoiding the family reception, he traveled to a nearby bar and sat omitted in a corner booth. To his surprise that night, an angel sat beside him. Elizabeth Meyers, Zabbie to her friends, offered him an ear and a shoulder. Zabbie had been at the bar a week prior and misplaced her cell phone. The bartender had contacted her, and she returned to retrieve it. During her cell phone rescue she saw a familiar figure hunched down in a corner booth. She approached her best friend's cousin, Adrian, realizing the pain he must be in over his Aunt Faye's death. Zabbie offered her warmth and kindness, and Adrian accepted it openly. By the night's end Zabbie found herself engulfed in Adrian's arms. She was not sure if it was his grief's need to feel love, but it was her need to fulfill a long time crush she had for her friend's dark, handsome family member.

When morning came a part of Zabbie regretted the impromptu encounter, but she continued to allow herself to repeat that night several times in the months to come. Though she was heavy into a relationship with Zach, she found she could not resist Adrian's calls. Was she using him? Zabbie wasn't sure but she was sure that it had to end. As fate would have it she asked Adrian to meet her at the same bar where their relationship had started. It was there she told him that their relationship could go no further. It was Adrian's expression of pure bewilderment and ache that she would remember for many years to come. Zabbie left him there quite the same as she had found him, lost and alone.

Seventeen months passed since being left in that bar, and now Adrian once again laid eyes on the source of his hidden anguish. Neither one of them shared their relationship with Jenna. Tonight he followed Jenna into the trendy club, NightOwl, feeling very excited about getting out and enjoying the evening. Then, when he saw Zabbie in a casual embrace with a man whom she was clearly in love with, sitting at the very table where he and Jenna were apparently headed, all excitement drained from him with an almost violent force.

"Hello you two." Jenna greeted brightly. "You guys remember my cousin, Adrian. I dragged him out with me tonight!"

Upon seeing Adrian standing next to Jenna looking down on her, the liquid in Zabbie's throat entered her wind pipe, and she began to choke. Immediately Zach patted her back. He looked up at them. "Hey, what's up, Adrian. Welcome back."

"Thanks." Adrian said, eyes fixed on the coughing Zabbie. Somehow that made him feel pretty good. He was still able to cause some kind of reaction within her. Yeah, that felt pretty damned good.

Jenna and Adrian sat down across from the couple. Zabbie was drenching her throat with the water Zach handed her. Slowly, she regained her ability to speak. "Hey." is all she could manage. She patted her chest while following Adrian's descent into the chair in front of her. Neither said a word, but their eyes exchanged volumes of conversation.

"What can I get you two in drinks? I'm buying all tonight!" Zach offered. "Wait I know, Margarita for you Jenna, and for you Adrian?"

"Corona." Adrian answered, glancing briefly at Zach. His eyes returned to Zabbie. "Are you ok? Something go down the wrong way?" He asked as one side of his mouth curled into a wry smile, mocking her.

Zabbie saw that he was deriving some kind of sick pleasure from her choking. "I'm fine." she retorted harshly.

"How long have you guys been here?" Jenna asked.

"Just long enough to get a drink and find a seat." Zach said.

"You two looked so cozy, I almost hated to disturb you." Jenna said, winking comically at them both. Zach returned her laughter, but Zabbie did not. Zabbie did not notice the humor at all.

"Well, there is a reason for that." Zach beamed, scooting a reluctant Zabbie in closer to him. "Babe, why don't you give them the good news."

Zabbie felt her new fiancé's arm slide around her back, but it was only when Adrian broke off his piercing stare and turn his attention to Zach that she woke up from the tailspin of the daze she was under.

"Good news?" Adrian asked Zach, his brow furrowing deeper and deeper by the second.

Zach, a bit confused at Zabbie's changed demeanor, answered. "Yes, we've finally set a date."

Jenna's face lit up. "Whoa! Finally is right! This is great news!" Jenna placed a hand on top of Zabbie's. "I can't wait, now we can get started on the real planning! This is going to be so much fun! Why didn't you tell me you two were so close to setting a date?"

"I didn't realize." Zabbie said somberly looking directly at Adrian.

"Oh, I am so happy for you two! This is going to be the wedding of the century!" Jenna put a hand to her chest, and then falling backwards in her seat. "I don't know why I'm so excited but I am! I love weddings!"

"Thanks, Jenna. I'm counting on you to keep her sane through this." Zach said. "I know how you ladies like to go a bit crazy planning weddings. I promise to stay out of the way and only surface when asked!" he said, smiling broadly.

"Are you sure?" Adrian asked the uncharacteristically somber Zabbie, who averted her eyes, by looking down at the cocktail napkin.

Zach looked at Adrian. "Why wouldn't she be?" he asked trying to maintain his smile.

"It's a big step." Adrian said, but his eyes didn't leave Zabbie's ever darkening face. "I want her to understand what she is doing. I want her to realize that when she sets a date, that date makes it final." Adrian watched, hoped, his words would cause Zabbie to hesitate, but his words did not.

Zabbie looked up at him with sudden anger. "It's final." she said with stark conclusiveness. "I love him." The directness of her words made her switch to Jenna and smile. "June 2nd this will be a Saturday next year. Perfect. It will be perfect."

"You better believe it will be perfect!" Jenna said still gushing. "Ahh, I am so happy for you two."

"I know you are." Zabbie said, which caused Zach to pause again and look at her. Her attitude was strange, and he did not like it at all. He was finding her gloominess to be highly inappropriate.

"Perfect, huh?" Adrian inquired. "Then why do you look and sound like you have just agreed to a death sentence?"

"That's a very good question." Zach said to Zabbie. He lowered his voice, leaning into her. "I thought this is what you wanted, what *we* wanted?"

"It is." she whispered back to him softly.

"Well, is it or isn't it?" Adrian demanded. "You sound really unsure right now."

Zach locked in on him, dropping the courtesies. "Excuse me, Adrian, but what business is it of yours?"

Zabbie clutched Zach's arm. "Zach." she pleaded gently.

"No! I have sat here and pretended not to notice his eyes on you, and you returning his gaze. What the hell is going on? Why do you care so much, man?"

"Just being a friend." Adrian answered him, yet the wrinkle in his smirk told another story.

"I don't think so, dude." Zach said then looked at Zabbie. "You want to tell me something?"

"No!" she exclaimed, her eyes widening. "Let's just drop it. Leave it alone." Zabbie pleaded with him as their drinks arrived. Zach's eyes narrowed as he saw Adrian's smirk widen.

"Nah, this is some bullshit." Zach said after the waitress left. "How do you two know each other?" he asked Adrian.

"They don't. They only know *of* each other, right Zabbie?" Jenna offered, trying to diffuse what was about to occur.

Zach looked at Zabbie for confirmation, and he got it through her violent nods.

"She *knows* me." Adrian admitted sternly. He avoided the shocked daggers coming from Zabbie's eyes.

"Really?" Zach asked him, while straightening up, readying himself for what he was about to do next. "How does she *know* you?"

"Baby," Zabbie almost yelled. "He doesn't know me; he's just screwing with your head. Now sit back and enjoy your drink."

Zach ignored her while watching as Adrian spoke, "Good advice, my man." Adrian said, and waited.

"Zach," Zabbie started scooting in as close to him as possible. "I love you. WE are getting married. Baby, don't listen to him, don't listen." Zabbie mustered up the sweetest voice she could. Her tone always seemed to calm him, and for a moment it was working. She could feel his muscles begin to relax under her grip.

Adrian and Zach's eyes were locked for the longest time and, yes, Zach was relaxing. He was just about to sit back and pick up his drink when these words entered his ears, cutting deep into his soul. "Don't you love that voice of hers?" Adrian began, "I used to love it when she would talk like that to me in the morning…" Adrian watched as Zach focused back in on him, "She would speak so gently, and moan so sweetly…"

Zach's face contorted into a painfully perplexed grimace, "What?" he asked, barely audible.

"Don't you love that tattoo deep inside her left thigh? What are the words written beneath that tiny heart? *Just for you?*" Before Adrian even got out the three word tattoo Zach had jumped across the table and punched him square in the mouth. Jenna was knocked backwards onto the floor by the force of the blow. Zabbie began to scream uncontrollably, begging her fiancé to stop pounding her ex-lover in the face. It took two large, bulky bouncers to pull Zach off of him.

Even as the blood flowed freely down Adrian's face he managed a private smile. As he pulled himself up into an upright position, he heard the far away shout of Zabbie into his face. "Why couldn't you just shut up?" She yelled. When he looked up at her he saw her teeth grind in front of him, and then she was gone, running off to Zach's aid as he was being brutally escorted out of the bar.

Adrian grimaced at the pain starting to throb on the side of his right eye. "Did you get the number of that truck?" he quipped, as Jenna plopped down in the seat where Zach had been seated. He could feel her eyes boring into him. Instead of meeting Jenna's gaze Adrian opted to take a drink of his beer.

"What the fuck just happened?" Jenna asked. Her expression was of pure puzzlement laced with rising irritation.

"I shattered a few bubbles is all." Adrian finally offered, after taking a few painstaking swigs of his bottle.

"Bubbles?" Jenna asked. She could not even begin to imagine what her cousin was finding so funny about all of this, yet that ridiculous grin never left his face. "You think this is funny? "

"A little." Adrian replied as he reached into his jacket pocket and retrieved a Marlboro box. He lit a cigarette and sat back looking into her angered face. "What's wrong Imzadi? You look a little disheveled."

Jenna shook her head. Her expression went from anger to pity. "You know, it's just like you to whirl back into town and fuck everything up. You get some sort of pleasure out of it don't you? I mean this is entertainment for you, isn't it?"

"It's not a party until someone gets their ass kicked." Adrian said then flicked his hand at her glass. "Finish your drink. No need to let previous unpleasantries ruin the evening."

Jenna had always heard about the fights, arguments, and sexual entanglements that her cousin would get into from other family members. She used to laugh at them when Adrian would give her the drama filled scoop after the fact. Jenna's mother used to love his stories, as well, especially the parts where Adrian's mother, her sister, would lose her cool. Yet now, looking at him from across the table, and after witnessing it first hand, it didn't seem so amusing. In fact, it was downright disgusting to her. Her mother was dead but life continued on for him as if nothing had ever happened. When you lose someone so close, weren't you supposed to learn something from it? Weren't you supposed to grow and change somehow? There would be no need for a riveting tale from Adrian this time. The news has a different effect when you're in the middle of it rather than just watching it on TV.

Jenna wanted to ask Adrian about the affair he and Zabbie had been involved in, but she suddenly didn't care to hear it. What difference did it make right now? None, as far as she was concerned. Instead, Jenna reached over the table and retrieved her purse. "I'm going home." She said. "I will check in with my best friend to see if she's ok, then I'm going to bed." She stood and paused for a moment, looking down on him. She didn't say anything but was waiting to see if he was coming, too, more as a courtesy than anything else. She knew he would not be.

As if on cue, Adrian spoke. "I'm gonna stay here and finish my drink. Don't wait up." He looked into her displeased eyes until she walked away. When she was gone, Adrian wiped away the blood on his face and ordered a stiffer drink this time. He sat alone for only a minute before making his way to the bar where he gulped down several more shots before finding a comforting female torso to ease his wounds. It didn't take long.

EIGHT

While Adrian Franklin's face was being pummeled by Zachary Emanuele, Samantha Mills was gripping the arm of her seat and clenching the paperback novel, she was reading, to her chest. The captain had just asked the passengers of Delta Flight 2131 from New York, LaGuardia Airport to be prepared for a little turbulence as they entered into the darkening clouds above Detroit Metropolitan Airport. The two-hour flight had seemed like an eternity to her. Samantha hadn't flown in over ten years. She had enjoyed driving back and forth from her hometown of Bloomfield Hills, Michigan to New York City, a drive that added eight hours to her trip but one she liked more than flying. Samantha's father always joked that it wasn't the flying she was scared of; it was the falling out of the sky, an old joke she was sick of hearing.

Samantha had chosen to fly home this time because her health had taken a sudden turn for the worst, and she honestly felt unable to make that long drive. About a month or so prior, Samantha had been leading a meeting with colleagues in the ad agency where she worked, and in the middle of speaking, suddenly, her knees buckled and she toppled over. Her co-workers came to her assistance and helped her to a nearby chair. She had blamed it on the wires from the LCD projector, but after days of continued fatigue and odd sensations in her fingers when she typed, she finally made an appointment with her doctor. What he told her drained the blood from her face.

"Samantha, you have Amyotrophic Lateral Sclerosis, ALS commonly known as Lou Gehrig's disease. It's a disease in which certain nerve cells in the brain and spinal cord slowly disintegrate. These nerve cells are called motor neurons, and they control the muscles that allow you to move the various parts of your body, which is why you fell down at your meeting." Dr. Muhammad Zaire had explained this to her rather mechanically.

"Lou Gehrig's disease?" Samantha repeated trying to search her mind for meaning.

"You may want to put your health care choices in writing in the form of a living will." Dr. Zaire continued. "This will give you control over your own medical care when you can't make decisions or speak for yourself. You may also want to choose someone to handle decisions for you medically with a durable power of attorney. It's a good idea to make these plans ahead of time."

"Living will? Power of attorney? Doctor, am I going to die?" Samantha asked. She wanted Dr. Zaire to stop making a speech and give her real answers, preferably any answer than the one he gave.

"There is no cure for ALS." Dr. Zaire replied. "However, with treatment and assistance you may be able to stay independent for some time. Your illness if quite advanced, however, I would suggest you begin to put your affairs in order, contact your family, and begin to prepare." He added.

"Are you sure it couldn't just be low blood sugar or low iron?" Samantha asked hopefully. "I haven't been taking care of myself lately. I've been so busy at work; I haven't been eating…" A bird flew up to the window and perched on the window sill. It was a small bird, a sparrow possibly; it was simple in color, swatches of browns. It had a white patch on its head like a little hat. The wings twitched as if adjusting itself. Cocking its head to one side the two stared at each other for some time. As Samantha watched the sparrow sitting there, it was then she knew in her heart it was not low iron.

"I'm going to write you prescriptions for Lioresal, Dilantin and morphine to help with the pain." Dr. Zaire scribbled out the prescriptions and handed them to Samantha. She was still watching the sparrow on the window sill, he waited patiently. Peripherally, Samantha, saw his outstretched arm and turned away from the bird, absently taking the papers from him.

Dr. Zaire further explained about the symptoms Samantha could expect, the progression of the disease, and treatments, and he ended by offering her the option of getting a second opinion. When Samantha started heading towards the door, as if he just remembered, Dr. Zaire picked up a pamphlet from off a shelf and handed it to Samantha. Now, as the plane was making its descent into Detroit, she remembered reading only one word on the brochure: Hospice.

In the air the clouds had been threatening, yet on the ground it was just a typical partly cloudy evening in springtime Michigan. Samantha had scooped up her one travel bag and hopped into the nearest taxi. She rattled off her parent's address then sat back in the seat silently. Thankfully it would be a forty minute drive. She had the time to reflect as the cab whizzed through the late evening freeway traffic. I-275 to I-96 to Telegraph, then to an aptly named street called Hidden Lake. It was very appropriate for what she was doing, going back to hide in her high school bedroom. She was back to the posters of Prince sitting ominously on his motorcycle in all his purpleness, back to the real Michael Jackson propped up on one elbow from the Thriller album, and even back to a hot poster of Apollonia 6, but only because, back then, many people thought she resembled the lucky Prince costar.

Samantha's mother kept her room exactly as she left it. She went in periodically only to change the sheets and dust. Samantha found it comforting to step into the time capsule of her old room. The only thing new in her room was a fresh coat of lilac paint to replace the old lilac color. The posters were brought down, then carefully replaced just as they had been in the 80s. A few times on her trip back home Samantha thought of telling her mother to turn her room into a guest room or library, or something but she was glad she never had the courage to say that. Samantha thought once she got married and had kids that it would be a bit obscene to still have the room that way, not to mention embarrassing, but the marriage never came, neither did the kids. She supposed she never grew up enough for those either, however, that was not the real reason.

Samantha had come close to marriage and children only once in her life to Kenneth Ford, age 22, Samantha's age was 21. He asked, and she said yes. Samantha remembered the day vividly. She had awoken in Kenny's arms the day after her college graduation. He had booked a gorgeous five star hotel room complete with a Jacuzzi. The room was a welcome escape after the exhausting day smiling relentlessly with family and friends. He understood her need to flee and always planned little private excursions away from the world. Kenny understood everything about her. He understood her love for the color purple; he understood her love of pink roses, and he understood her love for him. Because of this love, when her eyes opened on May 24, 1996, he greeted her with a smile, a pink rose, and the smells of freshly delivered breakfast. As soon as she was fully wake he produced the ring he was hiding behind his back and asked Samantha to marry him. Through joyful tears Samantha said yes.

Now, fourteen years later, Samantha saw the rest of that morning as a euphoric haze of images, the two of them enjoying breakfast, making plans, making love and creating a future. After they had checked out of the room that afternoon, Kenneth dropped her back home. The plan was for Kenneth to return to her house for dinner where they would share the good news officially with her parents. Her mother had cooked lamb chops with gorgonzola butter and vichyssoise soup. While waiting for Kenny to arrive, Samantha's parents sat at the dining room table with Samantha. She jumped up at the sound of every car and would peek out the window. The call finally came at 8:45pm. Kenneth's car had been struck by a semi truck as he was merging onto the freeway. He had been killed instantly.

Samantha had retreated back to her bedroom where she stayed in virtual isolation and grief for almost two straight years afterwards. Samantha's mother had begged her to seek counseling and then demanded she get on with her life. Samantha did; she escaped to college in New York, some six hundred miles away from her mother's intrusion. Samantha received her MBA in marketing in record time. She landed a respectable job before the ink was dry on her degree. New York was the perfect hiding place. The noise, the crowds, and the independent mentality of each resident gave her plenty of buffers from her life in the Midwest, a life that had died along with Kenneth. Everyone on the streets of Manhattan seemed to be running from something; they were all island refugees, with no desire to return to the normal world where they seemed to no longer fit.

It was approaching the hour of ten and Samantha knew what was occurring in her parent's home. Her mother, Lynnette, would be getting out of her nightly bath with her hot chamomile tea cooling bedside. Her father, Joseph, would still be downstairs in his study. After the usual dinner and primetime TV with her mother, Joe was happy to be in his man cave where he checked stock, played online games, and watched CNN. Her mother hated the news and loved her solitude before bed.

Samantha's taxi pulled into the circular drive halted under the cement balcony. Motion lights clicked on as the car pulled in. Joseph Mills was really big on security. Samantha knew that the security camera clicked to their location on the screens in her father's study, no, sneaking in there. Sneaking in was Samantha's wish, but she knew it wouldn't happen. Her mother might not respond to the screens that were also located in the master bedroom, but her father would, which is why Samantha had contacted her father to tell him when she would be getting in. Samantha had also spoken to him throughout her progressing illness. Joe was good at keeping secrets from his wife, especially when his only daughter had asked him to; otherwise, he was an open book.

Joe met his daughter at the door and tipped the driver. As the taxi pulled away, Joe pulled Samantha into a long strong hug. No words were passed between them and it took an extra second or two before Joe could release his daughter. Samantha did not mind. Once he let her go, he asked Samantha, "How was your flight?"

"A little turbulence on landing, nothing serious." She answered, following him into the house.

"You packed awfully light." Joe remarked, heading up the stairs to her room.

"We'll send for the rest." Samantha answered distantly.

"How do you feel?" Joe made it a point not to sound too probing.

"Tired." She said. Samantha watched as he carefully placed her bag into the wicker rocker. She thought he put a bit too much precision into the act.

Joe stood for a moment as they exchanged a knowing look. "Get some rest. I'll see you in the morning." He said.

All Samantha could manage was a fleeting smile and nod. She watched as her father slowly left the room, closing the door behind him. Samantha went to her bedroom dresser and pulled the 5x7 photo of Kenneth from under her folded nightshirts. She placed it on her nightstand. "See you in the morning." She whispered to his smiling image. She slipped off her shoes and slid under the covers fully clothed, and she slept.

NINE

Matthew made his way into the large conference room on the staff side of the building. The Interdisciplinary Team Meeting, or IDT, was held weekly on Tuesday starting at 8am. It was Matt's turn to provide breakfast so he set down two boxes of bagels along with an assortment of jelly donuts. He also bought a gallon of orange juice for the non coffee drinkers. There was a list on the door where the team could sign up to bring in breakfast, and each team member took their turn, or at least they were supposed to. He had been lax in remembering to provide the morning snacks, but last week Matt made it a special point to sign up.

Shannon made the coffee for the crew. She had already set out the first round of caffeinated goodness right before Matt came in. Soon after setting up, he quickly dashed out and retrieved his laptop and notes for the meeting. Each Monday afternoon was spent preparing to share the prior week's updates which were sent to Matt by volunteer's electronic documentation, phone calls and emails. He put all of this together into one formatted list by patient name. Matt also included any volunteer requests that he had received in the last week and his progress on filling these assignments. It was a tedious process making sure he had outlined the items proficiently, but through his own experience this was the best way to have the information readily handy when he was called upon in the team meeting.

Not every volunteer director did it this way in the organization, Susan just winged it each week, recalling from memory any updates, and Brandon just opened up each patient's electronic record and read from the clinical notes in the system. Brandon realized that sometimes the meeting moved faster than he could actually open up each patient file, but that was how he did it, and he really did not care for reorganizing all the information again into one document as Matt did weekly. Brandon commented that even though it was more efficient to do it Matt's way, he felt it was counterproductive because he could use that time working on something else. Matt felt that Brandon and Susan were being lazy because it really wasn't as complicated as they made it out to be. Matt just ran a few reports, and boom, he had his formatted list.

The long tables were filling up with team nurses and social workers. Matt sat at the far end which, by habit, was where the managers of grief support, spiritual care and volunteer services sat. This wasn't the rule. There were no assigned seats; it's just the way it always played out. The nurses were at the front of the class, then the social workers, then them; maybe it was a pecking order of some sort, a hierarchy if you will.

"How is that boy of yours doing, Matt?" the deep soothing voice of Judy Norm, the spiritual care advisor, caused him to look up from his laptop. She was an ex-Catholic nun. Matt had never met an ex-nun before; heck, he had never met a nun. Judy was a petite woman in her mid 50's. She set down her computer and the books stacked on top of it. Matt reached out a quick hand to stabilize the books as they were about to topple.

"He is growing like a weed, Judy, thanks for asking." Matt stood up and handed the books back to Judy.

"You have the reflexes of a cat, sir." Judy said. "I was trying to carry everything in one trip, not the best decision!" Judy's dark grey eyes sparkled in laughter.

Judy's laughter was infectious because Matt found himself smiling along with her. "So what inspirational reading do you have for us today?" He watched as she tapped a green book under her fingers.

"If I tell you, it wouldn't be a surprise, but I think it should be a good one." Each week before the IDT meeting began Judy would read a passage to inspire the team and refocus them on the work they were doing with the patients. She would often interject her own pieces of wisdom, refraining from sounding too preachy but also reminding them of why they were all there. Whether it worked or not, Judy was not sure, but she was confident that some of her words would seep into their hearts. Yes, she was sure of that.

"Hey Matt," the unmistakably loud commanding voice of Trish Kramer, RN extraordinaire, tore Matt away from his conversation with Judy. He managed a slight smile. Trish looked like a linebacker, an out of uniform linebacker with a C cup. "Did you ever get a volunteer for the Zimbowski family? I know I requested it like two weeks ago." Her stocky solid frame was turned austerely towards him. She stood like a statue waiting, impatiently, for his answer.

Matt's brow darkened and he searched his brain for a second to sift through the many volunteer requests that he received in one week, let alone two weeks. He didn't remember the name right off hand, which led him to the conclusion that the assignment was not filled and also that he was not currently working on it. The name Zimbowski was not a part of his current list of patients that were being reviewed today in the meeting either.

Trish saw he was perplexed, and her eyes narrowed with contempt. "The daughter, Brenda, is very overwhelmed. I had hoped you could find someone *this time*." She placed icy emphasis on the last two words.

"You're trying to say I don't usually get assignments filled?" Matt asked her. The unintended harshness of his tone caused a few eyes to gravitate in their direction.

"It doesn't seem like it when it comes to my patients. I ask for a volunteer and one either never gets placed or it takes weeks."

"Sometimes it happens that way. I don't have volunteers sitting in a closet waiting to be called on. They can say no to assignments."

"No other branch seems to have this problem, just ours." Trish responded. "And I'm getting really sick of promising families that they will have the help of a volunteer and then no one shows up. It makes me look like an idiot, and it looks bad for the agency." Trish announced this with her authoritarian voice.

"I've never had a problem getting a volunteer." another nurse, Terri Jessup, chimed in. "And Matt, everyone just loves Sylvia down at the nursing home. She is fantastic!" Terri further exclaimed. Matt gave Terri a pleasant smile and thanked her.

The temperature of his gaze lowered significantly when he looked back at Trish. "Volunteers take assignments that work best for them. I'm recruiting all the time. It's hard to find a volunteer in this economic climate. What do you think I'm doing here all day and weekends?"

"I don't know what you do to tell you the truth." Trish's tone was dismissive. "All I know is I don't get my assignments filled so I'm going to stop promising my patients something that you can't deliver." She almost shouted at him.

Karen McBride, the Clinical Manager, walked in with a hospice aide in tow waiting to get her schedule confirmed. Karen heard the exchange as it began heating up from her office. "Hey, hey guys." She began. "Let's take it down a notch shall we? We're all on the same team. So what seems to be the problem? I guess we can start with problem patients."

Trish spoke up first. "I can't get volunteers once I request them. I was asking Matt about an assignment I put in for the Zimbowski family. It's been over two weeks, and they haven't heard anything."

Karen mulled over Trish's statement then looked at Matt. "Have you spoken with the family, Matt?" she had placed her mediator hat on.

Matt had opened up the Zimbowski chart on the computer and found a notation he had made in clinical notes two weeks prior. "Yes, as I see here in the chart, I did speak with the daughter, and what she is needs is someone to be there with her Dad and change him. Currently, we do not have a volunteer who can do hands on care."

"I thought they could change diapers?" Trish challenged.

"Yes, they can when they have the experience." Matt corrected.

"Don't they get training for that?" Trish asked. "I mean what good are they if they can't help out with basic needs?" she looked at Karen for an answer.

Matt began to fume. Karen could almost see the steam rising from his head so she quickly answered. "Trish volunteers are not meant to do that sort of task, which is what we have hospice aides for. Now, did the family express to you that this was their need? How often does the aide go out?"

"The aide is already going out three times a week." Trish informed her.

"Yeah, well maybe we need to up it to four or even five. Educating the family may be necessary as well. Have you instructed the family how to change diapers, Trish?"

"No, she doesn't want to do that. She said she can do anything but that. She does not want to clean her father down there, she is very afraid of doing stuff like that which is why I ordered a volunteer. Of course now I see they are even more useless than I thought!"

"Useless?" Matt yelled.

"Trish you are out of line." Karen told her sternly. "Volunteers are the backbone of hospice. We need them and they are not useless! I don't ever want to hear you say that again! Without volunteers you wouldn't even have a job here because we would not be in business, understand that. Also my question to you is, if Matt's note was in the chart, why didn't you know that he had already spoken with the family?"

"I don't have time to check the clinical notes every minute because I have patients to see." Trish sat down, and her words were barely audible.

"We all are stretched to the hilt here, Trish, but it is your responsibility to check the clinical notes just like everybody else." Karen told her.

"I have a twenty patient case load! If I sat behind a desk all day, then maybe I could check every note, but there are only so many hours in the day, and my main priority is to see patients, not check notes." Trish said emphatically.

"I don't sit behind a desk all day." Matt told her.

"Trish, I would like to see you in my office after team meeting." Karen said to her.

"Well, I would love to, but I have a family meeting to attend at the hospital across town. Me and the social worker are due there by eleven this morning."

"Then on our first break." Karen ordered. Trish grinded out a "fine" between her teeth. Karen's eyes held onto the nurse for a long two seconds before she moved on. "Ok folks, let's get going with the meeting. Aaliyah, would you mind getting bereavement going please? Thank you."

Aaliyah Parks was the grief support manager for the East Branch. She was a very warm young woman with a soft spoken voice, and that was much needed in the room at that moment. "Yes, good morning everyone. I think this would be a wonderful time to gather in as Judy reads our inspirational passage this morning."

"Thank you, Aaliyah." Judy stood up opening her book to the marked page and began to speak. "Everyone here has heard of Mother Teresa. She is regarded as a saint, and I will read some of her words:

I will tell you a story. One night a man came to our house and told me, "There is a family with eight children. They have not eaten for days."

I took some food with me and went. When I came to that family, I saw the faces of those little children disfigured by hunger. There was no sorrow or sadness in their faces, just the deep pain of hunger. I gave rice to the mother. She divided the rice in two, and went out, carrying half the rice. When she came back, I asked her, "Where did you go?" She gave me this simple answer, "To my neighbors; they are hungry also!" I was not surprised that she gave-poor people are really very generous. I was surprised that she knew they were hungry. As a rule, when we are suffering, we are so focused on ourselves; we have no time for others.

Judy paused for a moment and looked up at the gathered team members. "This is an important message because as hospice workers this is who we are, we are our patient's neighbors. We are the ones who are going to help and provide aid to the families. As I listened to the exchange this morning, with all of its anger and fury, I have to remind all of you why we are here, why we do the work that we do. Here is another passage from Mother Teresa that speaks to that, as well:

> *In 25 years, we have picked up more than 36,000 people from the streets and more than 18,000 have died a most beautiful death.*
>
> *When we pick them up from the street we give them a plate of rice. In no time we revive them. A few nights ago we picked up four people. One was in a most terrible condition, covered with wounds, full of maggots. I told the sisters that I would take care of her while they attended to the other three. I really did all that my love could do for her. I put her in bed and then she took hold of my hand. She had such a beautiful smile on her face and she said only, "Thank you." Then she died.*
>
> *There was a greatness of love. She was hungry for love, and she received that love before she died. She spoke only two words, but her understanding love was expressed in those two words.*

"As we go through our day and our work, please try to remember that our role is to support the patient and to support the family. Our work is hard; our work is not for the weak willed or faint hearted. Remember, even though it can be trying at times, we have chosen this job, and it has chosen you. Our patients say thank you. Now, let us bow our heads in a moment of silence?" Judy lowered her head and the rest of the team followed suit.

For the remainder of the meeting, Matt only answered in short simple words. His eyes did not venture towards Trish's direction for fear he would lose his composure. During the discussion covering new patients Matt informed the team of the new volunteer requests. He inquired about what the family wanted and needed. When the patients who were up for recertification were named, Matt gave the volunteer report from his handy sheet. If more information was needed, he opened up the patient's electronic medical chart on his laptop and retrieved it, but he only had to do that a couple of times. When the break mercifully came, he hopped up immediately, went outside, unlocked his car, and did something that he had vowed not to do. Matt opened his hatchback, lifted the covering over the spare tire, and pulled out the week old box of Marlboros.

Matt lit a cigarette and, instead of replacing the box in the trunk, he slid it back into his jacket pocket, its original home. After his drink with Dave a few weeks ago, he had decided to try to quit again. He had been doing well. This pack was the last pack that he bought, and by the tenth smoked cigarette he decided he would stop and threw this last box into the trunk. Maybe he should have tossed it out altogether, but he didn't. Right now he was very glad he didn't. The first few days of quitting had been brutal. Matt hadn't realized how many of his habits had cigarettes wrapped around them.

When Matt woke up, he would immediately have a cigarette; when he drove into work he would have approximately two with his coffee. Depending on the work day, if he had no appointments or meetings, he would allow himself a cigarette break outside. Then on the way home he would smoke a couple unless he was picking up Jake. When Jake was staying over, he would not smoke until Jake left. Matt supposed there was some credence to second-hand smoke so he didn't subject Jake to any, although he was sure Connie still smoked inside and out of the house.

The morning's heated exchange with Trish made a cigarette necessary. It was either have the smoke or go a few doors down and have a vodka tonic at the Marriott's lounge. Matt opted for the most appropriate work day response. He usually didn't join the other smokers out on their break, especially since Trish was the main ringleader, so he opted to be hidden from view on the far side of his SUV. Besides, a break meant just that, a break from the team, and that meant everyone, but his break would not last long.

"Mr. Ames?" Matt jumped, startled at the sound of a slightly familiar voice. He frowned, looking past his car to the source.

Matt saw a person who made him drop his cigarette to the ground and crush it under his feet. "Yes, Miss Steele." He transformed into director mode.

"You don't have to stop smoking on my account. I'm a smoker, too." Jenna confessed granting him a bright smile. She pulled out her box. "You wanna share another? We don't have to go inside I just wanted to ask you a quick question."

This took him off guard. His new volunteer, Jenna, did not look like a smoker at all. He was also not used to having a cigarette or anything that casual with a volunteer. All he could manage was an inaudible "*umm...*"

"I'm sorry, you're on your break. I can wait inside." Jenna recognized how uncomfortable Matt looked.

"No, it's cool." Matt moved back and grabbed another cigarette out of his jacket. Jenna lit one herself. "You just don't seem like a smoker." Matt said.

"I know I should quit." Jenna replied.

"Me too, actually this is my first cigarette in about a week. I was quitting."

"Oh wow, and just like the devil here I am to tempt you."

"No, I had kind of a bad morning and of course this is the old habit." Matt said reassuringly.

"I hear you, the old bad habit."

"When did you start smoking?" Matt asked Jenna.

She thought for a moment. "Hmmm, I think I was fifteen."

"To look older?" Matt quipped.

Jenna chuckled. "Maybe at the beginning, I only did it with friends to look cool. Were we stupid or what back then?"

"Well, we're still smoking, and you don't look stupid." Matt responded.

"You're right. So we have no excuse now." Jenna said and they both had to laugh at the ridiculousness of their continued actions.

"So, what can I do for you, Miss Steele."

"Jenna, please." She watched him nod in agreement.

He placed a hand to his chest. "Matt, please."

"Matt, I know I went through training, which was very informative, by the way, but I keep thinking about the different types of volunteers."

"Ok."

"When I came to volunteer, I was thinking of mainly working with patients. But the more I think about it, the more scared I become with being assigned a patient. Does that make any sense?" she asked but didn't give him a chance to respond. "I mean, I want to work with patients, but the other day I went to get fingerprinted, and it suddenly hit me that as soon as the results come back I could be called out, and then thoughts of my mother start surfacing. Should I have waited?"

"Jenna, that is not a quick question. If you asked me where to go to get fingerprinted, then that is a quick question. But what you are asking is more of a sit down discussion for my office. Let's go in."

Jenna touched his arm. "No, do we have to? It's so nice out here, unless you're busy."

Matt thought about that for a second. His break was over, which meant he was due back in the meeting. This was much better. He definitely considered this a welcomed diversion, and a warranted one. Whenever his volunteers showed up, Matt took the time to speak with them. This is what he told each of them; his door was always open, and he was always available, even for drop-ins. Besides, she was right; it was a nice day. The sun was shining; there was a gentle breeze which was calming him down from his previous confrontation. "I'm never too busy for a volunteer." He said.

Matt hadn't realized how soft Jenna's light brown eyes appeared to be until seeing them in the sunlight. A smile instinctively crept across his face. "Jenna, you can start out doing so many other things. Most volunteers work with patients, but not all, as I explained in training. There are office volunteers, public speaking, community volunteers, those who work on projects, sing, or play an instrument..."

"I don't play an instrument, and for God's sake you don't want to hear me sing." Jenna replied.

"I was just naming different options." Matt paused for a moment then a light shined, "You know, we have a race coming up, it's a fundraiser. You can man one of the tables. It's too late to participate in the race, but we will need help at many stations."

"Oh, that sounds like fun, when is that?" Jenna asked.

"It's this weekend actually, Saturday."

"Perfect! Thank you!" she clapped like a cheerleader. Jenna was afraid she would chicken out of volunteering altogether if she didn't do something. This is why she came by; she knew Matt would lead her in the right direction.

"No, thank you for being able to help." Matt reached into his car and grabbed a pen and paper. "Here is the address to the event." He scribbled it down. "Now, if you take 75..."

"Oh, I can Google map it." Jenna said, taking the small note paper. Matt told her to be there by 7 a.m. Jenna assured him she would be. He put out his cigarette and was about to leave. "Matt, thanks for understanding. I promise I will be taking on patients. I just need a minute."

"Take as long as you need. Remember, you don't have to work with patients." Matt reiterated. They left it at that and he watched Jenna walk back to her car in the visitor's section. He was really glad she came by. As he made his way back to the meeting he realized it wasn't a cigarette he needed, it was refocusing, just as Judy was talking about in her reading this morning. *Why you are here.*

"What perfume was she wearing?" Matt thought to himself, then shook it off. Back to work.

TEN

When Jenna entered her home she was horrified to see Adrian laying in a heap on the living room floor with two treacherous looking men standing ominously over him. It was clear that they had been the cause of his bloody state. By appearances, both of them could have been boxers. The one who turned in Jenna's direction when she approached looked a bit too old to be a working athlete; the other man was shorter and his eyes never left Adrian's battered body.

"What the hell is going on here?" Jenna demanded of them. The older gentleman produced a wry smile but it was Adrian who answered.

"Hey, Jenna, this is Tony and Raul. They are from the west and are in town to see the Lions game and thought they would drop in to say hello." Adrian's speech was a bit garbled from the swelling of his lips.

The older man, Tony, stepped a few inches towards her. Jenna instinctively retreated backwards, and he held up his hands to steady her. "Sorry for the intrusion, Miss. Adrian, left town without saying goodbye, so we made sure to look him up the next time we were in Detroit."

"Football season is over." Jenna informed him.

"Did I say Lions?" Adrian spoke up. "I meant the Tigers." He was trying to make his way back onto his feet. Raul helped him up, a bit roughly Jenna noted.

"What do you want with him?" she asked, trying to remain calm.

"Jenna is it?" Tony asked. His cold eyes bore into hers. "This is a nice house. How much do you pay for a house like this in the D? Great location, just close enough and far enough away from the city, you know what I mean?"

"Look, just tell me what you want or am I going to have to call the police?" Jenna blurted.

Tony shook his head. "No, you don't want to call the police, Jenna. This is just a friendly visit. You don't want to make it unfriendly, do you?"

"It looks like it already is." She pointed out.

Tony looked back at Adrian. "What that?" Tony asked, gesturing at Adrian's bruises. "Nah, Adrian is just a little clumsy is all."

"I want you out of my house or I am calling the police!" Jenna yelled.

Tony's eyes darkened even more, which Jenna was sure could not happen. "I see you are not going to keep things cordial." He said. In less than a second he had advanced on her swiftly seizing both of her shoulders in his large hands.

"Leave her alone!" Adrian protested, which caused Raul to respond with a punch to Adrian's jaw.

"Does he owe you money or something?" Jenna's voice trembled as she spoke while under Tony's strong grip. His cologne penetrated her nostrils. Oddly it was a pleasant smell. Tony apparently liked the finer things.

"Clever girl." Tony said.

"How much? I'll pay you." Jenna told him.

Tony released her and stepped back. "Fifty Thousand dollars." He quoted easily.

"Fifty? It was forty!" Adrian yelled.

Raul responded with a punch to Adrian's gut. Adrian doubled over and then fell back onto the couch.

"That's for making me come to Detroit. You know how I hate this fucking city." Tony answered frigidly.

Jenna fished hastily through the purse that was still slung over her shoulder and produced a check book. She quickly scribbled out the check for cash. "Here!" she slammed the check into Tony's hand.

Tony smiled, and then examined the piece of paper. "Raul." He handed the check over to his partner, and Raul immediately began dialing a number. "If everything checks out then we'll be out of your hair. Should only take a moment." Tony reassured.

Jenna diverted her eyes from the ex-boxer, and looked down at Adrian. The fear inside of her began to shift to pure anger. It was so typical that Adrian would be mixed up with obvious mob guys or whatever the hell they were. A gambling debt no doubt and, of course, he carelessly brings his bullshit to her doorstep, inside her home. Jenna even thought that could have come here purposely to get the money from her. That's how Adrian was, how he always was. He cared about no one but himself. Jenna stupidly thought that she was different, that he would not endanger her because of their bond, but she was wrong, like so many of her family members had been wrong about Adrian.

After reciting the account number into the phone and waiting, Raul finally looked up at Tony and nodded. Then he hung up the phone and walked towards the door. Tony followed but not before turning back to them. "Again, forgive the intrusion, Miss." He tipped his head to her and looked at Adrian. "Adrian, always a pleasure. I'll see you the next time you're in Vegas."

"Not if I see you first," Adrian responded facetiously. With that, the men were gone. Adrian waited patiently for what he knew was about to come. Jenna did not make him wait long.

"What the fuck, Adrian!" Jenna screamed, throwing her purse at him. "You brought this shit to my house? What in the hell is wrong with you?" Jenna pronounced each word slowly and harshly to stress each one. She advanced on him in only two wide steps. "Get the fuck out!" Jenna ordered.

Adrian's heart dropped as he saw the distorted grimace on Jenna's face. She immediately turned and went upstairs out of his sight. He sat there with his head down and cupped in his hands. He stared at the few dots of blood left on the light beige carpet. He had come to the house to gather his things and leave but Tony and his sidekick had followed him. Adrian had spotted them in his rearview mirror late last night as he left the hotel room he had been staying at since his encounter at the club. Adrian led them into the cavernous streets of east side Detroit thinking he could lose them, and for awhile he thought he had. That was the opportune time to come and gather his belongings at Jenna's, but now, as he sat on her couch he realized it was the wrong thing to do. He shouldn't have come back. Jenna was right, it was time for him to go.

Adrian stood, and his body was aching. Raul had really laid into him, which was his purpose, Adrian knew. It was another streak of Vegas bad luck coming back to hurt his family. Only problem was this time it wasn't Aunt Faye. She had kept all of his transgressions quiet and never seemed to be affected by his most heinous faults. Faye only smiled, gave advice, then asked him to play a song on the piano. She would choose one of her current favorites or ask him to pick one, and Adrian knew that all was forgiven, all was forgotten.

Adrian took his hand and ran it down the photo of Faye on the mantle as if he was stroking her cheek. Tears welled up in his eyes, and he let them fall. Faye was gone, and he had burned the bridge with the only other family who truly loved him. Why he did the things Adrian did he did not know. Or was it that he did not want to know? Either way, it was time for him to go.

"Now I know what the two of you had in common." Jenna said, as she watched him standing in front of the mantle bleeding. It was becoming more and more common these days, watching Adrian bleed, she realized.

Adrian didn't look at her, just diverted his eyes. "What is that?" he asked.

"Self destruction. The two of you were partners in crime. I don't think I ever saw her truly happy. And you? You're just like her, waiting to die. Go, do it somewhere else, Adrian. I already watched my mother die."

Adrian stared at her for a long moment then started towards the door but stopped beside Jenna. "Now I know that you didn't know her at all." He paused, waiting to see if she would respond. Jenna did not. Adrian left the house and stood for a moment on the landing while looking up to the sky. His destination? Back to the hotel, he supposed, from there he had no clue.

Inside the house, standing in the same place, Jenna whispered to no one in particular, "You were both born dead."

ELEVEN

Samantha almost jogged down the stairs after a full week in her parent's home practically cocooned inside her old teenage bedroom. The only thing that stopped her from taking two and three steps at a time was the sheer reality that if she did she could have broken her neck. Even though she was aware that the disease coursing through her body would surely take her in under a year, Samantha was not ready to die by simply slipping down the stairs. How humiliating would that be?

"Where are you off to?" Lynnette Mills, Samantha's mother, had positioned herself purposely inside her pathway to the door. Samantha stopped at the bottom of the stairs. A harsh grimace slid across her face like ice. Lynnette was used to this expression from her daughter. "Even well into adulthood you are still insistent on me repeating myself."

Impatiently, Samantha checked her watch. She was meeting friends at a bar in Birmingham and didn't want to be late. "I'm just going to The Bistro." She replied.

"Really? Alone?" Lynnette asked, crossing her arms and narrowing her eyes, a most typical posture for her.

"No. I'm meeting Kyra, Shelley and Nina."

"Wow, the old gang's back in town."

"Yes, Nina's up from L.A., and I'm here, so it's the perfect time to get together." Samantha scooted past her mother and pulled a light jacket from the foyer closet.

Lynnette laughed to herself. "I remember when you girls were all this high." She said and as she placed her hand at her mid thigh. "Oh the trouble you girls would get into. You would run around this place like it was your private playground. Remember when Nina almost drowned in the pool? That scared me half to death."

"Yes, good times," Samantha responded. "Well I'm gonna head out. Don't wait up." Samantha opened the door.

"Hold on!" Lynnette exclaimed. "Jesus Sam you have been here for over five days and we haven't said two words to each other. We need to talk."

"We will." Samantha promised.

"You haven't even explained why you're here. Did you lose your job? On vacation? I know something is wrong, what is it?"

"Nothing is wrong, Mother. Everything is perfectly fine. I promise we'll talk tomorrow. But right now I'm late so if you wouldn't mind."

Lynnette briefly touched Samantha's shoulder. "Are you still upset about Charles? I told you he wasn't right for you dear."

"Yes, you told me."

"You have to let these things go, you can't dwell on the past, Sam."

"Well I sure can't dwell on the future." Sam quipped darkly.

"What does that mean?"

"It just means I gotta go." Samantha reached around and gave her mother a quick hug, a wave and then swiftly closed the door behind her. It wasn't until she was in the driveway that she took a breath. "*hump*, Charles." She snorted under her breath.

Samantha got into her father's Expedition and headed toward the bar. She missed having her own car but it couldn't be helped. Besides this car was extremely comfortable and asking her Dad to borrow it was effortless. He understood everything. He was definitely her ally.

Samantha rolled her eyes, taking the curves in the road, as she thought of her mother bringing up her ex-boyfriend, Charles. The fact that she would even bring him up, as a source of her anger towards her, proved to Samantha that her mother never listened to her and never took the time to understand her. The relationship between Samantha and Charles was not going to go anywhere. He was a boyfriend, it lasted barely seven months and he was not her type.

Charles' family lived in Chicago. She and Charles had decided to take the long drive to Illinois and stop off in Michigan to visit with her parents. Bad idea! A very logical idea, because it was right on the way, but a bad idea all the same.

Lynnette Mills was in rare form. During dinner she had downed two healthy glasses of Sauza Hornitos Gold on the rocks. Charles Oigbokie was a first generation American born Nigerian. His parents were both physicians, and he had an auspicious air about him that Samantha found revolting.

After topping off her second glass and after ignoring many side glances from her husband, Lynette had gone into a tirade about how Africans hate African Americans.

"So Charles, why do your people hate Black Americans? I mean, didn't we come from an area of Africa by force? And didn't your people help catch us? So what are you guys mad at us for? Shouldn't we be angry at you?" Lynnette asked her eyes boring into his.

"I'm sorry, Mrs. Mills?" Charles asked her clearly a deer caught in headlights.

"Mom, what are you talking about?" Samantha had practically yelled while trying to smile.

"Lynn, you're being rude. Forgive her Charles, please have some more potatoes." Joseph offered, hoping his wife would take the hint. She did not.

Lynn shot her husband a dismissive glance. "Joe, you don't understand, you're half French and Spanish."

"Creole." He corrected.

"Exactly," Lynn said to him then turned back to Charles. "So you don't get it. Charles, I don't mean to be offensive but you're an educated young man, I am sure the topic has come up before and I wanted your opinion, straight from the horse's mouth, so to speak." Lynn had waited for an answer.

The poor 28 year old tax attorney looked very bewildered and was not sure whether to have the political and cultural conversation that Lynette wanted. If he told her that his parents felt that African Americans had not rebounded in a healthy fashion, in their opinion and according to the crime rates, he would have to agree. If he had divulged that the only success that the black American seemed to be able to achieve was in the entertainment field and that President Obama was an exception to the rule, he was sure that not only would he be traveling to Chicago alone but the mother of his current girlfriend would have kicked him out into the streets without a hint of remorse. Therefore, Charles collected himself and in his most respectable voice, he stated: "Ma'am, I don't have an opinion except that all people of color have to fight and struggle in this world. We're all on the same side. Yet, to speak to what you are saying, I feel that is a myth rather than real fact. No one in my family has ever voiced such animosity."

Lynnette Mills sat back in her seat, took another sip of her Tequila and watched the young lawyer. She remained silent. It was her husband who gratefully spoke.

"Alright then, well said Charles. Why don't we have our coffee by the fire?" Joseph didn't wait for a response; he stood and headed towards the family room.

Lynnette was the last to leave the table. Samantha remembered standing in the dining room doorway watching her. She wondered why her mother was hell bent on ruining everything in her life. Even though Charles was not the one, for her, Samantha's mother didn't know that. For all her mother knew, she had caused the man Samantha loved to walk out of her life. Had that been her Mother's life goal? Was she sitting in her seat feeling triumphant at accomplishing just that?

Whether her mother was the catalyst of their relationship's destruction was of no consequence, however. It was the drive home that solidified her desire to be done with Charles. He had remained silent about the conversation on the way to Chicago, but it was on the drive home to New York when he inquired, "Has your mother ever considered looking into Betty Ford?" It was after that remark when Samantha said goodbye to Charles. Their relationship only lasted for the seven months because Charles was a "winer-diner". He loved the good life and they attended many events, which, for Samantha, were great distractions but, after this trip it went downhill, and the relationship ended soon after she and Charles got back to New York.

As Samantha pulled up to the valet parking at The Bistro, she watched the young valet make his way around to her door. Eyeing him, she got the distinct feeling it was her last valet parking experience. She felt that she would remember his face forever. His face was thin, contoured, his eyes remarkably green, skin remarkably fair. His uniform fit perfectly as if tailored. As she handed him her key, Samantha was sure he worked out many times a week; toned, chiseled, paying close attention to the detail. She instantly envied him. He would probably live well into his nineties.

As if a beacon of light turned on, Samantha heard the loud shrills of laughter coming from Kyra. She was grateful for the pleasant sound which helped to point out her friends with ease. Samantha eyed them appreciatively in all of their glorious feminine exquisiteness. She was one of them, she thought with pride. She was part of their splendor, a part of their gaiety, a part of their illustrious world.

Samantha had always loved being part of their crew. Ever since high school none of them knew the true meaning of teenage sadness or loneliness. Sure her mother tried to make her teenage life a living hell, but, because of her friends, her mother did not succeed. Once the front door was closed, once Nina's car door was closed, and once Seal's Kiss

From A Rose came onto the radio, Samantha's teenage home trappings disappeared and their own teenaged fantasy world revealed itself. It was heaven. For Samantha, though, it wasn't until Kenneth died that she knew the true meaning of sadness.

"Diva!" Kyra yelled out from across the room. They all waved displaying the sweetest smiles she hadn't seen in what seemed like ages. Samantha returned their greetings and made her way through the evening crowd. Passing by the bar drinkers, the sports fans watching their game on the flat screens, and the diners, Samantha felt familiar eyes on her. The admiration made her smile slightly to herself. In the past she might have allowed her eyes to wander and seek out the more alluring prospective daters but now her mind couldn't have been further from that. The time of dating is over for her she felt.

Before sitting Samantha affectionately gave out hugs to her friends. When the waitress promptly appeared she ordered a Mimosa and loaded tortilla chip appetizer for all.

"How are you feeling, hun?" Nina touched Samantha's hand gently.

Samantha stared at her for a long moment. Did she know? How could she? "I'm fine..." she said suspiciously.

"Was the break up amicable? You were talking about wedding dresses not long ago." Nina explained.

Samantha gave a sigh of relief. "Oh well, yes, it was okay. Charles went his way, and I went mine."

"Aww sorry, I hadn't heard." Shelley said.

"It's been a few months. I'm ok with it." Samantha assured.

"Well I'm glad." Kyra said, causing the other women to shoot her a confused look. "Seriously, you would have been Mrs. Samantha Oigbokie. Hell, I can't even pronounce it."

"You are so crude." Nina scolded. Shelley only shook her head, hiding amusement.

"You have to admit, it's an odd last name. Am I right, Sam?"

"I hadn't really thought about it, but I guess it is." Samantha admitted.

"Of course you didn't think about it," Nina said. "because it's not important!"

Now Kyra shot her a confused look. "What? Not important? You better believe it's important. Your name says a lot about you." She said.

"And what, pray tell, would his name have said about her?"

"That she's foreign or that she's married to a foreign man. Sam is in advertising! Her name precedes her. It's important." Kyra replied adamantly.

"I don't think so." Shelley added. "She lives in New York, not Utah, it wouldn't matter. In fact, some may have seen it as chic."

"Well, it doesn't matter anyway because I am stuck with Mills." Samantha broke in. "I don't want to talk about me and Charles. It's over. We were not right for each other. There it is. Can we change the subject?"

"Of course." Nina said, making a final warning glance at Kyra, who responded with a wry smile. "How long will you be in town?"

"I don't know, for awhile." Samantha said vaguely.

"You get fired?" Kyra asked bluntly.

"No, just taking a leave of absence." Samantha replied.

"Are you ill?" Nina asked, growing concerned.

"I've been tired lately. I just need to get away from the city, you know, to reevaluate things."

"I know what you mean." Shelley said. "John and I just bought a new home. It's huge, and I hate it."

"What are you talking about?" Kyra asked. "It's a small mansion! It's gorgeous."

"Exactly!" Shelley retorted. "And who has to take care of this small mansion? John will not hire help. He seems to feel I can clean this whole house, care for the kids, care for him, all without batting an eye. He has no idea what it takes to maintain the type of lifestyle he wants to be accustomed to."

"I should have such problems." Kyra quipped.

"Don't be so damned insensitive." Nina shot at her.

"Insensitive?" Kyra cocked her head to the side. "Shelley, sorry hun, but you have the life of June Cleaver. You have three beautiful boys, you have a husband who got a promotion instead of getting canned from his executive GM job, you just moved into a million dollar home. Forgive me, but what in the hell are you complaining about?"

"I am not complaining, I'm expressing the fact that it can be overwhelming." Shelley responded. "And you have no kids, Kyra; you do not know what it's like. And who the heck says I wanted this life anyway? It's not my life, its John's life." She added.

"Really?" Kyra stared at Shelley incredulously. "I think I'm gonna need another drink over here!"

Samantha began to laugh uncontrollably. "Man, I missed you guys!"

Kyra joined her laughter. "Okay, let's take me." She paused long enough to top off her drink and flag for another. "I've been doing my photography thing. I've been getting a few good gigs, mainly modeling stuff, yet still low key, no fire. I got my website up, you know, whatever. But this is

Detroit. I've been thinking about moving to New York so, you can't leave the city now, Sam, I need a contact!"

"I can put you in touch with a few people. I'll make some calls." Samantha promised.

"Really, would you do that? That would be great!" Kyra exclaimed.

"No problem." Samantha assured her.

"But Shelley," Kyra continued, "I would love to have your life. I'm single, mid thirties; I mean when is it going to happen for me?"

"Change your brand of men." Nina told her.

"Oh, here we go." Kyra said.

"No really, change your brand of men. You like them too attractive and shallow."

"I love my men well put together." Kyra agreed.

"No, you like ballers." Shelley corrected. "Those kind of guys do not want marriage and kids."

Kyra let out a sound like a tire losing air. "Yet there are plenty of married athletes. Now how does that happen?"

"Because they go back and marry their high school girlfriends." Samantha interjected.

"Yeah Miss Homely-USA." Kyra looked at Shelley, "No offense."

"None taken. Kyra, you do not appear to be the marrying kind. How many times have I gone to your Facebook page to see pictures of yet another event you're partying at?"

"You mean another event I am hosting! Have you forgotten that another one of my side jobs to the pay the rent is event planning? I plan the events, I promote them, and I take the pictures! All inclusive!"

"Yeah, but you're in the pictures drinking, wearing tight low cut dresses. You're very beautiful, but a man does not want to marry the life of the party. Sorry they just don't." Shelley emphasized.

"I'm mingling!" Kyra shouted back. "I'm in the crowd trying to keep the party going. I'm working, Miss Shelley!"

Nina held up her hands at them "Okay, can we take it down a notch? We're supposed to be enjoying this dinner after not seeing each other in a few months, and about a year for all of us even being together."

"You're right." Kyra said. "Sorry, Shelley." She apologized.

Nina picked up her menu. "So what are we all having?" she asked, and with that the conversation lightened to their careers, Shelley's kids, and the reminiscence of their teenage years. For the next two hours the friends ate, drank wine and were transformed back into the girls they once were without a care in the world. Samantha so needed this escape. She needed to feel alive again and whole. For those moments she was not a woman facing a debilitating disease, Shelley wasn't a housewife who considered divorce; Kyra wasn't a single woman wondering when her prince would come, and Nina wasn't living in California feeling so disconnected from everyone. For those moments they were the crew again, laughing, joking, thinking about the cutest boy on the football team, they were young and free again.

It was going on ten when the reunion started winding down. "I better get home before John puts out an APB on me!" Shelley said, gathering her things.

"When do you head back, Nina?" Kyra asked.

"In the morning. I have a nine a.m. flight." Nina replied.

"Next time we'll all fly out to L.A. and you can show us the night life." Samantha said, or at least that's what she thought she had said. Inside of her head those were the words she was saying, but actually her garbled speech sounded like *"markeeeet…shhhaw…lokida…rammmmmbdu…"*

"Sam?" Nina dropped her purse and bent down next to Samantha's chair. Samantha's face seemed to have melted on one side and a clear liquid was oozing from the edge of her mouth. Her eyes rolled back into her head, and her body began to shake violently.

"Oh my God!" Kyra gasped. "Oh my God, Sam!"

"Call 911!" Shelley screamed at the waitress and on lookers. "Call 911! Get us some help! Please help us!"

TWELVE

"Jerry, hi this is Matthew Ames calling from Community Hospice hoping that you would have availability this evening to do a vigil?" Matt waited for a response, listened, and then spoke again into the receiver, "Ah, I see okay, no problem, I will try someone else. Thanks Jerry." Matt hung up, looked at the next name on the list, dials, then speaks. "Angela, hi this is Matthew Ames calling from hospice to see if you can do a vigil for us tonight..." Matt listens... "Yes, tonight....as soon as you can get there...at the hospital...I see....yeah....no that's fine, I understand. Thanks Angela."

Matt used his fingers to go down the list of volunteers who had signed up to be called out for vigil assignments. These assignments always seemed to come at the end of the day, or the weekend, and they needed to be filled immediately because the patient is actively dying. Sometimes Matt would get it filled on the first call, and then there were times like these. He called another, then another, and then sat back in his chair glancing up at the clock. It read 6:30pm. Luckily, he didn't have to pick up Jake this weekend because he had to work the next day, Saturday at the race. He was actually excited about working the race because Jenna would be there. He knew she was a volunteer, but she was a woman too right? And he was a man, and why is he even thinking about this? Back to work! He chided himself.

"Mary hi, Matt here, how are you?....good......I'm calling to see if you can do a vigil for us tonight?......at the hospital......yeah.......ok.......well as soon as you are able to go......no, if you're busy....uh huh.......yeah.......you can?....are you sure, Mary?....Thanks so much!" He read off the name of the patient and the name of the hospital where the patient had been moved to. The daughter had been freaking out about being alone with her father once he was dying. She had requested that he be moved to the hospital as soon as he was active. The frantic call came in about an hour ago as Matt was leaving the office and heading home for a night of beer, pizza, and the Tigers. Something told him not to answer the call; however, the work of a volunteer director never ends. There is no official clock out time with his job. Calls such as emergency volunteer requests, vigils, RN checking on updates of a request, volunteers needing guidance on a patient situation, their documentation, and a whole host of other issues can come after hours.

Matt had considered ignoring the calls, and his counterpart, Susan, often said she turned her phone off when she left wok, but he wouldn't do that. First of all, it's Matt's job to be available to at least answer work related email, and with the vigils that can come at anytime, if he is going to service the patients he must be available. Susan says that her family comes first and that it's not like she's an executive, or a nurse, or even treated like a real manager at the company so why should she be available at all hours? Matt knew she definitely had a point. Although in their job title the word director appears, they are not on the status level as other directors in the corporation.

Secondly, the role of the volunteer director is complicated. No matter where the job's level lies, the description is clear. He is the human resources manager of all of the volunteers on his team, which are well over a hundred people. He has to maintain their files, make sure they are keeping up with the rules and regulations, maintaining HIPAA regulations, making sure that they have their TB tests, and competencies up to date. He is their direct supervisor. Not only is he responsible for recruiting the volunteers, training the volunteers, he must also keep tabs to make sure they are actually visiting their patients, doing the assignments they are given, and reporting what they do in an efficient manner. If they do not do their job, it is then his responsibility to reprimand them. Yes, volunteers can be fired from their position as a volunteer. All the while he is doing this he has to make sure that each individual volunteer is getting what they want out of volunteering.

The volunteer is not just a non-paid staff member, they are also potential customers. They are the voice of the community and he has to make sure that he treats them accordingly while also making sure they do what is required of them as a staff member of Community Hospice. In his role as the volunteer director, he must also make sure that he is fulfilling the Medicare requirement of the Five Percent. What is that? Well he has to make sure that his volunteers contribute at least 5% of the patient care hours by adding to the cost savings of hospice. If this is not achieved, then the hospice falls out of compliance. This means he must keep accurate records, accounts, and budgets which have to be reported to his boss who reports to the executive team. This is a lot for a person to do who is not considered a real manager. This is a lot for a person to do whose job is not fully respected by the clinical team or the executive team. It is hard for him to hear what *special work* he does as if he is a volunteer himself. He is not a volunteer; this is his career, a career that is not fully recognized nationally as actually being a career. It is frustrating, yes. But does this mean that he should not do the best he can do? Does it mean that he can say "sorry patient, I'm a glorified clerk, I leave at 5pm, try not to die until I return at 8am."

Of course not, it is not fair to the patient, not fair to his volunteers, and not fair to himself to slack off on his role as volunteer director because what he does is important, at least he used to think it was important. Some days he began to think that maybe it wasn't all that important or at least shouldn't be to him. Some days the offer that his old college chum made for him to move up and out of this role was looking not only pretty good to him, but downright logical to him.

Matt hung up the phone, sat back in his chair, and despite his low level, felt pretty darned good about himself. The vigil assignment was filled! Yae! As he sat back, one of his dedicated volunteers was on their way to the hospital to comfort a daughter who was having one of the worst nights of her life. His volunteer will be there for her, sit with her, hold her hand, get her some water, and not leave her side. That is what hospice is all about, a neighbor helping a neighbor. How could he not feel good about that? Rewarded? Yes he was rewarded thinking about the work he had just done. He was rewarded thinking about the work one soul would be doing for another that night. It was God's work, not to get religious or existential, but it was. So what the executive team thought of him as a lowly paper pusher? He did well tonight, he did his job, and that is all that mattered...*for now.*

A tapping came at his office door startling him. "Hey, what are you still doing here?"

Matt looked over to see his boss, Sarah Evans, Vice President of Volunteer Services, standing in his office doorway. He instantly smiled. "Boss, what are *you* doing here?"

Sarah came in and seemed to collapse in the chair in front of his desk. "I was on my way home, saw your car, thought I'd drop in." she said dropping her purse onto the floor.

Matt knew she wanted more than just a simple visit, but he was sure she would eventually get to it. This late meeting should prove to be more interesting than a baseball game, he thought to himself. "I just filled a vigil assignment." He informed her proudly.

"Great. We have to make sure we give them what they want." She said with a severe hint of sarcasm.

"What's wrong?" he asked almost comically.

She took in a long breath, paused, and then examined the edge of his desk for a long period of time. Matt was about to speak and more seriously ask what was going on but Sarah begun to talk. "I just got out of a late meeting with the clinical managers and executive team."

"Sounds like fun."

"Surprisingly it wasn't." Her eyes bore deeply into his. With her expression, if her next words were *'the CEO shot everyone and then himself'* he would not have been astounded. Fortunately, these were not her next words. "They've taken away my budget, our budget."

"What?" Matt responded, shocked.

"I mean you guys still have your individual accounts to draw from, it's just that I won't be the one approving them. If you want to order anything, or get a check release, you would still submit the forms to me but I have to get them approved through the CFO."

"The Chief Financial Officer? Why?" Matt asked, but he knew this was part of the restructuring Dave Chatman was telling him about.

"I don't know why," Sarah said, "but that's the new way they're going to be doing things, something about streamlining departments."

"That seems so unnecessary for the CFO to approve pens."

"I'm not finished." Sarah cut Matt off abruptly, and then gave him a softer look so he would not take offense. "The human resources department will oversee things like fingerprinting, volunteer applications, and volunteer files. Also volunteer training will be absorbed into regular staff orientation."

"What?" Matt was beginning to sound like a broken record. His face was a distorted sack of puzzlement.

Sarah continued. "You guys will still need to train the volunteers after orientation on specific volunteer stuff such as documentation, the assignment process, etc." Before continuing, Sarah looked up in the air trying to remember. "Let's see, what else...marketing will begin handling a lot of the recruitment ads in the paper for volunteers, and just a whole bunch of other stuff I can't friggin' remember at this point." Sarah stood up suddenly. She crossed her arms and began looking at the pictures on Matt's wall. "Basically, they're taking my job, Matt." She announced still staring at his collage of photos.

"Did they say that?" he asked.

Sarah turned to look at him because she didn't hear that much shock in his voice. "No, not in so many words, but what do you think they're doing?"

"I know they talked about layoffs and restructuring." He said vaguely.

"What do you know Matt?" she asked accusingly. "What did Dave tell you? I know you guys are friends."

"That's it." He lied. Matt didn't want to betray Dave's trust, and he was unsure about his own future within the company. "Calm down, they're not taking your job."

"Oh really?" Sarah said disbelievingly. "They are slowly chipping away at my position. They are filtering it out to other departments. First it's the budget, then I have to go through the CFO for every little thing, so what's next? And don't be surprised if your titles go from Director to Coordinator!"

"So was the meeting just about volunteer services?" Matt asked.

"No, no…" Sarah waved her hands impatiently. "It was mainly about the first round of layoffs which begin as early as next week, but you didn't hear that from me. Not to worry none of you guys are affected. They did, however, talk about elimination of positions which stirred up the room, to put it mildly. The directors and managers are not safe. No one is safe. The word from now on is *streamlining*." Sarah paced a bit then returned to her seat. "I lied." She said directly. "I came by to see if you knew anything, off the record." She paused. "So do you?"

Matt sat back in his seat looking away from her, frowning a bit. He honestly didn't know what to say. Dave had told him specifically that she would be losing her job. Should he tell her this? On the one hand he thought he should, but what if that changes? What if she's not one of the ones whose position is eliminated? Then what? What if she takes the information and confronts him or goes to the CEO for protection or just up and quits? He thought about the position that Dave offered. He needed that money, for sure, but is that really what he wanted to do? No matter what, he would never make eighty thousand dollars a year as a director of volunteers, but could he and Sarah lobby for more money? Should he fight for the department? He just was not sure what he wanted at this point.

"I don't want to put you on the spot; however, I can tell you do know something." Sarah said, after watching him contemplate.

"Sarah, Dave did offer me a position, Tom's position." He admitted.

"VP of Marketing huh? Wow, okay."

"I don't know what I'm going to do about it, because I love being director of volunteers, but he offered it because he knows I want to move up."

"And he's not sure about the future of this department." Sarah interjected.

"He just said there will be a lot of changes with these layoffs." Matt added.

"Did he tell you about the merger with All Saints Hospice?" Sarah asked.

"No." Matt answered, looking even more perplexed.

"Yeah well, that is practically a done deal. Amazing how they were able to keep that one under wraps."

"Wow, they're a big hospice." Matt said surprised.

"You bet they are." Sarah continued. "They have branches across the state. When I first heard about this merger I was very excited. I thought bigger expansion for us as well, but All Saints Hospice only has volunteer coordinators and they're paid much less then we are. My position does not exist. The coordinators fall under the human resources department."

"Hmmm….I see." Matt said, seeing Sarah's point.

Sarah nodded her head. "So you see where I'm going with this? I bet you anything I am being eliminated. They never wanted volunteer services to be its own department. That was the last CEO's undertaking. She felt it should be its own department, only adjacent to human resources, not necessarily a part of it."

"Even if we did fall under human resources, that does not mean they'll take away your role." Matt replied.

"You're not hearing me, Matt – REDUNDANCY! They don't want redundancy. If they feel the director of human resources can handle it then why keep the VP of volunteer services?"

"How about Director of Volunteer Services, I mean if they make us coordinators."

Sarah stared at him incredulously. "You want to be a *coordinator*? You want to make less money? I for one do not."

"No, I'm just trying to think of ways, if they do change the position, your role or job stays, just with a different title." Matt explained.

It was now Sarah's turn to sit back. "You're gonna take that VP position, aren't you?" She asked. Matt's intent just dawned on Sarah.

"I haven't been officially offered anything yet. This conversation is probably way too premature." Matt replied.

"You think so? Dave wouldn't have mentioned anything to you if it wasn't a done deal."

"None of this is happening tomorrow." Matt continued. "This is six months down the road, and six months in corporate years means at least eight months or a year down the road."

Sarah narrowed her eyes trying to see through Matts' bullshit. It was an odd side to Matt she had never seen before. He was practically corporate himself. Could she really blame him, though? He had been watching his college chum surpass him by leaps and bounds in the same company. That's gotta hurt a man's ego, especially if the chum is as flamboyant as Dave Chatman. "Maybe you're right." Sarah finally responded. "We have some time."

Sarah Evans, mother of two, grandmother of one, swept up her purse and stood. "Oh yeah," she began as an afterthought, "Ever heard of the CVA?"

Matt thought for a moment as he followed suit and started gathering up his things to leave. "Ummm.....yes I believe I have."

"CVA, it's the Certification in Volunteer Administration. You take the exam and get to put those three letters behind your name."

"Right, yes. You're thinking of getting it?" Matt asked.

"I think we all should. I'll take it out of the budget; as long as I still have one I think I will use it. It may add a bit of credibility to the department. What do you think?" Sarah asked Matt.

Matt hunched his shoulders as he switched off his desk lamp. "Yes, I suppose it could. Everyone here seems to have something behind their name besides their degree."

"Yes, I think it says 'hey we're certifiable too'!" Sarah roared.

Matt looked at her and laughed. "Certifiable? I have to agree!"

Sarah swatted at him playfully. "You know what I mean!" she joined him in laughter. They began to walk out of the deserted public side of the building. Shannon, the secretary, and all the clerical staff, left promptly at 4:30pm daily but especially on Fridays.

"Hope I didn't keep you from any hot dates tonight?" Sarah joked.

"Nah, just beer, pizza, and baseball." Matt said. He clicked off the main lights and left only the emergency lights for illumination. "Besides, we're up bright and early tomorrow for the race. See you there?" He asked Sarah.

"Yeah..." Sarah answered as she headed towards her car. "I won't be there as early as you guys, but I'll be there. Did you get plenty of volunteers to staff it?" she asked.

"You know it."

Sarah held up one thumb. "Good job. And I will send you the information on Monday for the CVA. Good night!"

"You can give it to me at the statewide meeting on Monday. That's still taking place, right?" Matt asked watching Sarah closely.

Sarah paused as if she had completely forgotten. "Yes, the meeting, yea it's still happening. See you on Saturday and see you on Monday, too." With a final wave, Sarah got into her car.

Matt waited and watched Sarah's car pull out, as a manly safety gesture. Once she was safely driving away, Matt went to his car and got in. He sat for awhile thinking about their conversation. Matt knew what Sarah wanted to do. She wanted to fight for her job and fight for the department. Matt wasn't sure he wanted to do either. He wasn't sure he wanted to fight a losing battle.

THIRTEEN

The world slowly began to ebb back in for Samantha. Sounds of people talking, footsteps, doors opening and closing were the first confirmations that she was waking up. She tried to open her eyes but found that her eyelids were strangely heavy. Just the act of attempting to will them apart exhausted her. *"Dr. Connell, pick up line two please. Dr. Connell, line two."* The apparent distant sound of an intercom made Samantha aware she was in the hospital. Somehow with that realization opening her eyes became easier. The stark brightness of the room caused her to squeeze them shut again, grimacing. Samantha opened them again, much more slowly this time, to allow her eyes to adjust. They blinked frequently as she looked from one side of the room to the other.

Samantha couldn't make them out, but there were people in the room with her. A cluster of bodies stood to the right of her bed a few feet away. To the left of her, one person stood closer to the bed. It had to be a nurse or aide because as soon as Samantha's movement was detected the figure began to touch her and speak. The nurse's voice sounded very far off for standing so close, but Samantha assumed it was an effect from whatever drugs they had given her.

Samantha's pulse was being taken, and the nurse rattled off vital signs to the physician in the room. The other figures moved in closer, from the right and once they came into view she recognized them immediately. It was her mother, father, and their old family physician, Dr. Phillip Rosen. Samantha hadn't seen him in years.

She noticed how intently her mother and father were listening to him. As Samantha lay there staring at them she realized that her mother was hearing for the first time the finality of her condition; from the moment of her diagnosis Samantha had made it a point not to tell her mother. She withheld this information specifically not because she wanted to shield her mother from the pain of learning her only daughter was dying but because, frankly, Samantha felt it was something very private and only wanted to share it with her father. Samantha loved her mother but there was a wall between them that was built years ago.

Samantha lowered her eyes when her mother shot a look of horror her way. This was in response to the news she was hearing from the physician. Her mother's eyes seemed to double in size, and her head began to shake back and forth in sheer astonishment at the words she was hearing. For a moment Samantha felt bad that she had not informed her mother, preparing her, because she did look like a deer in headlights, a poor creature in the middle of the highway about to become road kill. The moment passed as soon as Samantha saw her mother walking over to her bedside. Her mother's expression had gone from terror to anger in all of the two seconds it took for her to say "Thank you, Doctor."

"Why didn't you say anything to us?" Lynnette Mills demanded to know in no uncertain terms. "How could you keep this from your father and me? You have been home for over a week!"

"Sorry." Samantha's voice cracked from dehydration.

"Don't you think this is something your father and I should have been informed about? I knew you were selfish, but I didn't realize you were this self centered and cruel!" Lynnette barked.

"Lynn," Samantha's father started, "she told me." He confessed.

Lynnette looked at her husband as if his face had begun to melt in front of her. "*What?* You knew?"

"Yes, Sam called me a few months ago when-"

"A few *months* ago?" Lynnette couldn't believe what she was hearing. She looked down at her daughter then back up at her husband, but neither looked familiar to her anymore.

"I didn't want to upset you." Samantha lied.

"Bullshit!" Lynnette yelled.

"Hey calm down!" Joseph Mills scolded. "We should have told you, but right now we have to make some serious decisions."

"Well, it seems like the two of you are doing fine without me, so whatever decisions you have to make do it on your own. I'm going home. It is obvious I am not wanted here!" Lynnette clutched her purse close to her and headed for the door with Joe quickly following on her heels.

Joseph blocked the door. "Where do you think you're going?"

"Didn't you hear me? I'm going home." Lynette spat back.

"Did you hear the doctor? They are recommending hospice, do you understand what that means?"

Lynnette looked at him blankly. "Get out of my way, Joe. You two do whatever the hell you want." She shoved him out of the way and left the room. Joe stood frozen, agape, staring at the closing door. *What had just happened* he thought to himself?

"Dad?" It was his daughter's voice that brought Joe back to the reality at hand. Joe turned and quickly made his way over to her.

"Samantha, everything will be fine." He reassured her. "You know your mother, she is over dramatic. Everything is going to be fine, we're going to get through this."

Samantha placed her hand in his. "I know Daddy."

Lynnette Mills walked in a hurried fog through the halls of St. John General. Her mind was a haze of turbulent thoughts; she barely knew where she was going. At one point she was in an elevator, the next she knew sliding doors leading to the outside were opening and closing in front of her. Eyes were on her wondering why this strange woman was standing motionless in the doorway. She darted to the side to allow people to pass. Like a lost child, she wandered into the parking lot not sure about her destination. Suddenly, she could not remember where she had parked the car. Did they park outside or in the structure? As she moved further away from the door, Lynette remembered that they had used the valet service. She jerked her head up, looking around, and noticed that she was on the other side of the hospital. Her car was in the front of the building, she had walked out of the wrong door.

Lynette's confusion morphed into helplessness. She felt lost and alone in a bizarre desolate world. There was a bench nearby, close to the grassy median, and she sat down before her legs gave out. On the wooden bench under the sulfur lamp post she dropped her head into her hands and sobbed uncontrollably. Even though her cries carried over to the back entrance of the hospital, causing glances to come her way, she did not care. Her daughter was dying. Her precious little girl was being taken from her before she was even able to become a mother herself, before she was able to even walk down the aisle. Gone was the anticipation of that wondrous day of that pure white, that something blue, and all of the Chantilly lace. Lynnette's arms will forever remain empty of grandchildren, empty of love, empty of the hope of their name carrying on.

It wasn't fair. It wasn't fair that there was talk of death and hospice at such a young age. Was it right that her child would die before her? Wasn't the opposite the natural order of things? What had she done in 35 years to deserve her child dying before her time? What had she done in 55 years? What transgression had she made? Had she sinned somehow? Hadn't she followed the teachings of Dr. Spock, hell of Mr. Spock?

Lynnette tilted her head back and looked up. She peered into the devastatingly beautiful blue sky with soft wispy white clouds. How dare the sky be so dazzling on a morning like this? Would she forever now look up at the clear vanilla sky and think of this moment? God has taken all of her futures, has He not? Yes, He has.

    Lynnette buried her chin into her chest and took in one last deep breath before rising to her feet. It was not the time for her to feel self pity. Nor was it time to wallow in her own failures. It was time to turn back around and go upstairs to comfort her daughter. As she walked back into the bright lights and distant murmurs, of the hospital she realized that hospice did not have to be the answer. She was not ready to give up on her daughter. Not today. Not ever.

FOURTEEN

Jenna stood in a dark corridor with grime oozing down the walls. Dirt, seaweed, and puddles of muddy water covered the hallway floor. She was in a hospital, but it was too filthy and shadowy to be any medical facility she had ever been in before, but she recognized her surroundings immediately as an intensive care unit. She could hear howls and what sounded like distant screams coming from all around her. Her blood ran cold but she had to continue forward. The room was at the end of the hall. When she took her first step toward the closed door, she began to see an ever brightening light illuminating from beneath the doorway.

The light was more brilliant than it should be, this frightened her yet she knew she had to continue. A few more steps and the walls started to raise and descend like a chest breathing in and out. The closer she got the more she heard the voices wailing and moaning. Pain was inside those walls, pain of patients dying, yes she was sure of it, and they were all dying just on the other side. This made her want to turn and flee, yet when she did look behind her she saw the darkest pit of void she had ever seen. It was beyond darkness it was a pit, a black hole of nothingness that would suck her down if she tried to retreat, so forward she continued at least in front of her there was light.

The breathing walls drew in closer and closer. Soon it was harder for her to walk forward but she pressed through turning her body sideways in order to etch down the hall the best she could. The light under the door was much brighter now so bright that she had to shield her eyes. Jenna reached the threshold and saw that the radiance had fully engulfed the doorway now, so much so that the illumination itself was the doorway. She started to reach her hand into it when she heard her name spoken by a familiar voice. She gasped when she realized it was her mother's voice.

"Jenna. Come to me...help me..." The voice spoke over and over, calling to her from within that room. Jenna was no longer afraid; now she had to go in, she had to help her mother. *"I'm coming, Mama!"* she called out to the voice.

Jenna stepped through the passageway. Inside, was not quite what she expected. Inside the room looked normal. It was a hospital room complete with a nurse, a doctor speaking to family members, and a patient in the bed. Jenna stopped and watched the interaction of the people. The nurse was checking vitals, then she left. The doctor was giving bad news, then he left. The female family member became apparently upset then left the room. The male family member ran to the door to possibly stop the female but came back and sat with the female patient. The patient and male family member talked then eventually he left. Jenna was alone with the patient.

The patient sat up in the bed and looked towards her and smiled. She didn't look ill at all. Jenna moved towards her, their eyes locked. Sunrays entered the room, and a fog started to obscure the patient as she walked closer. Soon Jenna was unable to make out the girl in the bed, and soon she wasn't able to make out anything at all. The mist was thick, cold and wet. She walked steadily forward, but she seemed to make no progress. She should have reached the bed by now. The mist swallowed her up like a soft blanket. Jenna was in a white blindness. She stopped walking, looking desperately around her for some hint of shapes she could recognize. Soon the mist lifted. She was in a field of green which went on for miles. There were hills in the far off distance. She looked to her left, and there was nothing but a field of green, so beautiful she thought. To her right someone stood beside her. It was a woman from the shape of the outline. The woman was wearing a flowing white dress billowed up by a supple breeze. Jenna could not see her face, for the woman was wearing some sort of hood over her head. "Jenna, look." The woman said to her. The voice was coming from the distance, but Jenna was sure the woman beside her had spoken the words. The woman held up her arm and pointed in the direction directly in front of them. Jenna followed her arm and looked forward. At first she saw nothing but a grassy field, yet, after a moment, she began to see....something in the distance.... A circle...no...a perfect sphere of light... sunlight?.... It grew and grew until the horizon of hills was nothing more than blank whiteness... *"Jenna!"*

Jenna woke up, and sat up in bed trying to catch her breath. She felt as if she had been under water. She put an instinctive hand to her chest looking around the room to verify that her dream was over and reality was surrounding her. That dream was weird and left her with an eerily odd feeling. She looked over at the clock on her bedside and saw that it was 5:30am.

Jenna's eyes widened. "Shit!" she cried. The alarm had not gone off and she was supposed to be down at the race/walk by 6:30am. Jenna jumped out of bed and hurried to the bathroom to take a quick shower. How in the world was she going to be able to get ready and drive to downtown Detroit in one hour? It wasn't possible. She was going to be late, no doubt about it. She showered quickly, swiftly found her matching yoga pants and tank, pulled her hair back into a tight ponytail, and fished her tennis shoes out of the closet. Her first volunteer event and she was going to be late. By the time she dashed down the stairs it was 6:15.

Once she was in her car speeding down the highway headed for the river front, Jenna relaxed. It was too early on a Saturday for the traffic to be heavy so it was smooth sailing. Her mind drifted to her new "boss", Matt. Matt with the hazel eyes, shadow beard, and rugged good looks. She giggled like a school girl in the car. "Get it together, Jen, you're dreaming about your boss." She said aloud to herself. Dreaming.... What a dream she had this morning. So odd, who was the girl in that hospital bed beckoning her? And that field, it was so green, so lush... It all seemed so real somehow. Her mother, she heard her mother's voice, so clear.

The cosmic bells of her cell phone began to chime, kicking her thoughts back to reality. The caller ID read "unknown", which caused Jenna to frown at the read out. She started not to answer but thought it might be about the race. "Hello?"

"Don't hang up." It was Adrian. His voice was raspy meaning he probably hadn't slept that night.

Jen rolled her eyes. "What do you want?"

"Wow, it's like that, cuz?" Adrian responded.

Jenna remained silent on the phone, so he continued. "Sorry to bother you but can you come down and open the door?"

"Why?" she asked.

"I left something at your place. And I was hoping I could take a quick shower and possibly a nap?" Adrian had walked from the bus stop to Jenna's home. His car was now nonexistent, after crashing it hours before.

"I'm not at home. I'm on my way downtown." Jenna informed him.

"Really? For what?"

"None of your business. You can get whatever when I get home. I should be back by 1pm or so."

"hmmm 1pm huh? I guess I have to wait..." he left the front entrance and started around the side of the house. One of her neighbors was outside grabbing the paper and paused to eye him suspiciously.

"What did you leave?" Jenna asked.

"Nothing really, I just need to crash." He lied. Adrian did leave something in her house, twenty five thousand somethings strategically stashed in her basement near the furnace. He needed to wait until things died down with his friends from Vegas before he retrieved it. So, like it or not he would wait out the six hours on her patio. He jumped the fence, a very high fence, dropping the phone.

"What are you doing?" Jenna heard loud thumps and Adrian breathing hard.

"I had to jump your fence in the back. It was a challenge but I did it so you might want to get some barbed wire or a dog or something."

"Adrian, you're the only criminal I know." Jenna heard him chuckle through the phone. She thought for a moment, then relented. "Okay Adrian, go to the garage side door. Locate the key pad. Punch in 0666 and a digital card key will pop out. You can use that to swipe the back door and get in."

"Look at you! 666 huh?" Adrian headed for the side of the garage and got the key.

"Yeah, well, it will automatically reset to my next code once the card is removed so don't think you can use that code again to gain access."

"No worries babe, I wouldn't break into your place."

"What were you going to do, lie on the lounger for six hours?" Jenna asked.

"Yup. But it probably wouldn't have been that long." He swiped the card and the door unlocked. He was inside where he immediately made his way downstairs to the basement.

"Why not?" she asked merging into the right lane to make her turn off the freeway.

"Because your nosey neighbor gave me the eye, and I am sure he would have been calling the police within the hour."

"Well that's nice to know. I am at my destination. I suppose I will see you later?"

"Unless you want me outta here before you get back?" he asked.

"Tempting, but no need." Jenna told him.

"So I'm forgiven?" Adrian got down on one knee and reached his hand behind the furnace grabbing out the vinyl bag stuffed between it and the wall.

"Let's not go that far." Jenna said.

"Okay, love you too, cuz." Adrian smiled as he opened the thin bag and saw his crisp twenties were still intact.

"Sure Adrian." Jenna hung up the phone.

Jenna followed the signs and the festive people wearing clown outfits who directed traffic to the designated parking areas. It was a beautiful day for this event. The sun was shining, and it was a pleasant seventy-one degrees with a slight warm breeze. She exited the car and breathed in the tranquil air. However the only thing tranquil was the air. All around her people were changing into their running clothes, slipping on tennis shoes, hats, and calling out to their partners. Most of the people wore bright blue t-shirts with the logo of Community Hospice emblazoned across them. Happy cartoon graphics of people running in lilac and greens were also burned onto the t-shirts.

Jenna walked through the crowd of smiling people. She responded to the greetings of each nodding head. The area was filled with volunteers working to set up tents and stock tables with fresh juices, granola bars, and sign in sheets. She could hear a band tuning up in the distance and was almost run over by a few teenage girls. "Mr. Ames!" they called out in unison, causing her to look in their direction.

"Over here, ladies." She heard Matt's familiar voice. He was heading in Jenna's direction balancing two large boxes. Jenna followed the girls to the table where he dropped the boxes down.

"Mr. Ames, where do you want us?" asked one girl.

"Mr. Ames, my friend Paige came along. She's not a volunteer but can she help out?" asked another girl.

"Why yes, of course!" Matt exclaimed. "As long as you are willing to work, all are welcome!"

"Goodie!" All three girls screeched.

"Now each of you take a t-shirt with STAFF written on the back and go find Mrs. Cobbs, and she will assign you a job." Matt fished out 3 black t-shirts with the same design as the others she saw but with the bold identifying letters on the back. Each girl grabbed one and headed off. As they brushed past Jenna she heard one girl whisper to the others, "he's so cute!"

"Hello Ms. Steele." Matt greeted brightly. He flashed his famous smile that apparently made school girls giddy.

"Hello, Mr. Ames. Where do I go?" Jenna asked.

"You are here. You're going to work with me at this table. Let me get you a t-shirt" he handed her a black one. "Extra small?" he inquired making a funny questioning expression.

"Aren't you kind? Better make it a medium." She hadn't worn extra small since her high school days.

"Here you go." Matt handed her the larger sized shirt. "Come on around and start laying out each of these shirts by size. The black ones on the right end there, and take the blue ones to the next table for me. The blue are for the participants and black are, of course, for the workers." Matt instructed.

Jenna slipped on the shirt and quickly got to work. She felt a bit invigorated to be doing something. This was fun, she thought. She officially felt like a fully fledged volunteer.

Matt began setting up sign in sheets at the far end of the table closer to the entrance gate where people were walking in. "Make sure every staff member signs in and grabs a shirt." Matt told Jenna. "The participants sign in elsewhere, and they will get their numbers at the next table."

Jenna looked to her right and saw another long table with a huge sign behind it saying "Runners/Walkers Stop Here!" she looked behind her and saw a sign behind their table saying "Staff Stop Here!" She scooped up the blue t-shirts and placed them on the next table.

"Hello, I'm Brandon." She was greeted by an ample sized man in blue jeans and black staff tee. Jenna responded with a hello. "I am Matt's counterpart from the West branch."

"Oh hello. I'm Jenna and I'm a new volunteer."

"Fresh from training." Matt announced from behind her.

"So is this your first job?" Brandon asked. As she looked at him he seemed very familiar, then realized it was because he had a striking resemblance to Theo from the Cosby Show. Jenna smiled to herself at that. She used to love watching that show.

"Yes, this is my first." She answered him.

"It's a great first job." He told her. "This will be a fun day and not that long. We always get out of here before noon." He came closer to her. "But I don't know how easy it will be working with Matt over there." He said, pretending to whisper to her. "He's a slacker you know."

"I heard that!" Matt said comically.

"Hey, I'm only speaking the truth my man." Brandon said laughing heartedly.

Jenna liked Brandon immediately though she suspected that most people did. He was definitely the kind of person who never met strangers. "Do you have anyone working with you?" she asked.

"Nope." Brandon answered. "But don't worry if I need you to run and grab something I will let you know."

"Oh no! She is working MY table!" Matt corrected. "If you want help get your own volunteer." He chided.

"Don't be stingy! And besides Jenna looks like she can handle working both tables." Brandon said.

"No problem, I can stand sort of in the middle. I can do both!" Jenna told Matt.

"You're going to wear her out before she even gets started!" Matt said. "She'll walk off and never come back!" he continued and gave Jenna a quick wink to ensure her he was only kidding.

"Then it's a good test of her fortitude." Brandon said laughing.

"I assure you, I'm here to stay." Jenna told Brandon.

Brandon put a hand to his chest dramatically. "Ah, if all the volunteers would only say that!"

Matt walked over to them. "Nope only MY volunteers say that!" He put his hands on Jenna's shoulders as if to shield her from Brandon.

"Don't you want to defect to my side?" Brandon mock pleaded. "We have better snacks." He went on.

"Snacks?" Matt interjected. "You barely feed your people!" Matt looked at Jenna "Don't let him fool you; I have to remind him to buy food for events. If it wasn't for me the volunteers would have only water and coffee at his events."

"You Lie!" Brandon said taking a stance as if holding a dueling sword. "En Guard! For you have wronged me for the last time, sir!"

"Do you guys play like this all the time?" Jenna asked, giggling.

"That's him. I came here to work." Brandon said going back to set up his table.

"I see I have to watch you two." Jenna said.

"Good, you can have my job." Susan Cobbs said, coming up to the tables. She held out a hand to Jenna. "Hi I'm Susan, the director of volunteers for the South Branch." Jenna greeted her. "I remember you from training. Welcome."

"Thanks." Jenna said. "Glad to be here."

The morning progressed with an onslaught of participants and staff coming through. Jenna smiled and greeted while Matt took pictures of the staff and their families. He chatted with them, laughed, and stood for a few photos himself. Volunteers greeted him and even stopped to discuss their patients. Jenna supposed that a volunteer director's job is never done. Once the line of people had tapered off, she and Matt walked over to see the beginning ceremonies which were commencing, and listened to the Community Hospice CEO give a welcoming speech. Then an exercise trainer took the mic to get the runners and walkers warmed up for the rest of the day. Something surprising, at least to Jenna, was a special part of the beginning ceremony. An actual hospice patient came up to speak. He was a young man who couldn't have been more than thirty, if that.

Jenna listened as he told his story of having lung cancer, not from smoking but from a genetic condition. He said he was there because he used to be an avid runner before his disease forced him to stop. He also told how his mother was beside herself and did not know what to do until hospice came and helped his mother deal with taking care of him. He said that even though he was able to be there to speak that morning that he knew soon he would not be. He thanked all of the volunteers for supporting Community Hospice because their support helped hospice bring peace and dignity to patients, like him, in his final hours.

Jenna held back the tears as she listened to the patient speak. She was also aware that others in the crowd were experiencing the same heart wrenching emotions as she was.

"He puts a face to it." Matt said to her.

"You're right. Amazing that he was willing to even speak about something so personal." She said to Matt.

"True, but people with cancer speak all the time about their disease. What's wrong with hospice patients doing the same?" he asked.

"Well, most of those with cancer are fighting for a cure and usually it's the survivors speaking." Jenna replied.

"But that's just it. We have to educate people on hospice that death is going to happen to us all. It's about living all the way up to the end of your life with quality."

Jenna thought about that and began to understand what he was saying, and he was right. Death was scary, sure, but you don't have to be alone and that was the point. That patient was dying, but today he was still very much alive, and he was not alone. Jenna got it.

When the runners and walkers were off on their respective event, Matt and Jenna decided to take a walk along the river front. As they walked, the clowns and jugglers popped in and out of the path making funny faces and performing. Other volunteers and participants strolled the walk, as well. It was such a beautiful morning. "This is such a great day for this." Jenna said.

"You are so right." Matt replied. "Last year it was cloudy but still a bit warm. This year the weather is perfect, 72 degrees and sunshine. Who could ask for a better day?"

"Hmmm..." Jenna sighed, taking in the sun. She stopped along the path and leaned on the railing looking out at the glistening Detroit River. Matt joined her. She looked at him, and he had such a polished look about him, more like a model than a manager. "What made you pick hospice as a career? Why not a doctor or a lawyer?"

Matt was shocked to hear the question. He looked at her and thought for a moment. Which answer to give, the generic one or the truth? "I went to school for business. After getting my MBA I came here to work because a friend recommended a job in marketing. I took it but it kept me away from my family more than I wanted so when this position came open I applied for it. I was able to get the same basic salary, without the bonuses." Matt finished.

"So you're an ad man? I can see that." Jenna commented.

"Advertising allowed me to be creative, though sometimes it's hard to make it in that business. But, I had a knack for spotting trends and where the public's mind's were at, sort to speak. I did the ad game for about five years after college."

"Then you heard about hospice?" Jenna asked.

"A college buddy worked here and gave me a lead. It was a better paying job so I took it. I learned a lot about hospice. And felt it was the right place for me. I connected to it." Matt admitted.

Jenna watched his eyes drift and she knew. "You lost someone." She said.

"Just one someone, my mother." He said, looking back at her.

"That very important one." Jenna added. "Did she die in hospice?"

"No. It was just one of those things. She was at the wrong place at the wrong time. She was walking to her car at the mall. Two people were fighting at a car a few rows down. One of them pulled a gun, shot, and it missed their target and hit her." Matt hunched his shoulders.

"Oh my God I'm so sorry, Matt" Jenna said.

"Yeah, it happened just a few years ago. My son was only five. That was his favorite Nana."

"Did they catch the guy?" she asked.

"It was a woman. She turned herself in. She had a gun because her estranged husband abused her and he had been waiting for her to leave work. She worked at Orange Julius. She came out and he grabbed her. It was the first time she ever fired it."

"Wow." Jenna said mainly to herself.

"I don't blame her." Matt continued. "It was an accident. She was just trying to protect herself. I guess it was my mother's time, you know?"

Jenna reached over and instinctively touched his arm gently. "I'm so sorry. I don't know which is worse, your mother dying so quickly, or me watching my mother die of cancer."

"They are both equally bad. But at least you had a chance to say goodbye." Matt paused and thought a moment, then continued. "That's one of the main reasons I have stayed in hospice. We make sure each of our families has a chance to say goodbye. It's important."

FIFTEEN

When Lynnette walked back into her daughter's hospital room she found Samantha alone. She glanced at the bathroom, but it was empty. "Where is your father?" Lynnette asked, a bit accusingly.

"I made him take a break and get some coffee." Samantha answered. She looked up at her mother. Her mother's face looked old, haggard. "Maybe you ought to join him. You look tired."

Lynnette took a seat near the bed. "I'm sorry about storming out before. This is a lot to take in."

"You're telling me." Samantha said facetiously. Lynnette ignored her comical tone.

"Your father and I are here for you, we love you, and we're going to get you the best doctors to help you fight this. There are wonderful advances in stem cell research, experimental treatments, we will explore them all. We don't have to give up. This is not the end for you, Samantha. You are going to live a long and full life!" Lynnette declared.

"They're letting me go home in a couple of hours. The hospice nurse will be by the house this afternoon. The medical equipment will be dropped off by today or tomorrow." Samantha told her mother.

"There is no need for those vultures to stop by; you are not going into hospice! We are going to fight this, we are not giving up!" Lynnette said forcefully.

"They wanted to know if I wanted to keep my bed or get a hospital bed delivered." Samantha continued. "A hospital bed is safer, but I like my bed. They said we didn't have to make a decision right now."

Lynnette stood up. "Your bed is just fine. Now I will make some calls to UofM on Monday. There are new drugs being created all the time.

Meanwhile, you'll come home and get your rest. I remember reading something about John Hopkins Medical Center research. I know its in Baltimore but we want the best in the field. Also…"

"Mother, will you just stop it!" Samantha yelled sitting up in bed. "I have seen doctors! I have had the tests! While you were out having your temper tantrum, I signed onto hospice. I did! This is my decision. I am going to die! I will get weaker and weaker, soon I won't be able to fucking move. I'm going to need help! Dad can't do it alone!"

Lynnette's face contorted into a tight grimace. "What? Of course he's not going to have to do it alone, I will be there! And don't' you talk to me like you don't have any sense. You may be ill, but I am still your mother!"

"I am not ill, I am dying which means I can talk to you any way I damned well please!" Samantha swung her legs over in an attempt to get out of bed. The world spun.

"You have always been a rebellious child. If you think you are going to use this incident as some sort of way of getting back at me for whatever you have created in your mind you've got another thing coming Missy!"

Samantha reached out and grabbed her mother's arm for balance.

"Lay back down, Sam!" Lynnette tried to steady her and just as she was reaching around Samantha's back her daughter suddenly vomited onto her mother's shirt and pants. Lynnette let out a scream of shock and revulsion.

Joe ran into the room. "What's happening?" he asked, seeing Samantha coughing and gagging over the bed. He looked at his wife covered in yellow slimy ooze and went to his daughter's aid while yelling for a nurse. It didn't take long for a nurse to arrive and begin steadying Samantha.

"It's the medication," the nurse informed Joe. "sometimes it can have this effect. Samantha, you got it all out?" she watched as her patient nodded. The nurse scooted in between a stunned Lynnette and the bed. "Lay back Samantha, your Dad is going to get you some water." Joe quickly poured a drink from the night stand.

"I feel okay, I just got dizzy." Samantha said, lying back down in bed.

Lynnette was locked in place, eyeing her daughter who she secretly felt did it on purpose. Joe came up beside her, rubbing her back. Lynnette jerked away from him and headed off to the bathroom to wash up.

Joe shot his daughter a knowing glance. He was greeted with a weak, though obvious, malevolent crooked smile. "No…" Joe began, coming in closer to his daughter. "Tell me you didn't."

"There was time to turn the other way." She said. "Besides, she deserved it." Samantha was feeling sleepy again so she allowed herself to rest back into the softness of the pillow.

""What is it between you two?" Joe asked as he smoothed back the stray, sweat-stained hair from Samantha's face.

Samantha felt her father's love as he did this; her eyes closed and her smile broadened. "I'm sorry, Daddy."

Joe was instantly transferred back into the past when his daughter was only five years of age. She had broken a plate in the kitchen, on purpose. Sam did not want to digest another broccoli stalk so as soon as her mother turned around to leave the room she had smashed the plate onto the floor causing the vegetable and cheese to go flying to and fro. After listening to her mother scream, Sam finally said *"I'm sorry"* to her father when he bent down on one knee, looking questionably into his daughter's young eyes.

As Joe watched his daughter turn and drift off into a deep sleep in the hospital bed, he realized that whatever the trouble was between his wife and daughter started long before either of them could properly categorize it. It meant there was no solution that he was going to be able to give.

Joe left his daughter's room and ran into her friends, Kyra, Shelley, and Nina. Nina was the first to approach him. "Mr. Mills, how is she?"

Joe furrowed his brow because he was not ready to have this conversation outside of the family, but then he thought again, he had to at some time, and Sam's friends had a right to know. "Look girls..." he gently touched Nina's arm and led them away from the room. He spoke to them as if they were still teens from force of habit. "Sam is sleeping right now, we can't disturb her."

"What's her condition?" Shelley asked.

Joe paused for a moment then said bluntly, "Samantha has ALS, Lou Gehrig's disease. It is quite advanced."

"What does that mean?" Kyra asked bewildered.

"It's advanced?" Nina clarified, then asked soberly, "How long does she have?"

"Well we don't know. We're admitting her to hospice."

"Hospice?" Shelley gasped.

"What's hospice?" Kyra asked even more confused.

Nina turned to her, "Hospice is where they send you when you're dying."

"Oh my God!" One of Kyra's hands instinctively went to her chest.

"It's not quite as final as all of that." Joe tried to soften the reality.

"She's right." Lynnette said coming up from behind him. "It's where people go to die. Or better stated, it's where your family sends you to die."

"This is not the time or the place, Lynn." Joe scolded his wife, who paused yet with a look of such malevolence Joe wished he had not said anything.

"What time are they releasing Sam?" Nina graciously asked.

"Around three, the doctor wants to see her one more time before she goes home." Joe glanced at his wife because he knew she had not heard this. "Why don't you girls come by tomorrow afternoon?" he said. "She should be doing much better by then." Joe informed them, while ignoring the cynical snorts coming from Lynn.

The three friends all nodded and agreed. They slowly walked away. As Nina and Kyra headed for the elevator, Shelley paused at Samantha's hospital door. She gazed at it as if she could see inside. She did feel that a part of her could see her friend sleeping alone in the room. Shelley's heart sank because she knew that an end to an era was upon them. Samantha was dying and nothing will ever be the same again. Shelley held out her hand and placed it on the door. Her body leaned forward, allowing its weight to rest against the door; her head fell down into her chest.

Kyra, thinking Shelley was fainting, ran to her. "Come on, now." she said, holding her up but Shelley was not fainting, at least not physically. The thought of Samantha's life ending just got the best of her, and, emotionally, she had no more strength to hold herself up. Even though Shelley was in no danger of falling, she was grateful for Kyra's support because had she not come, Shelley did not think she would have been able to move. With Kyra's assistance, Shelley made her way to the elevator. After a moment of waiting for the car to come to their floor the friends entered and disappeared behind the closing doors. Shelley had looked up at Samantha's door one more time and stared at it as the two doors closed in front of her.

SIXTEEN

Matthew pulled his SUV into the office parking lot and shut off the engine. It was Monday morning and they all had a meeting in the central area of the state. Community Hospice was statewide, with a total of ten Directors of Volunteer Services covering the area, Sarah was their boss. This statewide meeting took place quarterly like clockwork, but Matt had a feeling that this particular meeting's agenda would be altered. Things were changing in Volunteer Services and he felt an ominous announcement may be in the works. A part of him was secretly hoping that they would hear the words "layoff" or "restructuring" today so he would have a plausible excuse to leave his current position for the executive team, if he made that decision. As Matt waited for his counterparts to arrive for the "meeting carpool", he thought why should he feel guilty about leaving a position that clearly did not pay enough, did not warrant enough respect from upper management, and, frankly, did not bring him pleasure? What was the guilt all about, anyway? Was he not justified to want a better life for himself, a better career, more child support for his son? Were these not worthy goals? Despite this, Matt felt an ache, the numbing ache of guilt. He could not deny it, but he truly struggled to do just that.

Matt's cell phone rang, jarring him back to the reality of the day. He swiped the tab that said "slide to unlock" and answered the call. "This is Matthew, may I help you?" Even though this also served as his personal phone, Matt always answered in this stoic business fashion.

"Hey Matt, this is Shannon." The voice confirmed, though no clarification was necessary; he knew her voice anywhere. "I know you're off to your meeting, but patient number 57678 Kochenda would like a volunteer for today at 1pm."

Matthew frowned instinctively, "What? Today? Are they for real? How many times do I have to tell the nurses not to promise, or even ask for a volunteer less than 48 hours out?"

"I'm sure many, Matt." Shannon said in a voice that was way too sweet to be professional. This caused him to sit up and act more managerial.

"Thank you, Shannon, I'll give the family a call." He said, in the most sober voice he could muster.

"Do you need the caregiver's phone number?" Shannon asked in that same charming tone.

Matt cleared his throat. "No, I'll look it up. Thank you."

"You're welcome." Shannon hung up. Matt did the same staring at the phone for a moment. Quickly he shook off the thoughts running through his mind and opened his laptop which had been nestled inside his brief case. It was his turn to drive the hour and a half carpool to the meeting so he waited outside his own office for his fellow directors to arrive.

Matt logged into the computer. He was close enough to tap into the company's Wi-Fi, as well as sign into AllScripts, their medical record database. As he waited for it to load, Matt was startled by a loud rap at his car window. Displaying a clear expression of annoyance, he looked up and into the moon face of Trish Kramer, RN. "Morning, Matt!" she said without even the slightest hint of delight, but it wouldn't be Trish if she did.

Matt hit the button to electronically roll down his car window. "Morning, Trish, what did I *not* do now?"

"Ha Ha, Matt." Trish lit a cigarette before she continued. Matt looked at her in the morning sun and realized that when she wasn't frowning she was actually a very lovely woman. But frowning was her strong suit. "Okay Matt, I'm glad I caught you. I saw your email about having an all day meeting in Lansing."

"Yep, just waiting for my colleagues now." he replied.

"Don't want to come off bitchy, but what the hell happened to the volunteer you promised the Roberson's yesterday?" She was leaning against an adjacent car, and her short, spiny, dark red hair reminded him strangely of a female devil.

Matt was very confused. He remembered talking to Carol, the volunteer he scheduled to go out on Sunday afternoon while the caregiver and family went to an event. He remembered talking to her, sending her all the information on the patient via email and confirming with the family.

He knew she went out so what is Trish *talking* about? Which is exactly what he said to her.

"Nope." Trish corrected. "Three o'clock came and no volunteer. The daughter called triage and triage called me while I was at the beach, laying out trying to get a tan, and here is Sandra Roberson in my ear, pissed! She missed their grandson's bar mitzvah or something."

"What? I had a volunteer all set up!"

" Carol, right?" Trish asked between drags.

"Yes!"

"She said she talked to a Carol on Friday, everything was arranged, and she was happy. Come Sunday, no Carol. She waited, and waited, no Carol..." Trish watched as Matt exited his SUV. Matt towered an easy five inches over her. He was clearly upset and confused, but she did not care. Trish continued. "The caregiver had to stay home and miss it, so she starts screaming at me! *I thought hospice could provide all these services? I thought someone would be here to watch my Mom? This was a very important event in our family! I had to let everyone go! I had to stay here! What happened? What happened? Who was this chick who called? Why do you make promises you can't keep?* Blah blah blah!"

Matt shook his head uncontrollably. "This is not possible. What the hell?"

"That's what I said." Trish responded.

"Look, I talked to Carol on Friday; she said she was fine to do it. She called the family, and all was set. All weekend I have not gotten an email. I was at the race but my emails pop up on my phone so I can always be reached. Didn't hear anything Sunday so I didn't think about it."

Trish reassured, "I know it wasn't your fault, Matt but the bottom line is the volunteer didn't show up, and the caregiver was stuck." Trish hunched her shoulders in a dramatic "I don't know" stance. "I talked to the caregiver, but if I were you I would call the family and try to smooth things over."

"Shit, she's pissed, she won't want to talk to me."

Trish put a rare hand of support on his shoulder. "That's your job." She said.

Matt looked at Trish, and for a split second a wave of understanding exchanged between them. There was no resentment, no my job is more important than yours, no doubt, no distrust, for that moment it was only a look of oneness. For that moment she was saying, *I need you to make this right for all of us.*

Matt relented. "Okay. I'll make sure to call her today."

"This morning." Trish clarified.

"Yes, this morning." He guaranteed her.

Trish threw her cigarette to the ground, stomping it. "Well I'm outta here. I have to admit a 35 year old today."

"Wow, that's young." Matt replied.

"Yeah, sad case, she has ALS, and it's aggressive. Parents are beside themselves. The mother is angry. She already hates us."

"Great." Matt said sarcastically.

"Yeah, the patient and father are on board with hospice. She knows she's dying. But the mother? No way! And who are they assigned to?" Trish waited for an answer.

"You, of course, you get all the juicy ones."

"Don't I though?" Trish threw up her hands and started walking towards the building. She stopped suddenly and turned. "Hey, I'm already thinking volunteer for this one. Lots of emotional stuff there, I can feel it. This patient, I know, is going to need a companion to take her away from her mother sometime." Trish started back towards the building. "I'll task you!" she yelled back and walked into the staff entrance.

Even though Matt and Trish butted heads frequently, she did care a lot about her patients. This was more than just a job for her; Matt knew that this was her life. She was like many hospice nurses, dedicated, head strong, knowledgeable and above all, compassionate. She would do anything to make sure her patients received the care they needed, and she did not give a damn if she was talking to family or the physician, she made sure the patient got all that they needed. If Trish could make it happen, Trish made it happen. Matt respected her, even though her personality was, at times, a bit brazen.

As soon as Matt got back into his car and rebooted his laptop, he saw Brandon's Ford Taurus pull in. It was a simple car, but Brandon was a simple guy. Matt always joked to himself that Brandon took the comparison with Theo Huxtable too seriously. Brandon did have a striking resemblance, but Matt thought that if Theo was grown up, with a wife and kids, he would be Brandon. Yet, deep down, Matt knew the real reason he thought like that about his colleague. He was jealous. Pure and simple, he was out and out envious of the life Brandon led. Brandon was happy with his job; he loved his wife and kids, and he was the ultimate everyday happy family man. Brandon's life was what Matt had wanted his marriage to be. Truthfully, he would have needed to marry a woman like Chloe, Brandon's wife, a sweet plain girl, instead of the glamorous wannabe like his ex, Connie.

Brandon tapped on the hatch. "Pop it, man." He waited for the click, then opened the back of the truck and slid in his rolling computer/file bag. "Working already I see?" he asked the back of Matt's head. Brandon looked up and saw Susan's car pulling up so he left the back open.

"It never ends." Matt said without looking up.

"Tell me about it." Brandon answered, more to himself than to Matt.

Susan Cobbs was being dropped off by her husband, not a usual occurrence. Brandon walked over to her car and relieved her of her identical carrying case. "Why thank you, Brandon." She said. Susan bent back down and looked into the car at her husband. "You see, Paul, that's what a gentleman does, he helps out! But you wouldn't know anything about that would you?" Susan's tone was icy, and she slammed the passenger side door.

Matt looked up from his computer after hearing her tone and the slam of the car door. He raised a hand in greeting to Paul, who waved back with an awkward smile. Matt watched as Susan blocked his view of her husband. She stood with a hand on one hip, then barked at Paul. "Just make sure that you're sitting in this parking lot at 4pm. Got that? 4 pm."

"Why don't you call me when you get close?" Paul suggested, wrong thing to do!

"No!" Susan yelled. "4pm Paul. I don't care if you have to sit here for over an hour waiting for me. Be here at 4pm!" Susan then turned swiftly getting into Matt's vehicle.

Paul hollered out the window. "Hey Matt, why don't you do us all a favor and leave that one on the side of the road?" Although Paul was smiling, Matt thought he may have meant what he said.

Brandon thought it was hilarious because he let out a roar of laughter as he got into the back seat of Matt's car. Susan shot him an evil glance, and then looked back at her husband who was pulling off. "Yeah you're just a regular comedian, aren't you?" she yelled at him, but Paul was quickly turning out of the parking lot before she even finished.

"And how are we this morning, Mary Sunshine?" Matt quipped.

"Just drive the car, okay?" Susan said, adjusting her seatbelt.

"What in the world happened with you guys this morning?" Brandon asked. He leaned back into the seat and got comfortable. He secretly wanted a large SUV himself, but his wife liked sensible cars like the

Taurus. He loved it when it was Matt's turn to drive because there was plenty of room for him to relax and listen to the stimulating conversation the three of them would have on the way to and from their statewide meetings. From the sound of it, this trip was not going to disappoint.

Susan ignored Brandon's question and just looked out the window as Matt drove out of the parking lot and headed for the freeway. "Now you know you have to tell us what that was about." Matt said.

"Why do I have to tell you? Can't I just ride in peace before I have to sit through eight grueling hours of a useless meeting?" Susan answered.

"If you don't spill, woman!" Brandon said lightly tapping her seat with his foot. Another cold eye was shot back at him. He raised his eyebrows to her glare as to inform her that they were waiting.

Susan let out an exasperated gush of air. "Men are stupid babies!" she yelled.

"Yeah, so what's your point?" Brandon quipped.

Matt looked over at Susan, "Paul is a good guy. What did he do now?"

"Paul is a twelve year old kid who dresses up like a man. I am married to a twelve year old!" She announced, as if just realizing it. "Last night we were all at dinner. We went to that classy Italian restaurant in Farmington Hills. The boys were getting on my nerves so I decide why not have a glass of wine with my meal? Then HE decides he wants a glass of wine too. I told him no because he's driving and we have to set an example for the boys. Does he listen to me?"

Both Matt and Brandon say in unison "Of course not!"

"Right! So we're leaving the restaurant," Susan pauses, "stop up here at Starbucks, I need a coffee." She told Matt, pointing out the window. Matt pulled into the drive thru. Susan continues, "We're leaving the restaurant and what happens?"

"He backs into someone?" Brandon interjected.

"No, he thinks he has the car in reverse, but nope he has it in drive, and boom, goes head first into the friggin' light pole! Completely destroys the front end!"

"Oh wow." Matt says. He drives up to the window and they all get a round of coffees. Soon they were on the road and headed for Lansing. This was going to be an easy hour and a half trip.

"Thank goodness no one was hurt." Brandon told Susan.

Susan let out a snort. "Instead of owning up to the fact that he had too much to drink he decides to blame it on me. He said that if I hadn't been yelling at the boys to be quiet then he wouldn't have been distracted, and none of this would have happened. To which I retorted to tell his stupid butt, that if he had *not* have had the drink, like I *told* him not to, then he would have been more clear of mind and none of this would have happened!" Susan looked over her shoulder at Brandon, then at Matt. "Why do you men have to be such babies?" she asked, and actually waited for an answer.

Matt furrowed his brow and tried to accommodate her. "Look Suz, men are not babies. I guess he didn't realize how the wine would affect him. And it really sounds like a mistake."

"Oh please." Susan dismissed.

"Susan, my wife and I went through this." Brandon said. "She thought the only way to get through to me was to treat me like a child, berate me. She found I was not responding. So we had a talk, and I told her how her attitude only made me defensive. She stopped and started speaking to me as an adult. It worked miracles."

"Well, if I was married to a man then that might work, Cosby kid." Susan remarked.

"Cosby kid?" Brandon appeared confused.

Matt quickly stepped in, "Who read the agenda for today?" He felt changing the subject would be a good idea.

Brandon agreed, grabbed the proverbial baton, and ran with it. "I did. Looks like the same stuff. I mean how many times do we have to talk about the utilization rate? That's really something we can't do much about. The nurses requests a volunteer, we provide them. We can't just make them request one."

"I think what they want is for us to speak up more in the weekly clinical meetings." Matt said.

"Speak up?" Susan chimed in. "All I do is talk about volunteers and how they can be utilized. Frankly, I'm sick of being ignored!"

Hearing her say that sent a charge through Brandon, "I hear you! I'm sick of it, too. But I keep saying 'do they need a volunteer?', 'Hey I think they could use a volunteer', 'Please, please, please ask for a volunteer!"

The car roared in laughter at Brandon's mocking voice. Not only was he funny, he was right!

"Sarah came into my office Friday. She did not look good. She thinks they're trying to take away her job." Matt announced.

"I've been hearing some rumblings." Brandon said.

"What kind of rumblings?" Susan asked.

"Well we all heard about the layoffs. That was announced and is official. The unofficial piece is that the volunteer services department will fall under the VP of Marketing because marketing is community focused and so is volunteerism."Brandon informed them.

"We're also human resources. Why not just fall under that?" Susan countered. Matt only listened, not wanting to reveal what he had been told by Dave.

"I think being shifted under the marketing department makes more sense, plus Sarah could keep her job because they would still need a VP to supervise us." Brandon answered.

"That doesn't mean she'll keep her job. I also heard that titles may be changing too." Susan said as she shifted a bit in her seat to see Brandon. "Now this is just a rumor, but I heard that we could all go from being directors to coordinators."

"What?" Matt said shocked.

"The job descriptions would stay the same but I heard that since most other hospices use the term coordinator instead of directors for our position that they want to be more in line with the profession's most recognizable terms." Susan explained.

"If that shit happens, I'm leaving." Matt said.

"I ain't no Juliet but what's in a name?" Brandon joked even though he was serious. For him the job title really didn't matter to him as long as he could keep his benefits and current rate of pay. He was not looking to be the next executive of the company. He liked his job, and he was looking forward to retiring from it. It was all semantics to him, and this is what he said out loud to them.

Matt retorted back quickly. "Semantics? Oh no, man, it is much more than semantics. You think we get treated like crap now as directors? Wait until they slap coordinator in our title and you can forget about any more respect. At this company, what is a coordinator, nothing more than a glorified secretary. I didn't work this many years and get an MBA to be a secretary, no sir!"

"I really don't care," Susan offered, "as long as I still have a job at the end of the day. But if they have to let any of us go in the region, I will volunteer, guys. I mean I have been thinking about staying at home full time anyway, been thinking about starting a cooking blog." She added.

"Cooking blog?" Brandon inquired.

"Sure, if I can get some good advertisers, I can make a nice penny off of it. Maybe I could write some accompanying cook books." Susan replied.

"I never knew you were a good cook, I never knew you were good with computers for that matter." Brandon admitted.

"Well, I don't disappear when I leave work, you know." Susan said. "I do have a full life beyond Community Hospice."

"Hopefully the layoffs will not affect us much, if at all." Matt said. "If nothing else this should be one interesting staff meeting."

Brandon sat up. "Agreed." He leaned forward toward Susan. "So let's hear more about the life of Chef Susan!"

For the rest of the trip Susan regaled them with her ideas for the cooking blog, her cooking skills and ambitions. Matt chimed in here and there but, mainly, he was zoned out thinking more and more about how appealing the VP of marketing position was looking.

SEVENTEEN

Trish Kramer, RN was greeted at the door by Joe. She could see that he had not slept for many days. She followed Joe into the living room, a room which was obviously reserved for guests. The experience of driving up to the home gave Trish an idea of the type of family she would be dealing with. Of course, it was mere speculation, and downright stereotyping, but she was usually right. The home must have cost well into the millions, she was sure, especially for this area. Trish guessed about four million, including renovations and landscaping. As she sat in the living area, she was sure that a professional decorator designed the Corsican-styled foyer and furnishings. It was old world and straight from an opulent magazine. Trish was sure that not many guests traveled beyond this point.

Trish unpacked her hospice admission packet and opened it, as she had done many times before, and placed it onto the oversized glass and mahogany coffee table. She gently scooted back the two candelabras and two large art books. The top art book was one that was professionally done of the family. The cover showed her new patient as a child and her parents flanking her. It was a gorgeous photo that could have donned any high fashion publication.

"Can I get you anything?" Joe asked. Lynnette walked into the room just then and took a seat directly in front of Trish. She was dressed in a silk peach blouse and matching wide legged pants. Trish thought she looked ready to go on a prestigious luncheon. Lynnette did not say a word to her, only nodded minimally. The woman was stiff and, to Trish, she looked as if she was ready to pounce. Her stare was ice cold. This did not bother Trish because it was a gaze she had experienced many a time before.

"No, I'm fine, thank you." She responded to Joe. "Is Samantha coming down or can we do this in her room if that's more convenient."

"Do you need her?" Lynnette asked frigidly. The only thing moving on Lynnette's body were her lips.

Trish maintained a smile. "Yes ma'am we do." She said. "Samantha is still alert and oriented so she has a say in the admission process. She needs to hear this and understand and sign off on it."

"Of course." Lynnette stated.

Joe was still in the doorway. "I can go get her." He said. "One moment." Joe awkwardly turned and headed up the semi-spiral staircase.

Samantha was fully clothed. She woke up early and dressed and was ready for the arrival of the hospice nurse. She was not in her room but was out in the back yard sitting in one of the lounge chairs and looking out at the expansive acreage of their property. It was a sea of green. Samantha remembered running across the field as a child. As a teenager she lost her virginity in the woods bordering the property and a multitude of family outings occurred here. She was thinking of none of those. This was the spot where Kenneth had first asked her to go steady. She had only been 16. The sun was just setting on that day. It was a rare seventy degrees in September, and they were the only ones left from a small family barbeque. The remaining guests had retreated to the basement game room so she and Kenneth were alone. He was a traditional man, even then, so he got down on one knee as if proposing and asked her to be his girlfriend.

The wind was blowing a soft breeze that day, and she remembered wearing a long white sundress that bellowed in the mild gusts. Kenneth had the promise ring ready in his pocket, and it was like magic the way he produced it so easily. Samantha remembered smiling from her soul. She could not be sure if she actually verbalized a yes, or maybe it was the silly giggles and tears that rolled down her face that gave Kenneth a clue. Now, as she sat alone in the chair, and thinking back, she felt Kenneth sitting next to her. Was he there, she wondered. Samantha looked over at the empty lounger and tried to imagine him smiling knowingly at her, as he always did.

"Sam?" At first, Samantha heard her name in Kenneth's voice, and she jerked her head around expecting to see him standing beside her chair. Her eyes refocused, and she clearly saw her father there. "Samantha," he repeated. "The hospice nurse is here, would you like her to come out here?"

Sam was a bit disappointed she did not see Kenneth standing there, yet also relieved that it was not her mother. "No, I'll come inside." Her voice was soft and seemed to come from a far off place.

Joe stood there for a moment. "Do you need any help?" he asked cautiously because he had always known his daughter to be a very independent person. He was not sure how this illness was affecting Samantha emotionally. He would just have to watch her and play it by ear.

"No, I'm fine. Here I come." She told him. Her father watched as her hand tightly gripped the arm of the chair; it trembled a bit as she pushed herself up. Samantha's legs were too weak for her to stand without that push. Joe heard a muffled grunt during her maneuver. No, she is not going to be able to do this on her own for much longer. His heart sank.

Sam noticed how the world blurred and spun as she started towards the door. Maybe meeting outside was a better idea, but, nope, she was up now and wasn't going to change her mind. She may feel weak but didn't want to appear that way...just yet. She stood in one place for just a second while the merry go round she was on slowed down enough for her to get off. It didn't take long. Samantha walked with her father noticeably right behind her. A part of her wanted to scold him and tell him again that she was fine, but she was not fine so she allowed him to remain without saying a word.

Both ladies in the living room looked up when Sam and Joe rounded the corner. Lynnette saw that her daughter looked pale. It was odd seeing her with no make up on of any kind. Trish saw that her new patient's legs were weakening, and her gate was unsteady even though she was walking without assistance. Trish immediately decided to order a walker, wheelchair, bedside commode, and to suggest a hospital bed with railings.

Samantha sat down in the large chair equipped with an ottoman. She eased down into the seat, and Trish noticed a bit of a grimace as she did so. Sam placed her feet onto the ottoman and relaxed back into the chair. Trish saw that her breathing was labored, as well.

"Hello, Samantha, I'm Trish, and I'll be your nurse case manager."

"You can call me Sam. I remember meeting you in the hospital." she said.

"Yes, that's right." Trish said. She reintroduced herself because sometimes patient's memory can be affected by the medications and the in and out of consciousness they experience. "I'm here to sign you onto the hospice program, but first I want to ask if you're in any pain?"

Samantha instinctively looked over at her mother, which was something she always did when she was about to lie. Even at 33 years old, she had reverted back to feeling like a child. "Just a little." She said, when she looked back at Trish.

Trish intuitively recognized that she was lying. "On a scale of one to ten, one being a pin prick and ten being the worst pain you have ever experienced, where would you say your pain is right now?"

"Right now?" Samantha asked. Trish nodded. Samantha glanced again at her mother. She did not want to let her parents know that ever since she woke up she had been in excruciating pain. It was a pain as if she had started a rigorous exercise routine and was feeling the after effects in her muscles. Yet, instead of the pain being in just her thighs or arms, it was all over her entire body. The pain was also a bit numbing and not sharp enough to make her cry out. When Samantha woke up she was okay, yet as the morning progressed so did feel the pain. She felt it was the pain killers from the hospital wearing off.

"I would say I am at a seven." Sam admitted.

"Seven?" Trish repeated. "Do you know if they sent you home with any pain medication?"

Joe spoke up. "A bottle of Percocet." He said.

"Sam, have you taken any this morning?" Trish asked her. She watched as Sam shook her head. "Okay, Joe, would you mind going to get that bottle? We're going to have you take a dose now and I'll call in an order for some Oxycodone."

"Oxycodone?" Lynnette asked shocked. "Jesus Christ, don't you think that's a bit extreme? She just got home from the hospital. I think the Percocet is quite enough!"

"Actually," Trish explained, "Oxycodone sounds scary to a lot of people, but for Sam's disease the pain she is feeling now will continue to escalate. It's best to get her started on a medication regime now to control her pain." Trish further informed Lynnette.

"Yeah, but opioids?" Lynnette challenged.

"Mrs. Mills, it is quite common and necessary for your daughter's condition." Trish told her.

"That's all you hospice people love to do, isn't it? You just dope the patient's up, sing fucking Kumbaya, and let them die!"

"Mother shut up!" Samantha screamed.

"Ma'am, I understand your concern, but again, for the kind of pain your daughter is experiencing and will experience in the future, she needs this level of pain medication." Trish assured.

Lynnette wasn't having it. "She needs a narcotic? She needs to be addicted to drugs? Is that your idea of medical care? Hell, I can get her heroin on any street corner! This is ridiculous!" Lynnette got up from her seat and stood by the fireplace.

"Ma'am, it's really not like that at all. It is an opioids, but it is not the same as heroin by any means. Mrs. Mills you have to trust that we know what we are doing. We're here to provide palliative care for your daughter." Trish stated.

"Palliative? What the hell is that? Is that just a fancy way of saying legal drug dealers?" Lynnette shot back at her.

"Mother, please." Samantha said, barely audible. The pain was really beginning to get to her. Thankfully, Joe was soon at her side with the medication and water.

"We were thinking Sam should take the medication as needed." Joe explained apologetically.

Trish opened the bottle and handed it to Sam. Joe handed Sam the glass of water. "That's the usual course people take in normal circumstances but Sam, you must take your medication like clockwork, even if you are not in pain at the time. The reason is so your body can adapt to the medication so your pain stays regulated. If at anytime you feel that the pain is getting worse then let us know and we will adjust your prescription. Okay?" Trish smiled at Samantha, and she tried to smile in return.

After Sam had swallowed the pills, Trish returned to her seat. She picked up her packet and handed a duplicate packet to Joe who had returned to his seat. Lynnette was still peering down at them from across the room as she leaned on the mantle.

Trish looked at Samantha, "Would you like a packet?"

"No, I'll just listen." Samantha said.

Trish mouthed an "ok" to her. "The purpose of this visit is to sign Sam onto hospice. I will be explaining what hospice is, the services that are provided, the hospice benefit, and answering your questions. I will also need to take a look at all of Sam's medications she is currently using. I will be filling out a schedule so each of you will know how and when to administer her medications. Before I leave I will also order the medical equipment which will be delivered within 48 hours. Before Sam signs any of the paperwork I am going to try to explain every detail as much as possible. Please stop me and ask questions, at any time. I realize that this will be a lot to take in all at once but hospice has a team that can assist you. The team consists of our physician who will be coming out, our social worker, and spiritual care, home health aide who can help you, Sam, with bathing issues when the time comes, and we have a team of volunteers who can assist you in a variety of ways. So let's get started."

EIGHTTEEN

Jenna awoke to a sunray beaming insistently through her sheer curtains. It beamed to the middle of the floor just beyond the foot of her bed. It gave her the sensation of being in a deep wooded forest where the sun forced its way through the tops of the trees, down the twisting branches, falling fast until it hit the dark cold dirt of the earth beneath. Jenna stretched lazily while her eyes tried to focus on the clock hanging on the far wall in front of her. The little hand was on the eight and the big hand was on the four. She sunk back down into her pillow cupping both hands under her head. Jenna's eyes closed, not to sleep, but to rest them while she decided on the course of her upcoming day. When she was working her day was dictated by the time clock; now it went as she pleased, however, she found coming up with a reason to get out of bed was becoming increasingly difficult. There was a time when waking up to a nothing day was anticipated; now, for her, it was dreaded.

Jenna turned herself under the covers, switching her body over to the side facing the television, and searched for the remote. As her hand snaked its way between the sheets to locate the device, her nose and ears perked in alarm. She heard a faint clinking sound coming from downstairs and smelled bacon. Jenna sat up straight in her bed, no longer feeling listless. Her brow furrowed in fear and confusion. Her only thought was, *Adrian?*

Still fearful, she hopped out of bed and paddled cautiously downstairs. Her bare feet made no sounds on the thick carpeted steps. When she hit the fifth step from the bottom it creaked as it always did, and she paused, her heart in her throat. She cursed herself for leaving her cell phone upstairs. It wasn't until she heard the familiar melodic rhythms of R&B music that she allowed herself to breathe again. She continued down the stairs, crossed the large foyer and walked on the cool wooden floors towards the kitchen. When she rounded the corner and saw the back of Adrian's head bouncing slightly to the music she smiled shaking her head.

"Morning, sunshine." Adrian greeted as he stirred the eggs. "Lightly scrambled correct?"

"Yep." Jenna replied sliding into the nearest island barstool. "How long have you been here?" she asked accusingly.

"Four a.m.?" Adrian said picking up the pan as he plated the eggs onto two plates. Then he also extracted the bacon from another sizzling pan and placed three strips of bacon on each of the plates. He brought them over to the kitchen island and put one in front of Jenna and sat himself down opposite her.

"Do you know I could have killed you?" Jenna told him. "Why couldn't you call instead of sneaking into the house in the middle of the night like a burglar?"

"I didn't want to wake you. I was in the neighborhood." Adrian replied. The sound of English muffins popping out of the toaster made him rise and grab them. He plopped one muffin onto her plate and carried the other back to his. Adrian saw how Jenna's eyes were boring through him. "Okay, I'm sorry. Next time I'll call." He promised not too remorsefully she noted.

"I don't remember giving you a key." Jenna stated. She was starved so she began to eat.

"No, I had one made." Adrian informed her.

Jenna, shocked, looked up from her food and stared at him. "Adrian, where are you staying? If you want to stay here then fine, I'm not going to kick you into the streets, but at least have the common courtesy to let me in on your plans. Don't come and go crawling in and out of my window in the middle of the night!" Her voice rose with each syllable.

"I'm sorry, I didn't think." He picked up the strawberry preserves he had been spreading on his muffin. "Do you want some?" he asked her.

"Are you listening to me?" Jenna demanded.

"Yes. I said I was sorry." Adrian had the tone of a child and this infuriated Jenna.

"I'm not my mother." She said forcefully. "You did this with her at her home, and she must have thought you were Peter Pan and she Wendy, because she quite enjoyed it. I, on the other hand, do not! You wanna stay here Adrian? Fine, but show my home some courtesy." She scolded.

"You know, you sounded just like my mother, just then." Adrian joked.

Jenna ignored his humor. "This is not a flop house or some kind of fraternity house where you come in after the club in the wee hours and crash on the couch." Jenna put her hand to her chest. "This is my home, Adrian! I'm sick of you bringing all of this chaos into my life."

"Chaos?"

"Yes! Thugs coming to my door, you sneaking in and out, me not even knowing you're in the house, and that ridiculous fight you had with Zabbie's fiancé." That made Adrian snicker. "You think this is funny?" Jenna asked. Adrian didn't say anything only shook his head.

Jenna continued. "We are not teenagers anymore. We're not even in our twenties. I am almost 35 and you are almost 40! This is your life? Beebopping from town to town, staying with friends? Don't you want a family of your own? Don't you want a life?"

"What are you talking about, I have a life." Adrian protested.

"You call this a life? Leaving the club at 4 am or some chick's bed."

"At least I'm having sex. When was the last time you had some?"

"That's none of your business!" Jenna stuffed the rest of her eggs and bacon into her mouth just to finish and took the plate to the sink.

"And you're saying I don't have a life?" he laughed. "You're becoming an old maid, Imzadi."

"Just because I am not sleeping around with every Tom, Dick, and Harry..."

"You don't have to sleep with Tom or Harry, just Dick."Adrian made a comical expression, and then burst into laughter again.

"You can turn a perfectly serious conversation into jokes. I'm trying to talk to you about your life."

"I don't like serious conversations!" Adrian said, spreading his arms out. Then, in an absurdly mocking tone he asked her, "What happened to you man, you used to be cool?"

"I'm done." Jenna concluded throwing up both hands. Just then the doorbell rang. "Saved by the bell." She whispered to herself mainly.

"Yep, you were!" Adrian smiled. He watched Jenna walk to answer the door. "Oh, and you're welcome for the breakfast!" he quipped, calling after her.

Jenna only rolled her eyes shaking her head. Once she was out of the kitchen, she allowed a faint grin to creep across her lips. *The comic relief*, she thought to herself.

Jenna opened the door and there was Zabbie standing with one hand on her hip and her long straight hair falling carelessly below her shoulders. "Zabbie?" Jenna greeted looking quickly over her shoulder, then back at her friend.

"I'm sorry to barge in on you this early, but my mother is driving me crazy." Zabbie gave Jenna a brief yet strong hug, then walked past her into the house. She began to speak without taking a breath and continued into the living room as she had done so many times before. Jenna was forced to follow. "You don't know what I've been through the last week. After that fight at the club, I had to do some serious Zach Damage Control. I spent that entire night and next morning explaining who Adrian was and who he was not. After Zach finally seemed to get over it, I retreated to my mother's, and she has trapped me into a whirlwind of wedding planning."

Zabbie plopped down onto her favorite spot on the couch. "I spent the entire day Wednesday doing nothing but discussing plate patterns." She put a questioning hand to her head. "Plate patterns! Should they be white, yellow, gold tipped, silver tipped? Should they have flowers or be elegantly plain? And did you know that there are over 80 shades of white?"

"No, I didn't." Jenna said sitting on the arm of the couch where she could easily see if Adrian started heading down the hall.

Oblivious, Zabbie continued. "The rest of the week we pondered over flavors of chocolate and the design of cakes. I spent hours with my mother sifting through wedding magazines. Oh, and she seems to feel that Tiffany Blue is a divine color for the bridesmaid's dresses." Zabbie touched Jenna's arm. "Jenna, we haven't even set a date yet!"

Jenna shrugged her shoulders and smiled at Zabbie while glancing back down the hall.

"I know what my mother's doing. She's trying to make sure she has a leadership position on the planning committee for my wedding. My sister forbade her from taking control of her wedding so she is honing in early on mine." Zabbie sat back scooting down further into the couch. "And, you know, I'm fine with it because I can't even think straight, not ever since that night, and seeing...*him*. Thankfully, Zach took me up north to his father's cabin for the weekend. It was gorgeous, quiet, and we did not talk about the wedding the whole time. We were just like an old married couple staring at the water for hours. Zach always knows what I need." Zabbie thought for a second then spoke softly, "But Jenna, my God, seeing him that night. What am I going to do about Adrian?"

"Someone say my name?"

Both women stood up in alarm as if a bomb had gone off in the next room. Adrian's eyes never left Zabbie's as he moved into the living room and positioned himself directly in front of Zabbie.

Adrian and Zabbie just stood and stared at each other for what seemed like a horribly long time filled with tension and private conversation which only the two of them were privy too. Jenna could only imagine the thoughts running through both of their minds, but she was only concerned with how Zabbie was feeling.

What was going on inside their minds? Adrian was thinking simply how beautiful Zabbie was and how he wished he was the kind of man that Zabbie could have fallen in love with, maybe more like the one who she was engaged to. What exactly did this Zach character have that he didn't? Judging from the cold in Zabbie's eyes, Adrian could clearly see what he didn't have, and couldn't have, the respect of Zabbie's family. He could never fit into the mold of her world. His hair was a bit too wavy, his skin a bit too tanned and his beard a bit too shadowed.

Zabbie was thinking how in the world was she going to be able to move from this spot without falling into Adrian's arms? Was it possible for her to just walk away? Was it possible for her to go to her dress design appointment with her mother and pick out the perfect design for her wedding, a wedding with Zach, a wedding that did not include the man who held her heart? The man standing in front of her? For that moment, Zabbie was sure she could not. She was sure that the next move she would have to make would be with Adrian. Thank God for Jenna.

"Zabbie, don't you have to get to that *bridal* appointment?" Jenna made sure to stress the word bridal as she glanced at Adrian, but he only acknowledged her with a sideway glance.

The words did snap Zabbie back into reality. "Yes." She managed to utter. "I have to go." She said in the direction of Adrian. This caused his stoic stare to drop into agitation.

"Okay." Jenna said as she grabbed Zabbie's arm and pulled her towards her. "I can meet you there."

"Um…" Zabbie was, amazingly, able to move. She stepped to the side towards Jenna releasing herself from Adrian's proverbial hold. When she was passed him and heading towards the door, Zabbie spoke again in the direction of Jenna, "On second thought, why don't you ride with me?"

"Okay, give me a minute. I'll meet you in the car." Jenna said almost pushing her out the door. After closing the door in the face of her friend Jenna turned back to Adrian. His stare sent daggers through her. He didn't say a word only stared for a moment then after a chilly gaze he retraced his steps back into the kitchen.

Jenna watched his back disappear around the corner, "Adrian…" she called out.

"Leave it." He said from the kitchen. His voice was faint. The only reason Jenna heard it was because she was acutely listening for his response. Jenna couldn't see, but Adrian had sat back at the island bar in the very seat she sat in earlier. There was a sinking in his stomach, so deep, so wide, that he hoped it would swallow him whole. He loved Zabbie, but she was probably better off without him. Adrian flipped on the TV, and it was playing a commercial with a blonde woman swishing her hair around and a young man running his fingers through it. The model looked into the camera and mouthed something about her conditioner. Zabbie's hair color was the same. He remembered the nights his hands ran through it. Suddenly he realized that they were from very different worlds. What could a man like him give to a woman like her? Would her parents accept an African American Arab into their family? He could see his mother at their wedding in full Abaya cloak; others would probably think she's a damned terrorist, he thought. Adrian quickly flipped off the television set. His cousin, Jenna, though reckless in her dealings with his emotions, was right. He should leave Elizabeth Meyers alone.

"Talk about saved in the nick of time!" Jenna said, as she got into the passenger side of Zabbie's car. Zabbie didn't respond; she only sat on the driver's side gripping the steering wheel so tightly that Jenna was sure her fingers would meld into the leather. "You can relax, it's over; we're out of there so you can relax."

Zabbie looked back at the front door. "Maybe I should go back and talk to him? He's not this horrible guy that I should just cast aside. I mean I know I did already but I should explain it to him..."

Jenna looked at Zabbie as if she was speaking a foreign language. "I don't know exactly what happened between you two, but was it worth what you and Zach have? I don't think so! Zach is your fiancé; you're going to be married. You're going to give all that up for a ... fling?" The words caused Zabbie to sit back in her seat. Jenna continued, "I love my cousin, I do, but you have to be realistic. Zach is solid. Adrian is not. I would give anything to have what the two of you have. Don't mess that up for lust."

Zabbie put a hand to her head as if a migraine was coming on. "What if it's more than that?" she looked at Jenna. "What if it's more?"

Jenna let out a hard sigh and shifted in her seat, turning closer to Zabbie. "It's just cold feet. People get that. They start questioning themselves because they think they are missing out on something. Tell me, if Adrian had not have come back, would he even be on your mind this heavy?"

Zabbie thought for a moment, "I don't know."

"No, the answer is no, he wouldn't be! Maybe this is one of those cosmic tests to make sure that your love for Zach is pure. I don't know, but I do know that you have a dress to pick out for the man you are going to marry, for the event that all of your friends and family will be there to witness. Don't ruin it just because you're scared." Jenna turned back straight in her seat and clicked on her seatbelt. Zabbie didn't respond, instead she started the car, pulled out of the driveway, and headed for the bridal store.

NINETEEN

Matt entered the conference room at the Lansing office of Community Hospice and immediately went over and pumped fists with Thomas Finnerty, the Director of Volunteer Services for the Traverse City site. Tom was an easy going simple guy with a wife and four kids. He loved to hunt deer and dress up as Santa Clause on Halloween. Matt had once asked him why he would mix holidays like that, and Tom answered with a wry smile, "Because everyone loves Santa any day of the year." Matt's only response to that was, "I think you're right."

"Killed Bambi yet this year?" Matt asked Tom as he moved to his usual seat in the expansive conference room. The Lansing site was often referred to as the second corporate office because it was so large and included offices to rival the executive spaces located at headquarters in the heart of Detroit. This location was set up like all the other branches however, one entrance for the public and managers, and another entrance for the clinical staff.

"Hunting season doesn't start until fall, you city dweller." Tom informed Matt. "Hey," Tom leaned down glancing over his shoulder as Sarah Evans walked into the room in full power suit and frantic expression. "Hey Matt, what do you think we're going to talk about today?" he asked trying to be stealthy.

Matt followed suit, glanced at Sarah, and replied "According to the agenda, we're talking about volunteer utilization rates and how we can get ours up to seventy percent." Matt unpacked his laptop and positioned his paper notepad at the ready, along with his trusty pens.

"It may say that on the agenda but we better talk about our jobs." Tom sat up. "Things are a-changin'." He said cocking one eyebrow up.

Matt hunched his shoulders carelessly, but he wondered how much Tom knew. There were so many rumors flying around, but who had the real story? He thought he did, yet did he? How much could he actually trust Dave, college friendship withstanding?

"Okay we have a lot to talk about today so let's settle down and get started." Sarah announced as she fiddled with the power point projector. Her fingers smashed the remote over and over with no results. Sarah tilted her head dramatically trying to get a closer look at the ceiling mounted machine. She hoped this would tell her why the little green light wasn't coming on and why in the hell the chime didn't sound alerting all that a connection had been made. Sarah looked from the remote to the projector, then from the projector to the remote. "Fuck!" she cursed loudly, under her breath. Yes, Sarah Evans was extremely frustrated this morning. "Matt! Help me, please!" she pleaded. Sarah called out to Matt without hiding a shred of her desperation.

Matt quickly made his way around the large conference room table. Soon he was relieving her of the "get the darned machine to work" task. Matt easily realized that Sarah was pressing the Play button when she must first press the Source button to get the projector to power up. The familiar and blessed ping of the computer chimed and the blue square light illuminated the wall screen. He pressed the CTRL + F10 keys twice and her desktop was splashed across the screen. The room burst open with laughter and applause. Matt made a comical bow and handed the remote back to Sarah.

Sarah tried to manage a smile "Thank you, Matt." She said. Her eyes darted around the room. The prepared agenda was basically useless. She planned to discuss the future of the Volunteer Services Department, or lack thereof being more to the point. The guest Sarah was expecting to assist her had not arrived yet, and she was very happy about that because she wanted to do some in house talking before he arrived. Matt had gotten her power point up and she easily clicked on the file called simply "future.ppt". Sarah wasn't going to be presenting it but wanted to have it ready for her guest. When she loaded the file, the screen showed the title slide, "What the Future Means For You" over a graphic of a door suspended in clouds.

"Okay, let's everybody settle." Sarah began. "Please close your laptops and shut your phones down, or at least mute them. I realize that during these meetings you like to continue to check email and answer incoming calls..." Sarah was interrupted by Matt's phone going off and she shot an impatient look at him.

"It's the Call Center." Matt told Sarah after reading the ID. He waited for her response as to whether he should answer. When the Call Center called, it meant the call had to do with a volunteer situation, whether a request for a new volunteer or regarding a current volunteer visit.

"Don't answer it." Sarah instructed him in no uncertain terms. She looked down at her secretary, Janice. "Jan send out an email companywide stating that all of the directors of volunteer services are in a departmental meeting and are unavailable for the remainder of the day."

"All day?" piped up Jessica Reynolds, a director from the Lansing site. "Not even at lunch time? Because I have a lot going on, and I need to be somewhat available to my staff." Matt and Susan exchanged a quick glance. Matt smiled when Susan rolled her eyes. The best word to describe Jessica was persnickety; however, Susan referred to her lovingly as a snotty bitch. To Susan Jessica did not think of the other sites as part of her team; it was as if the Lansing site was completely separated from the other 12 sites that encompassed Community Hospice. Maybe it was the fact that it was located in the state capitol, and Jessica participated in a lot of the governmental events, fundraisers, etc... Jessica intermingled with the hospice board on the political side of hospice statewide, which could make her feel that her role was a bit more important than the others. Today, though, Sarah could care less about her commitments.

"All day, Jessica." Sarah's tone was uncharacteristically harsh, and this made everyone look up at her. "We all have a lot on our plates. I know that each of you are pulled in many different directions at once and take on more than what your job descriptions account for. I will tell you; also, that after this meeting today you may not feel any better about any of it. The agenda in front of you will not take place. There are some key issues on it that we do need to discuss, but we'll have to do that at a later date." Sarah looked directly at Jessica. "So that means phones off, computers off, no interruptions of any kind. Hopefully, Jan's email will stave off most of it. I want everyone focused today on the task at hand. It will be a working lunch, guys." Sarah said.

"Sounds pretty serious." Tom commented. "Does this have anything to do with the layoff announcement?"

"Yes." Sarah answered.

"No." came the voice of Dave Chatman from behind her. Dave entered the conference room setting down his briefcase in the reserved seat beside Sarah. "Sorry to refute you and sorry I'm late." He offered. Dave's grand smile was ever present. When he walked in the mood changed from the usual comfortable feeling of being around colleagues to the more tension laden atmosphere that always surrounded an executive entering a room. "Something that I want to stress upon you, as our CEO,

Frank Jacobs, pressed upon us at a flash meeting we had at seven a.m. this morning, Community Hospice is in a Restructuring Period not layoffs. Layoffs may be a part of this transition but not our main focus. Most of the layoffs will occur on the clinical side and with redundancies in management and administrative positions."

"Redundancies?" Tom asked.

"Yes," Dave continued, "such as where there may be more than one of the same position at the same site, such as secretaries, receptionists, clerks etc.."

"What about the management positions? Could we see regions combined like with our southeast region of directors in our department?" Brandon inquired.

Dave paused and made an exaggerated thinking expression. "Brandon, there will be several adjustments to just about all departments. We're not sure how things will play out. Right now what we're focusing in on are stark redundancies and combining positions. Many people whose positions may be eliminated will be absorbed into other areas. If they're not able to be absorbed or wish not to be, Community Hospice will provide severance packages for them as they search for other employment opportunities. Thank you for that question, Brandon, because that is an excellent segue into my presentation." Dave moved over to the computer and took the remote Sarah was handing him.

Brandon leaned over to Matt whispering, "and thank you for not answering my question."

"What the future means for you." Dave read the title slide, then commenced to discuss the financials of the hospice organization. He then discussed the future of hospice in America, the sacrifices and hopes and dreams of being a non profit organization, blah blah blah. Matt leaned into Brandon and whispered, "executive speak." Matt watched Dave in his eight hundred dollar Hugo Boss suit. Matt knew the price because he had ventured onto the Hugo Boss website to take a look at how a well dressed executive presented him or herself. He was well aware that Dave loved this site so Matt thought, why not. The eight hundred dollar slim fit, eagle-shelled, dark blue suit was one of the more "reasonably" priced suits on the site. Purchasing it, Matt had thought, would take a severe chunk out of his two week net pay, and even though he could do it, it would be ridiculous to do it. Heck, the shirt alone cost over a hundred dollars. Nope, Matt shopped at Macy's primarily where, if he was lucky, he was able to score a suit in the three hundred dollar or less price range, and his shirts never cost above forty bucks.

Matt watched as Dave prattled on about how secure Community Hospice was making itself in the coming economic industry storm of new technologies and changing climates. Matt wondered if he were to take the executive position offered to him, would he have to learn to speak like this. Would he have to learn the catch phrases and power words to use to confuse and intimidate lower employees? Would he have to learn to smile in the right places and look pensive in others? Matt could use a power point laser with the best of them so he figured he had that one down, at least. Basically, Matt wondered, would he have to appear as plastic, glossy and unfeeling as his buddy Dave seemed to have mastered so effortlessly?

"Now I know this is a lot of information we're asking you to digest; however, that's why I'm here today. I want to try to make this transition as smooth as I possibly can for all departments. Sarah and I are now going to take your questions. Remember, if we're not privy to all of the information we will make sure that your answer is researched and delivered to you at your next meeting or as soon as possible." Dave had taken off his jacket throughout his forty-five minute presentation. Matt assumed that was a tactic to appear extremely engaged. Dave shot a glance down at Sarah, who immediately got up and turned up the lights.

"Any questions?" Dave asked. He crossed his arms, a stance that was supposed to symbolize closed-off resistance yet was one of Dave's favorite postures.

"Mr. Chatman." Jessica began.

"Dave, please, we're in this together." Dave assured her with a quick wink.

"Dave," Jessica corrected herself. Was that a shadow of a smirk that ran across her face? Matt took note. "You speak of new technologies; I noticed that all of the nurses were upgraded with new laptops. Is that something that all of the management team, specifically the volunteer services directors, will see in the future?"

"Great question, Jessica." Did Dave know everyone's name? Matt wondered. Dave continued. "Yes! We like to pilot our new computers with the core clinical team in order to make sure they work in the field. However, for the management teams, like yourselves, you would not get tablets as the nurses have. You need laptops, and that's another animal altogether, so please do not compare your resources with the clinical team's resources." Dave quickly turned to another director. "Yes, Susan."

"In the last few years, we've been in talks with human resources about upping our pay grade. We can never seem to get a definitive answer. Our titles say director, but we are at least five grades below the rest of the organization's directors. As part of all of these new transitions, will elevating our grade status be one of them?" Susan asked and waited for a response.

For the first time Dave's confident demeanor cracked. With a definite frown, Dave looked down at Sarah who was sitting next to him. He shook his head. "Not sure about pay grade changes…? Can you speak to this Sarah?" Matt saw that Dave's expression really meant *"can you shut her up, Sarah?"*

Sarah cleared her throat first. "Yes, Susan, we're still in talks with human resources." She turned to Dave. "It is true, Dave, the directors of volunteer services is about five grades below any other director in the company, and we've been trying to get this raised to a higher and more accurate level." She watched Dave nod his head in acknowledgment. He said nothing to this so Sarah continued. "I'm hoping this does not hinder anything or put it on the back burner, but, as you guys know, our initial request was rejected pending further research." She said.

"What research?" Susan asked. "Take a look at our job description, what other director speaks out in the community, recruits their staff, trains that staff, then turns around and supervises that staff? Not to mention we have to do marketing, budgeting…"

"Don't forget fundraising!" Tom chimed in.

"Right!" Susan said, giving him a strong nod of understanding. "And we have to run our individual programs." Susan looked at Dave. "Now sir, you may think that just because a person doesn't get paid they are lower down on the totem pole, but you would be mistaken! And let me tell you uncertain terms, you have to be a pretty talented manager to get a staff of over a hundred people to do a job that they don't get paid for, and it's an extremely astute manager who has to keep smiling when a member of said staff can tell you No! I'd like to see you executive directors handle that day in and day out!" Susan never broke her gaze at Dave, as her colleagues cheered and applauded her.

Dave rose up from his seat; he did not break her gaze. "Everyone, lets settle down. Now I hear what you guys are saying, and I, for one, am very proud of the work you do for this company and for our patients. Hospice could not run without the aid of volunteers. I am in awe of the amount of hard work each of you put in on a daily basis. But, folks, I know a little bit about salary scales, and they're based on market value; it's not a company thing but a national industry thing. Your salary, therefore, is based on the FLSA or the Fair Labor Standards Act. That's what HR means about research. They have to follow the national standard." There was a finality in Dave's voice that silenced the room. Dave sat back down, quite pleased with himself. He shot an aggravated glance at Sarah, because he was not pleased with her at all.

Sarah stood and took over the rest of the Q&A. The questions that came were met with similar non-committal answers and even a few "I don't know but will get back with you on that." By the time lunch arrived, the smiles and easy going demeanors that were usually prevalent in these statewide meetings were replaced with brooding scowls and silence.

"Hey, a taco bar!" Brandon praised absurdly. His tone was clearly sarcastic.

"Everyone grab some food and then we'll get back into it." Sarah said.

"You know, Sarah," Tom said. "I think it's illegal for us to work without stopping for lunch. Besides anymore of this meeting and I don't think my food will digest on its own. Give us a break."

Sarah looked up from her conversation with Dave. "Fine, you got thirty minutes." She said with a smirk.

"Oh gee, thanks." Tom laughed.

Dave got up from the table, put on his sports jacket, bent down briefly to relay, very sternly, a point to Sarah then he grabbed his briefcase. As if it was an afterthought, he turned and called to Matt. "Matt, do you have a minute?" Dave gestured for Matt to follow him, then put up a hand to the rest of the group, "Guys, enjoy your lunch, I'll talk with you soon."

"Not going to break bread with us?" Tom called back.

"Nope, it smells fantastic, but I gotta run to another meeting." And with a flip of his hand Dave exited the room.

Matt also left behind Dave. The two men passed through the hallways and out the large reception and foyer areas. Matt watched as Dave peeked into several offices, saying goodbye, and also watched him place a warm hand on the front desk as he passed by the young receptionist who presented him with a smile and friendly wave. Outside, Dave electronically greeted his roadster which saluted him back with the familiar *bloop* sound. Dave opened the car door and placed his case on the passenger seat then pulled a cigarette out of his glove compartment. "So, have you been thinking about the position?" Dave asked, lighting his cigarette and going around to the back of the car to lean on the trunk.

Matt joined him. He figured Dave chose this spot so their backs would be to the building and any on lookers would have a difficult time figuring out what they were discussing. "Yes, I have, it's hardly left my mind." Matt answered.

"Good. So what are you leaning towards, staying or coming over to our side?" Dave inquired, spreading his arms outward.

"Our side, huh? I always knew there was a separation between the execs and the lower ranks." Matt noted.

"Of course there is." Dave replied. "We make the decisions; you guys follow them. That's the separation. It has to be that way." Dave explained.

"Why?" Matt asked.

"You'll find out why when you come aboard."

"No chance of the directors being elevated?" Matt asked already knowing the answer.

"Not a chance, Matt, at least not now and never up to the level of the other directors."

"Why not?" Matt continued to plead.

"I already explained that." Dave glanced behind him and saw Susan and Sarah coming outside.

"And Susan explained why it should be..." Matt was cut off.

"Matt, forget about this department, will you? It's a dead end career move!" Dave pointed at Matt's chest for emphasis.

"No, it isn't!" Matt protested. "In the government sector, volunteer management is at a high level position."

"Then go to that sector, Matt, but in hospice and healthcare it's not! We are not the Peace Corps or United Way. In healthcare, clinical people run the show, doctors and nurses okay?"

Matt shook his head. "The volunteers contribute so much, why can't you people see that?"

Dave let out an exaggerated sigh. "Look man, you wanna go on this hippy crusade, be my guest, but I brought you out here to discuss *your* next move."

"Okay sorry, I'll get off my soapbox." Matt said, throwing up his hands. There was no talking to his college buddy about this so he gave up trying.

"Thank you. Can we talk now? You got it out of your system?"

"Yeah."

"Okay then." Dave said opening his jacket and pulling out two long tickets. "Here are two tickets to the Martinique Ball in July. Find a girl, rent a tux, a nice one, and come rub shoulders with the rest of your soon to be colleagues." The Martinique Ball is the major fundraiser for Community Hospice and held every year in July at The Townsend Hotel, a prestigious venue in Detroit suburbia. Eleanor Martinique was a philanthropist who died on the hospice program when Community Hospice was first beginning. She had left over five million dollars to the organization, and the family continues to sponsor the ball to help bring in even more donations annually since their matriarch's death, which also took place in July. It's one of the most lavish events in Detroit history for a local charity and definitely for any single hospice agency. It's also a big deal for Michigan high society to be invited. Unless employees were able to purchase a $500 a plate ticket, they were not in attendance.

"Find a girl..." Matt repeated to himself.

"Nice looking guy like you, it shouldn't be hard, pick one." Dave reminded.

"Yeah right." Matt responded.

"Hey, just make sure she's clean; this is a classy event you know? Leave the nighttime ladies to the night, pick one of the ones you see in the daytime."

Matt laughed out loud, and Dave joined him. Matt knew exactly what he meant. When they were in college the two roommates often identified their girlfriends as either nighttime or daytime. The nighttime girls were the ones who you could visit without taking them out; they had a reputation of being easy so they remained in the dark. The daytime girls were the ones you took to the dances, out to dinner, basically the girlfriends, sweet girls who rarely gave it up; hence they were clean. Matt had laughed so loud because he hadn't used those terms since college and, of course, Dave had made them up.

Sarah Evans had come outside to smoke with Susan Cobbs, and Susan only smoked when she was around Sarah. They stood by the side of the building. Neither of the guys saw these women stare at them while they laughed and acted like a couple of frat brothers. "What do you think that shit is all about?" Sarah asked, with a scowl so deep she could feel each wrinkle.

"College buddies, you know how guys are." Susan offered.

Sarah narrowed her eyes in suspicion. "Matt knows something about what's going to happen, but he's not sharing anything with me."

"You mean about the layoffs? What do you think he knows?" Susan inquired.

"The layoffs, the cuts, the reconstruction. I asked him about it, and he played dumb. But the two of them have their heads together for some reason." Sarah took a long drag of her cigarette as she watched the two men. She whispered to Susan, "It's a fucking man's world, Sus, and they never let you forget it." Sarah walked further down the side of the building, away from eyeshot of Matt and Dave. She leaned closer to Susan. "Do you know that Dave just cursed at me?" she asked Susan.

"What? Cursed at you?" Susan cocked her head at Sarah in shock.

"Yes all because you asked that question about the position elevation."

"Really? Damn, I'm sorry." Susan said honestly.

"No, I'm glad you asked it, but you see, all of the executives are going around to their departments and presenting the same exact speech Dave gave today. In the flash meeting I attended this morning, before this one, I was told to make sure the questions from my staff were limited to what Dave talks about and to discourage outside questions like what you asked. I was supposed to announce that before he came in, but I was fiddling with that stupid ass power point machine, trying to get ready, and just that quick, I forgot." Sarah revealed to her.

"Wow."

"Yeah, so right as Dave was leaving he bends down to my ear and said, *get your staff in line, do your fucking job.*" Sarah deepened her voice for effect.

"No!" Susan stomped her foot.

"Yes! I was shocked. Hell I was waiting for him to say *bitch*!"

"Oh my God, I don't believe it." Susan put a hand to her chest.

"Believe it! He's a bastard! We call him Dick Cheney because even though he's not the CEO he acts like it. Frank does basically whatever the hell Dave Chatman tells him to do. And if you don't kiss his ass you might as well sign your resignation. The only person who ever stands up to Dave is Mark Tobolowski, the VP of Marketing. He always challenges Dave in meetings. It's kind of funny actually." Sarah said laughing. She leaned back on the wall. "I remember last year when our census was way down and Dave was prattling on about too long nursing visits, overtime, etc. Mark had said, *I don't know why we're talking about long visit times when you just got a $10,000 bonus.* Everybody stopped, and was like what? $10,000? Dave lit into him! Dave told him he didn't know what the fuck he was talking about, to stop listening to idle gossip, blah blah blah. And when Dave gets pissed his clean polished speaking voice reverts back to his Brooklyn days. He turns back into a *guido*! It's really quite entertaining." Sarah chuckled.

"So what do you think is going to happen to volunteer services? Off the record." Susan asked Sarah.

"I don't know. They tell me nothing, that the department will stay the same. On the one hand, that's good news, but on the other that means that no raise in our near future. But off the record, I think they're going to get rid of me."

Susan cocked her head back in surprise. "No way, we need you! They wouldn't do that."

"Yes, they would. I have been hearing things, but all pure speculation. And me being paranoid of course, but I have my suspicions."

"Where would we go, back to clinical services with Dave as our boss?"

"Yeah I guess or maybe marketing. I don't know. Let's get back in there. You know we're not supposed to have meetings after the meeting." They both laughed at that.

TWENTY

Darkness has a way of engulfing you ever so slightly. Its torso creeps around the corners of the room; its legs slither along the creases in the rugs, and finally its arms encase you so gently, so completely, it leaves you dangerously unaware. Lynnette Mills sat in her study with her eyes peeled to the ever brightening screen. When she sat down after dinner, around seven thirty, the sun was still beaming through the windows. Her private office captured the setting sun beautifully yet this evening she was not experiencing it as usual. This evening Lynnette only watched the stark blue light of the computer screen. She was trying to find out as much as she could about the disease that was killing her daughter. Her right hand moved the mouse around the pad as she browsed website after website. Her left hand rested at times on her mouth, then rubbed her chin, then supported her forehead. Lynn read medical jargon after medical jargon and only some of what she read made sense. *"When the motor neurons die, the ability of the brain to initiate and control muscle movement is lost..."* Lynn whispered, as she read to herself. *"With voluntary muscle action progressively affected, patients in the later stages of the disease may become totally paralyzed."* Lynn shut her eyes tightly – *paralyzed*, she thought to herself.

"The progressive degeneration of the motor neurons in ALS will eventually lead to their death." Lynn further read catching the breath in her throat. Once again she closed her eyes firmly. Lynn took her hands away from the mouse and keyboard, set her elbows firmly down on the desk, clasped her hands together in a fisted prayer, and rested her forehead on them. She had cried so much that the well of tears seemed to be empty. All that was left for her to do was to mouth some kind of prayer to a God she hoped was listening. "Lord, if you haven't completely ignored me by now, please hear me. My daughter is dying please help us dear Lord, please help her. I know that it's in your power to heal, please spare

her life, don't take her..." Lynn repeated louder and stronger, "don't take her; she is young, too young. It's not fair, it's not right! God damnit don't you take her! Don't...don't you fucking dare take my baby!" Lynn collapsed her head onto the desk, and the tears she thought had dried up poured out of her like a river.

Lynn's husband, Joe, stood unseen at the doorway. He was immobile watching his wife cry and pray out loud. He sat down in the nearby loveseat across from her desk. "I'm not the greatest Christian, but I don't think that is how you're supposed to pray, baby."

His voice bolted her head up. Through her water logged eyes Lynn spotted Joe. "Fuck him."Lynn said venomously as she grabbed two tissues from her desk holder. "He never listens anyway." She said wiping her face. "Probably doesn't even fucking exist."

"Come on, don't keep doing this to yourself." Joe told her.

"What am I doing, Joe?"

Joe pointed at the computer. "You keep searching the web for more clues and answers. There are no answers. Sam has ALS. It's not your fault, it's not my fault. It's not God's fault."

"No? Then whose fault is it? Who the hell am I supposed to blame if not God?"

"Lynn..."

"No, seriously, did our child step on a bug? Did she kiss the wrong boy? Did she share the wrong needle? Did she smoke too much? Drink too much? Is she too fat? Too thin? Did she eat too much red meat? What? What Joe? You tell me what the fuck she did to cause this?"

"Lynn..."

"NOTHING! She did NOTHING! We didn't do anything so what does that leave? It leaves God! But you know what, I take that back, it doesn't leave God because there is no God! It's all bullshit! There is no God in the sky watching over us; there are no angels making sure we stay on the right path. It's all bullshit! Jesus was just a guy who wanted change and got himself killed for it. We made up this shit, so in times like these, we have something to turn to but when we get in situations like this we realize that there is no one to turn to, no one holding our hands guiding us, no one and nothing." Lynn stood up and walked to the window in her office that overlooked the expansive backyard. She peered out across the field and saw Samantha in the middle of it, near the gardens, standing in her long white lounger. It was not an odd occurrence; Sam loved the blooming flowers and often walked far out into them. "Joe," Lynn said, as she gazed at her child. "In a matter of months, maybe even weeks, Sam will be dead, and there is not a damned thing either one of us can do about that." Lynn turned suddenly, and her eyes bore into his. Joe could do nothing but return her stare. He suddenly realized that he had been doing everything in his power to make sure that Sam was dealing with this; he never once stopped to think how this was affecting Lynn.

Samantha had donned her white lounger/gown her father had bought for her only days before. She had been in an odd mood that morning. Strangely she had not been feeling ill; the nausea had subsided, and she was able to enjoy a breakfast of toast and eggs over easy, her favorite. The nurse had visited earlier that morning and set Samantha on a schedule for taking her pain medications. Samantha had to admit, they were great. When can someone consume narcotics and not feel like a criminal? In a sense, all of this was kind of great, she never had to go to work again, never worry about a bill, never worry about planning for the future, and she could stay high all of the time. What a fucking trip!

Samantha reached down and plucked a large closing white rose and placed the flower under her nose. She inhaled the delicate scent while looking around. *Lynn's Garden;* her mother had hired a gardener to tend to it. Even though someone was paid to do the work, Lynn used to force Samantha to come out to the garden to dig up weeds, spray pesticides, and water the freaking plants on most of her weekends, yet Samantha was never allowed to just come out here and enjoy them, and God forbid if she ever picked a few of the flowers for an unauthorized bouquet. Her mother was the only one with enough clearance to enter this domain of loveliness and extract from it. Only Lynnette Mills could create a bouquet for the dining room, the foyer, the bathrooms and, of course, her private office. No one else could enjoy the flowers except within those specific parameters; therefore, Samantha plucked a rather large rose for herself. She marveled, just a bit, at not using the proper cutting utensil and had ripped the rose from the earth, thereby, hurting not only the aesthetics of the garden but also breaking one of Lynn's primal rules.

A breeze blew across Sam's face, causing her to lift her head back to enjoy the feeling. She began to walk beyond the garden and into the field. The yard space was a full acre, ending where the manmade lake began. You would think in a state full of lakes that you wouldn't have to actually build a lake but, apparently, they did. The lake was masked by a row of pines and maples. On the other side was a golf course. The state could easily change its name from Great Lakes to Great Golf. California and Florida had Michigan beat in the number of courses, but they were also bigger and longer states, making Michigan golf particularly abundant.

The sun was setting fast, and the solar lights had popped on. The lights bordered the paths around the garden and one path that led out to a lone gazebo swing surrounded by natural shrubs and brush. Vines climbed the white arbor, and Joe had built a small cascading brook beside it. He had also placed a rather whimsical looking sulfur lamp post next to it. It was a special place for Joe and his daughter. As Samantha had reached her teenage years, she rarely made the trek all the way out there to sit but, occasionally, when she was really depressed or grieving the loss of Kenny, she would walk out to this most private area and swing.

Because of the curvature of the path, this area was not viewable from the main patio. The trees in the yard also made it very hard to view from the house windows. The only thing that could be seen was the sulfur lamp in the darkness but you could not see or hear anything from the house. You actually had to walk the path to find out if anyone was out there. It was an excellent spot for daydreaming, reading and stepping off into another world. This was exactly why Joe built it. Lynn did not want it there; she had wanted it much closer to the garden, but Joe put his foot down and reminded her that he had designed and built it so he could have a place to read and nap if he so chose to do so. Joe also used it to smoke his cigars and pipes.

As Samantha got older, she realized that her dad used it as his sanctuary from her mother. It was probably the real reason he even thought of building it. Lynn was not the easiest person to live with, how he did it for over 40 years was beyond Samantha's imagination.

Tonight, Samantha noticed, it was harder for her to walk the quarter mile out to the gazebo. When she finally reached it, she brushed off the leaves and sat down hard onto one of the throw pillows. Her breathing was labored so she rested for a moment just to catch her breath. In the distance she began to see the fireflies start to light up the night. The lamp did not give off much illumination at all, which was Samantha's intent. Emblazed windows were seen off in the distance; the only sounds were the crickets, and maybe a dog barking here and there. The loudest sound right now for Samantha, however, was her breathing, but soon she was able to close her mouth and breathe through her nose. Sam kicked off her flip flops, touched her toes to the ground to start the swing's motion, and then she tucked her legs gently up onto the swing and leaned to the side on the pillow. If she died right now, Samantha would be ok with it. Suddenly, that thought alarmed her, if she died...*when* she died. Would it be like going to sleep? Would there be pain in the end? Would Kenny be there to greet her?

The thought of Kenny lead her to wonder how it was for him when he died. Did he feel pain? Was he panicking as his car crashed? Was there a moment of clarity for him? Did he see a bright light and go into it? Sadness washed over Samantha at the thought of Kenny being terrified and alone in that car, his life was drifting away from him. Samantha was not very religious and barely believed in a God as it was written in about books but she hoped there was an angel who went to Kenny at that moment of his death, an angel who appeared next to him on the passenger seat and eased Kenny into whatever lay beyond.

Samantha rested her head on the swing's pillow. She kept the swing moving by reaching her fingers up through the rails and tugging on the wooden panels. She no longer concentrated on the homes around her but on the stars above her. It was a clear night, which made the midnight blue sky enchanting. Kenny used to know all about the constellations. He was a space junkie. A year before he went into high school his mother had signed him up for the Space Camp in Alabama. Kenny always remarked on how the Space Camp address was One Tranquility Base. And he had thought that was pretty funny. He really hadn't wanted to go to the camp, but when he came home, he was a full-fledged space junkie.

Kenny loved to grab blankets, spread them on the ground and lay with Samantha on their backs, looking up to the night sky. He would be blathering on about constellations called Little Bear, Lion, Archer and even one called Chained Princess. Sam didn't care one bit about constellations; she just liked looking up at the stars. She would rest her head on Kenny's chest and adored hearing his voice. His voice was deep so it seemed to vibrate his chest at times, and that always made her tingle inside.

"They call the constellation Chained Princess because the stars are so bright but, actually her name was Andromeda. You see Andromeda is the beautiful daughter of Queen Cassiopeia and King Cepheus. Sadly, the princess was killed because her mother, the queen boasted so much about how beautiful her daughter was, I guess it made people jealous." Kenny had explained.

"Mmmm hmmmm...." Samantha interjected at the right moments.

"Yeah, but Andromeda is also the name of our neighboring galaxy. One day Andromeda and the Milky Way will collide into each other. But don't worry; humans will be long gone before that happens."

"Mmmm hmmm..." she had moaned again.

Kenny was catching on so he tested her. "Humans will be gone but the Klingons will still be alive because they are a warrior race and can out live anything, hence the term Kling-on – you know clinging on."

"Yeah, that's nice." Samantha had purred.

"You're not listening to a word I'm saying are you?"

"What? Yes, of course, baby, I am."

"Sam, then what did I just say?"

Samantha had thought for a moment, sitting up to look at Kenny, "Um…you said that the princess was killed by Klingons, but then they collided with Andromeda?"

"Yes, that's exactly what I said, and here I thought you weren't listening." Kenny replied sarcastically, feigning disappointment.

"Oh, I'm sorry, Kenny, but I really do love lying here listening to you talk about space. You get this sort of energy in your voice that I love to hear. Please keep talking about it; I'll listen more closely this time. I promise."

Kenny looked down at her. He took a finger and removed a hair from her face. "I love you." He said.

"I love you too, Mr. Spock."

"Lieutenant Spock." He corrected with a smile.

"Lt. Spock." Samantha repeated. Kenny then bent down and kissed her lovingly on the lips. They had spent many nights sharing their love under the stars.

As Sam lay on the swing now her eyes became blurred with tears. She closed them and tried to keep the memory of his touch in the forefront of her mind. Soon, the stars filled her dreams as she slept.

"Joe, I've been thinking." Lynn said when she came into the family room where Joe was reading the paper. Lynn had given up trying to get Joe to just read the paper online. He looked up from the news, and she said, "I think we should get Sam a volunteer."

"Samantha is a grown woman; she doesn't need a baby sitter." Joe responded.

"Sam has been depressed, she won't talk to me, she spends hours just sitting staring into space, and she needs some interaction."

"We talk all the time." Joe declared with a hint of haughtiness, Lynn noted.

"I'm sure." She said, sitting on the arm of an adjacent chair. "But you work and can't be with Sam all the time. This person would come out and give her companionship, talk to her, keep her company. This person wouldn't be her parent."

"She has friends that come by." Joe reminded her.

"Yes and how long do you think they'll keep that up? Nina lives in California; Kyra is busy with her career, and Shelley has a family of her own to take care of. Sooner or later no one will visit. She needs someone."

"I thought we were hiring a full time caregiver?" Joe replied.

"That's just another nursing person. I just think the companionship will help Sam." Lynn said.

"Have you asked her?" Joe inquired.

"Have I asked her...?" Lynn repeated. "She thinks she has everything under control. Besides she's not talking to me."

"Whose fault is that, Lynn?" Joe retorted.

Lynn stood up, shooting a cold stare at him. "I'm calling hospice in the morning. I'm ordering a volunteer. I'm going to bed." Lynn left the room and headed upstairs without giving him a chance to respond.

Joe had no intention on responding. He closed his paper and walked out of the room to the patio doors. He peeked out, trying to see if he could see Samantha sitting in the patio lounger as she often did most nights now. She was not out there. Joe looked up at the ceiling as if he could see through it to Samantha's bedroom. He didn't remember her coming in, so he walked outside and headed down the lighted path. Once he passed through the garden and made the turn down the curve to the gazebo, Joe saw a white form on the ground blocking the path ahead of him. He immediately recognized the form. "Sam!" Joe cried out.

Samantha was lying on the ground and struggling to get up. She held up a hand to her running father. "I'm ok," she said. "I miss stepped. I think I tripped on my gown." She lied. Samantha had awakened from her nap on the swing and decided to go in and go to bed, but after only a few feet, her legs grew strangely weak, and she tumbled ungracefully to the hard ground. She was finding it very hard to get back on her feet.

Joe quickly took Samantha's arm and gently raised her up. He noticed instantly that she was not able to assist him. Without warning Joe lifted Samantha off her feet and into his arms. He hadn't lifted another human like that in years and, he wasn't quite sure if his fast approaching 60 year old back could take his Samantha's weight but his daughter was not heavy to him at all. "Let's get you upstairs." He said.

"Oh Daddy." Samantha whispered, surrendering herself to his aid. It would be stupid to fight it. *Stupid to fight it.*

TWENTY-ONE

It had been almost two weeks since Zabbie came over and ran into Adrian. Since then Zabbie had seemed to snap back into her old self. Jenna had been helping her with the planning of the wedding, thinking of color schemes, plate designs, and, of course, what kind of wedding dress. Zabbie had decided on a Vera Wang sweetheart mermaid style, yet hadn't honed in on an exact dress, but it was obvious Zabbie's excitement level had tripled. Zabbie's mother, Donna, was beside herself with the joy of planning the particulars of the wedding, and Zabbie was happy to let her mother handle most of it. Meanwhile, Jenna had been feeling a bit out of sorts and envious. She didn't mean to have these feelings but with watching Zabbie look at gowns and talk cake, Jenna began to wonder if her day was ever going to come. The last couple of years had been a whirlwind with her mother dying and Jenna, herself, moving into her new home. She had time to think about her own social life.

Before her mother's illness Jenna had dated, but she never felt she had any real significance to the men. Her last relationship was with a man who was in a word, beautiful, but only the outside, on the inside, he was pure sewage. He had been a local model and even tried to break into the reality TV biz, but to make a living he worked as a car salesman. His name was Devon Patrick, aka The Devil Incarnate, at least that is what her mother used to call him. Jenna would joke to her mother that Devon wasn't the devil, a demon maybe, but not the devil. It was the only way Jenna could deal with defending their relationship. She had stayed with this man for more than five years before finally releasing him back into the void from whence he came. He did all of the usual, he cheated on her, even in her own bed once. He had manipulated her out of money, and that was when she was working as a lowly receptionist. Devon even made her have an abortion, not once but twice. Devon's reasoning was that he wasn't mature enough to be a father, yet he did have a child with an ex-girlfriend and ended up marrying her only months after he dumped Jenna. The devastation Jenna felt was beyond reproach, and depression soon followed. She was ripe to be a constant caregiver to her mother at that point.

So this house, Devon Patrick could definitely be blamed for Jenna spending a large portion of her inheritance on the monstrosity. She needed to look at surroundings that did not remind her of the past, Devon especially. Zabbie said that Devon was a product of Jenna's low self esteem. "Devon is Golden Opulence" Zabbie had said about him once. "He is that ridiculously overpriced ice cream sundae that runs for a cool thousand dollars. He's as sweet and delectable as eating pure gold but when you finish you are left with nothing but a large bill and an excruciating stomachache."

Jenna laughed out loud to herself remembering Zabbie's words now as she sat at the computer desk in her bedroom. She rolled out of bed around nine thirty on this Monday morning. She began checking her email before heading down to make breakfast. Jenna had heard Adrian coming in around six that morning. She decided to just let him sleep. At least he was sleeping in the bedroom she gave him instead of passing out on whatever couch was closest. They hadn't talked much since the Zabbie encounter, only simple greetings. Adrian left early and came in late. What he was doing while he was out and who he was with was none of Jenna's concern. Yesterday Jenna had went over to Adrian's mother's house for Sunday dinner, as she did on occasion, and her Aunt Regina had questioned Jenna about her son's whereabouts, but Jenna had no information to offer her. Her aunt only gave her a knowing nod and changed the subject. Her aunt was actually relieved that Adrian was close by and with family.

Jenna answered a few emails, and posted a few twitter responses, she liked a few comments on Facebook, when her phone rang. The ID read Community Hospice, and she quickly answered. "Hello?"

"Hey, is this Jenna? This is Matt Ames from hospice." Jenna had instantly recognized Matt's voice.

"Hello, Mr. Ames; I thought you'd forgotten about me." She said.

"Not at all, Jenna, and remember, please call me Matt."

"Okay. Matt." She responded, and smiled. "What's going on?"

"Well, first, how are you doing?" Matt asked.

"I'm doing pretty good. How's your son?" Jenna asked and immediately cursed herself, wondering if that too personal?

"He's doing really good, Jake's enjoying his summer, and he was with me this weekend. We played baseball in the park."

"Aww, that sounds nice, you guys had good weather for it."

"Yes, it was great. Jenna, the reason I'm calling is that I have an assignment I think you would be perfect for."

"Really? That's fantastic, tell me about it." Jenna said.

"We have a patient who is about your age. She has ALS, still verbal and mobile. She lives with her parents only about five miles away from you. No smoking in the home, no pets. The mother thinks she would benefit from a volunteer for companionship. She does have a paid caregiver, but the patient has become a bit isolated and depressed."

"Aww, okay. Well I'm pretty open. What days were they looking for?" Jenna inquired.

"The mother doesn't care, she thought a couple of times a week if possible. Would that work for you?"

"Sounds fine. So....what do I do now?" Jenna asked, feeling anxious and unsure, which was to be expected prior to a first assignment.

"I'll email you the patient's medical information sheet and details. The patient's name is Samantha Mills. The primary caregivers are both of the parents, Joe and Lynnette Mills, but you can speak with the mother and work out the visit times. I'll put her phone number in the email. Are you up to calling the family?" Matt asked.

"Yes. If I can remember from training, I am to ask about what the patient likes to do, if she has hobbies, and how the house looks for directions?"

"Yes, and introduce yourself as the volunteer from Community Hospice. I believe the patient's mother will probably want you to come by for a meeting first before you begin visit, and don't worry, Jenna, you'll do fine. If you have any questions please don't hesitate to call me. In my signature is my cell phone number and I check my email regularly especially after hours so I'm always available to you, okay, Jenna? Remember, you can go out with a mentor a few times if you would prefer to do that before having your own patient, but I think because you two are so close in age, I think you'll do just fine with her."

"No, no problem, I'll give it a go without a mentor."

"After you set up schedule times and everything, reply to the email I'm sending you now with what you've worked out with the caregiver, or call me with anymore questions." Matt concluded.

"Got it. Is it too early to call?" Jenna asked.

"No, the mother's an early riser. You can call her now." Matt responded.

"Okay, will do." Jenna agreed. They hung up, and Jenna took in a couple of deep breaths and waited for Matt's email. Within a few minutes she had it, and she dialed the number listed in his mail.

"Hello Mrs. Mills, my name is Jenna Steele from Community Hospice. I'm the volunteer you and your husband requested for your daughter." Jenna greeted stumbling a bit.

"Ah yes, hello Jenna, thank you for calling." Lynn responded.

"I just spoke with my manager and he said that you wanted me to come out a couple of times a week to visit with...Samantha?" Jenna had almost forgotten the patient's name; thankfully, Matt's email was still up.

"Yes, my daughter Samantha has been feeling down as of late and it seem to be getting worse. I'm here most of the time but I think Sam would like company other than me and her father."

"I understand." Jenna responded.

"There's a caregiver who comes everyday so no need to worry about that. Samantha needs to interact with people. She gets around, but her illness has made her very weak, and she may need assistance moving. She won't ask for help until she's practically falling so you have to just keep an eye on her when she walks. I have asked her repeatedly to use her walker, but she won't. How old are you?" Lynn asked Jenna suddenly.

"Thirty-one." Jenna replied, a bit startled by the question.

"Good. Sam is thirty-five. I only ask because I want someone close to her age. I know most volunteers are much older or much younger, like students."

"Yes they are." Jenna said.

"The nurse said that the volunteer manager had someone in mind so I am very glad you two are about the same age. So...Jenna is it?"

"Yes, Ma'am."

"Can you come by on Wednesday around noon for lunch? I would like to have an introductory meeting to make sure it's a fit for everyone."

"Absolutely no problem." Jenna assured her.

"You have our address, Jenna?"

"Yes, you guys are not too far from me."

"Really? Where do you live?" Lynn asked.

"I live off of Forest Lake."

"Ah, yes, a very nice area; you live close indeed. Has your family lived here in Bloomfield long? I may know your mother."

"No, I just moved here a little under a year ago. I grew up in Pontiac." Jenna informed her.

Lynn paused a moment. "I see. Well, this is really the township. So I'll see you on Wednesday at noon, then, Jenna. We're not too far off of Telegraph. It's a beige home, a few winding roads, but it's not too hard to find. If you have any trouble just call the house I will be happy to guide you."

"Okay thanks, Mrs. Mills. I am excited to meet you all." Jenna said.

After hanging up, Jenna replied to Matt's email and gave him the time and day for the first meeting her first assignment. Jenna printed out the information sheet for her patient, Samantha Mills. She read over all of the information. For one eight by eleven piece of paper it was chock full of facts. The first part was the demographics and directions. She did not need directions because she knew exactly where they lived. While searching for the house she was now living in, Jenna had been taken to that area to look at homes, a very nice area of older homes and larger homes. These are rich people, Jenna thought. "Oh, jeez, am I going to be dealing with a princess?" she asked herself leaning back in her chair.

Jenna rocked as she read the rest, age 35, *wow young,* she thought. Mother and father listed as primary. Patient was at risk for falls. Equipment in the home, walker, wheelchair, and bedside commode. Patient mobile, verbal, depressed. Well, that about sums it up. Jenna went on to read the different disciplines on the case, RN case manager, Trish Kramer, social worker, Karen Richter, and spiritual care, Judy Norm. There were a few spaces without names, and then her name was listed as Volunteer, Jenna Steele, followed by the name of the Volunteer Manager, Matthew Ames.

Jenna danced a bit in her chair, smiling at the sight of her name. "Volunteer, ladies and gentlemen, introducing Miss Jenna Steele – aaahhhh..." She lifted her hands to add to the crowd cheering effect.

"What in the hell are you doing?" Adrian asked Jenna as he appeared in the doorway. "Talking to yourself now?"

Jenna turned around, startled by Adrian standing there. "How long have you been there?" she asked, embarrassed.

"Long enough to think about committing you."

"Please, if anybody needs to be committed it's you."

Adrian nodded. "You could have a point." He said.

"What can I do for you dear cousin?" Jenna asked him.

"Oh, nothing, just wanted to let you know that I'll be gone for a few days and, but I'll be back by...um...Friday." Adrian announced.

Jenna stopped rocking. "What? Where are you going?" she asked, alarmed. Although she shouldn't be, alarmed, this was Adrian's M.O.

"New York."

"Why are you going to New York?"

"Business, and I know people in the city I like to hang with, so business plus a pleasure trip."

"Business? What *kind* of business, Adrian?" Jenna asked suspiciously.

"Whoa, I just heard Gina's voice there, yeah?" Jenna sounded exactly like his mother to him at that moment.

"No, I'm just inquiring or can I not do that?" Jenna asked him.

"Of course, nothing to worry about, I just have to take care of a few things. I wanted to let you know so you wouldn't wonder where I am."

"I can't help but be worried, I come home and men are beating you up, demanding money. You go away and we don't see you for months at a time without any contact."

"Who's we?" Adrian asked Jenna skeptically.

"Me, your mother, the rest of the family; I know sometimes it feels like it's just me and you now, but it's not, Adrian."

Adrian paused, looking at Jenna strangely, and then he smiled his famous million dollar smile and touched her chin. Outside, they heard a car horn blow, as if on cue. "That's my ride. Gotta go, Imzadi." He reached down and kissed Jenna's forehead, then grabbed a bag that was in the hallway and headed down stairs. Jenna was close on his heels.

"Whoa, you weren't kidding!" Jenna said.

"Yeah, I was coming to tell you I was leaving."

"Sure, but I didn't think you meant right now!" Jenna made it to the bottom of the stairs.

Adrian opened the door and sent up a hand and dropped his bag outside the door. The driver saw this so he exited the car and came to retrieve Adrian's bag.

"A limo?" Jenna asked then cocked her head to the side. "What's going on Adrian? I mean really, what's going on?"

After watching the driver get his bag and return to the car, Adrian turned to Jenna. "Listen, Jen…" He placed both hands on her shoulders. "I know I've been a fuck up. I've hurt people…but trust me, when I finish with this deal, I'll be on the straight and narrow, I promise. You were right, its time to grow up. I want to be someone that you can be proud of, that my Mom can be proud of. I know you've heard it all before, but I mean it this time."

"I haven't heard *this* before." Jenna let out a deep sigh. "Adrian, please, don't do anything stupid."

"Who me? Do something stupid? Now you know better than that." He winked at Jenna and smiled. "You don't worry, when I get back, you'll see, things will be different."

"Adrian, you do not have to prove anything to me, or to anyone else for that matter." Jenna assured him.

Adrian nodded. "I'll see you Friday. We'll get drunk and sing at the piano." They both smiled at each other. Adrian turned to leave, then spun around. "Oh shit, almost forgot." He pulled out an envelope from his back pocket. "Give this to Zee, I mean Elizabeth."

Jenna took the thick envelope. "What is it?"

"Tell her she's going to make a beautiful bride and that I'm sorry for complicating things."

"Jeez, sound like you're saying goodbye." Jenna gave Adrian an agonizing stare.

"Just to her. We all gotta move on sometime, right?" Then, without another word, Adrian turned and left. He flung up a quick wave and disappeared into the long black car.

Jenna watched the car pull away, then went back into the house. She stood in the foyer for a moment staring at the standard white envelope with one letter written on it: "Z". Jenna could not help but feel that something was wrong...very wrong.

TWENTY-TWO

Jenna pulled up to the Mills' household at 11:40am, Wednesday morning. She wanted to be early but not twenty minutes early. The stone carport was a bit intimidating, she had to admit, as she sat in the car, not sure whether to park there or wait for a valet. She didn't have to make a decision because soon the large wooden door was opened by a woman who had a striking resemblance to Diahann Carroll, so much so it made Jenna look twice.

"Hello, I'm Lynnette Mills." Lynn said after Jenna got out of her car. Lynn extended a perfectly manicured hand to her daughter's new volunteer, and said "Follow me inside."

Jenna smiled warmly. Mrs. Mills seemed like a very nice person, she thought immediately. The mother's demeanor made the splendor of the house seem more inviting. As Jenna walked through the corridor of their home, a space large enough to land an airplane in, she felt, her 4000 square foot home was a small cottage in comparison. This actually made her feel better, more like herself. Jenna had grown up in homes which were always smaller than her school counterparts; therefore being in the Mills' home gave her familiar territory, which strangely, was comforting. She knew how to act in this environment. It came easy to her. She knew when to smile, when to grimace and nod, when to laugh out loud, and when to say "yes, I understand." She executed them all perfectly.

Lynnette led Jenna into a small dining room. Jenna figured this was the informal dining room, judging from the size of the home. It may have been the informal dining area, but it was still decorated lavishly.

"Hello, I'm Joe Mills." Joe said, entering the room through the double swinging doors. He was carrying a large wooden salad bowl and serving spoons. He set them down easily and shook her hand. "My wife tells me you don't live too far from here." Joe gestured for Jenna to have a seat at the table.

"Just five miles away, an easy drive." Jenna told Joe.

"That's good. Did you grow up around here?" Joe asked.

Before Jenna could answer, Lynn entered the room with a large plate of mustard-dill tortellini salad skewers. "No, hun, she grew up in Auburn Hills." She said.

"What high school did you go to? Northern or Central?" Joe asked.

"Actually, I received a scholarship to Notre Dame Marist Academy." Jenna said.

"Excellent school!" Joe exclaimed. "Are you Catholic?"

"No. My mother didn't want me at the public schools. She said they were too dangerous so I went to a Catholic School."

"Bet you hated wearing those uniforms everyday." Joe commented.

"I would have had to wear them at the public schools so I guess I didn't mind, much." Jenna responded.

"Much." Joe laughed and Jenna joined him. They continued to chat about the school system, how it's failing students and about the poor educational options in the surrounding counties; as they talked, Lynn walked in and out with drinks and bread. She went around filling each plate, even the plate with the empty chair belonging to Jenna's new patient.

Lynn listened to the conversation, interjecting that their daughter, Samantha, attended Cranbrook, the prestigious boarding school in town. She told Jenna to go ahead and eat while she went to find her daughter. Lynn was headed upstairs but noticed that the sliding door leading to the patio was open. She jogged towards it and there was Samantha, of course, sitting in the same spot as she always did, looking out at nothing.

"Sam, didn't I tell you that the volunteer is coming for lunch today?" Lynn called.

"Yeah, so." Samantha answered without turning around. This made Lynn walk in front of Samantha's chair and look at her daughter defiantly.

"So get your butt up and join us for lunch! She is here to meet you! You're being unnecessarily rude!" Lynn whispered rude.

"Why are you whispering; she can't hear you." Samantha said looking up at her mother.

"Get up now!" Lynn commanded.

"In case you missed it, I'm fucking dying. So if I want to sit in this chair, I'm going to sit in this chair. Leave me alone."

Lynn sucked in air, putting a hand to her chest. "I should slap your mouth right now, Samantha, you are still my daughter, living under my roof, and you will not talk to me that way!" Lynn bent down pointing into

Samantha's face. "You've always been a disrespectful child! Spoiled little brat!" This time Lynn did yell.

"Good, you're getting in touch with your feelings. The social worker did say you needed to do that. I would offer you one of my pills but you might get addicted." Samantha laughed wickedly. "Oh, but forgive me, you probably already have your own stash."

Lynn drew back a hand and slapped Samantha's face as hard as she could. As soon as she did it, Lynn regretted it. "Sam, I'm sorry."

"What's going on here?" Joe said appearing at the doorway with Jenna right behind him. They both had seen what had transpired between the two women. Jenna suddenly thought she should go.

"Nothing, Daddy." Samantha said, looking behind her at him. "Mom was just getting in touch with her emotions."

Joe walked over to Lynn. "What's gotten into you?" he asked his wife.

"You deal with her." Lynn hissed at Joe, and then brushed past him. She stopped short beside Jenna, conduct in check. "As you can see, Jenna, we need you." Lynn walked past her inside of the house disappearing around a corner.

Jenna stood for a moment not knowing what to do. *This is her first assignment? Great,* she thought. She watched as Joe knelt down and said something privately to his daughter. She saw Samantha nod her head then Joe rose and walked back over to Jenna. When he reached Jenna, he touched her shoulder lightly, leading her over to where Sam was still sitting. He guided her around so Sam could see her.

"Sam, this is Jenna Steele; she's your new volunteer. She will be coming out a couple of times a week to visit with you..." He said awkwardly.

Samantha turned and looked up at Jenna and smiled. It was clearly fabricated but Jenna took it. Jenna watched as Joe made his way into the house. As he closed the door he made an expression at Jenna that seemed to say "go on talk."

When Joe disappeared into the house, Jenna sat down in the chair beside Samantha. At first she was going to talk as her father suggested. She was going to ask the usual questions such as "how are you today?", "can I get you anything?", or start into her own life story, but she remembered something she learned in training: "meet them where they are." This was something she had not done with her mother. She had gone out of her way to make her mother feel comfortable and well looked after before her mother had died, but Jenna noticed that this often made her mother agitated. When Adrian came to visit, he didn't do that. Sometimes he would just sit with her mother, not saying a word. Jenna recalled late one night she had gotten up around to check on her mother, and Adrian was sitting in the chair next to her mother's bed sleeping. Jenna watched as her mother stirred, opened her eyes, smiled, and touched Adrian's hand. He woke up but did not say anything, just squeezed her hand back. Then her mother went back to sleep. That was all her mother had needed at that moment.

So Jenna sat down and looked out at the Mills' huge backyard. It seemed to go on forever. Jenna wondered if they owned the part where the trees bordered it, but probably not because she knew beyond the trees was a lake. She thought that they probably had a dock down there with an attached boat like most of the people did in these lake areas. Her own neighbors owned boats, Jenna did not, nor had she any plans on purchasing one.

The garden, how magnificently beautiful, all of the different flowers and colors in bloom. She could only imagine how many hours someone spent out here watering, toiling in the soil, hard work for sure but well worth it to be able to sit and marvel in it. What was missing from this yard was a pool. Jenna thought that odd for such a large property. Yet the patio definitely made up for it. It was surely designed for entertaining with the outside kitchen area, bar, and fire pit surrounded by concrete seating. Jenna had not done much to her back yard. It was still as it had been when she bought it. There was a built in barbeque grill, but it was still a blank canvas.

"Why are you here?" Samantha asked suddenly, breaking the silence. The tone in her voice was not pleasant.

"I'm here to sit with you and keep you company." Jenna replied, not really knowing how to answer.

"I don't need company." Samantha said flatly.

"Well, your mother seems to fe…" Jenna started but was cut off.

"Seems to feel? My mother doesn't feel." Samantha pointed in front of her. "It's like that garden you've been admiring. It's immaculate, manicured, bullshit. I call it Pedro's garden." Samantha looked at her visitor. "You know why? Because my mother hired a gardener, Pedro, to plant, till, toil, grow and maintain it. It looks the way it does because of Pedro, not because of Lynnette, although she claims it as her own. She parades people around it, sucking in the praise like she spent hours upon hours cultivating it. It's really quite pathetic."

"My mother had a garden, too," Jenna said, "but not as big and beautiful as this. It was mainly a rose garden with some perennials, no real structure, she just liked roses. She also planted tomatoes, spinach, carrots, stuff like that. She loved working in it. When she died, I didn't keep it up."

"Sorry to hear that. When did your mother die?" Samantha asked.

"A little over a year ago." Jenna told her.

"How did she die, if you don't mind me asking?" Samantha turned towards Jenna. Jenna turned to her, as well. She was a beautiful woman, Jenna saw. Samantha didn't look sick at all, just a bit tired around the eyes.

"Ovarian cancer. She fought it for five years, maybe longer, yet by the time she told me about it, she was in her final stages. I watched over her for two years until she died."

"Were you two close?" Samantha asked.

"Yes, I suppose so. I was an only child, so it was just the two of us."

"Me too, an only child." Samantha said putting a hand to her chest.

Jenna thought that she had better bring the conversation back to Samantha. *Gear it back to the patient*, she could hear Matt saying. "How was growing up alone for you?"

"Not bad." Samantha admitted. She was beginning to loosen up. "I wasn't alone a lot. When I was little me, my dad and my mom would take vacations together. We had family game night where we'd play board games, and my favorite was charades. My dad used to make the silliest faces and gestures. I knew he was only trying to make me laugh. My mom would get mad because he would be making movements that had nothing to do with what he was trying to act out." Samantha sat up in the lounger, snickering. "You know what we used to do? We would make up gestures to words that made no sense then when it came time to play I would guess what he was saying and he would guess mine, and mom didn't have a clue what we were doing so she would always lose! She used to get so pissed!"

"Oh my God, you guys cheated!" Jenna laughed.

Samantha nodded. "Yep! But it was fun. Me and my dad used to do stuff like that all the time. We would have private games, secrets, and stories. I guess that was his way of making me feel like I had a playmate."

"He sounds like a special guy." Jenna said.

"He is. He's my buffer from the wicked witch." Samantha said without jest.

"You have a strained relationship with your mother?" Jenna asked.

"You could say that." Samantha shifted again, grimacing.

"Are you in pain?" Jenna asked concerned.

"Just achy." Samantha reached down into a bag lying on the patio and pulled out a bottle of pills, popping one. Jenna immediately looked around and saw water sitting on the outdoor end table. She poured Samantha a glass and handed it to her. "Thanks." Samantha responded taking a large sip of the offered water.

"Just give me ten minutes, because in 10 minutes I'll be fine!" Sam seemed to be acting out a line from a movie. "Do you know where that's from?"

Jenna shook her head. "A movie?" she asked.

"Dolores Claiborne. I might have mixed it up a little bit but it was when her daughter, Selena came home to their old house and she popped some pills to get herself through an argument she and her mother were having."

"I don't think I've seen that movie, but I've heard of it, though." Jenna said.

"You gotta see it. Great movie, better book. Although they did a really good job with the movie I must say, so hard for people to depict a Stephen King novel."

"I don't like horror movies too much, probably why I haven't seen it."

"Big misconception about Stephen King's works. He doesn't really write horror stories per se. He writes about regular, ordinary people, like you and me, but he tells the story of what happens to them emotionally and how the things that happen to them can be very horrific. You have to read the books. When his books are turned into movies, it seems they only play up the horror parts. It's like taking the story of a husband and wife who have been married for 50 years and turning it into a porno." Samantha further explained.

"Ah, I see. I'll have to take another look at his stuff." Jenna said.

"Well, if you don't like horror, then don't go renting "Cujo" or "It", but do watch "Dolores Claiborne" or "Misery". He has a knack for telling interesting stories about women. Those two stories are really good ones."

"Kathy Bates, right?" The actress popped into Jenna's mind.

"Yes! She was made for both of those roles. They couldn't have found a better actress to play the parts. So watch those. Don't watch "Pet Sematary." Samantha chuckled.

Jenna lifted her hands. "Oh, I did see that one. That scared me! That little kid coming back to life? Ohhh, freaked me out!"

"Yeah, that was pretty creepy!" Samantha leaned back in the lounger. "Hey, any more of that lunch left, you think?" she asked Jenna.

"I'm sure it is. You want me to fix you a plate?" Jenna asked.

"You don't have to do that. I'll go in and fix me something."

"That's what I'm here for, Sam, and besides, you wanna make me look bad to the wicked witch?"

Samantha looked at her and smiled. "You're ok with me, Jen." She said nodding. "Alright, I'm going to go over to the table. And make sure you bring me some of that papaya juice, its good stuff." Samantha steadied herself and started to get up. Jenna could see she was struggling so she quickly placed a hand under Samantha's elbow to balance her. Samantha paused but then leaned into her, allowing Jenna to assist her up. Samantha patted Jenna's arm with an appreciative look. Jenna nodded back at her.

The two ladies sat and ate the chicken salad Lynn had made for lunch. Jenna sat with Samantha talking and laughing for another couple of hours before she left her first assignment. On the drive home that day, Jenna felt good, accomplished, as if she had made a small difference in Samantha's day. Jenna had walked into the home scared. She had met Samantha and thought she would tell her to get out, but now Jenna knew she had made a connection, an important connection. They had made plans for her to come back every Tuesday and Thursday, starting the next day. Jenna was looking forward to it. She had found her purpose.

TWENTY-THREE

Brandon walked into Matt's office and slammed a green book down on his desk. "What the fuck is this?" He stared at Matt irately.

"Morning to you too, man." Matt said comically. He looked down at the book and read it. "Volunteer Administration Professional Practice. Well, it looks like the book we have to study in order to pass the CVA exam. I have one, too." Matt reached down and pulled it out of his briefcase. "It came yesterday." He said.

Brandon let out the sound of air seeping from a tire. He plopped into a nearby chair. "CVA *ppbbsstt*! I don't have time for this! I'm out recruiting for more alternative therapies. I'm out bribing hairstylists and massage therapists left and right. Do you know how many interviews I've had in the past week?" He watched Matt hunch his shoulders. "Too damned many!" Brandon answered. "They all want to be on the payroll! I'm like what part of volunteer do you not understand?"

"I know man." Matt stated. "But we gotta do it. Offer them free advertising. That's what I did and I recruited two new massage therapists from it."

"Ads? Where do you put them?" Brandon asked.

"In my newsletter, and I put their business cards around the office." Matt replied.

"That's a good idea." Brandon admitted.

"Yeah, I just put "Donated Services by blah blah blah and then I put please patronize their businesses. I'm also going to see if I can get permission to have their logos on our website."

"Good luck with that." Brandon said.

"You never know, don't hurt to ask. These people are giving their time and expertise, and they should get something back for it, something more than just a good feeling. They do have a business to run after all." Matt added.

"What about training? I had so many of them say they can't come for training, so they back off."

"Yeah, I give them a special training. I skip all the history and medical stuff and focus in on what they NEED to know such as HIPAA, Confidentiality, and how to fill out their documentations. Then I give them the volunteer manual and tell them to go online and do the refresher courses at their leisure. I also give everything about 90 days to get them turned in."

"When did you start doing all of this?" Brandon asked.

"Right after the meeting when the demands came down. I had to start thinking outside the box! I mean we need the massage therapists and hair stylists, so we have to make it work for them, not for us."

"Right." Brandon said and picked up the book he had thrown down and started thumbing through it. "Have you looked at this book yet?" he asked.

"Not yet," Matt said, "hopefully, I'll be able to look at it tonight." Matt then checked his emails. The three volunteer directors had a quarterly regional management meeting scheduled that day. At this meeting, similar to the statewide meeting, they discussed upcoming trainings and mutual strategies to keep them on track.

"Listen to this…" Brandon said, reading aloud from the book. "Financial Management and Fiscal Development. Assets minus liabilities equals net assets. What? Why do I have to know this? Am I an accountant for this company?"

"We do have a budget to manage." Matt replied, jogging Brandon's memory.

"Yeah, well the only budget, I'm worried about is my home budget and I have to do that on a secretary's salary." Brandon cursed under his breath.

"What is your major malfunction, buddy?" Matt asked his friend, "I rarely see you upset like this. Is it because we have to take this exam to get our credentials?"

"That's only part of it." Brandon said, as he stood up and walked over to the window, "Chloe and I had a fight last night which continued into the wee hours of the morning. I didn't get any sleep." Brandon said as he rubbed his eyes.

"Ah, wife troubles." Matt said, understanding.

"My oldest boy, BJ, is going into the eighth grade this year." Brandon stated. BJ was short for Brandon Junior.

"That's right, he's in junior high." Matt recollected.

"Yes, and this year they closed the junior high school so all of the eighth graders are going to the high school and the seventh graders will be moved back to the elementary schools."

"What? That's crazy." Matt exclaimed.

"Chloe is livid," Brandon said. "Remember the shooting that happened last year at the public high school. Since then, she's been trying to convince me all winter to sign him up for a private school. Do you know how expensive private school is?" he asked.

"Yes, I do." Matt said because that's exactly what Matt's ex wanted, but he shot her down every year.

"Well, I kept telling Chloe that we cannot afford it. So what does she do? She goes behind my back, applies for financial aid, he gets it, but you still have to come up with five hundred a month for the remaining balance. She's signed him up for school and everything. Where am I going to get five hundred dollars from? Then she starts talking about she wants another baby. I'm like what dream world do you live in woman?"

"Wow man." Matt said sympathetically.

"Then she goes into *'well you were supposed to go back to school to finish your bachelors and get your masters.'* So we have that old argument again. And I remind her that she was supposed to stop working part time at the mall like she's in her twenties and get a full-time position. Oh no, she doesn't want to do that. Talking about she made a commitment to her friend who owns the boutique she works at and that she likes being home when the boys get out of school. And I remind her spoiled ass again that we can't have it all. But all of this is my fault! You know what she said to me?" Brandon asked Matt, who waited patiently for the answer. "She tells me it's my fault because this life is not what I promised her when we got married some fifteen odd years ago. I was supposed to be the boss of my own company by now and we supposed to be living in a much nicer house and driving brand new cars. She actually said this to me. She was serious like I'm in breach of contract right now! When you're twenty years old you say a lot of shit, then life happens!" Brandon threw up his hands in exasperation.

"I remember those arguments with Connie. Women think that just because you're a man, jobs come easier." Matt said.

"Eh, it probably is my fault." Brandon relented going back to sit down.

"What? It's not your fault." Matt said.

"I knew what kind of a woman she was when I married her. She was so beautiful, so poised, you know? I would have said anything to get her to marry me and I did. Even after we were married, I was still wooing her. I bought her all this shit, borrowed money pretending to be what I wasn't.

Took out a mortgage on a house that we couldn't afford, cars I couldn't afford. Then the kids came and I had to get a real job and work. I stayed working here because this company gave great benefits and retirement. I always assumed I would move up into a better position. But this is healthcare. Without a nursing degree you're pretty much screwed. And when positions did come open not requiring that, you needed a masters. I'm stuck man. So, sorry, when I stopped by my office on the way here and saw this book sitting on my desk, I guess I lost it." Brandon sniggered to himself.

"Don't worry about it, Brandon, we all have those days. It's gonna get better." Matt tried to reassure him. Brandon only let out a small snort of disbelief.

"Thanks for listening, Matt. I appreciate it. Don't mean to dump all this shit on you. Nothing will ever be accomplished by complaining. I have to figure it out and make it happen, get a second job if I have to."

"We have to do what we have to do, right?" Matt told him. Brandon nodded. Matt looked up when someone appeared in his office doorway. He expected to see Susan, late as usual, but instead saw a tear-drenched, sniffling Shannon Silverman. Matt immediately got up and went to her.

"What's going on Shannon?" He placed his hands on her shoulders. Shannon was practically hysterical.

"I just got fired!" she whimpered, then collapsed into his arms.

Startled by her behavior he just held onto her while she cried. Over Shannon's shoulder Matt saw her boss, Maria Marano, coming up to them. She did not look happy. "What's going on, Maria?"

"It's Chatman. He's here handing out pink slips. Brave little fuck came himself." Marie put a hand on Shannon's back. "Come on now, honey. Don't do this to yourself. Let's go."

"What am I going to do, Matt?" Shannon cried.

"Sit down, Shannon. Everything's going to be alright." Matt told her. How did he become the consoler today? He thought to himself.

Brandon got up and let Shannon sit down. "Damn. So it's started huh?" he said.

"It's started alright." Maria said standing beside Shannon with a hand on her shoulder. "Don't go to the other side, its chaos over there." Maria warned.

"Who all got laid off?" Matt asked Maria.

"All of my staff, all of the LPNs, and a few home health aides, the part time ones." Maria's tone was pretty straight forward. She was a tough cookie.

"Jesus!" Brandon exclaimed. "*All* of the LPN's?"

"Every last one." Maria confirmed.

"What about you?" Matt asked her.

Maria shook her head. "Nope, not me. Someone has to hold down the fort." She said.

"Well, that's good at least." Matt said.

"So I quit." Maria said to him. She met his shocked eyes. "I don't need this job. I've been here a long time. I should have retired long time ago, Matt. But I believed in this company. I believed in the mission of hospice. But the way Chatman came through here like a bulldozer with his hundred dollar suit talking on his cell phone like it wasn't shit. I guess it ain't to him." Maria suddenly looked very sad.

"Oh my God." Matt said shaking his head.

"We knew it was coming." Maria said. She tugged at Shannon. "Come on. The guard is waiting, and we have to get our stuff out of our desks."

"Guard?" Brandon asked.

"Yep, human resources and Pete, the security guy from corporate. They have to watch us leave so we won't steal or break anything." Maria said. "See ya later Matt. I'll invite you and Jake over for lasagna one Sunday." Then she turned and left.

Shannon stood, wiping her eyes. She started to leave, and then turned back to Matt. "Can I call you later? I just need to talk to somebody." She looked at him with pleading eyes.

Matt glanced at Brandon who quickly looked away. "Yeah, of course, and don't worry, everything's going to be fine." What else was he going to say? Shannon managed a weak smile, then followed Maria out. Matt looked at Brandon again.

Brandon held up his hands. "I ain't sayin' nothin'." He said comically.

"Don't start." Matt said, going back to his desk.

Brandon whispered. "I thought that was over?" he asked pointing at the door.

"It is. You heard her; she just needs someone to talk to. She's pretty distraught."

"Ok...."Brandon said. "Hey you're single, nothing wrong with a little stress relief."

Matt held up a hand in protest. "Let's try to focus on today if we can."

"Sure, as soon as Susan ever gets here." Brandon said.

On cue, Susan appeared in the door. "I'm here, jerk." Susan said, putting down her laptop bag and purse. "Oh My God, have you heard what's going on?"

"Yeah, we heard." Brandon said.

"That little Napoleon shit is out there canning everyone. But it's happening at my office too, which is why I was late. I guess each of the execs took a location. Tomorrow they're headed out to the other sites. Today and Friday they're wrapping it all up, at least the first rounds."

"This is brutal." Brandon commented.

"As they said it would be. Lord, I haven't cried so much in years!" Susan let out a deep sigh. "So how is it here?" she asked.

"Horrible." Matt told her. "I've been warned not to go next door to the staff side."

"I'm wondering when it's our turn." Susan said, crossing her arms, looking at Brandon and Matt.

Brandon shook his head. "Nah, not us. Who else are they going to get to do this, for the same price?"

"Please..." Susan said. "There are plenty of hospices who combine grief support or social work with volunteer services."

"Small hospices. We're too big for that." Matt said.

"Okay..." Susan thought, "Then they can reduce it to regions. There are plenty of directors who handle more than a few hundred volunteers at a time."

"Sure at hospitals where there are other staff that they report to. We have to build relationships, not so at hospitals." Matt claimed.

"Yeah well, I still don't feel safe." Susan confessed.

For the next two and a half hours the three of them tried to concentrate on the agenda at hand. They poured over the calendar year left to undertake. They had three more joint trainings to deal with, plus the joint awards dinner that they held annually at the Whitney. The trainings, no problem, yet when they got to the awards dinner for the volunteers the same argument arose.

"We always get the same people at the dinner. What is the point?" Brandon asked.

"I don't care. We honor those who have gone above and beyond and also announce the statewide volunteer of the year. So what if the same people come. They are apparently the volunteers who care enough to attend, therefore, they deserve to have an appreciation dinner." Matt declared.

"Yeah, what's wrong with that?" Susan asked.

"Just, financially, is it viable?" Brandon asked.

"Well, we have the educational seminar in the spring so we capture the others." Matt informed.

Brandon shrugged his shoulders. "I guess."

"Hey, we get a band, it's a fun night."Matt remarked.

After agreeing on the scheduled events they started discussing the budget which led, harmoniously, into logistics. Although, between the three of them there was no real leader, Matt was always the one left to make the final decision, or his suggestion was usually agreed upon by Susan and Brandon. Also, Sarah Evans, VP, spoke with Matt more often about what to do. Sometimes Matt resented that because if his opinions were so valued, why wasn't he compensated for them? Matt knew he could not sit and ponder that for too long. He knew that if more respect and power were what he wanted them he had to accept the VP position.

The budgets for all three branches were dwindling down as they crossed over the half year mark, but Matt always encouraged the other volunteer directors to spend what was allotted, because if you wanted more, you have to spend up to the line of your budget. Only then are budgets kept the same or raised for the following fiscal year.

"Are we done?" Brandon asked suddenly. Both of his colleagues looked up at him, but it was Susan who spoke first.

"Look, after this morning I can't sit here all day." He admitted.

"Thinking it better to be at your desk?" Susan surmised.

"Yes, my home office." Brandon got up and stuffed his notepad into his computer bag, but he had taken no notes during the meeting, "I'm outta here, guys," he said. "If you need me, I'll be at home. I'll be reachable by email or cell." Brandon waved a hollow goodbye, then walked out of Matt's office towards the door. He ran into a very lost looking Jenna.

Jenna was used to having a receptionist greet her in the lobby area, but the window was closed and the door into the offices was wide open. "Hello, I'm looking for Mr. Ames." She said to a passing Brandon. "Oh, hello." She greeted him once she recognized Brandon face.

Brandon's demeanor instantly changed. He smiled pleasantly. "Hello, Jenna right?"

"Yes." She replied.

"Come with me, he's in his office." Brandon led Jenna back down the hall. "Have you gotten an assignment with a patient yet?" he asked.

"Yes, I did. I don't live too far from here so I thought I would drop off my documentation forms to make sure I completed them correctly." Jenna said.

"Great." When Brandon reached Matt's office he poked his head in. "Look who I found." He said and moved to allow Jenna into the room.

Matt stood up from his chair and smiled. "Hello, Jenna how are you?"

"Doing good. Sorry to come here unannounced. Should I have made an appointment?" Jenna asked.

"Absolutely not, nothing is more important than my volunteers." Matt beamed, pointing to a chair for her.

"I'm not going to take up too much of your time. I just wanted to go over my documentation forms." She said pulling them out of her oversized purse.

Susan stood as well. "Well, I'll let you two talk; I'm going next door to see what the damage is." When Susan left, she closed the door behind her.

Jenna's brow wrinkled. "Damage? Is there a problem?" she asked Matt.

Matt scratched his ear not exactly sure how to answer, and then decided to tell the truth, at least basically. "So you won't think we're closing shop, the company is making some layoffs today. All is fine in our department, but it's a bit tense around here today." He explained.

Jenna nodded. "That explains all the people in the parking lot." She said.

"Who's in the parking lot?" Matt asked. He hadn't even gone next door to see who was left.

"Just some people standing by their cars talking. They seemed to look pretty angry. Sorry to hear that."

"It's business. Companies have to that from time to time. I only told you because you are here and rumors have a way of taking on a life of their own." Matt said.

"Do you want me to come back?" Jenna asked.

"Like I said, my job is to make sure you're alright, so what can I do for you?" Matt looked down at the papers in her hand. "Documentation! What questions do you have for me?"

Jenna handed him the forms. "Just take a look to make sure I filled it out correctly. I wasn't quite sure about my comments. I can redo it, if you need me too."

Matt looked over her paperwork carefully. He noticed something. "Ok make sure to fill in the mileage section." He said.

"Oh okay. I didn't because I remember you explained this was something we can use as a deduction on our taxes. I probably won't take that deduction so I skipped it."

"No, it's not just for your taxes. We need to know this information, as well, because it correctly determines our cost savings, which is very important to our bottom line."

Jenna's eyes widened a bit. "Ah, I see. Okay, I'll make sure to correct that." She said.

Matt looked over the next few pages. "So you've gone out three times to visit Samantha Mills, I see."

"Yes. The first visit last Wednesday was just a get to know you visit. Her mother made lunch. Sam, that's what she asked me to call her, was a bit reluctant at first but I think she warmed up to me. I went again last Thursday, Tuesday, and again today." Jenna thought for a moment, "Oh, was I supposed to fill out documentation for that first meeting?" Jenna asked. "I wasn't sure since it wasn't a real visit per se; though we did talk for a couple of hours after I met her."

"Yes, you do. Anytime you have any contact with the patient, document it! Remember the motto: If you didn't write it down... it didn't happen." Matt responded.

Jenna repeated it. "Right, I'll remember." She said, and giggled at how much she had forgotten. Jenna felt like she was back in high school.

"So how was it? I got your email about your first encounter. How have things been since?" Matt asked.

Jenna relaxed in her chair and began to tell Matt about her visits with Samantha. On the second visit Samantha's father met Jenna at the door and just told her she was on the patio. It seems that the patio is Samantha's favorite place to be, or maybe she just liked being outside and out of the house, away from her mother. It was clear that she did not get along with her mother, although Sam had not explained why. Jenna figured eventually she might talk about it, but she was not a counselor so she decided it best not to press her.

When Jenna walked outside on the patio, Samantha didn't speak. Again she was looking straight ahead at the garden. Jenna didn't really think that Sam's focus was on the flowers but much further away. Jenna could only imagine what could be going through her mind. What do you think about when you're dying? She wondered.

Jenna called Samantha's name as to not startle her, "How are you today, Samantha?" she had asked sweetly, yet tried very hard not to sound condescending.

"Don't call me that." Samantha had told her firmly, and then her tone softened. "Call me Sam. Kenny used to call me Sam."

Jenna sat down beside her. "Okay. Sam."

"No one calls me Samantha but my family, or people who don't know me. I feel like I'm 12 years old when I hear it." Samantha had looked at Jenna. "You can call me, Sam." She had cracked a small smile so demurely that Jenna thought she would never forget her face at that moment.

"So you made a connection?" Matt commented. "Good, very good."

"Yes. She's pretty private. Sometimes we would sit in silence for a long time. At first I thought I should suggest that we do something, go for a walk or something, but she looked so peaceful I didn't mention it. Should I offer stuff like that?" Jenna asked.

"You can. Remember, though, that ALS is a degenerative disease on the muscles, soon it may be extremely hard for her to walk."

"On that second visit Sam told me about Kenny, about how he died in a car accident tragically. I just left the house and came here. Today she was in better spirits, but the nurse came and I left a bit early. I thought the nurse came earlier in the day."

"It's hard to know the exact time the nurse will get there. Sometimes her previous appointment will run long and she may be a bit late, but there's no real set time."

"It was okay. Sam wanted me to stay so I did for a minute but her mother thought it would be better if I cut the visit short. But I was going to be leaving in the next thirty minutes anyway so Sam didn't seem to mind."

"Well good. Sounds like the two of you are hitting it off, as I knew you would." Matt said. Despite himself, Matt couldn't help but notice how beautiful Jenna looked today. He wondered if she was dating anyone. A woman like her surely was. This thought led him to the request from Shannon earlier that he had received. Should he even call Shannon? Matt knew where an innocent phone call of support could and would lead. Did he really need another empty romance? For that matter, did he need another empty weekend alone? His son Jake was gone to visit with his maternal grandmother for the remainder of the summer. At first Matt had protested, but Jake loved his grandmother and since she had moved back to Tennessee after her retirement, it was an excellent summer diversion for Jake so Matt relented and allowed him to go without another fight. Matt was sure Connie was delighted because that meant more freedom for her. Matt, on the other hand, was a bit saddened by it because Matt had just bought the new Madden game and was eager to play it with his son. Matt was surprised how much he missed Jake. This "empty nester" feeling was very new to him.

"Well I'll get out of your hair." Jenna was saying.

"So what are you up to now?" Matt asked her.

"A bachelorette party planning meeting." Jenna announced.

Matt grinned. "Really? Who's getting married?"

"My best girlfriend, Zabbie." Jenna told him.

"Zabbie?" Matt thought the name odd.

"Her name is Elizabeth." Jenna said and laughed.

"Ah, that sounds like fun." Matt said.

"It should be interesting. It will be me, her sisters, and couple of her friends. I'm only true friends with Zabbie. We went to catholic school together. She was rich, I wasn't, hence I only knew her."

"I am picturing talks of g-strings and margaritas." Matt laughed.

Jenna joined him in laughter. "Yeah, pretty much!" she nodded. "The wedding is not for another eight months, but we want to get ideas started. And her sister is a bit of a perfectionist."

"Uh oh, sounds like a potential cat fight on your hands!" Matt joked.

"Boy, you guys love the whole cat fight idea, don't you?" Jenna chuckled.

Matt hunched his shoulders like a little kid, "Sorry, but yeah!"

Jenna couldn't help but shake her head at him. "Oh I forgot to tell you, I got an invitation to The Martinique Ball."

"Oh yeah?" then it dawned on Matt, Jenna's donation of twenty-five thousand dollars.

"Yeah, it said I was part of the Diamond Club. It looks like it's going to be really nice, black tie event. Are you attending?" Jenna asked Matt.

"Actually, I am. I wrangled a free invite. The plates are too expensive for me." Matt confessed.

"Mine is free, too." Jenna said.

"Well, you've already given a very generous donation." He reminded her.

"Glad you'll be there, I'll have someone to talk to." Jenna laughed nervously. "I don't think I've ever been to a black tie event before. I'm a little scared, I may not even go."

"Oh no, you gotta go." Matt encouraged. "I believe they honor the big donors, and that means you. You'll have a lot of fun." He paused a moment then suggested, "You can bring a date, of course." Matt said.

Jenna met his eyes with an expression of confusion. She hadn't thought about bringing anyone. "No, I just planned on going alone." She said.

"Alone?" Now Matt returned her expression. "You can't go alone."

"Why, they won't let me in?" Jenna asked sarcastically.

"I mean you must have someone, beautiful girl like you." Matt said it before he realized. It wasn't so much the words as how he said it. Did she hear his admiring tones?

Jenna looked directly at him with a hint of a blush. "I'm not seeing anyone right now." she told him leaving out the part where she hadn't been in any sort of relationship since she had moved in with and taken care of her mother until her death.

"I have an idea," Matt began gingerly. "Why don't we…" Matt stopped.

"Yes?" Jenna waited, was sexy Mr. Ames about to ask her out?

Matt cleared his throat. "I mean, why don't we sit together? I'll see if we can get side by side seating, that way it won't feel so awkward for you?"

Aww he chickened out, she thought to herself, or maybe he was never going to ask in the first place. "Okay, that sounds good. Thanks." Jenna said somewhat disappointed.

"No problem." Matt said, returning to his business tone. He watched as she got up. "What's the date of the Ball again?"

"The 21st." Jenna answered.

"Hey, that's next Saturday. I gotta get a tux!"

"You mean you don't own one?" Jenna asked as Matt walked her to the front entrance.

"Sorry, I'm not the kind of guy who owns his own tux." He revealed.

Jenna came in closer to him and whispered, "I don't believe that for a second."

TWENTY-FOUR

The corridor was long and dark. The ending of it could not be seen in all of this blackness. Samantha's feet were wet...no they were submerged in about two feet of water. *Is this a pool?* Samantha said aloud, startled by her own voice. *It's flooded*, spoke a male voice from all around her. She immediately recognized the man belonging to that tone, she would know it anywhere. *Kenny?* She called out into the nothingness. He did not answer. She tried to look deeper into the blackness and saw nothing but the void behind her, beside her, and in front of her. *Kenny?* She called again to no avail so moving forward was her only option. Samantha lifted her left leg, then her right. The more she moved through this ever thickening liquid goo, the harder it became. A desperate feeling of dread enveloped her, and panic squeezed on her heart. The aching was just as physical as it was emotional. She broke out in an uncalculated sprint as best she could through the murky sludge.

To Samantha's horror she began to sink down deeper and deeper; yet, something drove her to keep going, to keep moving through the darkness. That's when she saw it, beyond the water, there on the horizon, a sun was rising. She was no longer inside of a building but outside with the sea stretched out all around her. Far off in the distance Samantha saw a figure standing above the water. All she could make out was the silhouette of a man, but she was sure it was Kenny. *Kenny! Help Me!* Samantha tried to scream, but the water was up to her chin, and when she spoke, a little of it seeped into her mouth and down her throat. She could not see Kenny's eyes, but could feel him staring at her, wasn't he going to try to help her? *Ke- please-he-* the water took her. Down into the depths she sank deeper....deeper. A futile arm rose upward towards the far reaching surface. There he was, his dark shadow dancing on the waves above her looking down at her. She could no longer speak, and then it dawned on her, *go to sleep. Close your eyes. Stop fighting.*

"Samantha!" Trish Kramer, Samantha's case manager, was shouting into her face. Trish gently shook Samantha's shoulders, lifting her a bit off the bed. Lynn and Joe stood on either side of Samantha's bed peering desperately down at their daughter who was experiencing some sort of apnea. Joe had thought he heard Samantha calling out in her sleep so he went into her room, and her breathing had become obstructed; then she had stopped breathing altogether. Joe had thought she was dying so he quickly picked up Samantha's bedside phone and dialed hospice. In less than twenty minutes, Trish was knocking at the door.

Trish credited her quick arrival on the fact that it was three am and no one was out on the roads at that early hour. Trish woke up beside a snoring husband when the phone rang with Joe's call. It didn't take long for her to slip on jeans and a t-shirt. Before her husband, Chris, had turned over in bed, Trish was already placing two fingers on Samantha's carotid artery. "She has a pulse." Trish said as she listened to Samantha's heart with a stethoscope.

"I think we should get her to the hospital." Lynn almost yelled.

"Remember Lynn we talked about calling 911?" Trish said to her, without averting her attention away from her patient.

"Yes, but clearly something is wrong with her. You just checking vitals, is not going to help my daughter." Lynn's tone was so nasty that it caused Trish to raise up from what she was doing and stare at Lynn for a moment.

"Mrs. Mills, Mr. Mills, can you give me a moment here?" Trish said finally. Although she was speaking to both of them, she only continued to glare at Lynn. It was like a western movie standoff. Who would make the first move? Trish had encountered many families who were not accepting of their loved one's impending death, but Lynn added a new flavor to it that rubbed Trish the wrong way. It was Lynnette Mills' added haughty, condescending edge that often left Trish wanting hand over this case to another nurse. Yet, even if she screamed enough to her supervisor, Trish could have this patient reassigned, she was not about to do it. For one, Samantha needed her to fight for her needs, and not her mother's needs. And for two, she was not about to back down from this woman. Trish suspected that a woman like Lynn usually got what she wanted, but this was one of the times Lynn would not get what she wanted. Maybe Samantha never truly had someone in her corner before to stand up to her mother. Surely Joe, although obviously loving his daughter very much, stepped to the side for many of their disagreements. Trish did not know where the anger was coming from between Samantha and her mother, and frankly she did not give a shit, because this was one area of her daughter's life Lynnette Mills was not going to control.

Joe gestured for Lynn to follow him out of the room. "Let's let Trish do her job. She's a nurse; she knows what she's doing." Joe was halfway out the door as he spoke. Lynn's eyes narrowed; then she turned and stomped out of the room, almost knocking her husband to the ground as she did. Joe gave an apologetic look to Trish, who held up a hand in understanding. Joe closed the door behind him.

"Sorry, my mother's such a bitch." Samantha said to Trish. Trish's head popped up from listening to Samantha's palpitating heart and looked at her. Samantha's eyes were open, and aside from them being very glassy she appeared normal. Samantha's voice was scratchy, however, which prompted Trish to pour her a glass of water from the beside carafe.

"Welcome back, Sam, how are you feeling?" Trish asked her patient.

Samantha sat up just a bit and took a sip of water. She looked around the room as if trying to place where she was. "I am back." She responded weakly.

"You're okay now." Trish reassured her.

"I was dreaming I was underwater." Samantha said.

"What happened in the dream?" Trish gently spread Samantha's eyelids open so she could see the dilation of her pupils.

"I was in a long corridor. Then I began to sink. It was dark." Samantha told Trish.

"Anything else?" Trish asked.

"I don't know…. I was sinking… I couldn't breathe." Samantha struggled to remember. The dream was fading.

"You were having apnea." Trish told her.

"What's that?" Samantha asked.

"It's when you stop breathing in your sleep. We have to get you on oxygen, Sam. Your lung muscles are getting weaker." Trish explained.

"So I could just suffocate one night and never wake up?"

"That's what the oxygen is for. You'll be fine." Trish watched as Samantha nodded.

"Why aren't we fighting for our child, Joe?" Lynn was standing in the dining room with the lights off. Joe had found her in there after they both came downstairs. "It's so easy for you to give up, isn't it?" she was standing against the china cabinet far back into the darkness. Only the dim inner light silhouetted her. "You've always been like that. Why?"

"I don't want to keep having what's rapidly becoming an old argument." Joe said, standing at the foot of the sixty-seven inch hard wood table.

"Remember when we were in high school and I was dating that quarterback, what was his name?" Lynn feigned forgetfulness.

Joe's memory was fine. "James Johnson." He replied.

"Jimmy J." she said fondly. "I remember when he found out that you wanted to ask me to the sophomore dance. He and his buddies cornered you in the parking lot after a game. He kept poking you in the chest. Poke, poke, poke." She held up her forefinger and imitated the movement in the air. "You did nothing. Why was that? Why did you cower to him?"

"I didn't cower to him." Joe took a step forward. "What I told you then is still true today. I saw the coach pull up before Jimmy and his goons came over to me."

Lynn laughed, "Goons."

"Jimmy didn't see the coach, because his back was to the coach's car. I saw the coach light a cigarette, turn off his car, and watch."

"So what?" Lynn dismissed.

Joe looked at her incredulously. "You don't remember your quarterback boyfriend getting kicked out of school and off the team the very next day?"

"I remember him punching you in the gut three times solid, and I remember you falling to the ground. That's what I remember."

Joe's head shot back in disbelief. "Why do you think he was kicked out of school?"

"I don't remember him being suspended. Jimmy was always ghost during class time. That was Jimmy."

"And him not being at homecoming game?" Joe asked.

"He told me he had to go to Mackinaw with his family, some important celebration." Lynn hunched her shoulders.

Joe just stared at her. "He was lying of course. That was also Jimmy. Jimmy the liar, Jimmy the con artist." He paused and looked at his wife. "Jimmy, the poon hound."

"Still jealous after all these years, Joe?"

"Hard to be jealous of a man who was murdered in a prison cell in Jackson, Michigan." His statement was only met with silence, as he knew it would be. James Johnson had spent over 20 years in prison for the cold blooded murder of an elderly couple in a botched home invasion. The couple was not supposed to be home, so when they drove into their driveway Jimmy and his friends were waiting for them. His cohorts ran while Jimmy bludgeoned the couple to death with a crowbar he had found in the garage. Jimmy was later killed by a rival inmate gang. He had taken his harsh leadership skills with him to the penitentiary. Could Lynn still love her old flame after thirty years and ten years after he was dead and buried? "Answer me this, Lynn since we're going down memory lane," Joe said, "Why did you say yes to my invitation to the homecoming dance if you apparently thought I was a wimp?" Lynn replied to Joe.

"I didn't say you were a wimp."

"Oh, excuse me, coward."

"You want the truth, Joe?"

"I'm asking you." He said.

"Because I was Lynnette Copeland, popular, adored, and a cheerleader. How could I not go to the dance, let alone show up by myself?"

"So you used me from the beginning?"

Lynn took a seat at the table. "I was 16, Joe. You clearly liked me; my boyfriend wasn't around so I said yes. Simple."

"Okay." Joe conceded. "Then maybe the better question is why did you continue to go out with me? I mean why did you marry me, Lynn?"

Lynn thought about that for a second, looking down at her fingers intertwined on the table. She finally spoke, hunching her shoulders once again. "You were nice to me. No man had ever been nice to me before, not my father …not even Jimmy. I never told him about us. I visited him for a few months when he first went to prison." she shook her head. "Soon he stopped accepting my visits and my letters. I went to see him one last time, pretended to be his sister. I borrowed her ratty jacket and the hat she always wore. He almost left when he saw it was me, but then he came over and sat down. He listened to me talk; I gave him the news of the neighborhood, and when I was finished, he told me to never come back, to forget about him." Lynn chuckled mysteriously, "I pleaded with him to let me stay, to let me come back. I even asked him to marry me so we could have conjugal visits. I said I would do anything." Lynn snorted as she thought back. "He was so cruel. He told me I meant nothing to him. He said I was only a high school piece of ass, and he only dated me because I was popular, and his friends had dared him. But, when I looked back at him as I was leaving, I knew he wasn't telling the truth. He loved me, but he wanted me to have a life; he wanted me to be free."

"So you married me by default. And here I always thought you married me because you saw the difference between me and Jimmy. I thought you chose real love over bullshit."

"I chose life over death. I moved on, like he wanted me to. I have always chosen life over death. That's why I don't understand your insistence on hospice so soon. You didn't even try any experimental treatments for Sam."

"I did what our daughter wanted to do. Besides, I actually listened to the doctor while he was speaking. Her condition is advanced, Lynn. Sam's been living with this for awhile, long before she told us."

Lynn slammed her hand down on the wooden table. "Why don't you fight?" she yelled. "Fight for our family, fight for *your* daughter! Sam's weak, but she needs our strength! You can't think of her as an adult now. She's our baby and she needs our guidance. She needs her father to be strong for her." Lynn rose up from her seat. "Maybe you can't be. Maybe you don't know how to be strong, but I do." Lynn walked towards Joe and began to pass him when Joe took hold of her arm, stopping her.

"You asked why I didn't fight back that day. I didn't fight back because the coach was watching. I knew that if I did fight back, I would have been expelled. If I had gotten expelled, I would have lost my football scholarship to Michigan State. If I lost my scholarship, I wouldn't have been able to go to college, and I wouldn't have been able to land a good enough job to marry you and have kids. See, even then I was thinking of our future, I was thinking of us. You may not have loved me, Lynn, but I have always loved you."

Lynn turned and looked at her husband. "Yeah? Prove it." Lynn said flatly, then left Joe alone in the dark room.

TWENTY-FIVE

"Kenny?" Samantha said when she opened her eyes and stretched out a limp left arm to the body sitting in the chair by her bed. The sun was streaming in from the window behind the figure, darkening the features. Samantha wasn't sure if it was morning or evening. The more she reached towards it the further back the chair appeared to go. "Kenny?" she said again, *"Kenny please.....take me...."* Samantha's words were barely audible. A hand came towards her as the figure stood up and grasped her hand. *Not yet...* Samantha heard his voice clearly so she opened her eyes wider to the figure standing above her. It bent down closer to her face and she realized that it was not Kenny, but her volunteer, Jenna who had been sitting there waiting for Samantha to wake up.

"No, don't get up, not yet." Jenna said as she grasped Samantha's hand and arm, helping her back onto the bed after nearly falling off of it.

"Oh Jenna, it's you." Samantha said with a distinct sound of disappointment. Her voice was cracking. She tried to clear her throat, and Jenna was right there with a small glass of water. Samantha sipped it gratefully. She felt as if she had been sleeping for days.

"What time is it?" she asked Jenna.

"Almost three o'clock. Are you hungry? Your mother made you some soup." Jenna gestured at the tray sitting on the rolling food table that Lynn had purchased. It was an actual tray from a hospital supply store. Jenna walked over and rolled it from the foot of the bed to place in front of her. Samantha sat up with Jenna's quick assistance. She was getting used to assistance to move, but Jenna was the only one she didn't mind accepting the aid from. With her father it was okay; she just went into child mode. With Samantha's mother, however, never. Jenna made it tolerable somehow, allowing Samantha to lean into her when needed without a hint of humiliation. There was no judging with Jenna.

As Samantha grabbed the soup spoon, she noticed that her clothes had been changed. She was wearing her plaid pajamas instead of her usual pink gown. She looked from side to side trying to remember changing them or at least having them changed by someone. She couldn't remember. The last thing she remembered was her nurse Trish checking her pulse. There were new things in the room, new equipment. There was an oxygen tank by the bed along with an IV drip. Further into the room, over by her seating area where she had spent many days and nights watching TV, laughing with her girlfriends, and making out with Kenny and others, there was a wheelchair and bedside commode. All of it looked startlingly out of place around her things. It was as if her childhood bedroom was transforming into a hospital room right before her eyes. But had all of this equipment gotten here within hours of her apnea episode?

Samantha jerked her head to Jenna. "How long have I been sleeping?" she asked her.

Jenna heard a bit of panic in her voice. "Well, I came by on Tuesday. Your mother said that you had a bad night and that you were resting. So I called on Wednesday to check in on you, and your father told me you were still pretty much out of it. Then when I came by today, your mother told me to come on up and sit with you. I've been here since about one."

Samantha tasted her soup, it was still warm. "Oh man, I'm sorry you had to sit here for two hours."

Jenna sat back down. "I didn't mind, Sam, I had my book to read." Jenna flashed the book at Samantha then replaced it in her purse.

"Oh yeah? What's it about?" Samantha began to eat, and found she was really hungry. With each bite she felt better.

Jenna giggled, feeling embarrassed to say. "Just one of those silly romance novels."

"Romance? What, like Fabio romance where the hero rescues the damsel in distress?"

"Pretty much." Jenna said. "It's set in the early nineteenth century. A princess is captured after the king is murdered. She is locked in a dungeon, but the guard who's assigned to watch her falls in love with her and decides to help her escape. So, right now they're running through the back hills of France."

"So have they done it yet?" Samantha mocked.

"No, there is a lot of looking into each other eyes, and almost kisses, but no sex. The princess, of course, hated the gaurd because he was one of the guys who captured her, but she is learning to trust him since they are on the run."

"Ooooh sexual tension, I love it." Samantha laughed. "How do you read that stuff?"

Jenna hunched her shoulders, picking the book back up again. "My mother read romance novels all the time. She liked them because they were period pieces set in times and places that didn't remind her of what was happening today. She loved reading because she was engulfed in the story, the characters, the scenery, you know?" Jenna turned the book over and over in her hands as Samantha watched her. "I was going through some of my mother's things the other day and came across it. This was the last book she was reading. I don't think she got the chance to finish it before..." Jenna's words trailed off.

"Before she died." Samantha finished Jenna's sentence. The women looked at each other and nodded. Samantha saw the hurt in Jenna's eyes from the loss of her mother. It was a pain she had known herself with the death of Kenny. Suddenly she had a thought. "I have to show you something." She said, pushing away her tray and scooting up to get out of bed.

"Do you think you should get up, Sam? How do you feel?" Jenna asked rising up to assist her.

Samantha swatted away her hands. "I'm fine, just needed to eat. I've been in this bed, apparently, for days. I'm getting out!" she brushed past Jenna. Her legs were wobbly, but she chose to ignore it. She made it over to her closet and stripped off her pajamas, replacing them with her favorite comfortable jeans and an old UofM t-shirt. Jenna was right behind her as she left the bedroom and headed downstairs.

Lynn was coming up the stairs. "Sam, you should get back in bed." She ordered yet Samantha was not listening to her and skirted past her. Lynn looked at Jenna. "Jenna?" she said, with an expression of *do something*!

"She'll be fine Mrs. Mills, I'm with her." Jenna said surprisingly confident.

"Yes see, Jenna's with me. I'm fine." Samantha taunted her mother as she reached the landing, then turned and headed out to the back yard.

Jenna gave Lynn an apologetic look, but Lynn only glanced from Jenna to her daughter coldly; then she turned and continued up the stairs without another word.

"You like antagonizing her, don't you?" Jenna said to Samantha as she followed her past the patio out towards the garden.

Samantha paused and looked at Jenna. "Sometimes being a bitch is all a woman has to hold onto." She said in the voice of Vera Donovan from

Delores Claiborne. Samantha let out an evil snicker, then started walking again through the garden. She took a sharp left and lead Jenna down the long curving path to the gazebo.

When Jenna saw the white structure with the plants, flowers, and vines all around, it she had a strong memory of her mother for some reason. Jenna didn't know why, maybe from the sort of books she read because this gazebo was like it was placed here from out of one of those romance novels. Jenna would not have been surprised if a fairy or an elf stepped out from behind it.

Samantha sat down on the swing and Jenna joined her. "This is my private place." She told Jenna.

"It's beautiful." Jenna said, and then rethought it. "No, it's enchanting."

"Yes!" Samantha said and smiled brightly because that was the best way to describe the place, although that term had never really occurred to her. "It is enchanting." Samantha said, pushing her feet on the ground to start the swing's motion. "My father built it when he was putting down the pavers for my mother's garden and all that. He must have seen a little dirt path that lead back to this opening in the brush and decided to keep laying down the pavers all the way back here. I think he built it to get away from my mom, you know, to have a place to take a nap, work on the computer etc… You know there's even an electrical outlet back here?" Samantha told Jenna.

"Really?"

Samantha pointed at a cement block that had a metal panel with a hatch. She opened it and revealed two outlets. "I think it's there so he can plug in his laptop without having to recharge in an hour or something. He could stay out here for as long as he wants." Samantha tilted her head back on the swing and looked up through the trees at the blue sky. "I rarely came out here when I was younger. Too busy partying and being a teenager I guess. Kenny and I sat out here a few times when he would visit. That was nice, romantic."

"I could see how it would be very romantic back here. It's so private and peaceful." Jenna commented, looking around. Trees were behind them and to the side. Thick brush was all around except for the path. In the far distance, neighboring homes could be made out.

"Very, but since living back home, I come out here all the time now. One night I even fell asleep, and my dad carried me back into the house. I had fallen on the path trying to make it back in. I guess I was too weak that night. I fear the time when I can't make it out here at all. You can't even see this place from the house. You can see the lantern's light through the trees, but just barely."

"Do you get scared?" Jenna asked Samantha.

"About dying?"

"Yes." Jenna replied.

Samantha thought about it for a moment. "Not as much as you'd think. I think I get angry mainly, angry at the fact that my life has stopped. I'll never have any kids, never get married, and never have a home of my own like this. It's beginning to feel like I never left here, never went to college, never moved to New York. It's like I was just on vacation there. That life is becoming a blur, it's strange." Samantha said.

"Tell me about your life in New York." Jenna urged.

Samantha laughed. "It was busy! I loved it there. I remember when I first got there I was so terrified, so sure that I would be mugged every time I left my apartment building or left the office. I lived there for seven years, never mugged once. I feel like I've missed out on a New York experience I should have had." Samantha and Jenna both laughed at that. "But after several months that fear went away and I started enjoying the city. It's not like any other city. Manhattan was the downtown that went on forever. I got used to the constant noise, the cars, the people. I came back home to visit for the holidays, and I practically went crazy from the silence! It was odd."

"I don't think I could live in the city. I hate even going into Detroit with the traffic and parking nightmares." Jenna told Samantha.

"Yeah, but in New York people walk everywhere. I had a car but I paid a ridiculous amount of money just to keep it parked. Eventually I sold it and simply rented a car when I needed to. But I rarely needed to."

"It must have been expensive to live there."

"Yeah, I guess. But I had a good job plus I had savings, my Dad made sure of that. I couldn't imagine moving there with no money and no plan. Yet millions of people do. It didn't remind me of home. I think that's why so many people move to New York because of that. Now, in the Burroughs, like the Bronx, Brooklyn, Harlem people have lived there all of their lives, and grew up there, but, in Manhattan, most people were imported. They moved there to get away from their small town lives."

"And you wanted to forget?"

"I did." Samantha admitted darkly.

"But this house is so great, so much space and land. I would have loved growing up in a house like this." Jenna marveled, remembering the small home she grew up in.

"I don't deny that I had a pretty cushy life, never wanted for anything. I guess money doesn't buy you happiness."

"Most people who say that have always had money." Jenna told her.

Samantha nodded. "Yeah, I guess so. I admit I didn't think about money growing up. I mean, I knew people didn't have it as nice as I did, but I never really saw poverty around me. I went to a private school, I went to the mall, I hung out at my friend's houses, which were comparable to my own, and so it never really touched me. But that was also my parent's doing, mainly my mother to keep all things bad at arm's length. She has an idea of a perfect world and she made sure that everyone played their respective parts in it. If you deviated from that world, even a fraction, hell surely broke loose." Samantha explained.

"Were your parents wealthy growing up?" Jenna asked.

Samantha made an exaggerated face of repulsion. "No way! My dad's family was a working class family, and my mother's family was pure project ghetto trash, as she lovingly calls them, even to this day. My dad works for Chrysler. He's a mechanical engineer, by trade, but he has worked on the executive levels for a long time. He's a hard worker. My mom is a housewife, and loves it. I think my dad bought this house, which he probably couldn't afford back then, in order to give my mother a lifestyle she fantasized about. All of this is my mother's dream, except for this little patch of land."

"I see," said Jenna.

"Yeah, my father is a modest man with simple tastes, but because of her, he made investments to further strengthen their situation as well as working his ass off for *the man*, so she can shop at Neiman Marcus and have dinner parties."

"And he provided you with a good life." Jenna reminded her.

"Absolutely, yes, I love my father. I'm going to hate leaving him here alone with her." Samantha admitted somberly.

Jenna looked at her feeling a sinking in her stomach. "You mustn't think about that, they'll have each other. You just focus on each day and don't worry about the things you can't change." Jenna felt stupid giving such a stock answer, but she wasn't sure what to say to someone dying; however, she did think it unhealthy to dwell on what would happen after you are gone.

Samantha shuddered a bit next to her on the swing, "I hope he gets away from her. I hope he leaves this place and never looks back." She said, her voice quivering.

Her words made Jenna lean over and observe her more closely. Samantha was crying. Jenna scooted over closer and placed a calming hand on her back, rubbing her gently.

Samantha closed her eyes to Jenna's touch and without warning, she let out tortured sobs and fell to the side onto Jenna's shoulder. *"I'm scared...I'm so scared."* She wept desperately.

Jenna held Samantha tightly, instinctively rocking back and forth. "It's okay." She said and repeated it again and again as Samantha cried. Those were words Jenna's mother would whisper to her when she was a child when she had hurt herself or was feeling sad. Yet, for Samantha, it would not be ok; she was dying. There was no amount of soothing words or rocking that would ever change that fact.

Nevertheless, Jenna sat there with her as she released the pain inside. Jenna had logged over eight volunteer hours that day, and she was perfectly fine with it. She would have logged more, but Samantha was exhausted and Jenna had watched her fall back asleep. The sun was setting before they made their way back up to the house, and before Jenna got back in her car and headed to her own home.

TWENTY-SIX

Jenna drove up to The Whitney and pulled into the valet area. Saturday night came fast, a lot faster than she had anticipated. Jenna had spent the better part of the day at Somerset Mall looking for an appropriate dress for the Martinique Ball. Finally she decided on something only two hours before she needed to leave for the gala event. She had gotten her nails done that Friday, so that was not a hassle, only the dress. She had teased Matt about not owning a tuxedo, but she did not own a formal gown herself, and there was no renting that. Aside from running up and down the aisles of Nordstrom searching for the perfect thing to wear, Jenna was worried about Adrian. She hadn't heard from him since he left two weeks before. He was supposed to only be gone for a few days, yet that Friday had past and Adrian had not returned.

Adrian was a grown man, known to be flighty and would disappear for months, but still, Jenna was worried about him. It was also not unlike him to straight up lie about where he was going and when he would return just so he could get out the door without much of an explanation. Jenna finally decided to put thoughts of Adrian out of her mind and concentrate on the evening, instead. Even though she was going to this event alone, she didn't quite feel date-less. With a weird and wonderful feeling, Jenna felt that Matt was meeting her there, which was the reason why she painstakingly searched for the perfect outfit.

Jenna had settled on a form-fitting, long, black, lace gown with a beige satin lining. Without time to go to the hair salon, she just loosely pinned her hair up in a soft twist. "Welcome to The Whitney." The young valet said to Jenna as he offered a hand to help her out of her car. She immediately took it because she was not sure how she would be maneuvering in her five inch heels. Jenna stepped out of her car and, for a frightful half second, she thought she might slip on the end of the long gown but managed to recover quickly. The valet smiled as she regained her secure hold onto the concrete. She tried not to show her humiliation. The valet didn't seem to notice, for that Jenna tipped him nicely.

As she skip-hopped onto the sidewalk leading into the venue, Jenna's phone rang. She managed to pry it out of her little purse before it stopped ringing. Reading the caller ID she frowned in confusion not recognizing the number. "Hello?" she answered.

"Jenna?" It was Zach. "Sorry to bother you, but I didn't know who else to call." He sounded dangerously close to being frantic.

"Hey Zach, what's wrong?" Jenna replied and stepped to the side as other guests were arriving.

"Has Zabbie called you? No one has heard from her since early this week. A couple of weeks ago she said she was taking a quick trip to L.A. for the weekend but she hasn't returned."

Jenna was shocked. "What? She hasn't called you at all or her parents?"

"No." Zach replied. "Well she did call last week saying she was going to extend her trip longer but, after that nothing except a cryptic response to my hundreds of texts to her."

"When was that?" Jenna asked.

"A couple of nights ago. After me texting her for days she finally responded with: *Sorry I haven't called. I will be home tomorrow.* And that was it. That was Thursday, today is Saturday. I went by her place but she wasn't there."

"Oh my, well Zach, I know Zabbie was having some nervousness about getting married and planning the wedding; maybe she just needed time to clear her head. It happens." Jenna found it very coincidental that she hadn't heard from Adrian in two weeks either, but kept that to herself.

"She never mentioned to me that she was nervous." Zach said. "I mean the wedding isn't for months yet. I thought cold feet happened closer to the date."

"Yeah, but her mother has been pushing her to make plans. She's really been relentless. Zabbie has old friends in California, as you know, so maybe she just needed a final girl's away vacation. It's quite normal. I wouldn't worry about it, if I were you."

"Don't you find it strange that you weren't invited to this girl's away thing? Or did you know about it and were told not to tell me?" Zach accused harshly, but Jenna decided to ignore it.

"No Zach, I didn't know anything about it. Zabbie does have a group of friends that I don't really know. Zabbie is really my friend. I'm not friends with a lot of her friends. I guess it was a societal thing of old families knowing old families." Jenna responded.

Zach paused. "Yeah, that's true." Jenna was a little annoyed by the acknowledgement of the separatism of those who come from old money and everyone else, a fact that Zach clearly understood and endorsed. "I'm just worried." He said finally.

"What is her family saying, Zach? Have they heard from her?" Jenna asked getting a little irritated. This is a side of Zach, she's not used to.

"That's just it. Even though they've told me that they haven't heard from her, they don't seem real worried either." He said sarcastically.

"So, you think they're lying?"

"Yeah, a little bit, wouldn't be the first time." Zach admitted.

"Hmmm....well like I said Zach, I'm sure there is nothing to worry about, especially since her mother hasn't called the police. Sounds like Zabbie just needed some space." Jenna started walking again towards the entrance of The Whitney. "Sorry to break off so soon, but I am just heading into a fundraising event... black tie." Jenna told Zach.

"Oh wow, I'm sorry, Jenna." He said, sounding embarrassed.

"No problem Zach. I'll try and call Zabbie tonight to see if she picks up. I'm sure everything is alright." After hanging up with Zach, Jenna dialed Adrian's number; surprisingly he picked up on the second ring.

"Adrian? Hey, are you still in New York?" Jenna asked.

"New York?" he asked as if he didn't have the faintest clue what she was talking about. "Oh, New York, no I'm back. In fact I'm pulling into your driveway right now. I plan on taking a long hot bath and hitting the sac! I hope you've shopped, I'm starving!"

"Oh, so you're back?" Jenna again was shocked. "Adrian, have you heard from Zabbie?" she asked him. There was a long pause then he finally responded.

"Nope."

"Are you sure she hasn't contacted you?"

"Why would she do that?" Adrian asked flatly.

"Her fiancé just called me. He hasn't seen her and was asking if I knew where she was."

"Have you tried calling her?" Adrian asked.

"No, I haven't." Jenna replied.

"But you're asking me... doesn't make much sense."

"No, I guess not." Jenna admitted. Again there was a long silence.

"Okay, well I'm going to find me something to eat, get in the tub, and crash. Talk to you when you get in. Where are you by the way?"

"I'm at the charity ball for hospice. I told you about it." Jenna responded.

"Oh yeah. Okay, talk to you later." Adrian hung up, leaving Jenna to stand in the foyer area of The Whitney with a puzzled look on her face. She didn't quite know what, but something wasn't right. Zach never called her before. He had never sounded so off center. He was always a very light and easy going guy. Even if Zach dressed in tattered jeans and an old t-shirt, you would still be able to tell he was from money, old money. It was in the way he moved; it was in the way his eyes fell upon you. The air around him was almost imperial, noble, a trait that, Jenna was sure, could only come from growing up with generational wealth. Zabbie had the same air about her.

And Adrian had sounded distracted as if he was trying to get her off the phone. Jenna shook her head; she knew Adrian didn't go to New York.

"Wow!" came a voice behind her that made Jenna swing around. Matt standing with a look of boyish awe on his face that made Jenna blush.

"Mr. Ames, I see you found a tux!" she joked.

Matt comically posed for her. "You like it? I have to return it to my uncle, who's a waiter, tomorrow."

She swatted at him, "You're silly!" Matt presented his elbow to her. She curtsied and slid her left arm around it as Matt led her into the foyer where the grand staircase loomed before them. "Piezas Sobre Cantos Populares" by Granados was being piped in through speakers from the live orchestra playing in the bar area. The music created an atmosphere of enchantment.

"They say it's haunted." Matt whispered to Jenna.

"The staircase?" she asked.

"The whole place," Matt said. "People have reported seeing shadowy figures on all levels of the house." Matt wiggled his fingers in front of him for effect.

"You're lying, haunted? Really?" Jenna laughed looking around.

"Yep. Both David Whitney and his wife Sarah died here, and they still roam the halls."

"That's crazy." Jenna said disbelievingly.

"You don't believe in ghosts?" Matt asked.

"I don't know. I've never seen one, and if they're anything like Hollywood makes them out to be that would be really horrible. I would like to think that my family, who have passed on, are in Heaven sitting on clouds, not hanging out here walking around."

"I guess it would be pretty sad." Matt admitted.

"Do you believe in ghosts?" Jenna asked.

"I've never seen one either, but some of the stories I've heard have been pretty convincing." Matt replied.

"What, you mean like the story about this beautiful restaurant being haunted?"

"No, like my patients who have seen their loved ones right before its time for them to go. It's like the come and get them. Too many of those stories have been told to just shrug it off." Matt said.

Jenna thought about that. "That sounds kind of nice and pleasant. I would hope my mother would be waiting for me, you know, on the other side."

"That is a nice thought." Matt smiled at Jenna and she returned it warmly.

"But spirits here? It's just too creepy of an idea." Jenna said shuddering at the thought.

"My dear, the only spirits that are here are the ones inside your champagne flute." Dave Chatman said as he appeared in front of them and handed Jenna a glass of the sparkling wine.

"Jenna, this is Dave Chatman, he is the COO of Community Hospice. Dave this is Jenna, one of our newest volunteers." Jenna greeted Dave and accepted the glass he offered.

"Jenna Steele," Dave said in complete recognition. "I would know such a beautiful Diamond Club member anywhere. On behalf of Community Hospice, I would personally like to thank you for your most generous donation."

"You're very welcome." Jenna bowed her head slightly. "My mother was on hospice care at the end of her life, and I know she would have wanted me to give back."

"I see that you are continuing to give back by volunteering, which we genuinely appreciate." Dave said.

"Yes, I have my first patient and we're getting to know each other. She's finally warming up to me." Jenna beamed, glancing at Matt.

Dave moved in closer to her. "That's fantastic. I think it is so wonderful when volunteers, like yourself, are able to be there for the patient, to sit with them, read, just get to know them. I feel it takes a special kind of person to do that. You could have stopped with your monetary donation but you went further, very commendable and appreciated!"

Jenna was a bit taken aback by his comment, it seemed rehearsed. "Thank you, it's very rewarding." She responded and hoped he didn't detect the trace of sarcasm.

"Before dinner is served, there are a few people I would like to formally introduce the two of you to." Dave announced. He led them through the crowd of socialites, dignitaries, and donors with the grace of a humming bird. Jenna was sure this was Dave's expertise. He recited off names along with their brief bios with ease. It was like a dance the way he moved from person to person with perfect timing, smiling in the perfect places, laughing in others. Jenna also noticed when Dave got to the company executives he made it a point to highlight Matt's career accomplishments. It began to feel like she was in the midst of a mini marathon interview with Matt as the lead candidate.

After the whirlwind of faces and introductions, Dave, Matt, and Jenna made their way to the first rows of tables to be seated. "Wait, I think our table is back there." Matt said to Dave.

"This is a Diamond Club member, Matt; she sits up front. And, lucky for you, you get to be seated next to her." Dave laughed at Matt and slapped him playfully on the shoulder, which Matt did not appreciate.

"Looks like we got the best seats in the house," Jenna said, sitting down. Matt was still standing and watched Dave make his way to his own seat beside his wife. Jenna tugged at his jacket. "Sit down, Matt, it's okay." She teased him.

Matt turned and sat next to Jenna. He cocked his head at her, "It's okay?" he questioned her comment to get him to sit.

"You seem a little anxious when we were talking with Dave." Jenna said.

"No...not anxious," Matt answered awkwardly.

"Is he grooming you for another position?" Jenna asked and shifted in her chair to see him better. She waited patiently for a response. She knew she had just started and had only been volunteering a few months, but somehow, a future without Matt at the helm made Jenna feel uneasy.

Matt paused and returned her gaze. He never realized how striking the colors of her eyes were. They were brown with a hint of hazel around the rim. Her hair was pulled upward with soft strands that curled across her face and down her long neck. At this moment he was sure she was the most beautiful woman he had ever seen in his whole life. He was also sure that he couldn't lie to her.

"Yes. It's for an executive position in marketing, head of the department." He disclosed.

Jenna reached out and adjusted Matt's grey satin bow tie. His vest matched the bow tie. The suit was a stylish black that fit him well. Her eyes traveled over him, examining not only his choice of attire but his fresh new haircut. She noticed that the natural fine blonde hair shown even more when his hair was shorter. She knew that if he grew his hair out it would appear much kinkier. His African American roots would definitely dominate despite the bluish hue of his eyes.

Jenna was attracted to him; it was more than just some school girl crush she had developed when she first saw him. There was more to this man, something much deeper. It was the way he had spoken about hospice and volunteering at training. He wasn't just reciting an ever repeating lecture, no he meant what he was saying, she felt sure of that.

"What are you thinking?" Matt asked, after her gaze lingered.

Jenna woke up from her thoughts of Matt and asked, "How does a man who doesn't own a tuxedo suddenly decide to become a part of this world?"

Matt frowned a bit, not really understanding the correlation. "What do you mean?" he asked.

"You know, how they say the clothes make the man?" Jenna replied.

"Yes…" Matt was interested to see where she was going.

"Well, your friend Dave, he's wearing a simple black tuxedo, but I bet he has two or three more in his closet. He looks rather comfortable in it. But you, I can see you going around searching for the perfect one, but I can also bet that what you paid for yours he paid five times more."

"Does it look like I'm wearing a cheap suit?" Matt laughed nervously. "I mean I paid almost five hundred bucks for this."

Jenna placed a hand on his knee, which sent surprising chills through Matt. "No." she began clarifying, "What I mean is…" she lowered her voice, "and I don't know you very well, but I feel this is not you."

The server came by then and placed a light salad in front of Matt and Jenna, and that stopped the conversation. Matt sat back for a moment continuing to look at Jenna as she started eating. He wasn't sure if he had just been insulted or not. Was she saying that he was not the executive type? Wasn't he classy enough to wear a tuxedo or be part of this crowd? Granted, the room was filled with very wealthy philanthropists and influential people, movers and shakers, who did great things and made big decisions for the city and community, but didn't he also belong? Okay, he was at the front table because Jenna, his volunteer had donated twenty five thousand dollars. He was not sitting in the back where some of the other regular staff was seated, but couldn't he fit in if he wanted to? What's wrong with wanting more, Matt wondered? What's wrong with wanting to be a part of such a crowd? Is it the Jesus factor where you can only be good if you're poor and suffering?

As the night went on, Matt ate the fine meal placed in front of him. He drank the champagne and enjoyed the entertainment provided, but Jenna's words never left his mind. Once dinner was over and the event had moved out to the garden area, he snuck away to a corner of the garden and stared at the Detroit skyline. They were gifted a clear starry night with a cool summer breeze blowing. It was refreshing. Jenna mingled socially with many at the gathering. She had an easy way about her, he observed, and that drew people to her. You would have thought she had been volunteering for years the way she conversed about the topic.

"Things seem to be winding down," Jenna said, coming up behind Matt. He grunted in accord. "Are you okay?" she asked.

"Yes." Matt said, producing a smile. "Did you enjoy the music?"

"Oh yes, the string quartet was lovely. I don't always get to hear that kind of music live." Jenna explained.

"Do you like classical music?" Matt asked her.

Jenna nodded. "My mother used to listen to a lot of instrumentals, classical, jazz, R&B. One night she was listening to this local Detroit jazz artist, Brian O'Neal. She said that his main theme was No Words Necessary and she wholeheartedly agreed. She would say sometimes the words in songs got in the way, so I started just listening to the music and she was right."

"I think I've heard of him. He plays with Kem."

"Yes. I went out and bought all of his CDs for her. My mother had a thing for unsigned artists. She thought they were more authentic somehow."

"Is that how you feel? You see a kind of honor in not being commercialized, glossy, and glamorous?" Matt asked, still staring into the night.

Suddenly, Jenna got it. "Oh my goodness, I offended you earlier." She realized, touching his arm and making him look at her. Matt shook his head. "I did though, didn't I?" Jenna said. "I'm sorry I didn't mean to. I wasn't saying that you….I mean I was just saying that…." Jenna was trying to find the right words. "Look, I don't know you well enough to judge you like that, I'm sorry."

"You were right." Matt said, looking around at the people. "This isn't me. I like what I do. I love working with volunteers; I love training; I love hearing a family go on and on about how wonderful their volunteer is. I'm always in awe when I know a volunteer leaves the comfort of their home to go out in the middle of the night to sit with a patient taking their last breath. I'm proud to be a part of that."

"What you do is important, Matt. I was so scared; I was thinking who am I to volunteer with dying people; maybe my monetary contribution was enough, but you coached me, you encouraged me to try. With your words from training and what you said to me, I stepped out of my comfort zone and, in fear, went to my first assignment. I met Samantha, who is a wonderful woman and someone I greatly admire. She did something with her life; she went to college, and had a great career in New York! Hell, I didn't even complete community college. Now Sam is dying, and it's so unfair! She's so young and should have her whole life ahead of her! But if I can be there for her, if I can sit and just listen to her, and hold her hand, I know it makes a difference to her, Matt. Sam's mother is a pill, Sam has practically isolated herself from the world, and if it wasn't for hospice, if it wasn't for a volunteer visiting with her. I shudder to think of her sitting alone in that back yard, staring into nothingness. I mean I'm no nurse, I barely know what to say, but I think it means something to Sam that someone is there just to sit, just for her, you know? So it matters; what you do matters, greatly."

Matt marveled at her enthusiasm. "I know that's why I've stayed. But Jenna, it doesn't pay."

"Who cares about that? The work is more important!" she protested.

"I have a son. There's child support, private school, sports. It takes money to be a father. Being a director of volunteer services may be a virtuous job but the salary is for shit. It's just not enough. As my son gets older it's only going to get worse, Jake will need more, and college? Let's not even talk about that. I have to be realistic, Jenna." Matt's smile went away.

"I do understand that. Have you asked for a raise?" she suggested. She watched Matt chuckle at that. "I mean if they're willing to promote you to an executive position, you should be worth a raise."

"It's not me; it's the position. It's not the company; it's the profession across the board, at least in hospice. The salary cap is pretty low. It is what it is." He told her.

"Wow, that's pretty defeatist." Jenna responded.

"Like I said, it is what it is."

"You gotta fight for it, Matt! Not to keep bringing up training, but I do remember you saying that hospice could not be a hospice without volunteers! I would think that the person who recruits, trains, and manages these volunteers would be pretty damned important to the company!"

"You would think," Matt agreed flippantly.

"No, I'm serious. You have to fight! You have to make them see your worth." Jenna said adamantly.

"They don't respect us." Matt tried to explain.

"Well then, you have to make them respect you! You can't quit! Going off to work in marketing may make your pockets richer, but will that help volunteer services?" Jenna asked.

Matt hunched his shoulders pointing his hands dramatically to his chest. "What am I supposed to do? I can't change anything!" he said.

"You just told me that you love your job, that you love volunteers and what they do. I just told you how much you encouraged me to keep at it. I just told you how grateful I am. Don't you believe in this?" Jenna asked.

"What do you want me to do, march on Washington?"

"I want you to fight for us." She said somberly.

"Fight for you?" he asked.

"If they don't think what you guys do as managers is important, then it's the same as saying they don't think that what we, as volunteers, do is important. There's this mandate to have volunteers but, if across the board, they don't really think we're valuable then that mandate could change. If nothing else, you feeling this way could trickle down to how you do your job. Maybe good people like you will quit and be replaced by people who only see the position as a stepping stone to something better." Jenna explained.

"That's already the case. People take this job for a few years; then they often move on; that's if they want a real career. Or they move into another field of volunteer services, like the government, who take volunteering a lot more seriously."

"Hmmm…" Jenna thought for a moment. "What could be more serious than being with someone at the end of their life, than holding their hand while they take their last breath? You tell me, what's more serious than that?" she asked.

Matt knew Jenna was right. He had thought about it, yet with the pressures of the here and now it was often hard to look to the future. Fight the good fight? Sure it was a great concept, but did he really have the time or the luxury of pursuing it? Even as he agreed to take the credentialing exam that Sarah so desperately wanted them all to take, he had to question, was it really worth it? What really was the point? Yet, as he looked down at Jenna on this peaceful night, hearing her strong words of uprising, it did make Matt think again.

Jenna gasped loudly, putting a hand to her chest. Matt was startled by her sudden wide eyes. "We have to dance!" she proclaimed and without waiting for his response, she grabbed Matt's hand and led him back into the building straight to the dance floor. "I love this song!" was all the reason she gave to Matt. Soon they were on the dance floor and danced to the song "The Way You Look Tonight", no words, just the band playing.

Matt hadn't danced in years and couldn't remember dancing to a song that did not require him to grind. None of that mattered because the proximity of Jenna's body to his melted away any thoughts of making a fool of himself in front of his colleagues. It was her smell, her hair, her soft movements, it was her and, God help him, he couldn't stop the emotion welling up inside of him. Crossing the lines, be damned. He couldn't help what was happening inside of him, Matt wanted Jenna desperately.

Matt hoped Jenna would forgive him for pulling her closer to him, the same way that she hoped he would forgive her for resting her head on his shoulder. And as the song ended and other dancers started shaking their bodies to the higher tempo of an old Bee Gees tune, Matt kept her close, lifted her chin with his hand and kissed her, a kiss Jenna did not resist.

TWENTY-SEVEN

Matt opened his eyes to an out of focus dark winged creature peering down at him. At first all he could make out was the silhouette of a woman's body, possibly naked, standing in a graceful ballet stance with arms stretched up towards her head. The wings appeared to be enormous in comparison to the body. Matt took in a breath and began blinking in an effort to bring clarity to his surroundings. This naked winged woman was not real; she was a bronzed figurine sitting prominently next to a bedside lamp. The room was unfamiliar and quite large, he noticed, definitely not his rather average sized bedroom in his own home.

Things were fuzzy as he awakened, yet he did know where he was and what had transpired the night before. He remembered walking Jenna to get her car from the valet. He remembered a rather long good night kiss, which had been quite intense, though not as intense as the events that were to follow. They had mutually agreed that the night should not end at the charity ball; therefore, he followed Jenna to her home, a very large and beautiful mini mansion where they enjoyed more drinks, snacks and intriguing conversations. He remembered Jenna's soft laughter at his ridiculous jokes and how she felt in his arms. And the rest, yes, he did remember the rest. The rest was more vivid than any other part of the night. He had to admit he had gotten tipsy but not drunk, and neither was Jenna. It was mutual; it was wonderful; and it was a mistake!

Matt slowly, carefully, turned to look over his right shoulder. If Jenna was sleeping he did not want to wake her. It was morning but still quite early, only around seven a.m., if that. To his surprise Jenna was not in bed with him. The covers on her side of the large California King had been thrown aside when she had gotten up and left the room. Undoubtedly, she was feeling just as guilty as he was. He canvassed the room and saw that it was a suite with a small living area equipped with a TV and chairs, rather nicely decorated. To the left there was a bathroom, and this is where Matt was headed. The plan was to quickly splash water on his face, dress, and make a not-so-graceful hasty retreat. He was successful in the first part of his plan; he used the bathroom, and washed his face with hand soap. The world had come completely back into focus; his mind had definitely caught up to his actions.

What in the hell was wrong with him? Granted he had not made love in a few months, granted he could barely remember his last one night stand, but did that allow him to sleep with his volunteer? *"But she's beautiful"*, Matt whispered to his reflection in the mirror. His brain agreed with that, but Jenna was his employee for crying out loud, was he really that desperate? *"She's smart, funny, and the attraction is unbelievable!"* he whispered aloud again. Sure, all those things were true, but it was clearly a mistake. How are they supposed to have a working relationship now? *"She's not a one night stand."* No, of course not, how could she be? There were only two options Matt could come up with logically; he would have to fire her or marry her. *"I can't afford to lose a good volunteer! I'm going to have to marry her."*

"Matt?" Jenna was knocking gently at the door. "Are you okay?" she was asking.

Matt looked at the door in a slight panic, searching his mental directory for the most appropriate response, but he couldn't come up with one. He opened the door to see Jenna standing there draped in a flowing African caftan. His expression immediately changed from one of dread to one of elation. *God, she's gorgeous*, he thought and then spoke. "I gotta go." He slid by Jenna grabbing up his tuxedo which he had thrown carelessly on the floor by the bed.

"Um...would you like some coffee at least?" Jenna pointed at the small table in front of a large window.

Matt saw that there was not only coffee but two plates of eggs, bacon and bagels. *I need a cigarette*, he thought. "Oh wow, thanks." After slipping into his shirt and zipping up his pants, Matt walked over and sipped a bit of the coffee. He nodded in approval. "It's good." He told her.

"Then sit down, enjoy." Jenna sat in the seat across from Matt. She watched as he slowly made the decision to sit. He was doing what most men do; he was running. "Matt, I can see you're nervous," she began once he was seated.

"Nervous? No...just have to pick up my son...I had forgotten..." he lied.

Jenna just looked at him knowingly. "I know what we did last night was spontaneous and maybe a little crazy. You can blame it on the champagne but I wanted to be with you. I have no regrets." She reassured him.

"Neither do I!" Matt exclaimed. He reached out and touched her hand. "Jenna, I don't regret last night. It's just that you're…" he searched for the right word.

"Your volunteer and you're my boss?" she asked.

"There's no *rule* against it. Many managers have their spouses, girlfriends or whomever as volunteers. It just never happened to me. Most of my volunteers are either in their sixties or in their twenties. I'm in unknown territory." He admitted to Jenna.

"Don't worry, Matt. I'm not going to stalk you, I'm not going to quit. We're both adults. It was just sex." She told him matter-of-factly. Jenna paused, waiting for a response but Matt didn't give one. They shared a very pregnant awkward stare. She had to break it before she went mad. "Eat your eggs before they get cold."

Matt didn't have a clue what to say, so he ate his breakfast while they downgraded into small talk. They conversed on the charity event, their favorite foods, music and about hospice in general. Jenna told him about her patient and mentioned she would do more events. Matt opened his phone and checked his email to see what assignments he had available. Jenna agreed to take on two patients located in a nearby nursing home, as well as agreed to work a couple of upcoming health fairs. Matt made sure that she was not over extending herself, which she assured him she was not.

After breakfast he finished dressing and Jenna walked him to the door. To her delight, Matt took her in his arms and kissed her passionately. Despite her adult and logical speech of the night just being a casual event, Jenna could not lie to herself; it was much more than that for her, much deeper. She only hoped that he felt the same way, yet, with men, you could never really tell. Before he left, Matt promised to call her later that evening. Jenna nodded and watched him walk to his car and drive away. When the door closed, she leaned on it for a moment, closed her eyes, and remembered their fervor of the previous night. She just wanted to hold onto that sensation for awhile. Jenna smiled as she breathed in his scent still lingering on her. She giggled like a teenager thinking of him kissing her back, her neck, and her inner thighs.

"Well, well, well…" Adrian's voice broke her pleasing visions.

Startled, Jenna's eyes shot open, and she stood up straight. Adrian was smiling mischievously down at her from the top of the stairs. "Good Morning, Cousin." She greeted.

Adrian came downstairs. "Good morning to you too, Miss Mary Sunshine! I thought I was going to have to call the paramedics last night with all of those moans, groans, and shrieks coming from your room. I was like, damn, he's going to kill her! Or was it you killing him?" Adrian laughed wholeheartedly.

"Oh shut it!" Jenna said, heading away from him down the hall into the kitchen. Adrian was right on her heels.

"Come on, who was this guy?" he asked.

"None of your business!" Jenna protested.

"Look my cousin, my Imzadi, who has not had a relationship in years, who suddenly wakes me up from a deep sleep with mating calls that vibrate the whole house, I think I should at least know who he is!" Adrian demanded.

"Just a guy," Jenna said dismissively while cleaning up the skillet she had used to cook breakfast.

"Just a guy?" Adrian responded, "I thought I would see a repeat performance at the doorway just now the way you two were going at it. Nah, this is not just some guy."

"Jeez!" Jenna said and slammed the skillet into the sink and turned around to glare at Adrian. "So what if I had sex, big deal! Am I not entitled?"

"Absolutely." Adrian sat at one of the island stools. "I leave you alone for a couple of weeks and you bring home Don Juan. What did you do pick him up from that dance last night?"

"It was a charity ball, not a dance, and he is Director of Volunteer Services at the hospice where I volunteer."

"You slept with your boss? Look at you!" Adrian let out an amusing cat call, and then a bright light went off in his head. "That's why you started volunteering! I couldn't figure it out! I was like she donated some cash, okay sure, but why is she volunteering with hospice of all places, people dying and all that. Now I get it! You think you're slick!" he shook a comical finger at her.

"That is not why I'm volunteering, Adrian. Everyone is not as heartless as you. I want to make a difference, I want to give back." Jenna said unwaveringly.

"You gave back a lot last night! Bang! Bang! Bang! Bang!" Adrian stuck out his tongue while he did a little dance.

"Oh, will you shut up! I can do whatever I want. This is my house and if I want to bring a man home, I can bring a man home! I do not have to explain myself to the likes of you!" Jenna was getting upset.

Adrian held up his hands in surrender. "I'm sorry. You're right. I'm just teasing you." Adrian then got up, giving Jenna a quick hug which she rejected. "I'm glad you opened up, figuratively and literally. After everything, you needed a release. I was beginning to worry about you. You were about two steps away from buying a cat!" Adrian teased.

"Oh, ha ha!" Jenna was not amused. "So what happened to you? Where have you been for the last two weeks?" she asked.

Adrian paused, frowned, and looked up at her. "New York. Don't try to change the subject."

"I'm not changing the subject. Where were you…really?" she asked suspiciously.

"I told you. New York. I was helping a friend and getting paid. Anything else?"

"Yes, was Zabbie with you?" Jenna placed two stern hands on her hips.

"No, Elizabeth was not with me." Adrian said each word distinctly.

"Why don't I believe that?" Jenna asked.

"I have absolutely no idea why you don't believe me. Elizabeth is getting married. She has clearly made her choice. Not like there was much of a choice to make. You think her parents would have allowed her to end up with me? Nope, they do not want half Black half Arabic blood running through their WASP lineage. And you know that."

"Oh come on, Adrian, the Myers family is not racist. They're philanthropists, very liberal, and they have never given me that vibe."

"Yeah well, you never slept with their daughter either." He paused comically "or did you?"

Jenna waved him off. "Look, the Meyers are not racists. If they don't like you, it's because you're flighty, you have no real career…"

"What? I'm a jazz pianist." Adrian said, defending himself.

"Whatever Adrian, jazz pianist. You're a gambler, you hang around the mob." Jenna shot back.

"Now who's being racist? Just because a guy is Italian and his family owns a string of casinos does not make him mafia."

"Tony Bandino is not in the mafia?" Jenna asked disbelievingly.

"No! He's just Italian; he's a paisan from New York; he's a businessman."

Jenna shook her head in disbelief "Okay, whatever, Adrian. I'm going to get dressed." Jenna left him there.

Adrian stood there a moment listening to Jenna walk upstairs. His phone had begun to vibrate as she was leaving, so he waited for her to be out of earshot. Once it seemed the coast was clear he answered his phone. "Hey you…" If Jenna could see her cousin, she would have seen something she rarely saw on his face; he was blushing. Upstairs Jenna was trying to call Zabbie, but it went straight to voicemail.

TWENTY-EIGHT

Lynnette Mills was awake and dressed by five a.m. on Monday morning. With her husband still sleeping she closed the bedroom door behind her and hurried down the hall to her daughter's room. Samantha was asleep as well. Lynn shook Samantha's shoulders to awaken her. "Sam, Sam, I'm going to need you to get up." She ordered Samantha softly as soon as her eyes were open. Samantha moaned an inaudible murmur and tried to come to life as requested. She saw her mother dart back and forth in her room, grabbing her weekender bag from her closet and haphazardly stuffing underwear and clothes into it. Lynn ran into the adjoining bathroom and picked up Samantha's toiletries.

"Come on, Sam, we gotta go, let's go!" Lynn said as quietly and as sternly as she possibly could. She picked up Samantha's baggy jeans that she had pulled out of a drawer. Then Lynn removed Samantha's legs from under the covers and proceeded to dress her daughter. Samantha protested, not just from being handled like a five year old, but because of the piercing pain that was coming from every muscle in her body as her mother proceeded to dress her.

"Ahhh stop!" Samantha growled as she pushed her mother's hands away. "What are you doing?" she asked.

Lynn looked up at Samantha, realizing that her daughter's speech was extremely slurred. She could barely understand her. "We have a plane to catch, now let's go."

"Where's Dad?" Samantha asked. Her words were slurred because she was finding it increasingly hard to move her mouth and tongue.

"Don't worry about that; just get your shoes on." Lynn said and placed a pair of slip-on sneakers on Samantha's lap. She then ran over to where she had packed the overnight bag for Samantha's and scooped it up. Lynn looked around the room in a frenzied manner making sure she wasn't forgetting anything. She thought about hauling out the wheelchair but realized there was no way to get it on the plane so she abandoned that idea. Lynn swirled around and gazed at her daughter's progress. Samantha was just looking down at her shoes. Lynn quickly came back to her daughter's side and slipped the shoes onto Samantha's feet.

"Where are we going?" Samantha asked, although it sounded more like *wha eee goeeen.*

Lynn snapped her fingers in front of Samantha's face. "Are you okay? Can you walk?" she asked.

"I'm fine!" Samantha attempted to scream. The finger snapping was very annoying to her. Samantha tried to get up as Lynn helped her. Her legs were weak, feeling like they were about to buckle, but they didn't as she walked down the stairs with her mother guiding her.

"Okay, I'm going to take your bags to the car, Sam. If you need to rest just sit on the steps. I'll be right back...okay?" Lynn said while holding onto Samantha's shoulders as she assisted her to sit on the second step.

Samantha watched her mother fumble with her car keys, open the door, kick the door all the way open with a foot, then scoop up each of the bags and run outside. Samantha didn't understand why her mother was rushing around, nor did she understand why her father wasn't helping them. But what was even more alarming to Samantha was where they were going. Her mother had been very vague about that information. It was as if Samantha was being kidnapped. It was a ridiculous thought but then again this was her mother.

Once Lynn was outside, it gave Samantha a moment to focus on her speech. She moved her jaw around, listening to the bone pop inside her head. She tried to say hello. It came out "Haaallooow." It was like trying to talk with a mouthful of cotton balls. Samantha's eyes darted around in a tempered panic. She couldn't speak? What in the hell was going on?

"Heeeelllllow" Samantha attempted again, better this time but not normal. Samantha gripped the wooden stair post, taking in a deep breath as she did so. She cleared her thought; surely this was happening because it was so early. She took in another breath and tried again, "Hhhhelo." A wave of relief wafted over Samantha. It was not perfect, but it was better. She was just tired, the pain medication, yeah, that was it, the medication was making it hard for her to speak; that's all it was.

"Baby, are you alright?" Joe asked as he was he bounded down the stairs in a sudden sprint. He was awakened by the opening of the front door and by his bed being empty on Lynn's side. His alarm clock was not set to go off for another half hour, and it usually took the alarm to get him up. He tried to wake up as soon as he heard the alarm because Lynn did not like the sound. If the snooze button was pushed more than once, Joe had hell to pay. In the beginning of their marriage, Lynn was his alarm. She would wake up before him, fix breakfast and coffee, and gently woke him up so he could jump in the shower. Once he was dressed, Joe would stroll into the kitchen and eat the meal Lynn had prepared for him, but that was before Samantha was born and before they moved into this big house. Joe often longed for those days of living in their nice, yet small, bungalow and waking up to the smell of coffee and bacon. Those days ended quickly; it was almost as if Lynn was waiting for him to purchase this house but also to get pregnant because once both of those events occurred, Joe had to be awakened electronically.

"Did you fall, Sam? Did you get weak coming downstairs? Why are you dressed?" Joe asked the questions almost simultaneously.

Samantha turned around looking up at her fretful father. "I'm okay, Dad." She said and patted the hand he had placed on her shoulder.

"What's going on?" Joe asked and stepped past Samantha, heading for the open door. He looked outside. "What are you doing, Lynn?" It was still dark out even with the lights. Lynn was bent down in the back seat and did not rise up when he called. Joe took a mental note of his wife's disregard, then turned back to Samantha. "Where are you going?" he asked her.

"She didn't tell me." Samantha told her father. Her words were clearer but still labored.

"We're going to the Emory ALS Center in Atlanta." Lynn said as she appeared in the doorway. "Our flight leaves at 7 a.m."

Joe was, simply stated, dumbfounded. There were so many words running through his mind, making him unable to formulate them into rational sentences, so he just asked, "What?"

"Let's go, Sam." Lynn said and attempted to walk by Joe to help Samantha onto her feet. But Joe, however, grabbed Lynn's arm, stopping her in her tracks.

"You're not taking Sam anywhere until you tell me why you think she needs to suffer a plane ride all the way to Atlanta." He demanded.

"It's called a second opinion, Joe! It's called not taking shit at face value, it's called not giving up on your daughter, damn it!"

"You just don't get it do you?" Joe asked her.

"No, you don't get it!" Lynn yelled and jerked Samantha out of his grasp. "She is thirty five years old! She has a right to live, and we have an obligation to try! I know that concept may be hard for you to understand, but trying means fighting for her life, our daughter's life!"

"You don't think I want my daughter to live? You don't think I'm fighting for her? I'm fighting for her life, Lynn! I'm fighting for her to live the rest of her life in peace. And, goddamnit, I'm fighting you to let her have that peace!"

"I'm trying to save her life, but you've given up on it." Lynn said to him.

"Why do we have to argue about this every single minute? Have you even asked Samantha what *she* wants? Or is this all about you?" Joe asked his wife.

"How dare you! How dare you question what I'm trying to do here!" Lynn rebounded.

"What are you trying to do, Lynn? We're already spoken with her doctors, more than one in fact. How many times do you have to hear that our daughter is dying?" Joe placed a gentle hand on Lynn's shoulder. "Come on; let's talk about this before you do something rash."

"You wanna talk about it? You wanna talk and talk and talk, well talking is over. I'm doing something about it, now! I'm sick of this shit!" Lynn shouted and went over to Samantha who was still sitting on the steps. "Come on, Sam, we have a plane to catch." She said.

Joe watched Samantha grimace as she made her way to her feet even with Lynn's help. "Leave her alone!" Joe yelled, immediately wishing he hadn't.

Lynn led Samantha to the door before turning around. Samantha leaned with her arm against the wall. "This is my child!" Lynn suddenly screamed, startling Samantha with her rage. "You have always been a punk ass! But you are not going to kill my child just because you don't have the balls to man up and do what it takes to save her life!" she shrieked.

Joe was struck backwards by her words, but they did not come as much of a surprise to him. "You finally said it. You have always thought that I was less than a man. You probably wish you had of married Jimmy, am I right?" Joe asked Lynn.

"YES!! You are right! Jimmy was a real man! I should have stuck by him and married him because he was the one I loved! I never loved you!" Lynn shifted her position to be as close to his face as possible. "So how does it feel knowing you were second best, Joe? How does that make you feel?"

Joe thought about that statement for a moment. He felt strange for feeling no emotion at Lynn's outburst and pity for his wife swept over him, at that moment. He also felt their daughter's eyes glaring at him. "You would have married a dead man." Joe said to Lynn. "There was no other future for him than where he is right now, six feet under, but maybe that's where you belong, as well."

"Daddy, stop it! Both of you!" Samantha yelled. She walked over to stand in between her parents, placing a hand on her father's chest. "Stop it, just stop." She said softly, unexpectedly out of breath from her sudden scream. "I'm going to the clinic with her, okay?"

Samantha's tone was irrevocable. This calmed him down. "Okay." He relented. "I'll get dressed and go with you." he said.

"No!" Samantha pleaded. "You stay here. This shouldn't take long and we'll be back tomorrow." She watched as her father nodded in reluctant agreement.

"Alright, let's go Sam." Lynn said and tugged at her daughter. Samantha followed after giving her father a kiss of peace on his cheek. Lynn flashed one last cold gaze at Joe, which he correctly read as *this is not over*. It was at that moment Joe realized that the argument they had may not be over but, for him, their marriage most certainly was.

The car ride was quiet, and Samantha tried to go back to sleep. Even though she was unable to do so, she was grateful for the peace and quiet that her mother was allowing her. Lynn only spoke when needed, such as to alert Samantha that they had arrived at the airport, which way they were going once they got there, and to tell her it was time to board the plane. Lynn had booked first class seats, which was a relief to Samantha. The comfort of the larger seats was a blessing, as was being able to have a window seat. Samantha was looking forward to the moment she herself would rise above the clouds. She felt soon she would be doing that without the aid of an airliner.

Lynn was more subdued now because, once they were seated in the waiting area, she stole away from Samantha and sought out the closest water fountain. Rarely would she even consider using the public water hole, but she needed to take a Valium immediately. Now on the plane the pill was taking effect. She hadn't spoken to Samantha but not because she didn't have anything to say. Quite the contrary, Lynn wanted to talk about the clinic and how she had discharged Samantha from hospice and that the plan now was to fight and manage this illness, not to let it defeat her. But after the quarrel with Joe she didn't feel like communicating at all. All Lynn wanted to do was get to the clinic. She wanted to walk into the clinic, have her daughter examined, and be told by a doctor, with some hope in his voice, that everything was going to be fine. Lynn wanted to be told that all Samantha had to do was eat right, exercise and stay on her medications. She was sure this was the message this doctor would give them. The other doctors didn't because they were not specialists. They couldn't figure out what to do so they had given up on Samantha and thrown her into hospice as some last ditch effort to pump her with pain medications and watch her die. Well, Lynn had no intention of doing that, not at all.

While she couldn't talk, Lynn could think, and think she did. She rested her head onto the back of the seat and wondered why she had said those words to her husband; *he was the one I loved! I never loved you.* Though the words were true, Lynn had never fallen in love with Joe. He was a great provider, a good man, easy to get along with and he had made her life very comfortable, and love never entered her heart for him. The most she had ever felt was familiarity. She had grown accustomed to him. The sex had been tolerable. He was not an unattractive man, but there was no passion for him. Joe did exude quite a bit of passion for her, which made it easier for her to "play" along and to go through the motions, if you will.

Early on, she began to study her husband both romantically and practically. She memorized his desires, when to moan, to sigh, what he liked in the bedroom to bring him to the end as thunderously and quickly as possible. Lynn had learned the tricks of the trade to find the fastest way to please him, and when he tried to pleasure her, she learned ways to mimic the sounds so he would think she felt it and then it would be over. It worked for years. The rest of it was easy. Learning Joe's favorite foods, TV shows and sports interests was easy.

Joe was a man of comfort. Soul food and Italian cuisine were his favorites. They were fattening foods, but it kept him at ease. He loved watching documentaries and news programs, all of which were utterly boring to her. His favorite sport was baseball, another boring venture, but she persevered through it all. Lynn had learned how to look interested while her mind wandered. She would play silly games inside her head, like picking out the most ridiculous hairstyles of the political analysts, or counting the women at the baseball games who wore the most make up or were wearing yellow. And when it all became too much, Lynn would crush up sleeping pills into Joe's drinks to get a little time to herself.

The years passed, Lynn realized that she didn't have to have sex with Joe as much and that letting him go to the ball games or watch TV alone was the acceptable thing to do as an aging married couple. After a while, their lives had grown almost entirely separate. Romantic tussles in the dark had gone down to once or twice a month; sometimes three months would go by and once even six months. Lynn supposed Joe had given up on that; maybe he was having an affair. The thought of another woman pleasing Joe actually made her feel better because she knew that she didn't have to have sex with him, but Lynn actually didn't think Joe ever had an affair. Oh, he may have had a guilt-ridden, one-night stand or two, but a full-on affair was not his style.

But Lynn did. She had always kept herself fit by jogging or taking aerobics classes so she was still able to attract the opposite sex. She found it exhilarating to hire landscapers who didn't have much experience but were young and handsome. Joe must have noticed that all of the guys who mowed their lawn, or the carpenters, or even the plumbers could have made a living as models. He must have found this odd, yet he never said anything. Just every now and then she would hear from one of her lovers that they were quietly fired, and a new more experienced team of guys would show up, all with bulging bellies and thinning hair.

So Lynn moved further away from the home front to then have her flings, which was just as easy. She would venture to the gyms, the malls, wherever young men were to be found. Lynn found that being completely honest about her intentions, and buying them toys, kept it light and simplistic. She never fell in love with any of her lovers and the flings never lasted longer than a few months, sometimes only a night. Lynn would often wonder why there weren't more male prostitutes around for women.

The only male hookers she had ever heard of were for men and hookers in general. What a shame, she often thought; there were plenty of married and single women with her means, who would enjoy a simple affair with no strings attached, although Lynn assumed the need was not as plentiful enough to warrant an ad in the paper or them camping out at a casino or corner. Lynn felt there were lots of women who secretly wanted these services but society kept them from verbalizing it. Yet then, Lynn surmised, there were plenty of men who would sleep with women for nothing, just for the act, no ad needed.

Lynn looked over at her daughter who was sound asleep. She let her eyes travel past her and out to the clouds they were flying over. *Joe had to bring up Jimmy, didn't he?* She thought. Out of all the men Joe knew she was sleeping with in their marriage, Jimmy was the one that stuck to his soul. *You can't fight a ghost*, she had remembered hearing one day, and it was true. Her love for Jimmy had become frozen in time that day she left the prison for the last time. When she heard of his death, she went to the funeral, alone, and he was locked in her heart ever since.

Then the dreams started. Dreams of her with Jimmy as a young man, lucid, sexual dreams that made her feel as if she had actually spent the night with him, and the love became fresh again. Lynn had even visited a medium once to ask about the dreams, and the psychic had confirmed that it was Jimmy who was around her, his apparition visiting her in the night. The medium said they were no dreams. She said the experiences were real.

Once, when she had awakened from one of those "non-dreams", Lynn thought she saw Jimmy standing at her bedside looking down at her, smiling the way he always did, yet, when her eyes focused he wasn't there.

Maybe they were only dreams, maybe more, but she was sure that the memory of Jimmy prevented her from loving Joe. There was nothing she could do about that, and nothing she wanted to do about it. She would take Jimmy's spirit with her to the grave where she knew he would be waiting.

TWENTY-NINE

While Samantha was riding in a taxi to the Emory ALS Center, Jenna was getting ready to visit her new patients at Morning Glory Assisted Living which was only about three miles from her home. It was a little after 11 a.m., and the sun was high in the sky, and it was a typical cool late summer day in Michigan. Jenna was not as nervous as she was when she first went to Samantha's house. These patients were residing in a facility, with staff available to her, so she felt quite at ease. The first lady she was going to see had dementia. Jenna couldn't remember if that was a form of Alzheimer's or Alzheimer's was a form of dementia, anyway the woman was eighty-five, not bed bound but usually stayed in her bed and was very lonely. Her name was Irma Rizdorf. The next lady Jenna was seeing was Edith Borwoski, age ninety, diagnosed with debility, or old age as Matt put it, she walks with the aid of a walker and likes to stay in her room. Edith was classified as talkative and feisty. She should be interesting, Jenna thought as she pulled into the parking lot.

The outside façade of Morning Glory was very beautiful. The landscaping and small waterfall gave such a tranquil feeling to the building. Jenna walked through two sets of double doors to be greeted by a smiling young woman in a light pink nursing uniform. Her auburn hair was pulled back in a loose twist. "Good morning, welcome to Morning Glory. How may I assist you?" she asked brightly. Jenna was immediately put at ease.

"Hello, I'm a volunteer from Community Hospice. I'm here to see a Mrs. Rizdorf and Mrs. Borwoski." Jenna said and flashed her badge.

"Okay..." The young woman, whose nametag read Cindy, pointed a finger at an empty space on the notebook open on the counter. "Please sign in." she said as Jenna did so, Cindy continued, "Irma is in room 125, which is down the hall to the right. When you're ready to see Edith, she's on the second floor in room 244. The elevator code is 0115." Cindy wrote it down on a post-it note for Jenna. "You'll need this code each time you get on the elevator on any floor. This is our guest staff code to be given only to hospice and outside clinical staff. Please do not share this code with anyone else." Cindy spoke in a soothing yet rehearsed tone.

"Thank you." Jenna said, then started towards Irma's room. She had meant to ask if Irma was in her room or somewhere else, as Matt had instructed, but when she turned back, Cindy was with a UPS driver. Jenna decided to just go to the room. The hall was decorated lavishly with cream colored wallpaper with silver satin stripping. There were fine paintings amidst exquisite light sconces. At the end of the hall was a large sliding doorway leading out to a beautiful patio and, beyond that, a pond with a huge water fountain in the middle. Irma's room was the second to the last.

Jenna knocked on the door firmly but not too hard so she wouldn't startle the patient. She heard a woman say "come in" and Jenna entered. The room looked like a stately old bedroom in any home, not like a hospital room at all. The walls were filled with pictures of what Jenna assumed was the patient's family, a spectrum of photos from sepia, black and white, to rich color images. The patient's bed was made, and she sat by the window in her wheelchair. Jenna walked over and introduced herself. Irma nodded, holding out a hand for Jenna to sit next to her on the recliner. "This is a very nice room you have here. Did it come furnished?" Jenna asked, making conversation.

"You're gonna have to speak up, dear, I can't hear too well out of my right ear." Irma told her. Jenna repeated herself. Irma nodded in recognition. "Yes, my daughter brought over my linens and blankets from the old house, as well as all of my pictures from the living room. Each room here is different, you know. Bernadine, that's my daughter, she thought this one looked the most like our old house." Irma looked around the room. "It's close, I suppose, except for that ugly wallpaper. She switched out a few chairs and tables; you can do that you know. I guess its home now." Irma's voice was soft with a bit of a country drawl. She was clearly not from Michigan, Arkansas maybe.

"How long have you lived here?" Jenna asked.

"Oooooh I've been here a while now...one summer's worth at least."

"You like it here?" Jenna asked.

"Oh I like it alright, I suppose. My daughter moved me up here from Fairhope, that's Alabama, not long after Eustis died. Eustis, that's my husband." Irma paused, leaning in closer to Jenna, and said "Eustis has been visiting me every night for the past week, you know." She said.

"Your husband visits you?" Jenna asked, trying not to sound too disbelieving.

"Mmm hmm. I keep telling him I ain't ready just yet, but he says he knows, but he thought he would come early and wait for me. He was always that way, you know. He was early for everything. I used to drive him crazy because I would take my time getting ready for every little thing, so he used to call up to me when I'm getting dressed and he say, 'Irma, I'm waitin!' Child, I used to just sit on my bed all ready to go, and wait for him to say it twice, the I'd wait just a little longer, then I'd come downstairs, real slow like. Eustis say, all mad like, 'Now Irma you know I like to be on time!' and I'd say, 'Eustis, don't you know that all good things come to those who wait?" Irma starting laughing and Jenna joined her.

"So now, I got him waiting again!" Irma let out a hearty cackle.

Jenna touched Irma's arm. "Miss Irma, I can see already you're a mess!"

Irma pointed at her. "He sits right in that chair you're sitting in now. We talk about all sorts of stuff. I asked him what's it like over there, and he told me I'd see soon enough. I'll make him wait another week or two."

The visit continued for another hour while Irma ate her lunch. Jenna assisted her to eat and Irma asked that she come back again at lunch time so they could chat some more. Jenna agreed to come on Mondays and Wednesdays at lunchtime. Irma thought that was fine because her daughter visited on the Fridays. For someone with dementia, Irma seemed pretty sharp. There were a few times in the conversation when she would repeat herself or wonder what she was talking about, but, otherwise, she was on the money. Jenna thought her to be very pleasant and looked forward to visiting with her again.

When she left Irma's room Jenna fished the post it note out of her pocket and entered the elevator. Once inside, she punched in the code and went up to the second floor. As the doors opened, the difference from the first floor to the second floor was uncanny. The staff was still dressed in pink uniforms but the hallway was painted not wallpapered. The floor was not carpeted though it appeared clean. The color scheme was more medicinal with those familiar puke colored greens and light blues. Jenna noticed patients sitting in wheelchairs outside their rooms, sleeping and looking pretty sad. Jenna made her way to the nurses' station.

"My name is Jenna Steele from Community Hospice, and I'm here to see Miss Edith Borwoski." She greeted the much older nurse or nursing assistant. The woman looked up and did not smile.

"She's in her room." She said. Her nametag read, Sophia, she pointed down the hall. "Room 224." Sophia went back to the computer screen she had been looking at, and seemed very annoyed she even had to look away from it.

Jenna was put off by her attitude but continued on to the Edith's room. She noticed as she travelled down the hallway the absence of pictures and elaborate sconces. The light fixtures were just that, fixtures, and there was no scenery at the end of the hallway, only a wall with arrows pointing the way to other rooms. Jenna turned the corner and found Edith's room was the first one around the corner. She knocked as she had before, but did not get an answer. She knocked again, a little harder and heard something so she walked in.

The room was also a stark difference; it did look like a hospital room, no pictures on the wall, no added furniture, just the décor it started with. Jenna did not see the patient anywhere. She did hear what sounded like moaning coming from the cracked door of the bathroom. "Mrs. Borwoski?" Jenna asked and walked slowly towards the bathroom door. She placed a cautious hand on the door and tried to peek in without opening it any further. With the crack of the door opened, she not only heard what was clearly moans of pain, but she smelled the unmistakable scent of feces. At first, Jenna was not sure what to do so she called again to her. "Mrs. Borwoski, do you need some help?"

"Help me, please!" the patient called out fraily.

Jenna opened the door all the way and saw the elderly woman lying on the floor, holding onto the sink and trying to raise herself up. She was covered in feces from the waist down. Instantly Jenna placed a hand over her mouth. She paused a moment to gather herself. "Oh my," she said. "I'm going to get help!" Jenna said, and then ran out the door. She had heard the patient protest her leaving, but Jenna was out the door and running down the hallway back to the nurse's station, back to Sophia.

"My patient in room 224 has fallen down in the bathroom. She didn't make it to the commode." Jenna told her frantically.

Sophia was on the phone and held up a finger for her to wait. This infuriated Jenna. "Hello!" Jenna said to her more firmly. "The patient is on the floor!"

Sophia finished her conversation which from what Jenna heard, was of a personal nature and not business. "The towels are in the linen closet right across the hall there. Take what you need." She said.

"What? Did you not hear me? She has soiled herself and needs help!"

"Did you not hear me?" Sophia said in an aggravated tone. "Like I said, go to the linen closet, get what you need, and clean her up."

"Look, I'm not a clinical person. I'm a volunteer. I walked in and found her that way." Jenna explained.

"You're from hospice right?" Sophia asked.

"Yes."

"Well, clean her up!" Sophia reiterated.

"I'm a volunteer! We are not allowed to provide hands on care. You're the nurse; isn't that your job?"

"No, it isn't. That's your job! You're hospice; that's your patient, so get in there and clean her up. Stop bothering me with this." Sophia went back to her computer.

Jenna glared at Sophia, not believing what she was hearing. She pounded on the desk and Sophia looked back at her. "Where is your supervisor!" Jenna screamed, more loudly than she wished to.

"What do you need my supervisor for? She's going to tell you what I just told you. Go clean her up! Do your job!" Sophia screamed just as loudly.

Soon this caught the attention of a woman in a suit that came out of a flanking office. "What seems to be the problem here?" She asked, looking at Sophia and Jenna. It was Sophia who spoke.

"This girl is from hospice, and she is refusing to clean up the patient in room 224."

"That's Mrs. Borwoski, Edith." The suit lady said. Jenna read her nametag, and it said Ruth Epstein, Director of Nursing. Ruth looked at Jenna. "You're from hospice?" she asked.

"Yes." Jenna told her. "Like I was telling your employee here, I am a volunteer, not clinical, and volunteers don't do hands-on work so I was asking Sophia to clean the patient up, she's lying on the bathroom floor!"

"I see." Ruth said with more professionalism. "Just so you're aware, Edith will be charged $75 for an emergency clean up. Hospice is supposed to provide a home health aide for regular bathing. Will hospice be paying for this?"

"I don't know!" Jenna said, putting a hand to her chest. "Why is it extra? Isn't that part of your services here?"

"No. Edith has the standard package, which does not include clinical care, which is why I assumed her grandson put her on hospice." Ruth said without a stitch of compassion.

"So what happens when there's an emergency like this?" Jenna asked.

"We assist, but we let the family know that there will be an additional charge." Ruth explained.

Jenna held up a stern hand. "Forget it! I will take care of it, myself!" She stormed off back towards Edith's room. "This is ridiculous!" she said to no one but made sure it was loud enough where both women heard her.

Sophia and Ruth exchanged looks, and then Ruth said. "I'm going to lunch."

Jenna bounded back into Edith's room and entered the bathroom. "I'm going to help you, Mrs. Borwoski." She announced to her, and then proceeded to get her gently off of the floor. "I'm going to undress you." Jenna told her, and she went immediately into caregiver mode. She told herself that Edith was her mother or her grandmother, and she was the only one who was there to help her, which was the truth. Jenna slid off the patient's dress, making sure to keep the soiled side away from Edith's face. Like her mother before, Jenna assisted Edith into the shower stall and washed her off. Soon Edith was clean. Jenna dried her off and found a new gown in her bedroom drawer. She helped her dress and placed her back in bed.

Jenna asked her if she had eaten. Edith said she did have lunch, so Jenna told her to try to get some rest. Jenna turned to go back to clean the bathroom and she felt a hand on hers. "Thank you, thank you so much." Edith said to her, then laid back and closed her eyes.

Jenna placed a warm hand on the woman's forehead, "you sleep now." she said, the same words she had spoken many times to her mother when her mother had a particularly bad night. Jenna smiled at the woman who settled into slumber. It was apparent that on the first floor were patients who had a much better package deal. Her Miss Irma must be on the first class package deal because all of her needs were met; hell she had wallpaper for crying out loud. Jenna left Edith's bedside and finished cleaning the bathroom. Jenna did have to go out to the linen closet to get more towels. She exchanged a rather cold look at Sophia when she came out with an arm full of towels. Once the bathroom was spotless, she rejoined Edith at her bedside and sat there with her for another half hour as she slept.

When Jenna was back in her car, she started it, then switched the key off and sat there crying softly. Edith could have been her mother, her grandmother, her aunt, anyone. She didn't have any money so she was destined to be ignored as she sat in her own feces, not strong enough to call out. What an injustice, Jenna thought. Mrs. Borwoski was someone's mother, someone's friend, once someone's neighbor. Jenna knew nothing about her, but, from human to human, how dare she be treated this way, just because she couldn't afford a better package deal? "It's so unfair. She deserves so much more, so much more." Jenna whispered to herself as she wiped her eyes. An image of her mother lying in her bed replaced the image of Edith lying in her room. She felt that Edith probably had lived her life a lot like her mother, alone and sad. Jenna only hoped that Edith didn't live it on purpose like her mother did until the end.

At that moment she wanted to talk to Matt; she wanted to hear his voice, but she hesitated because she didn't want to disturb him. This was something she could handle herself. On the other hand, she should not be thinking of him on a personal basis at this moment. He was her manager and he should be informed about what was happening with his patients, as well as Jenna's volunteer experience. Jenna pulled out of the parking lot and headed for the hospice office.

If anyone would have seen Matt's face as he held the phone receiver to his ear, they would have been intrigued to know what was being said to him on the other end of the line to cause such an exasperated expression on his face. In a word, he was infuriated at the tone, the voice, the words, the insinuation, and the sheer candor of the woman speaking to him. What he wanted to say in response to the verbal bashing he was receiving was not professional by any means. Matt wanted to curse at her as she was doing to him. He wanted to call her an adjective, to let her know that he was aware she was acting like an old rabid female dog, but he couldn't do that. Instead he had to take every word she was saying and respond both calmly and adeptly.

"I am furious!" the patient's wife was screaming. "I have had these plans for weeks, and now you are telling me that you can't get someone over here so I can go? You have got to be the most incompetent person on the planet!" She shouted.

"Mrs. Logdon, as you know, your current volunteer has come down with a cold so he is unable to come out. I'm working on getting another volunteer placed for you." Matt said in the calmest tone he could muster up, and it was really hard.

"Working on it? Just send someone else out! You mean to tell me you have no volunteers? I thought it was your job to get me volunteers! What is your purpose if you can't get me someone to just sit with my dying husband while I leave? What kind of a place are you people running?"

"I assure you that every effort is being made to find a replacement volunteer for you."

"Well, maybe your effort is not good enough, ever thought about that? I have worked with hospice agencies before, and they get caregivers out to me in no time!"

"Was that a paid service, Ma'am?"

"Of course! Just like I am paying for hospice service. I was promised that I would have all of the services that you provide, that I am paying for, and that includes volunteers. So I suggest you go back to your little rolodex and start cold calling your people and get someone out here, do you understand me? And if, come tomorrow, you cannot get someone out here, I am yanking my husband from your fucking piece of shit service and taking my business to a hospice that can give me what I need!" With that, Mrs. Logdon hung up.

Matt sat back in his chair and stared at the receiver for a long while, stunned by what just occurred. He knew when he called Mrs. Logdon to tell her that a replacement had not been found for her that she would be disappointed. Most family members expressed regret that a volunteer was not able to be found for them, for whatever reason; yet, almost all were appreciative of the effort and understood that these were people who were giving of their time, without pay, and that every now and then their request could not be filled.

There are so many reasons why an assignment might not be met. It could be there were no volunteers available for that day and time, or all of the volunteers, who might be available, were already working with another patient at that time, or it could be something as simple as no one wanted to take that particular assignment. It could be any number of reasons. And, case to case, situations are different, and often complex. Most families understand that but, sometimes, on rare occasions, you get the people who do not understand or care to understand. You get families who are angry, belligerent, and just plain nasty to the hospice staff no matter who they are or what service is being provided. Sometimes Matt would just hear about the horrific things that happened to a nurse or hospice aide. He would hear that the patient struck them, or the family member cursed at them, or straight out argued with them to the brink of a physical altercation. Every now and then a volunteer would call back and describe what occurred on their watch. It does happen; yet, through it all, the staff has to be professional and courteous.

Matt slammed down the receiver. "Fucking Bitch!" He yelled at the phone. His office was empty; though he was sure someone in the hall or in the next office should have clearly heard him. Matt did not care. He took a moment to regroup. He placed his head in his hands and took a deep breath in, and let the breath out. He repeated the breathing exercise. He knew that people often are at the brink when they are caring for a dying loved one. He also knew that some people were just miserable jerks and, no matter the situation, they would still be miserable jerks. He was sure that Mrs. Logdon was the latter.

Five minutes had passed before he returned to normal, but peaceful normalcy would be short lived. "What the hell happened?" came the voice of Clinical Program Director, Karen McBride. Her expression was very similar to his expression only minutes before.

"What are you talking about?" Matt asked.

"I'm talking about the fact that I just had to promise Mrs. Logdon a hospice aide for tomorrow for four freaking hours or she was going to discharge her husband from hospice."

"What?" Matt asked in amazement.

"Yes! She said that you couldn't get a volunteer out there. You told her you would and didn't, so she is very unhappy with our services and that we better get someone out there guaranteed, or she's pulling the patient, hiring a lawyer, and going to the press and describe how horribly she was treated by Community Hospice!"

"How horribly *she* was treated? The woman is a fucking psychotic!" Matt stood up and pounded on his desk.

"What happened, Matt? I looked in her chart, the patient has a volunteer, so what is the problem? Isn't he going out there? Give me some explanation why I have to reschedule a hospice aide to go out and be there for four hours, which will take the aide past normal working time, so I have to pay her overtime, because *you* couldn't get a volunteer out there?" Karen's voice had the same accusing edge as the patient's wife did. This did not help Matt's mood at all.

"First of all she is lying! Her volunteer is going out there two to three times a frigging week! Check the damn clinical notes. Secondly, the volunteer is sick; he has a cold, meaning he is contagious. He cannot be around the patient therefore he cannot go out. So all day I have been searching for a replacement volunteer for her. I called Mrs. Logdon just now to give her the progress report on that, and she went ballistic!"

"So why can't you get a volunteer out there?" Karen asked.

"Because no one, as of yet, has responded! I learned of the volunteer's illness this weekend. He sent me an email on Saturday. He told me he would call me today, Monday, to let me know if he felt well enough, and he doesn't. In fact, he feels worse and is headed to his doctor today. He did call and inform the patient's wife, also."

"This prompted her to call the weekend staff to ask for a volunteer for Tuesday?" Karen asked, clarifying.

"Correct. So I immediately sent out a notice to the volunteers, even the one's in the other sites, to see if anyone would be willing to fill this assignment for tomorrow. No one has responded yet."

Karen made a face of confused doubt. "Out of all of those volunteers, no one has responded? Come on!"

"Look, it takes time for people to get the message, check their calendars, think about it, and get back to me. This is the process!" Matt told Karen.

"Well, your process is not working. Don't you have people on standby or on call?" she asked.

"What do you think this is, a temp agency? You think these people are just waiting by their phones for a job? They are volunteers! Key word: VOLUNTEERS!" Matt was yelling again. With each word, he was getting more upset because he had to explain himself to her.

"I understand that, but if we're telling people that we have volunteers who will sit with a patient while they get out and then when they need the service, and we can't provide it, then that is unacceptable! I shouldn't have to have an aide, who has better things to do with her skill and time, than to just sit with a patient for four hours. That's what your volunteers are for!"

"We never guarantee a volunteer will be out there. Your staff keeps giving people false information! It's not a guaranteed service. Every single assignment is not going to be filled!" Matt told Karen in no uncertain terms.

"In my opinion, if it's not guaranteed then what the hell do we need them for?" Before Matt could respond, Karen stormed out of his office and walked through the staff door leading over to the clinical side of the building.

Matt stood in his once again empty office fuming. It was Monday, and he had been yelled at by two people who thought not only was he incompetent but also they thought the volunteers are not even needed. Matt turned and went over to his office window. Through the blinds he watched the cars go by on the street. He suddenly wished he was in one of the cars driving away from this place, this office, this job. *What in the hell am I doing?* He thought to himself. Matt began to consider his life for a moment. He was a divorced father rapidly approaching his forties. He had two more years to be exact left in his thirties. He had a career which felt more like a dead end job to him most days, especially today. He wasn't able to make his marriage work and had no real positive thoughts on another one. Was this the way his life was going to be? A change had to be made. He could not keep going on this way. Matt was unhappy; yet, he knew that it was up to him to find a way to be happy.

There was Jake, Matt's son, who gave him immense pleasure. Matt only wished he had done a better in his relationship so he could go home to

Jake every day instead of only weekends and extended stays in the summer. Jake was a healthy kid, loved soccer, and seemed to have adjusted to the split up of his parents. Then there was Jenna. Just the thought of her gave Matt's mood a warm stillness. She was sweet, kind, and had a way of seeing into him. Had he moved too fast with her? Matt was scared that he had. He should have waited, and he shouldn't have been drunk. But what's done is done now; he could not dwell on that, just move forward. But to where? He wanted her in his life; that much he knew; he just had to take it slower. As for his job, he wanted it, as well, yet after a day like today, he wasn't so sure it was worth it. Matt rubbed his forehead hoping by doing so, it would massage out the kinks in his mind to produce clearer thoughts.

"Headache?" Jenna asked him, standing in his doorway.

Matt swung around at the sound of her voice. He instantly smiled. "Hey, what brings you here?" Matt went over to her and hugged her briefly. He wanted a kiss but thought against that here in the office. He only allowed himself a look into her eyes. Jenna returned his gaze, filling it with silent sentiment.

Jenna reached up her hand and placed her fingers on the temple he had been rubbing. "Why is it when I see you, you always appearing to be lost in thoughts and far, far away?" she asked.

"I'm sorry; it's been a long day. But you're here now, so it's picking up. Have a seat." Matt gestured at a chair, and he sat back at his desk. "So what brings you here? Please say you're not quitting." He half joked.

Jenna frowned in astonishment. "Quitting?" she asked and let out a soft chuckle. "Well, if you asked me that about two hours ago then I don't know if my answer would have been in the negative." She said.

Matt cocked his head to one side bracing for her next words. He knew that she had just come from her first visit with her new patients. "What happened?" he asked.

"I don't even know where to begin." Jenna started. After taking what seemed like a long pause, Jenna began to explain her mornings activities, from the rudeness of the facility staff to her cleaning up feces in her new patient's bathroom. Describing the incident to him Jenna felt as if she was reliving it and once again wanted to hit someone, yet she had been more appalled at the treatment of her patient and not at what the receptionist and nurse had said to her. Jenna realized how lucky her mother had been to be able to be called for at home. She realized how fortunate anyone is to have family who cares about them and who are willing to go the extra miles of inconveniencing themselves for however long it took to care for the person who raised them. When she was done reporting, Jenna just felt sad instead of angry. "No one should have to end their life like that." She said finally.

Matt sat back and absorbed her words. "I'm sorry you had to go through that. Volunteers are not assigned to do what you did today." Matt then picked up the phone. When the person answered, Matt asked, "Karen, could you come into my office, there's something I need you to hear." He listened as the Clinical Program Director resisted, informing him that she was about to head out to lunch. "It will only take a moment; it's regarding a patient we have over at Morning Glory." Reluctantly, Karen agreed and soon was once more standing in Matt's office.

Matt asked Jenna to repeat briefly what she had just told him. Karen sat next to her and listened intently. When Jenna was finished, Karen could only shake her head in disbelief and disgust. After throwing Matt an apologetic glance, she turned to Jenna and offered an apology. "Thank you so much for being there for the patient and doing what you did for her. You shouldn't have had to do it, but we so graciously appreciate that you took it upon yourself to do it." Karen took note as Jenna told her about caring for her mother and revealed that she had cleaned her up many times, so it was nothing she was not used to. "Be that as it may, Jenna, it was not your job to do so and again we are so very grateful."

Karen stood up. "I'm going to deal with this right now." She looked at Matt and said, "I'm so sick of dealing with the staff over there. Before you even told me what staff members were involved, I already knew. Today they have gone too far! Just because a patient is on hospice does not mean they get to wash their hands of them! They still have a job to do!" Karen let out an exasperated sigh. "Thanks, Matt, for letting me know immediately." Karen turned to leave then paused. "And Matt, sorry about this morning." She said.

"Don't worry about it." Matt told her.

"No, no..." Karen said firmly. "I was out of line. You were right, and I admit I was wrong for my attitude."

"We all have a hard job to do." Matt shared.

"Yes, yes we do." Karen looked back at Jenna and said goodbye.

Matt and Jenna exchanged a long stare. "I'm hungry." Matt said. "How about you?" He watched Jenna smile in agreement.

THIRTY

I wonder what the fish are thinking? Samantha thought as she stared at the sixty foot fish tank located in Dr. Jim Solaris' office. Samantha and her mother had spent the last two days at the clinic. It was a longer time than expected and much longer than she had wished to be there. At night, Samantha had hoped her mother would go back to the hotel, but Lynn, instead slept in the makeshift sleeper couch inside of Samantha's assigned room. She had tried to suggest, ever so politely, that her mother should go and get some rest in the beautiful hotel room she had purchased because it would be a waste of money if she didn't. Lynn had decided against saying that she did not want to leave Samantha's side. Samantha wasn't sure if her mother genuinely didn't want to leave her or if she wanted to keep an eye on the clinic's staff. Samantha figured it was the latter, yet, in any case, Samantha had the pleasure of her mother's company for twenty-six straight hours. The only reprieve Samantha enjoyed was when she was wheeled away to undergo yet another test.

Samantha was sure she had never been poked and prodded so many times. After awhile, she started to tune the world out. She had become quite the expert at this ever since returning home. Samantha's mother would be blathering on about something and, suddenly, her mind would be fixed on the trees outside the window, or the shadows on the wall, anything that took her away from the sound of her mother's voice. Samantha did find that her periods of daydreaming were becoming easier to go into and harder to come out of. She would hear her mother calling her name over and over before she was able to snap back to the reality around her, and this did alarm Samantha.

Now, as Samantha sat in the obligatory wheelchair the clinic provided for her exit meeting with the physician, she had zoned out again, only to resurface to hear words such as, *continuous, debilitating, illness,* and phrases such as, *what you can expect, what to do when this happens,* and *disease progressing rapidly.* Samantha felt quite safe in her apathetic attitude because she knew Lynn Mills would ask all the right questions and demand all the right answers so it really wasn't necessary for Samantha to listen. Besides, what would Lynn have to talk about on the plane ride home if not to regurgitate the doctor's every word. At least Samantha would be hearing something new.

It wasn't as if Samantha didn't care about her condition; strangely, she had adapted to it. The idea of dying did not seem as horrifying as it once did. She also wasn't as angry as she was in the beginning and no longer felt the need to ignore it as she had for years while working in New York. Maybe when you are closer to life, up and walking around, running from appointment to appointment and trying to live the most productive life possible in the corporate world, as Samantha had been doing, the idea of death was very frightening and very damned inconvenient.

Death to Samantha before came in the form of a dark figure appearing from behind a building, lurking in the dark, ready to pounce on her and beat her with a blunt object to rob her of her purse. Death was a moment of misjudgment in the car and running off the road or crashing into another unsuspecting driver in a fatal head-on collision. Death was also that distant visitor when you're closing in on your ninth decade that would come like a thief in the night and carry you away from your dreams.

As the ALS kept attacking Samantha's ever weakening body, death was more like a patient limo driver waiting just outside on the driveway and reading a paper while Samantha completed her journey. Sometimes, she would think of him out there, smoking a proverbial cigarette, flicking through radio stations, and taking a nap until it was time for Samantha to join him. Soon, she knew she would get up and walk down to the car. He would jump out, adjust his hat, and quickly open the back car door for her. She would wait for him to get back into the driver's seat, look in the rearview mirror at her and ask if she was comfortable enough. Samantha imagined she would nod at him, and he would slowly drive away, giving her the opportunity to look back at the world she was leaving behind. Once Samantha was done with peering out at her life as it faded into the background, she would turn and there would be Kenny smiling in the seat next her.

"Sam, the doctor asked you a question." Lynn said as she gently shook Samantha's arm.

Samantha looked away from Kenny and back at her mother and Dr. Solaris, they were both staring intently at her. "I'm sorry, what?" Samantha asked.

"I was telling your mother," Dr. Solaris repeated, "that the onset of your disease probably came on years before you remember. It is much more aggressive than many cases we've seen before. Some people who are afflicted with ALS have symptoms that are slight and progress at a steady but manageable rate, your ALS, Samantha, is moving quite fast, especially for your age. That's why it's getting more difficult for you to speak and walk. You've fallen quite a bit so I would suggest you utilize your wheelchair at home on a regular basis. I have consulted with your hospice physician, and we've agreed to changes in your medication. The pain meds have been increased, as well. They will make you more drowsy, and you'll have bouts of constipation as another side effect. We've adjusted other medications to ease this as well. How are you feeling today, Samantha?" he waited for her response.

"Fine." Samantha answered slowly. Gratefully, Dr. Solaris turned his attention back to her mother and continued updating her on Samantha's progress and what to do once she arrived at home. He also, thankfully, suggested that her mother be more patient with Samantha because speaking would become increasingly difficult and to expect only one word answers. Samantha thought she would begin that immediately.

Lynn was not as talkative on the plane ride home as Samantha had thought her mother would be, and she was able to sleep. When she opened her eyes, the plane had already landed, and that was a blessing. She was happy to note that this would be the last plane ride of her life. She hated flying, and now it was over. Great! When they walked out of the gate connector, the first person Samantha saw was her father standing and waiting for them. She immediately perked up and walked faster to him, leaving her mother to struggle with the bags. Samantha immediately tucked her arms into her father and snuggled close to him. She had missed him desperately. It was a weird feeling, but a part of her thought that she would never see him again. After the encounter he and her mother had before the trip, Samantha began to envision her father packing his things and moving out while they were in Atlanta.

"I'm so glad to see you, Daddy." Samantha said. "Glad you're still here." She heard herself saying before she could stop herself.

Joe gave her a warm squeeze. "I'm not going anywhere baby girl." He reassured her then walked with her upstairs and into her bedroom. Samantha peeled off her clothes as Joe helped her into the shower. He could readily tell that she was much weaker. Samantha leaned into him more than usual and also did not protest when he walked her all the way into the bathroom, his arm assisting her into the shower. Before, Joe would have been stopped at the door while Samantha went into the shower, on her own. He saw his daughter's condition was declining. "I'll be right outside the door, baby."

"Would you mind staying?" Samantha asked him. "I might need help getting out." There was a hint of embarrassment in Samantha's voice, and Joe was saddened to hear it. He quickly came back into the bathroom and sat down at one of the small stools.

"You bet, I'm right here for you, Sam." He said. Joe sat down, and they chatted about the trip, the weather, and just idle conversation, anything generic so they wouldn't have to discuss her disease process. Joe did not want to discuss how she was progressing moving closer and closer to death.

When Samantha was done with showering, Joe helped her dry off, change into her nightgown, and get into bed. "Dad?" Samantha asked, as she watched Joe settle into the chair beside her bed. "What's going to happen to you and Mom when I'm gone?" she asked.

"I don't want you to think about that." Joe responded.

"No, I wanna know, are you two going to be okay?" Samantha pressed.

Joe took a breath before continuing. "Listen," he began, "Don't you worry about us. I want you to concentrate on getting stronger."

"You and I live in the real world, dad, we both know I'm not getting any stronger. Even the doctor at the clinic said so." Samantha told Joe.

"Oh baby." Joe said taking her hand.

"I'm not scared anymore." Samantha announced with clarity.

"You're being brave." He surmised.

Samantha shook her head, "no, I just...I can't really explain it. Maybe it's the drugs, but I just feel more at peace with everything. When I was on the plane coming home, I realized that this is the last plane ride that I will ever have to take, something about that freed me."

Joe's heart sank. It was becoming all too real, too imminent, he realized. "Freed you? You mean from this world? Are you starting to let go?" he asked.

"I suppose." Samantha thought for a moment. "Remember when I was moving to New York after I got the job at Libman Advertising and I was so terrified?" she asked.

Joe cocked his head, astonished, "Really? You seemed so excited."

"Well, I was, but I was also scared out of my mind! I was headed to New York...to live!" Samantha held out her hands in front of her for emphasis. "Even though I had been back and forth to the city many times, I was always a tourist, but this time I was going to be living in one of those tall skyscrapers, all by myself. I remember being all packed and sitting right over there in a chair and feeling so alone. I literally thought about calling my new boss and declining the position. But, before I could dial something happened that changed all that." Sam said and looked up at Joe. "Do you know what it was?"

"No, what happened?" Joe asked.

"You happened." She told him. Again, Joe was stunned. "You came in and said something to me; do you remember what it was?"

Joe thought for a second, and the only thing he could remember was, "I told you that your room would never change." He said.

"Yes, that's it. Mom had been talking about making this room a guest room. She wanted it to look just like a hotel room." Samantha chuckled. "She was even thinking about actually locating one of those dark cherry armoires that you see in most hotel rooms now, you know with the stand that slides out the TV?"

Joe joined her in laughter, "Yeah, I remember that! She was even going to go to the Marriott and inquire. I thought she was insane. But did that upset you, Sam?"

"At first no; I actually thought it was kind of a cool idea. I mean guests would feel like they were at a hotel, but at your house. I didn't think anything of it until you came in that next day and said that to me, and I realized how much I would miss this room." Samantha looked around at her posters and stuffed animals. "Just thinking about it made me feel like a part of my life was over, and I got so scared." She said.

"I just wanted you to know that no matter where you went, no matter whatever happened to you, your home would always be here." Joe explained.

Samantha nodded. "Then I wasn't scared anymore." She said. "I felt safe." A tear escaped her eye, and Joe gently wiped it away. "It's like that now." she continued. "I feel safe. I don't know what's going to happen, but I feel that home will still be here."

Joe got up from the bedside chair and sat next to his daughter on her bed. Samantha immediately placed her head on his chest. No more words were spoken and soon Joe listened as her breathing became rhythmic as she fell asleep in his arms, much as she did when she was just a little girl. When he knew she was asleep, Joe did not move, but allowed himself to cry silently. It was not until this moment that he truly began to feel the pain of his little girl's approaching death.

THIRTY-ONE

In Michigan the winter sets in fast, barely into October and the winds have cooled considerably. August is really the only month where the warm air of summer grows hot; yet, once the eighth month has passed, it's a steady downward slope towards the frost. Matt began his certification exam study group with a reluctant Brandon Thames, an eager Susan Cobbs, and a pessimistic VP, Sarah Evans. They met every Tuesday afternoon in Sarah's office, ordered in lunch and hunkered down into the small green textbook recommended by the volunteer manager's credentialing site. It was clear that only he and Sarah were studying outside of the group. Brandon and Susan both argued that family life was just too hectic to devote much more time to learning the material. Sarah, on the other hand, was very determined to get certified. She felt her job would depend on it, and Matt shared her views.

Matt wanted his VP to succeed because it would bring more credibility to the department. Also, Matt was just as determined to succeed because he wanted to keep the department viable. "Fight for what you really want." This is what Jenna had told Matt during their almost nightly study sessions together. Jenna began helping him tremendously and would not let him falter. Over the last few months, Matt began spending more and more nights at Jenna's home. At first, it was just the weekends, and then he found himself leaving from her house on workdays. Matt would rush back to his place, get showered and head to work. Then it became more feasible to start bringing a change of clothes with him to Jenna's home on a just in case basis, until finally, Matt's apartment became more of a storage facility rather than a dwelling.

Matt was falling deeply in love, and it was apparent that Jenna was right there with him in his feelings. He had never been so happy and content in a relationship since his first year of marriage. Jenna was also good with Matt's son. Jake took a liking to Jenna almost immediately. She even transformed her expansive basement into a game room just for Jake. Matt was overjoyed with the weekends that Jake stayed with them. They truly felt like a family, the three of them. Matt did, however, have one or two heated discussions with his ex-wife regarding Jake spending time at Jenna's house, but he finally won the dispute when Jake went on and on about how much fun he was having there. Connie was noticeably envious of her ex-husband's new relationship, but Jake was happy and safe which was all that mattered to her.

Fully aware of the strong romance developing between Jenna and her new friend, Adrian made himself scarce around the home front. Although he was extremely happy for his cousin, Adrian was more pleased that Jenna was focused on her own love life, which meant she was paying less attention his. This is exactly what he and his own new, romantic partner wanted, at least for the time being, anyway.

"How are the wedding plans coming?" Adrian asked the naked woman lying beside him.

Zabbie was lying on her back looking up at the ceiling. The painted load bearing beams gave the vaulted ceiling character. She gazed up at the wooden ceiling fan, one of three in the master bedroom. This boat house where Zabbie and Adrian spent most of their time together was located on Duck Lake, discretely, about 20 miles away from her home. Zabbie's family owned the home, but she rarely ever went there. It was bought many years ago for her mother's elder sister, but she only stayed there for about ten years before she retired to Arizona. That was over five years ago. Zabbie often suspected her father kept it for his own surreptitious rendezvous. How ironic that she would be using it for her own stealth affair.

"I don't think you really want to know about that." Zabbie answered Adrian. She twisted her body around to look at him. The room was dark except for the full moonlight shining through the window. She had no clue what the hour could be but was sure it was well before dawn.

"I do actually." He told her. "Is it still a June wedding?"

"What difference does it make?"Zabbie asked flatly.

"It makes a lot of difference to me."Adrian admitted.

"Does it?" Zabbie returned to lying on her back.

"You still doubt me?" Adrian asked.

Zabbie let out a hard breath, becoming frustrated. "Come on, Adrian why do we have to talk about this?" she reached over and stroked his chin, scooting in closer to him. "Let's just enjoy this time together." She began kissing his neck and shoulders.

Adrian pulled away. "This is all I am to you isn't it? You're still going to marry Zach after all the time we have spent together?"

"I don't know if I'm going to marry Zach. I need time to think." She replied.

"What are you thinking about? You're saying you need time to decide whether or not you still love him?" Adrian's voice was rising.

"It's not that simple. My parents have already spent an incredible amount of money on my dress, the venue, invitations." Zabbie said. "Right now, my mother is planning this huge Thanksgiving dinner for Zach's family. I'm the last child. It's a big deal." Zabbie emphasized the last line.

"And I'm not?" Adrian asked as his body recoiled away from Zabbie even more. "How you feel about me is not a big deal?"

"You don't understand." Zabbie said.

"No, Elizabeth, all I understand is us, you and me." Adrian reiterated.

Zabbie jumped off the bed suddenly. She grabbed the closest clothing to her, which was Adrian's button down shirt; it fit her like a dress. She didn't want to have this conversation with him. For months they did not speak about Zach, her pending nuptials, or anything, for that matter, besides each other and the moment. It was not as if Zabbie didn't love Adrian, because she did. She could not see going to her mother and telling her that the wedding was off, because she was involved with someone else, someone she didn't even know wanted to marry her. She loved Adrian but could she even see herself *marrying* him? Those thoughts had never made their way into her brain on any reality level. Thoughts of marriage to Adrian were part of a fantasy she had had long ago when Adrian was only her best friend's dark wayward cousin. Adrian wasn't real in her mind. Zach, on the other hand, had always been very real in her world.

The Emanuele Family and the Meyer's Family were members of the same country club, spent summers in Europe, and spent winters in Aspen. Their parents even had the same financial advisor, an advisor who only handles families with generational wealth. Zach understood her world and the types of people who inhabit that world. She and Zach were simply, a better fit. Zabbie had always felt at ease with Zach. He was a wonderful guy; they had a lot in common both financially and culturally. It was a perfect match. That was, of course, until Adrian came back into her life. At first, Adrian was only a part of her teenage illusions, but ever since they had reconnected a few months prior, it had become very real, actually too real for Zabbie to grasp. Now, as she looked into Adrian's pleading eyes, begging her for some kind of response, she wondered if she had things backwards. She had to ask herself, feeling as deeply as she did for Adrian, which was a feeling she never truly experienced with her fiancé, was Zach actually the fantasy?

"How do you want me to respond to that?" Zabbie asked Adrian.

"I would hope you would respond honestly." Adrian's eyes fixated on Zabbie's in such a way that made Zabbie feel uneasy. She could not return his gaze. Instead, she studied a dark spot on the wall.

The more she stared at the wall, the more agitated she became. How dare Adrian put her on the spot like this? How dare he blindside her! "Do we have to do this now? Why do we have to talk about this all of a sudden?" she asked, clearly annoyed.

Adrian stood up, stepping two wide steps to be within inches of her. "All of a sudden?" he said and placed a stern hand on Zabbie's chin to pull her face forward forcing her to look directly at him. "These months haven't meant anything to you have they?"

"Adrian..." she sighed.

"Have I not been honest with you? Have I not told you that I love you? How *much* I love you?"

"Yes...but..."

"Do you not believe me?" he pressed.

"yes..." she responded.

"Do you love me?"

"You know I do." Zabbie said, but averted her eyes from Adrian. Adrian, somehow, shifted his head right along with her in order to force her to look back up at him. It was in that instant that he was sure.

"You don't." Adrian whispered and dropped his hand from her face and stepped away from her. He nodded his head. "This is what you want." He said and gestured around the room. "The two of us, in the dark." He watched Zabbie shake her head in dispute, yet she did not speak. They stood there, locked in a gaze, until he let out a deep "*hump*." Adrian's eyes rolled over Zabbie's body; then he turned away from her searching for his clothes.

Zabbie's heart sank as she realized he was about to leave. She broke her silence. "Adrian, please listen to me; things are not as simple as you think." He slid on his pants. "I mean you have to give me some time. I can't just drop everything, my whole world, in an instant!" Adrian sat on the bed and slipped on his socks as Zabbie continued, "It may be easy for you to just change your mind and go off in another direction without thinking, but I can't do that! Too many people are involved. Do you understand that, Adrian? I have to think of more than just myself!" she shouted.

Adrian paused, looking around the room, and realized Zabbie was wearing his shirt. He decided to slip his jacket over his bare skin; then he grabbed his car keys and headed for the stairs.

"Adrian!" Zabbie protested seizing his arm and swinging him around. "Where are you going? You can't leave me now! We have to talk about this!" she begged.

"I don't see that there's anything left to talk about." He answered, surprisingly calm.

"So that's it?" Zabbie suddenly screamed at him. "You're going to run away like you always do?" Adrian broke away from her and continued down the stairs. Zabbie followed him closely. "And you wonder why I'm hesitant to give up my entire world to be with you! It's because of this right here! You run! You've been doing it for years, your whole life! Who's to say that if I called off my wedding you wouldn't run again? Once it really gets real and in your face, huh?" Zabbie saw Adrian reach the door and opened it. A strange surge rose inside of her and she bolted between him and door causing it to slam shut. "You are going to stay here and talk to me!" Zabbie shrieked uncontrollably.

Outside in a parked car hidden by overgrown bushes and the darkness of night, Zach's head popped up at the slamming of the door and what was, undeniably, the loud voice of Zabbie. He had been sitting out there for hours. He wasn't able to find her at home or reach her on the phone so he drove by her family's boathouse on the off chance that Zabbie would be there. When he saw an unfamiliar car in the drive parked next to hers he decided to wait and see who would emerge. Zach had fallen asleep. He clicked his cell phone on to check the time, and then switched it off quickly to squelch the blinding, bright display. It read 4:16am. Zach scooted up in his seat, careful not to let his body be touched by the haze of the street light.

Adrian, shocked by Zabbie's sudden outburst, stepped back from the door and shoved his hands into his pants pockets. He watched her waiting for her to calm down.

Zabbie took in a long deep breath. She tried to gather her thoughts before she spoke. "Adrian..." she took in another breath. "I don't know what to do. I...what... what do you want me to do? What are you asking?"

With an even voice Adrian answered. "I want you to break off your engagement and come away with me."

"Away with you? Where would we go?" she asked.

He thought for a moment. "I have some friends in New York. I've been thinking about getting an apartment there."

"An apartment?" Zabbie said making an expression of slight disgust which Adrian took note of. "New York?"

"Yes. I've been doing a lot of thinking about my music. I think I want to take a shot at becoming a true jazz artist."

Zabbie made a face of pure bafflement. "What? Since when do you want to be a jazz artist?" she asked him.

"Since forever, really. I've played a few clubs in New York, Chicago, and here in Detroit. I've moved around so much that I never really had time to focus but, since I've been home, and with you, I'm thinking more about things I really want to do."

"I don't want to move to New York, Adrian." Zabbie told him. "This is my home. This is your home. We both have roots here. Why do you want to leave?"

"Fine, if you don't want to move to New York we don't have to. What I'm asking is for you to be with me." Adrian stepped closer to her. "Can you do that?"

"I want to, I do...b—"

Adrian held up his hands in aggravation. "Great! We're back to BUT! I can't do this." He brushed past her and stormed out the door.

Wearing only Adrian's shirt Zabbie ran out the door behind Adrian unaware that two very intense eyes were on them. "Adrian, wait! Please Adrian, Wait!" she cried desperately.

"Wait for what Elizabeth? For you to make up your mind? For you to walk down the aisle?" Adrian shouted.

"No! Just give me some time please!" she begged.

Adrian opened his car door, got in, and started the car.

"Don't leave like this...don't leave..." she pleaded with him. "We can figure this out."

"I get it now," Adrian said as he put the car in reverse. "I'm not good enough." He said, barely audible, then backed out of the driveway and headed down the street away from Zabbie.

Zach watched from his car as his fiancé cried out for her lover in agony. He saw her fall down to the cold concrete in tears. He almost felt pity for the half naked woman left alone in the darkness, but that feeling was quickly taken over by pure rage. Zach grabbed the door latch, about to get out and scream at her, but something stopped him. He wasn't quite sure what, but instead of confronting her like a pathetic jilted lover, as she was now, he decided to wait. Instead he took his hand off of the handle and sat back to watch Zabbie slowly lift herself off of the ground, wipe her eyes, and drag herself back into the house. After a moment he started his car and drove home.

THIRTY-TWO

"Are you here to read me my last rites?" Samantha asked, sitting in the living room in her wheelchair. She had begun using the chair more frequently since returning from the clinic in Atlanta. She was getting weaker, and even though Samantha detested the use of it, she did know it was necessary.

Judy Norm, Community Hospice's spiritual care advisor, sat across from Samantha on the couch. "You're referring to the anointing of the sick?" she asked. Judy had been waiting for about fifteen minutes in the room talking with Samantha's mother before she made her appearance, quite reluctantly Judy noticed.

"Yes. Isn't that where you pray over me before I die, so my soul goes to Heaven?" Samantha inquired.

"In a manner of speaking, its one of the sacraments." Judy told her.

"I've heard that before, sacrament, what is that?"

"In the Roman Catholic religion there are seven sacraments. They're ritualistic prayers meant to strengthen the faith of the believer, such as baptism, confirmation, penance or when you go to confession, matrimony, holy orders or when someone joins the ministry, and anointing of the sick or last rites as some people call it." Judy explained.

"So, if I get these then all my sins will be washed away?"

"In a manner of speaking. Are you religious, Samantha?" Judy asked.

"No." Samantha laughed. "And neither is my mother, so I am not sure why she called you."

"Your mother just felt that you would benefit from talking to me. I'm not here in a religious capacity. I'm a spiritual advisor, so I'm just here to talk about whatever you would like."

"Whatever I would like to talk about...*spiritually*?"

"Yes." Judy replied.

"um..." Samantha's eyes darted around the room to see if anyone was listening. "What will happen after I die?" she asked.

"There are many different beliefs out there about what will occur, depending on who you're talking to." Judy explained.

"What do you believe?" Samantha asked her.

"I definitely believe that the spirit continues on, that this is just one part of our journey. What do you think will happen, Sam?"

"I don't know. I used to go to church with my parents, but after I moved out I never went back. No time. And I believe that people in church are pretty much hypocrites. I mean my mother went and like I said she doesn't believe." Samantha watched Judy nod then continued. "I guess I believe in God. It could all be just stories we tell each other to make us feel better. The closer I get to...dying...I don't know." Samantha looked at Judy for answers.

"There is uncertainty even for the truest of believers, but that is where their faith comes into play."

"Faith..." Samantha said the word as if hearing it for the first time. "I don't know if I have much of that anymore." She said.

"Why not?" Judy's voice was soothing to her, Samantha appreciated her soft tone.

"I just don't. It's like getting your hopes up for something that's never going to happen. Life feels like a crap shoot, anyway. You make plans for your life, what you want to be, places you want to go, your future, and then it all changes in a blink of an eye." Samantha sunk deeper into herself. "Then it's all lost." She added.

"Do you feel lost, Sam?" Judy asked.

"I feel like what was the point?"

"What do you mean?"

" What was the point of going to school? I spent about seven years in college sweating over exams, eating cold pizza, not going to parties so I could study harder and harder. And for what? To graduate with honors, so I could stay at the top of the pile of resumes, so I could land a great job in New York? All of that happened but, within only a few years of it, all this happens to me." Samantha slammed her right fist down on the chair.

"It's not fair is it?" Judy said.

"No, it's not fair! A week before I went to the doctor for that fatal appointment, where he told me about my disease, I had just completed a huge ad campaign. I wasn't the leader of it, but I had my hands in just about every piece of it. My design, my model choice, and it's now displayed in Times Square."

"Wow that's fantastic!" Judy exclaimed. "You must be proud."

Samantha did not join in her excitement. "Yeah...wow." She said blandly. "I would have been the leader of the next project. This is what my boss said to me that night. I was finally going to get recognition. I was sitting in my apartment afterwards, we all had celebrated, it was early in the morning just before dawn. I was sitting in the window looking out over the city, and in the distance I could see the river, and I knew that I had made it. I knew what my life would be like in five years, ten years. Success! For the first time in years, I could finally start enjoying all the hard work. It wasn't all for nothing." Samantha sat back in the wheelchair. "I had no doubts. I felt so good about myself, and about my life. And then….poof!" Samantha made an explosion gesture with both hands. "In a blink of an eye, all gone."

Judy looked at the thinning woman whose face had begun to sink in, causing her cheekbones to protrude. Samantha's skin, though pale, had started to take on a yellowish hue, the onset of jaundice she imagined. Judy got up from the couch and walked over to her. She bent down next to Samantha, who was holding her head down into her chest.

"Let me say a prayer for you." Judy said and observed a small nod and the closing of Samantha's eyes allowing the moisture inside to spill over onto her cheeks. Judy took Samantha's weakening hands into hers and began to pray.

Jenna pulled up and parked under the stone parkway in front of Samantha's house. Her visits were more frequent now; she came three to four times a week and had begun talking with Samantha on the phone, as well. When she learned that Samantha had been temporarily taken off the program she called immediately. Samantha asked her to come out anyway, but from that phone call spawned many more calls, sometimes initiated by Jenna, sometimes by Samantha. Often Samantha would call in the middle of the night just to talk about a dream she had had or because she was feeling anxious.

Judy was walking out as Jenna approached the door. Judy held out a hand to her. "Hello, you must be Jenna, Samantha's volunteer." Judy greeted.

Jenna returned her greeting. "Yes."

"I'm Judy Norm, spiritual care."

"Oh, hello." Jenna replied.

"I've been hearing great things about you from the team and from Samantha. It's great how you handled that situation at the nursing home before. Have things improved there, Jenna? I'm heading over to see those patients now."

"Thank you, yes, it's gotten much better. I come in and make my visits without issue. That Irma is amazing; I think she will outlive me!" Jenna giggled.

Judy joined her. "She is a hoot! I heard you recorded her story?"

"Yes! That was astounding! Her memory is so intact. She talked for hours! I just delivered the Angel's Voice package to the family last week." Jenna said.

"I love that name, Angel's Voice." Judy admitted.

"Me too." Jenna replied. "The package is so beautiful; it has the huge leather cover over the scrapbook. Irma chose her wedding picture. She was a beautiful young woman."

"I don't want to keep you." Judy said. "I just wanted to make sure I said hello. Keep up the good work." Judy patted Jenna on the shoulder and walked off, then paused and turned. "Oh and Jenna," she began. "Samantha is declining very rapidly. I just said a prayer for her. She's kind of down right now, just thought you should know her current state."

Jenna nodded. "Yes, I've been noticing her decline. Ever since she came back from that clinic, she seems to be deteriorating at a faster rate."

"Yes. For someone Sam's age, patients do tend to live for years with her condition but from my nonclinical perspective, she's getting close."

"Thanks, for telling me." Jenna waved goodbye, then went into the house. She found Samantha where Judy had left her sitting in the living room alone. Samantha's back was to her, and for a moment, Jenna just stood there. A wave of sadness came over her as she remembered Judy's words, *she's getting close.* Jenna took in a quick breath and tried to brush off the feeling. She walked around to stand in front of Samantha giving her a bright smile. Samantha slowly raised her head. When she saw it was Jenna, she instantly lit up. It was a relief to see her friend standing there.

"Oh, thank God, it's you." Samantha said smiling.

Jenna chuckled. "Why?"

"Good to see a regular person." Samantha said. She moved her head, signaling Jenna to bend down, which she did. "You got them?" Samantha asked, conspiratorially.

Jenna comically looked around and patted her jacket and whispered, "Right here in my pocket." She said.

"Yes!" Samantha said, making a fist. "Come on, let's go." She said and placed a hand on the little joystick control of the electric chair and started toward the backdoor. Jenna knew where they were headed, their spot out back: the gazebo. It was indisputably their place now. Weather permitting, she and Samantha always went out there and sometimes Samantha was already there when Jenna arrived.

The wheelchair made it a much easier journey through the garden area. Jenna knew Samantha rejected the use of the wheelchair for a long time, but Jenna had gotten in it one day and zoomed around Samantha's room. "This is sweet!" Jenna had shouted in amusement. Lynn had been watching in the doorway, holding back from telling Jenna the wheelchair, to get off but when Lynn saw that Samantha relented and told Jenna to get up and let her into the chair, Lynn kept quiet. Well, it was worth a few dings in the furniture, Lynn had surmised.

Samantha and Jenna reached the end of the path in record time. "You're not cold?" Jenna asked. Just in case, she had grabbed the blanket lying on the couch as her and Samantha were leaving.

"Help me onto the swing and I'll let you put the *blankie* over me Mom." Samantha joked.

"Oh, ha ha!" Jenna positioned herself in front of the wheelchair, locking the wheels. "Place your arms on my shoulders." She instructed. "On three." Jenna counted, then bore the weight of Samantha and pivoted her to the gazebo seat. She unfolded the throw coverlet over Samantha's legs. After pushing the wheelchair aside, Jenna sat down next to her.

"You didn't forget the lighter?" Samantha asked, a bit giddy.

"Nope." Jenna reached into her jacket pocket and pulled out the fresh pack of cigarettes.

"Awe yea!" Samantha rubbed her hands together in anticipation. "I've been waiting for this a long time! I quit years ago, but now I'm like, who cares!" she watched as Jenna opened the pack and handed her a cigarette. In the same smooth action, Jenna flicked the lighter for her. Samantha took in a long drag, sucking in the smoke. She immediately coughed.

"Take it easy!" Jenna patted her back.

Samantha waved her away. "I'm good." She said and sat back on the swing tucking her legs underneath her. She took in another drag, leaned back, and let the smoke out. "You just don't know how good this feels. Thanks, man!"

"You got it." Jenna looked down at the pack. "What the hell, I think I'll join you."

"I was about to say, have a smoke, girl! Smoking is a social event."

"I've been trying to quit." Jenna told her as she lit one for herself.

"Really? I didn't know you smoked. You never smoked around me." Samantha said, surprised.

"No, I don't smoke when I'm visiting patients."

"I hope I'm more than just a patient. I think of you as my friend." Samantha said.

"You are more." Jenna briefly touched her shoulder. "Besides, your Mom seems like a non-smoker."

"*ppbbst!*" Samantha grunted. "That woman smokes like a chimney and drinks like a fish." Samantha and Jenna laughed. "She just doesn't want anyone to know about it, but I know she does. My mother is the queen of illusion. It's all smoke and mirrors with that one. Pun intended."

"You guys relationship getting any better?" Jenna asked, more seriously.

"It's gotten quieter, so that's better." Samantha said as she flicked an ash. "Let's not talk about her."

"Ok." Jenna agreed. "What do you want to talk about?"

"Let's talk about you. How are you are your hot boss doing?" Samantha lifted her eyebrows up and down smirking fiendishly.

"Aren't we nosey?" Jenna teased.

"Yep, now spill!" Samantha repositioned herself as if to hear her better.

"Well, things are getting kind of serious." Jenna revealed.

"Ooooh, how serious? Get him in the sack yet? You two doing the horizontal mumbo? You sexing him up?"

Jenna's mouth spread open. "What? Samantha!" her faced turned red.

"Oh come on, Jenna, I'm dying. I have no time to be coy." Samantha stated sincerely.

Jenna giggled. "Yes, he's been staying over more and more. He's practically moved in."

"Ah, you hoe!" Samantha playfully slapped Jenna's knee. "So, you like him, huh?"

"I think I'm falling in love with him. Sam, he's so sweet, so caring, and he has the cutest little boy you've ever seen!" Jenna pulled out her phone. "You wanna see a picture of them?"

"Wow, this is serious, you got family pics." Samantha waited for Jenna to scroll through her photos and finally she stopped on one with a man and a boy of about eleven years old. They were standing at what appeared to be a street festival, both holding their own huge ball of cotton candy. "Man, he is fine!" Samantha exclaimed. "He looks a little like that guy on Grey's Anatomy, the one with the green eyes and muscles. He looks like a tanned Jude Law too, but with more meat on his bones."

"Yeah, people tell him that all the time." Jenna replied proudly.

"So, wedding bells?"

"We just got together! We've only been dating a few months, Sam."

Samantha sat back again looking up at the sky. "Take it from me, kiddo, you gotta grab life while you can." She grew silent after that. Jenna allowed her to rest and didn't pressure her to talk more.

For a long while they just permitted the swing to rock back and forth as they each smoked their second cigarette. The silence engulfed them until there was only sound of the wind and of the creaking swing chains. This is how it was with them so many times. Soon another familiar sound wafted into Jenna's ears, the sound of Samantha's even breathing. She had fallen asleep. Jenna pulled up the cover to Samantha's chest, and sat back keeping the swing gliding.

Wedding bells? Jenna thought, smiling to herself. She hadn't even thought that far in advance. Yet, she had to admit it did cross her mind a few times, especially when Jake, Matt's son, was visiting. She did like the feeling of having him there. When Jake was around, there was a completeness that fell over her. Watching Matt with his son was very inspiring, as well. Matt loved him so much and they got along so well. Jenna often wondered what in the world was wrong with his ex-wife that she let go of such a wonderful man, a wonderful family. Was there a flaw that she wasn't seeing? Was she blinded by the newness of love that she didn't see a crucial piece of his personality, which would ultimately lead to the inevitable destruction of the euphoric allegory she was engulfed in now? Was Matt not the man he appeared to be? No, she was sure that he was much more.

Jenna thought maybe it was his job. Matt did mention to her how his ex would complain about financial issues, but he was working to make things better for them. Jenna suddenly shook her head, to shake away the thoughts. She couldn't dwell on his past relationship. It was about the two of them and, from her perspective; Matt was the right man for her. And Jake, yes, she could see herself in the stepmom role with him. But again this was all premature speculation.

Jenna looked over at Samantha and found that she had woken up. Samantha was smiling at her in such a way as if she was hearing her thoughts about Matt. Not possible she was sure. "Samantha, are you alright?" Jenna asked her.

Samantha nodded lethargically, "Yes, Jen…" she said sluggishly. "Please, take me to my bed."

Jenna frowned a bit, because there was something in Samantha's eyes that sounded a distant alarm within her. "Okay, Sam."

THIRTY-THREE

Matt was dressed in the most impressive business suit he owned. It was also the most expensive suit he owned. He sat nervously outside of CEO Frank Jacob's office. Frank's secretary, Mindy Koehler, had offered him a latte, which he declined. He was too nervous to drink more coffee, not to mention he had already downed two heaping strong black liquids, earlier in the morning. But Matt was not too nervous to watch the 5'6, 110 pound blonde walk back around her desk. He had immediately felt guilty about it and thought of Jenna. Matt had even whispered the words; *my lady is gorgeous*, under his breath. However, Mindy did hear him, and she smiled to herself, happy her outfit was working on the male species.

"Ready, buddy?" Dave Chatman said, unexpectedly appearing at Matt's side.

Startled, Matt responded. "Yes, as ready as I'm ever going to be."

"Okay, I'll be in there, so no worries, okay? You got this in the bag!" Dave stuck out his tongue and did a little jig.

"Mr. Chatman." Mindy called to him. "Mr. Jacobs is ready for you and Mr. Ames."

"Thank you, Mindy." Dave said giving her a curtsy. If Matt didn't know him, he would surely think he was drunk, or high. But, that is just Dave.

As Matt walked toward the CEO's office, he paused a moment to adjust his suit and to settle his mind. He glanced back at Mindy, sure that she could see how panicky he was, but she gave him a quick thumbs up.

Stepping from the front office where Mindy was sitting into the lush mahogany confines of the CEO's office was a monumental transition. Matt had never been into this office before so it was a shock to him to see such lavishness, obviously professionally decorated.

"Have a seat, gentlemen." Frank was a short stocky man with a stylish white, close-shaven beard. The trimmed gray hair against the darkness of his skin gave him a real distinguished look. His conduct suggested a cultured upbringing.

Matt sat down in one of the winged chairs placed in front of Frank's desk. It was a comfortable seat, but Matt still felt out of sorts. This was it, his interview for the vice president of marketing position. If this job was "in the bag", as Dave had assured, then when Matt walked out of here he may no longer be in volunteer services. Matt was not able to categorize his emotion. Was it excitement, exhilaration, anticipation, or sheer terror? If it was terror then what was he terrified of? Was he afraid of leaving what he had grown to know and love? Was he afraid of change, progress, or achievement? That could be it, the human nature's fear of progress, fear of the unknown, or fear of change?

"I've been looking over your resume and accomplishments here at Community Hospice, Matt." Frank started. "I must say that I am impressed. I've also spoken in great lengths with Mr. Chatman about your abilities. You come highly recommended for this position. Now I ask you, what do you feel best qualifies you to be the new Vice President of Business Development Chief Marketing Officer?"

For a second Matt only stared at the CEO as if he didn't know who he was, and then something clicked, and Matt spouted out his rehearsed response regarding the trends of the hospice industry. He spoke about the current strategic marketing plans, its successes and weaknesses. He informed Frank about his ideas to elevate patient census and the holes within the community that are being missed, such as the minority populations, and ways to break through the barriers there. Frank and Dave listened intently to Matt's detailed five year plan that he had formulated to engage not only the employees but the volunteer staff, as well, to play a more active role in the marketing of their services. Matt reminded Frank of how employee morale affects the word of mouth tool which is critical to people's selection of health care providers.

When Matt had completed his presentation, Frank was sitting up in his seat, and immediately asked follow up questions with which Matt had even more tactics to relay, such as how to carry out his ideas and find the financial backings to do so.

Frank sat back in his seat and looked at Matt for a long time before he spoke again. He had a list of standardized questions he usually asked someone being interviewed for an executive seat, but he didn't need to ask them because Matt had already answered many indirectly. To say that the CEO was impressed was now an understatement. "You have some fresh ideas that had not been brought to my attention before, Matt.

I've thought about some of them, but I wasn't quite sure how to implement them and still remain financially viable until now." Frank stood up, folded his arms, and placed a pensive hand to his chin. Dave shot a quick smile at Matt as to say "you got it!"

Frank walked over to his window and looked out for a moment. Then he turned and said, "Matt, whether or not you get this position I feel that your talents are being underutilized in your current one." Frank thought some more. His nickname, "The Thinker", is being seen in the flesh as Frank pondered more. After another moment, he returned to his seat. "Matt, I have to talk this over with the board, and there are a few more candidates that I must see, however, I don't think it would be too bold of me to say that I want you for this position. You're a great asset to this company and would be an excellent addition to the executive team."

Matt's mouth fell open in astonishment. A flush of triumph washed over him; it was a feeling he could not remember feeling in a long time. Finally, the recognition that he deserved, that he had always knew he should have. Dave slapped Matt's back with enthusiasm sporting a big grin. "I told you, Frank!" Dave exclaimed, "This is the guy!"

"I have to agree." Frank said with assurance.

"Thank you, Mr. Jacobs for your vote of confidence and for seeing me today." Matt said, trying his best to contain his joy.

"No, thank you for your interest, and I will get back to you with, hopefully, some really good news of an offer soon." Frank stated, and then paused. "Matt, one more thing, and this has been perplexing me."

"Yes, sir?" Matt answered. Dave had risen out of his seat to leave, then sat back down.

"With an MBA, past experience in marketing, and your obvious grasp of sales analysis, why did you take a position such as director of volunteer services?" Frank asked his expression of incomprehension.

Matt's first instinct was to briefly explain his marital situation at the time of applying for volunteer services but felt that would not truly answer the question. The question was not one of choice or direction, the question was really *"why did you settle for such a nothing job?"* It was the equivalent of asking *"since you are in fact a God why would you walk amongst the lowest of mortals?"* At least that's what Matt heard. It was a question he had been asked many times by Dave, his ex-wife, and even had asked himself. A few years ago, hell a few months ago, if he had been asked the same question, Matt would have replied how he needed less stressful hours, needed to be there for his son; in essence, it was just a pit stop, a layover, a pause in his career path for the greater good of his family. And, sure, that answer was actually true. Matt supposed the true root of the question is *why did you stay*? This was the question Matt decided to answer.

"Mr. Jacobs, thank you for asking me that question. I've thought about that answer for many years now working in volunteer services. It's not a simple answer, but I'll try to give you a concise one. When I started in volunteer services, I had the same confusion that you share now about how to make this job work for someone with my educational background and obvious ambition in the hospice industry. I had known before accepting the job that where a position is ranked in the company says a lot about the importance the agency places upon said role. Being relatively ignorant to volunteer services, I thought that maybe this was a company decision and a right one actually. I mean, sure, I was managing a staff but that staff was not paid, and volunteer services was not a reimbursed service, such as nursing, so how critical could it possibly be to patient care? For about a year I came in and did my job filling assignments, orientating new volunteers, etc. with only one thing in mind, my next position. This was just a pause, after all, and I needed to find something that, as you said, utilized my expertise.

Then something happened: I received a call from a caregiver; her mother was dying of cancer and she was only nineteen. She had no other family willing to help her, and she was alone and terrified. Her mother was in the active stages of dying so she was literally dying before the young woman's eyes. She had remembered the hospice nurse telling her that if she needed someone to be with her in the end she should call volunteer services and someone would immediately come out to stay with her. It was after nine at night, and it was raining cats and dogs, a tornado warning, a horrible night, but if you could have heard this young woman on the other end of that phone line; She had been crying and was hysterical. I had barely introduced the of vigil volunteers program, so I scrambled calling, and emailing, every volunteer I could, and just when I thought it was a lost cause and I was even prepared to jump in the car myself and head over there, I got a call back from a sweet elderly volunteer who just asked me one thing: what's the address? The patient died at 4:47am the next morning. The volunteer had gone out in that storm and stayed with the patient's daughter. Thank God she did too, because the power had gone out, and I don't want to think about how this patient's daughter would have managed alone in that house as her mother was dying with the storm and darkness. The volunteer stayed with her all night and well after the patient's body was taken away. The volunteer prayed with her, lit candles, held her hand. Needless to say, the girl was very appreciative.

After that experience I started to pay more attention to my role as director of volunteer services. I finally realized that there is a reason why Medicare and the Department of Human Services require hospice agencies to have volunteers and requires them to provide minimally, five percent of all care. I finally realized just how important volunteers are to the care that we provide our patient and families. Even though that this hospice, as well as many others, do not place the role of the volunteer manager on a higher level in their ranks, it doesn't mean that what I do is insignificant and it doesn't mean that the volunteers are insignificant.

So, do I think my talents are being underutilized? No. I need all of my talents to do this job well. I manage a staff that, even though we don't pay them, they are critical to our care. Therefore, it is crucial that I use my education and abilities to train them. I must use my marketing training to recruit them. I must use my human resources abilities to regulate them. I must use my business economics education to run this program and budget correctly. I must stay knowledgeable about the emerging trends in this field, and it is a field, Mr. Jacobs. Volunteer management is a growing field which is taken quite seriously, not only nationwide, but worldwide. I began to be less perplexed as to why I stayed as director of volunteer services, and more confused as to why the hospice field, whose very existence requires volunteer services, isn't shown in higher regard." Matt paused, and the realization that he didn't want to leave his current position dawned on him.

"Thank you again, Mr. Jacobs, for meeting with me." Matt turned to Dave. "Thanks, Dave, for your confidence in me." Then, after giving it one last thought, he said to the CEO. "I'm going to have to remove myself from consideration, I like it where I am. I will say this, sir, volunteer services should be its own department, especially within such a large corporation as this one. It should have its own corporate vice president as well as a budget. I know there are restructurings occurring in the company, but when you think of reorganizing volunteer services, please think of elevating the status of the department, and those in it, as opposed to diminishing them. I believe our status now is below the rest of the management teams, and the description of director and even our vice president is not on the level of the rest of the staff. It's in name only. This should not be, sir. This is a hard job with many high level complexities. Do you know that the trend now is for volunteer managers to be certified? I'm studying for it as we speak. And it is no easy study! The industry is taking notice, but no one wants to be the first to place volunteer management at the level it deserves. We have a progressive organization here, and we claim to be the forerunners in this industry. Well, I say it's time for us to prove it." Matt stood up and shook the hand of a very dumbfounded CEO. Matt thanked him for listening and left the office.

When Matt stepped back into the secretary's office he had to catch his breath. A trembling hand went to his chest; his heart was racing. He was glad that Mindy was on the phone because he wasn't sure he would be able to speak. He walked out of the office and quickly down the hall, making a bee line for the men's bathroom.

When Dave busted through the door behind him, Matt was splashing cold water on his face.

"What in the fuck did I just witness?" Dave yelled at him. "Have you lost your goddamned mind?" he glared at Matt then started pacing himself. "Okay, all is not lost. I'll tell Frank that you just got caught up in your little humanitarian speech and you were taken over by the moment. You do want the job, and to keep your name in the running, though it is assuredly a little lower now!"

Matt wiped his face off with a paper towel. "I don't want it. I'm fine where I am."

"You're fine in some piss ant job that, like you said yourself, is only director in name?" he said.

"Yes, Dave. Sorry to waste Frank's time, but I hope he at least heard me."

"You know what Frank heard? He heard a man turn down an executive level position because he's afraid of taking things to the next level. That's what he heard, pal."

"Afraid?"

"Scared shitless!" Dave stressed the last word.

"Is that right?" Matt asked, getting irritated.

"You damned right, that's right. Let me tell you something, man, you gotta grab this world by the throat and be willing to squeeze every ounce of life out of it. Get over this self defeatism crap and live the life you were meant to live." Dave argued.

"That's what I'm doing. I believe in volunteer services." Matt responded.

"I believe in world peace, Matt, but you don't see me joining the fucking Peace Corp do you? I give to charities but I'm not going to ruin my life to save a world that can't be saved."

"I'm not trying to save the world. I'm trying to do a job that I love doing. Why can't you understand that?"

"Because it's idiotic that's why."

"Well I've made my decision, Dave." Matt headed for the restroom door, and then looked back at him. "You know money isn't everything." He said.

"Nope, it's not. There is a little something called respect. Remember that word, Matt? You wanted it, but fine, go wear turtle necks and dashikis and eat brussel sprouts and receive paper awards that mean nothing, but you missed your shot man. This was it! *This was it*! When opportunity comes you have to take it or it passes you by. Well say goodbye to this one Matt. There it goes, bye bye, woo hoo!" Dave waved his hands in the air for emphasis. "And I don't have to tell you how hard I busted my ass to prime Frank to hire you. He was ready. But so what, big deal, go be admired by the little people. I'm done." With that, Dave brushed past Matt and out the door leaving Matt to stare in the mirror attached to the back of the door. He looked at himself for a long moment. "Shit."

THIRTY-FOUR

While Dave was ranting about how idiotic Matt's decision was, Jenna's phone was vibrating. It was a little before eleven in the morning, but she was moving rather slowly. She had practically been up all night with Matt going over his interview strategy. Jenna had also received an odd text from Samantha that read simply, *good night, Jenna*. The message wasn't strange, it arrived around nine last night, but usually Samantha called, not texted, but maybe she was still very tired. When Jenna had left Samantha the previous afternoon, Jenna noticed that she could barely keep her eyes open. Jenna feared it was the last time they would sit under that beautiful gazebo together. It was only a feeling, yet a very powerful one that she could not shake. After hanging up with Matt around 2 a.m., Jenna found it extremely difficult to fall asleep. She had finally drifted off around 4a.m. Unfortunately, the alarm was set for 7:30a.m. so she could call Matt to wish him luck, and going back to sleep after that, had been impossible so she got up.

Picking up the phone, Jenna did not recognize the number. "Hello?" she said, and when she heard the voice she knew.

"Hello, Jenna, this is Mrs. Mills. Sorry to bother you but Samantha is not doing so well. She's a bit delirious and keeps calling your name."

"Oh my. Did you call hospice?" Jenna's concern was growing.

"Yes, the nurse is on her way. I was hoping you could come, as well. You always seem to know how to calm Sam down." Lynn sounded very distraught, a side of her Jenna had never seen.

"Yes, of course, I'm on my way." Jenna told her.

"Thank you so much, Jenna, I hope I'm not disturbing you. I realize I'm not supposed to call you directly, but I got your number from Sam's phone."

"No problem, Mrs. Mills. I'm glad you called me. I should be there within minutes." Jenna hung up the phone and without delay, ran to the coat closet to grab her jacket and slip into her sneakers. Luckily, she had already showered, but she was only dressed in an old Detroit Lions jersey and jeans. Her hair wasn't even done, but she couldn't be bothered with that right now. She just wanted to get to Samantha as fast as possible. Jenna hoped her fears since receiving Samantha's text were not becoming reality.

Lacing up her shoes, Jenna began to experience an old, yet familiar, feeling: approaching death. It was an acidic, glacial sensation that crept up your bones seeping into your bloodstream transforming your platelets into ice. It was all around Jenna in the air she was breathing. Jenna closed her eyes and paused for a moment to catch her breath. She was reminded of the day her mother had died. Like today she had woken up with the sensation pulsating through her. Death was as close as the walls, touching her like the floor. When it was here, it was here, there was no escaping it.

Jenna had not thought about how she would feel when one of her patient's died. This was the warning that Matt had given to her when she was in training, to be prepared because it may come as a shock. He was right, yet the surprise was not about the death itself; she knew it was coming, but she was stunned at how soon Samantha's demise arrived. It was almost as if Samantha was beckoning it to take her, calling out to it and waiting. Had she not seen it in her eyes yesterday, right before Samantha had asked to be taken to her bed? Jenna had.

Purse? Jenna thought, looking frantically around for it and remembered it was upstairs on her dresser. She bounded up the stairs, rushed into her bedroom and snatched it. Heading back down the stairs, she almost ran into Adrian who was making his way to the bathroom.

"Where's the fire?" he asked.

"It's Samantha, one of my hospice patients, her mother called, they think she's close." Jenna said quickly.

Adrian's face wrinkled. "You have to be there when they die too?"

With no time to explain things to him, Jenna just blurted out, "No, not usually, but Samantha and I have a bond. Anyway, I gotta go. Talk to you later."

Jenna left Adrian standing there. When she got to the bottom of the stairs, she sprinted to the door, sweeping up her keys as she passed the hall table where she left them. Swinging open the door, this time she did run into the person in her path. Jenna recovered because Zabbie was able to place her hands on Jenna's arms, stabilizing them both.

"Whoa!" Zabbie said. "Slow down!"

Jenna looked at her friend, startled to see her. "Zabbie, what are you doing here?"

"Nice to see you too." Zabbie said walking into the house. Jenna followed Zabbie in to stop her and guide her back out of the house.

"Sorry, Zabbie, but as you can see, I'm on my way out. Bit of an emergency."

Zabbie's eyes darted around the house then up the stairs. "It's okay, I actually came to see Adrian." She said.

Her words stopped Jenna in mid stride out the door. She stepped back inside, leaving the door slightly open. "What?" Jenna asked, as if Zabbie had been speaking gibberish. "You're here to see...Adrian?" she asked her, carefully pronouncing each syllable.

"Yes, I am. Is he upstairs?" Zabbie started for the stairs but Jenna had seized her arm vigorously. Zabbie winced under the force of it.

"What do you want to see him for?" Jenna asked still holding her arm. When she noticed the pain in Zabbie's face she let go.

"I have to talk to him." Zabbie responded.

"About what?" Jenna pressed.

"That's really between me and Adrian." Zabbie told Jenna sternly.

"I don't think so. What could you possibly want with him?" Then it dawned on Jenna. "I see. You're sleeping with him."

"Again, that's none of your business, Jenna."

"Yes, it is! You're my best friend! What about Zach? Do I have to remind you that you are marrying him?"

"No, I'm not." Zabbie walked away from Jenna into the living room.

"What?" Jenna exclaimed and followed Zabbie, dropping her purse and keys on the couch; thoughts of her urgency forgotten for a moment.

"I thought you were leaving?" Zabbie retorted.

"I am but not until you tell me why you and Zach are not getting married."

"Because I called it off last night, I don't love Zach, at least not the way I love Adrian. That's what I've come to tell him with hopes that he'll take me back." Zabbie looked downright desperate.

"I'm in the goddamned Twilight Zone." Jenna said. "What is wrong with you?"

"Nothing is wrong with me. I'm in love. You know I've always been in love with Adrian."

"It was a school girl crush, Zabbie! And now it's not love, if anything it's just lust!"

"No, it's much more than that. I love Adrian and he loves me."

"You think so, huh?"

"Yes!"

"Adrian doesn't love you, Zabbie. Wake Up!" Jenna yelled at her, with hopes that her loud voice would do just that.

"I do love her." Adrian said from behind Jenna.

"Oh for God's sake, will you get out of here!" Jenna screamed at him. "This is not a soap opera, this is real life Adrian. Stop playing your games with her. You are ruining two lives!"

"Jenna, this really has nothing to do with you!" Adrian contested. "Go to your appointment."

Jenna turned and walked up to Zabbie. "Listen to me, I know you think you love Adrian, but you have a wonderful man in Zach. This is all just cold feet, pressures of the wedding, your mother, it'll pass. You'll see."

Reluctantly Zabbie took her eyes off of Adrian and looked at Jenna, shaking her head. "I love him and I don't want to live my life without him. Please try to understand, Jenna. I know what I'm doing."

"Do you Zabbie?" came a voice from the foyer, followed by the loud gun discharging.

The next thing Jenna heard were the screams of both she and Zabbie as they watched Adrian fall backwards onto the couch bleeding from his side. They hadn't heard Zach come through the doorway because the door was still open, but, as soon as he had seen the gun Zach was holding Adrian had leapt towards him, the impact of the bullet knocking him back.

Zabbie ran towards the fallen Adrian but Zach commanded, "Get away from him!" causing Zabbie to recoil back to where she had been standing.

Jenna held both of her hands out in front of her. "Zach please, stop, put the gun down."

His blood shot eyes fell upon her. "I'm sorry, Jenna, but it's too late." He started walking towards Zabbie, and Jenna instinctively edged next to her friend to try to block his path. "Maybe if I had stopped myself a few days ago when I sat outside the boathouse, maybe if I had driven off, not fallen asleep only to wake up to see the love of my fucking life fall down to the ground crying over that piece of shit that's dying on your couch. Maybe if I had of bashed his skull in when I had the chance months ago in the bar, or maybe, just maybe, if I had seen years ago what a lying, slut, fucking *WHORE* she was before I gave my life to her, maybe then what I'm about to do wouldn't' have to be done!"

"Zach please..." Jenna pleaded, still edging Zabbie away, "you don't have to do this..."

"Why did you do it, Elizabeth?" Zach asked tears pouring down his face, gun poised at the ready. "Why did you destroy everything? We could have had a beautiful life. We were meant to be, you told me that once, don't you remember? How can you stop something that was meant to be? I mean, if it was meant to be then it *has* to be, right?"

Zabbie looked over at Adrian lying on the couch, not moving. "Zach, you've killed him, you son of a bitch!" Zabbie shrieked.

"Don't worry, babe, you're going with him. Aren't you happy? Now the two of you will be together..." Zach held pointed the gun directly at her and cocked it. "Forever!" he screamed as he fired the gun.

Jenna didn't know if it was the adrenaline from her earlier rushing to get to Samantha, or the increasing anxiety of the moment, but Jenna instantly reacted pushing Zabbie to the floor and standing in front of her in time for the bullet to enter her body just beneath the right third rib, ricocheting off the sternum and exiting out the latissimus dorsi.

The world went black.

The corridor was long and dark. The ending of it could not be seen in all of this blackness. Jenna stood in this dark corridor with grime oozing down the walls. Dirt, seaweed, and puddles of muddy water covered the hallway floor. There was a room at the end of the hall. When she took her first step towards its entrance, she began to see an ever brightening light illuminating from beneath the doorway. The light was more brilliant than it should be....*wait I have been here before...* Jenna looked behind her and saw the darkest pit of void she had ever seen, a black hole of nothingness that would suck her down if she tried to retreat, so forward she continued, at least, in front of her there was light. *"Jenna"* The light under the door was much brighter now, so bright that she had to shield her eyes. Jenna reached the threshold and saw that the radiance had fully engulfed the doorway now, so much so that the illumination itself was the doorway...*Jenna...*

She stepped into the light that seemed to go on and on and on. Soon the lighted mist began to lift and she was standing in a beautiful field of green as far as the eye could see. *Jenna...* there it was again, that whisper from all around her. She wanted to call out but found she could not speak. Then she saw it, there in the distance, near a horizon, a ball of light like the sun hovering in the middle of the field. She didn't know why, but she was drawn towards it. The closer she got to it, the more she could start to make out some kind of white structure. It looked familiar to her. Jenna looked down and saw the gravel path under her feet. She knew where she was, she was headed towards the gazebo. It was much larger than she had remembered and the path was long and wide.

Jenna could hear the creaking of the chains, someone was swinging! She started to move faster towards it until the haze was cleared and Jenna saw her there swinging.

"Samantha!" Jenna called out to her. She saw Samantha lift up a hand motioning for her to come closer and sit down. When Jenna got to the gazebo, the first thing she noticed was Samantha's skin. It was no longer yellow from jaundice, nor was her cheeks sunken in. Samantha's skin was golden, shimmering, and dazzling.

"Sit down, Jenna. Let's swing." Samantha's voice was soft, deep, and melodic.

Jenna sat down beside her. It felt like it had always felt, so peaceful in the gazebo, the grass so green, the sun so bright, the breeze so warm. "I think I was coming to see you." Jenna said to her.

"Yes, I know." Samantha sat back, letting her head rest on the swing. "You made it."

Jenna looked around; things were not quite as she remembered. A strange feeling started to come over her. "It's...*different*." She looked at Samantha. "You look...*different*."

"No." Samantha said, sitting up. "Everything is the same." Samantha took Jenna's hand. "I'm glad you came. I wanted to see you one more time."

"It was you were calling to me." Jenna realized.

"Yes. I wanted to show you something." Samantha got up and stepped off the gazebo, and went to the back of it. When she came back around, something was in her hand, an envelope. "I'm going to leave this here. Will you give it to my mother?" she asked.

"You want *me* to give it her?"

"Yes." Samantha confirmed.

Jenna tried to take it but she could not grab hold of it. Her hand kept seeping through the paper. She frowned. "I don't understand." She said looking up at Samantha.

Samantha smiled at Jenna. "I'll leave it here for you. You must go now."

Jenna felt scared suddenly and hugged her. "No, I want to stay here with you. It's so beautiful here. Let's swing for awhile."

Samantha hugged her back. "Ah Jenna, he is waiting for me, see?" she pointed to someone walking towards them in the distance.

Jenna could not make out who it was, she could not see his features, he was a blur, but she had a feeling who it was. It was Kenny.

"You must go back." Samantha said to her. "Lay down, Jenna." Samantha told her and she did. The sun was being covered by that mist again. Once Jenna was lying down on the swing, Samantha pushed it gently. She bent down next to her. "Now you go back, and you'll see, it'll all be clear." She said.

Jenna found it hard to keep her eyes open. "Goodbye, Sam."

"Goodbye, Jenna." Samantha said, her voice trailing off.

Jenna could feel the soft pressure of Samantha's hand on her chest. It was comforting. The pressure became stronger and stronger. Soon it was so hard that Jenna could hardly breathe, and she could not open her eyes anymore. Darkness had returned, and the pressure was pulsating on her chest, again and again and again...

"Clear!" a man's voice said from some far off place.
"*one...two....three....four...five....*Clear!" the man yelled over and over. "Wait!" he shouted. "She's coming around! Get her on the stretcher!"

THIRTY-FIVE

Samantha Mills died on a cold morning in November while calling Jenna's name. Lynnette was sad that Jenna never made it to her bedside. She sat in the kitchen alone when the funeral home came to transport her daughter's body. Joe and the hospice nurse took care of everything. Lynn wanted to move from her chair but could not. Later that evening she learned why Samantha's volunteer could not be there. She watched on the news how Jenna Steele had been shot at point blank range by a gunman who had then turned the gun on himself. Jenna was in critical but stable condition. Another man was also shot but released after being treated for a flesh wound.

The next few days of funeral preparations were a blur to Lynn. Somehow, she was able to move her mouth and produce words. What she was able to say, she did not know. Whatever she uttered the people around her seemed to understand as they responded appropriately. Trish Kramer, Samantha's nurse, came and sat with Lynn during the viewing of the body. Lynn cried beside her as she held her hand. She had uttered the words to Trish, "the flowers are beautiful." And without warning she had broken down in Trish's arms.

Joe did not understand why or how his daughter's condition deteriorated so quickly. He felt that when she left the clinic in Atlanta, she just gave up, or maybe her body gave up, he didn't know which. Someone had said to him at the gravesite that "God needed his angel home." Joe had no clue who that person was. It was a friend of the family but he remembered walking away from them and the service to cry alone by a tree. A part of him was angry with the idea that God took his daughter away because he needed something from her. "Fuck you! I needed her!" he cried under his breath to the snow tipped branches.

The house was quiet now. All the equipment from Samantha's room had been taken away. Lynn had cleaned everything. She washed the sheets, shampooed the carpet, and replaced every stuffed animal back to its proper place. It felt like a tomb, Joe thought, some nights he would go in there and cry silently. He and Lynn kept their distance from each other, only interacting for the most basic of communication, such as coordinating meals, and saying the appropriate greetings, no real conversations at all. Lynn let him sit in his study and Joe let her stay in the master suite for days if she wanted without any quarrel from him. And that's how it stayed for a very long time.

Soon the day came when Joe announced he was moving out. Lynn had said nothing in response. It was the day after Thanksgiving. They had gone to his sister's home for dinner. The next morning he told her that he had to get away, get out of the house. Lynn had listened to his reasons and only nodded to say *I heard you.*

That same day the doorbell rang and Joe answered it, and there was Jenna standing there. When she came in, Lynn came over to greet her with a hug. It was strange to Lynn just how happy she felt to see her. "How are you doing?" Lynn asked her as the three of them sat in the living room.

It was almost like that first day, almost a year ago, when Jenna had arrived at their home. "Much better, thank you." Jenna told them.

"I'm so sorry you didn't get to say good bye to Sam." Joe said to her.

"We heard about what happened. How awful!" Lynn said.

"Yes." Jenna responded slowly. "I wanted to be with her too. But I truly believe that Sam and I said our goodbyes." Jenna told them, picturing the image of Samantha sitting next to her on the swing, her face glowing.

"Are you recovering?" Lynn asked.

"Yes, I am." Jenna paused for a moment not sure how to do what she came to do. She wasn't sure what to say so she just blurted it out. "Sam asked me to give you something."

Lynn and Joe looked at each other, it was Lynn who spoke. "Really? When, at your last visit?" she asked.

"This may sound a little weird, but when I was shot, the doctors told me that my heart stopped beating for almost three minutes." Jenna explained.

"Oh my goodness." Lynn put a hand to her chest.

Jenna continued. "While I was out, I saw Sam."

"I'm sorry, what?" Joe said.

"Jenna, are you saying…" Lynn began but Jenna broke in.

"I know it sounds unbelievable but she was calling for me."

"Yes, that's why I called you that day because she kept saying your name over and over." Lynn said.

"Yes, I heard her while I was unconscious." Jenna watched as they again exchanged glances. They did not believe her but she continued. "I was in this dark corridor, there was a door. Sam was calling me. At first I didn't know who it was, but when I walked through the doorway there was a bright light, and then I saw her...at the gazebo."

"The one in the backyard?" Joe asked.

"Yes, it looked like that one, only it was much larger. I went to her. We sat in the swing, it felt like before when we would talk out there for hours. Then she told me she wanted me to give you something." Jenna looked at Lynn. "It was a letter."

"A letter?" she asked.

"Yes. She said she would leave it for me to give to you. Then she said goodbye."

Lynn stood up and walked over to the other side of the room. She tried to take in what Jenna was telling her. "So, where is it? This letter?"

"I don't have it, but I think I know where it is." Jenna stood up. "She left it at the gazebo." Jenna started for the back door.

Joe stepped in front of her. "Jenna, I have been out there many times, since...since then. There is no letter out there. There isn't even a place to hide a letter out there. I would have seen it, Jenna."

"Mr. Mills, please, I'm sure it's there." Jenna didn't pause; she just headed out the sliding doors that lead to the backyard. She looked behind her and, thankfully, Joe and Lynn were following her, indulging her, humoring her. Jenna didn't care why they were following her, as long as they were.

Joe and Lynn were behind her as they made their way through the garden and veered off to the left down the winding path to the hidden gazebo area. Jenna stopped abruptly in front of the swing. Her body was blocking the middle part. Jenna just stood there looking down. Joe stepped to the side, Lynn stepped to the other side of Jenna, and they both were frozen in awe as they saw a crisp white envelope sitting there on top of the snow covered swing seat.

Joe moved in closer to it, cautiously. "That's impossible." He looked at Lynn. "This was not here before!" he protested.

"It's here now, Joe." Lynn stepped closer to it, picking the envelope up. "It's dry." She said.

"Did you bring this here and leave it for us to find?" Joe confronted Jenna.

"No, Mr. Mills." Jenna promised. Joe looked around and didn't remember seeing tracks in the snow. Besides he had spent so many nights out here before the snow came.

"It's Sam's handwriting." Lynn told him.

"It's for you." Jenna told them. "She wanted you to have it, Mrs. Mills. That's what I came to do. I'll leave you two alone, now."

"You don't have to go." Lynn said to her.

"No, someone is waiting for me in the car." Jenna started back up the path, and then turned. "Samantha was more than just a patient to me. She was my friend." Jenna watched as they acknowledged what she said to them; then she walked back up the path towards the house. She looked up at the window of Samantha's room. In the window she saw Samantha standing there smiling. Jenna was at first stunned because she was looking at Samantha's ghost. Jenna quickly recovered, then smiled at her and waved. Samantha waved back and dissolved into the curtains.

Jenna opened the car door and got in. Matt waited for her to get settled. "Everything alright?" he asked her.

"Yeah, Sam's letter was delivered." Jenna told him.

"Did they believe you?" Matt asked cautiously.

Jenna thought for a moment, and then smiled. "Yes. They believed me." She reached over and kissed Matt.

"What was that for?" he asked.

"For standing by me, for bringing me here, for introducing me to the best experience of my life, if I hadn't have walked into your office, I would never have met Samantha. Thank you."

Matt smiled. "Thank me? Thank you, for reminding me how important hospice is to me, how important volunteer services is to me. Without you, I would have never told the CEO to take the marketing VP job and shove it. And he would never have called me, to tell me that I was right, and that volunteer services needed to be its own department. I would have never gotten the new position of Corporate Vice President of Volunteer Services. Sarah got to keep her old job and the volunteer directors were elevated to their rightful levels, equal to the rest of the directors at the company. That's what you did, Miss." He leaned over and kissed Jenna passionately. "I want you to know," Matt added, "I love you, not just for what you've done, but for who you are. I love you."

Jenna stared at him for a moment, tears filling her eyes. *Oh my God, he said it first*, she thought to herself. "I love you, too, Matt." She said to him, and stroked his cheek sweetly. Matt wiped away the tears that fell down Jenna's face, and he smiled.

Jenna took in a cleansing deep breath, then said, "Now, let's get out of here before Adrian burns his new house down trying to cook us dinner!" Jenna said laughingly.

"I have to say. I'm looking forward to this double date. Adrian and Zabbie, you and me. I could really get used to this!" Matt said.

"You better get used to it!" Jenna said, playfully poking his chest. "I plan on many more nights just like this."

"Me too." Matt beamed, then started the car and headed out from under the Mill's stone driveway and into their future.

Laurie, hospice patient, with her volunteer, Marie

This novel was inspired by the amazing relationship between the patient above, Laurie, and her hospice volunteer, Marie. Although the characters and events are fictitious, the inspiration to write a story about the journey of a hospice volunteer was born from witnessing this glorious bond form.

-Crystal Hickerson

~ Note from hospice volunteer, Marie Appleberry

On a Tuesday morning in June of 2008, I was awakened from sleep by an overwhelming urge to volunteer for "hospice," at the time not fully understanding the meaning of hospice beyond being a program for patients who no longer have any hope for a cure for their particular condition and are seeking, instead, palliative care. That morning it seemed like God was compelling me to take the first step in a journey which, ultimately, has blessed and enriched my life in countless and priceless ways. A computer search led me to the website for local hospice, a nonprofit agency with offices located in several Michigan counties. Being impressed with what I read about hospice and, most importantly, the fact that no patient is turned away based on their inability to pay, I immediately downloaded a volunteer application, filled it out and delivered it to the Macomb County branch office without calling for an appointment. I seemed to throw protocol out the window and followed my heart and what I believed was the divine intervention moving me forward.

As it turned out, I was not only able to meet Crystal Hickerson, Volunteer Services Manager for the Macomb County office; she also took the time to give me an interview. Despite my somewhat unusual and spontaneous actions that day, Crystal accepted me as a trainee and sent me home with a three-inch-thick training manual to study prior to participating in the upcoming training sessions. She also scheduled me to work in the office one day per week before I completed the mandatory training program, which would then allow me to work directly with hospice patients and their families.

That same Tuesday evening, I recapped the day for my stunned but proud husband and confided in him that I felt there was "someone who needed and was waiting for me out there." He, of course, asked what I meant by that, but it was difficult to explain instinctively knowing I'd meet someone before actually meeting them, and all I could tell him was I just knew!

That someone turned out to be my first regular assignment, and her name was Laurie. From the beginning we had a very special connection because we both loved cats and loved the color purple. Laurie was bedridden, but she was blessed with a phenomenal sense of humor and always tried to lift the spirits of those around her. Right from the start, my mission was to bring as much joy into Laurie's life as I possibly could, and that was the basis of our 16-month relationship, to have fun when we could and just sit quietly when Laurie didn't feel well enough to do more than smile. The good days were always embraced and treasured.

When Laurie had to move from her apartment to a nursing home, the transition was, needless to say, very traumatic for her. I decided to surprise her with a purple Swarovski crystal bracelet to cheer her up, but first I had to learn how to make the bracelet. That one inspirational idea took on a life of its own once I learned how to do so. Laurie proudly wore her bracelet 24/7, and when I took classes to learn to make more difficult bracelets, and even rings, Laurie just shined with each piece. She was the jewel wearing the colorful bling! Laurie had beautiful hands and loved to have them manicured and always wore fingernail polish. She was elated with the ring and being able to show off her beautiful hands. When she subsequently asked if I could make bracelets for some of her favorite nurses and aides, I was especially happy because it gave Laurie the opportunity to make choices when so much of her life was out of her control. She was able to pick out the colors of the crystals and the style of bracelet for each person, and she would eagerly await the finished product so she could surprise the special people she cared about with a gift from her heart. This little project was such a small thing, but it helped to give some purpose and meaning to Laurie's days. Our bling project brightened many lives and turned out to be a wonderful blessing for both of us. Giving from the heart not only blesses the recipient, it especially blesses the giver.

Hospice volunteers are often credited for blessing patient's lives when, in fact, we are the ones who are blessed to be a part of this most sacred and final journey in their lives. Laurie will always have a special place in my heart. When she died, I started lighting tea candle at our dinner table every evening in remembrance and continue to do so to this day, not only in remembrance of Laurie but for all of the patients who have come into my life. Also, Laurie and I did discuss my premonition of meeting "someone" and knowing with certainty that she was that special someone. We did have a special bond, and we both thanked God for bringing us together, sharing joy and tears and making memories to cherish in small and meaningful ways.

Since joining the hospice team as a volunteer, I've also undergone grief support training and feel equally proud to be part of an agency that continues grief support services for 13 months following the death of a patient if or when needed by their loved ones. One of my assignments was to visit a lonely and grieving woman after she lost her beloved husband. She was homebound and was unable to attend grief support meetings held regularly at the office. She truly appreciated these visits, which enabled her to grieve by sharing her feelings and memories and giving her a shoulder to cry on.

      Other volunteer opportunities arose to do community outreach in the form of health fairs, memorial services and fundraising. I also received training for the "My Stories" program, which was newly implemented after I started with hospice. "My Stories" gives patients the opportunity to make an audio recording to leave for their loves ones, and it has proven to be an invaluable gift for the grieving loved ones. An additional service hospice provides is that of vigil volunteer. Every person deserves a dignified and peaceful death and, above all, they shouldn't have to die alone. It has been such a privilege for me to be with patients as they make their final transition and are actively dying. Sometimes the vigil volunteer sits with a patient's loved one so he or she won't have to be alone during such a sad but sacred time, a time which can also be frightening for them.

      The need for hospice volunteers is great in many different areas, but patient care is the heart and soul of the work. If wealth was measured by the number of hugs a person receives, then I'd be a very wealthy woman indeed. Volunteering for hospice gave new purpose and meaning to my life, and I'd recommend it to anyone seeking to make a very real difference in the lives of people embarking on their final sacred journey. To see a patient's eyes light up when you walk into his or her room truly is a joy to behold. The simple act of being there can make all the difference in the world.

Want More of Crystal Hickerson?
Check Out More Works from this bestselling author:

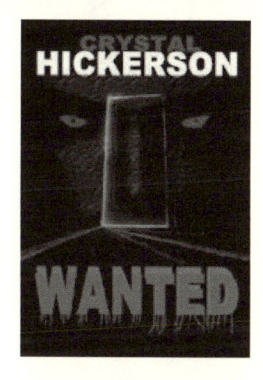

WANTED: A chilling tale of a woman's struggle to deal with the brutal death of her daughter, and the demon that is stalking her.

ISBN: 978-0-557-09133-1

Street Corners: A hot and steamy love story set against the backdrop of a world filled with crime, deception, and prostitution. Diane finds out that the boy you grew up with is not the man she's grown to love. *(also watch the animated movie)*

ISBN: 978-1-4303-2030-2

The Magician: A new age of man is about to dawn and an ancient battle is being waged all around us. Levi may be a simple magician trying to earn a living but it is soon evident that his powers are real.

ISBN# 1-4116-6009-9

Purchase books online at:
Amazon.Com
LuLu.Com
and at the author's website:
CrystalHickerson.Com

amazon.com